JONATHAN

BOOK 2

GUARDIAN OF DREAMS

A. CORRIN

Credits:

Cover illustration by Eva Soulu–www.evasoulu.com

Interior Illustration by Katie Hofgard

Map by Rengin Tumer–rengintumer.com

Other books by A.Corrin:

Jonathan, Prince of Dreams (Book 1)

CONTENTS

To my dear friend Pius, a wise scholar, a daring adventurer. Thank you for the knowledge you share, and the wonder you inspire. Enjoy your journey through the Land of Dreams!

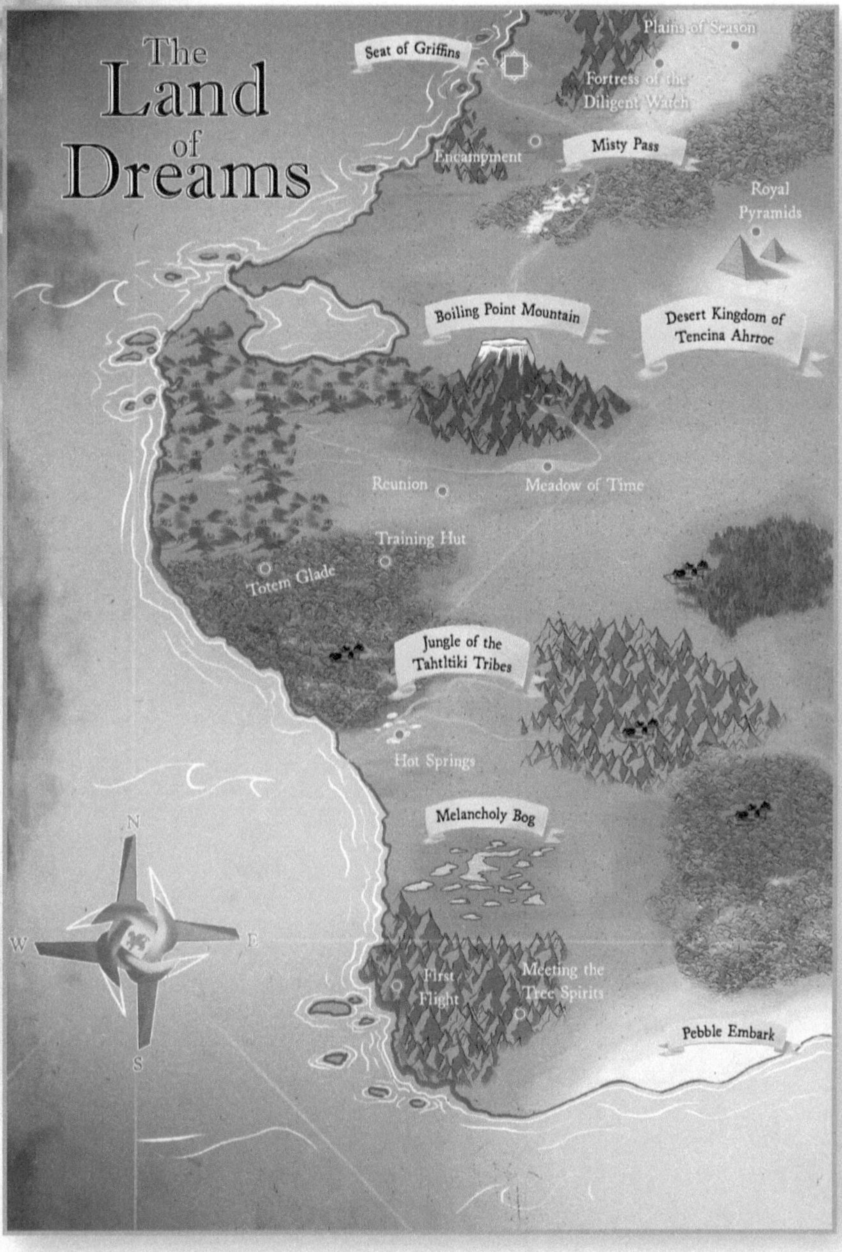

The Land of Dreams

Seat of Griffins
Plains of Season
Fortress of the Diligent Watch
Encampment
Misty Pass
Royal Pyramids
Boiling Point Mountain
Desert Kingdom of Tencina Ahrroc
Reunion
Meadow of Time
Training Hut
Totem Glade
Jungle of the Tahtltiki Tribes
Hot Springs
Melancholy Bog
First Flight
Meeting the Tree Spirits
Pebble Embark
N
W
E
S

CHAPTER ONE:

HOSTILE TAKEOVER

AT THE FIRESTONE TOWN MEETING CHAMBERS

The meeting chambers, situated in a large brick building, had been flooded with anxious, clamoring people.

Elders shouted in consternation to each other. Adults, arms crossed and stances wide, territorial even, kept their confused young children in check or searched for friends to mingle with. Teenagers exchanged the word amongst their own, glaring about belligerently as if expecting an attack like the one that had demolished the town's hospital.

The mayor, a portly, balding man in a black suit, ambled out of the building and held up a hand for silence, clutching a megaphone in the other. He pressed a button, and the megaphone gave a wailing whoop. People flinched, and someone's baby whimpered with discomfort.

Towards the edge of the gathering, Nikki stood tense behind Tyson's wheelchair. For the umpteenth time, she counted to make sure that her friends were all nearby, reading their emotions.

Lia, her blond hair bleached white as bone under the bright lights flooding the parking lot, impatiently checked the time on her cellphone, looking over the heads in front of her towards the agitated mayor.

Ben stood beside his girlfriend Kitty, who fiddled with the ends of her dark, curly hair. His gaze occasionally but discreetly flicked to

Donovan, the boy who had saved Nikki's life in the hospital explosion, as if suspicious. But Donovan was as stiff and blank-faced as stone.

Vince, hunched in on himself, shifted from foot to foot like a bear. He stared up at the stars, clearly wishing for all the world, as Nikki knew that all the others did, that their friend Jonathan wasn't missing, and that everything was as it had once been.

Of course, Jonathan was more than a friend to Nikki.

Nikki examined her shoelaces to keep from weeping. Jonathan, the young man she loved and her *best* friend, had been missing for weeks now, and she was losing hope that she would ever see him again. She looked up around her, at her friends and the other people gathered in the cold. That's why everyone was there.

People had been going missing. Natural disasters were tearing across the world in abundance and out of season. Crime sprees and general violence had spiked country-wide. Everyone wanted answers–and *needed* a plan of action.

The mayor's voice belted staticky from his megaphone and voices hushed into an attentive quiet.

"People of Firestone! As you may be aware, every few weeks, we meet to discuss local events and any issues that need to be resolved. It saddens me that we are all here on this particular night because of the grievous events of the past month. Terrorist attacks have claimed lives. Kidnappings take place on our safest streets. And gangs seem to be sprouting up in full force from the most unlikely of places. The question is, what are we going to do about it? Why doesn't anyone seem to know what's going on? I hope that by putting our collective minds together this evening, we can do more than just panic alone and live in fear. Perhaps we can create a game plan.

"There are almost four times as many people here tonight than ever before, so the board members and I have set apart six rooms, one for each of us to meet with perhaps twenty at a time. That should be enough. One of the rooms, the first down the hall and to the left, is for young adults fourteen to twenty only and will be led by our youth committee member, Josiah Fairbanx. All children younger than fourteen are welcome to wait in the hall or meet in room 63 down the stairs. Mothers and fathers, please take your babies there too if you wish; there will be daycare management."

It was miracle enough that the townsfolk had held their tongues even during this short speech. But now, they resumed clamoring as they bustled forwards towards the doors.

"Josiah, I like him," Nikki remarked. Josiah was hers and Jonathan's school counselor. He was a polite young man in his late-twenties who had always shown interest in Nikki and her boyfriend as if they were all close next-door neighbors. She began pushing Ty forward.

Tyson sat in still, subdued silence, but Nikki could see the cogs working behind his eyes. There was no doubt he was thinking of questions to bring up to Josiah. He had recovered extremely well from the plane crash he'd survived almost a month ago. Despite the haggard pallor in his face and the gruesome scars on his hand where he had almost lost three fingers, his eyes were alert.

"I don't know what they think'll happen," Ben muttered behind Nikki. She turned and frowned at him over her shoulder. With a spurt of irritation, she noticed he had purposefully fallen back to allow Donovan to walk in front of him as if he expected Donovan to stick a knife in his spine. His strange distrust of the kid who had saved her life frustrated her. When the hospital where Tyson had been recovering from the plane crash he'd survived had blown up, Donovan had rescued Nikki, catching her before she could plummet out a window to her death–and yet Ben treated her hero like he had sinister ulterior motives.

"You never know," Kitty said, her tone optimistic and encouraging as always, though the gleam in her eyes had dulled. "If we all share our experiences, then maybe someone can take our stories and put them together like a puzzle to make sense of them. Right, Donovan?"

To Nikki's surprise, Donovan flinched at Kitty's address, as if her words stung him. Avoiding her eyes, he gave a brisk nod but said nothing. Kitty gave Nikki a mildly offended look, but Ben reached forward, took her hand, and pulled her beside him to kiss her cheek.

Nikki heard him lean aside to mutter something to Vince, who cast Donovan a look of appraisal, and shook herself. Ben's suspicion and Donovan being startled at sweet Kitty's voice had to have been the result of tension, of stress. *Everyone* was acting strange, what with the whole world crashing around their heads. Tonight, she promised herself she would leave the meeting chambers with answers.

All sorts of kids packed the meeting room. Nikki and her friends recognized most of them from school. They had all gathered into their cliques: shy kids with shy kids, material girls with material girls, athletes with athletes, and so on. But all looked worried and sickly.

They brooded, arms folded and legs crossed at the knees, displaying nervous tics like chewing their nails, twirling their hair, and biting their lips.

Josiah sat at the head of the table, a long, polished hunk of wood bare but for a few pencils. He seemed comfortable compared to the kids, his feet up on the tabletop, his big leather boss's chair tilted back. His hands were clasped behind his head, and there was something about his pointed face that made him look important and authoritarian. His long-ish black hair, rather like Jonathan's but more shaggy, was clean and combed, his calico eyes taking in everyone's expressions and seeming to analyze them. Josiah always dressed festively, like a man going to a party. Tonight, he donned deep-green cargo pants and a scarlet button-up flannel shirt with yellow lines that ran up and down it in an orderly pattern.

He waited until the last person to enter closed the door and then spoke in that laid-back, calm way of his.

"Let's bring this to business, shall we? In an orderly fashion, might someone begin our discussion? We'll start with questions."

All at once, shouts rose like a riptide. Nikki winced, and Lia covered her ears. Josiah blinked furiously and managed to talk over the hubbub, though it didn't seem as if he had raised his voice.

"People! Please, please, please...*please*! Shhhhh..." The clamoring ebbed into frustrated murmurs as other kids struck up the task of quieting their fellows.

Josiah got everyone to raise their hand before speaking, and the meeting settled into a dull Q and A, except that hardly anyone had any A's. Throughout the whole thing, as questions became more pointed and specific, as other kids told of their experiences, of glimpsing strange people in dark robes and developing vivid, detailed night terrors, something like a memory nagged at the back of Nikki's mind. She felt as if something important hovered at the fringes of her thoughts, some sort of information she could contribute. But first, she had to remember it herself.

That evening in the park with Jon, after he had led the football team to victory against their school rivals... Something had taken place then that fit like a puzzle piece into this whole mess. A group of men had jumped them, taunted Jonathan, called him a prince... but that didn't seem to mean a thing. There was something else. Something Jonathan had said...

They had been so scary, so abnormal...and they had known Garrett.

In days Garrett had transformed from the brutal school thug that everyone tried to avoid into some sort of savage monster that had nearly, remorselessly, led a kid to getting killed snowboarding on the mountain. Garrett had always harbored an intense hatred for Jonathan–and his friends by extension. Once he had shamed Nikki, had touched her, and had it not been for her own intervention, she had little doubt that Jonathan may well have killed Garrett for it. Most of the school believed that Garrett had had a part to play in Jonathan's disappearance, including Nikki and her friends, but Garrett had vanished just as mysteriously as Jonathan had, his house as empty as if it had never been lived in, and the police, overwhelmed as they already were with the hospital bombing and the kidnappings and the uptick in violence had little time or resources to spare in launching an intensive investigation.

Nikki remembered her last conversation with Jonathan, discussing Garrett's potential for being involved in the strange things happening in town and across the country, even the world. Was that it? Was that significant? Was that what she'd wanted to share?

Nikki strained her mind like she was twisting water from a cloth. There was more to it... but she was getting closer. Beside her, Donovan slid his hand down on the arm of his chair, gripping it tightly.

The next day, after the incident in the park, Jonathan had said something about them... called them something and said they were pure evil. He had seemed to have known something... and then he had vanished. How could she have forgotten that? What was the connection?

A haze was lifting from her mind, unsticking as if it were reluctant. Donovan stood gracefully beside her and excused himself to the bathroom, sounding weak. Nikki nodded distantly.

What had he called them? In all the chaos with Jonathan going missing and her own near-death experience, she had forgotten. Or had she? She had been about to explain to her friends the day that vehicle had crashed into the hospital and detonated. The haze kept drifting away as if sucked through an invisible tube. Rakers... Rain... Rainer... *Rankers!* Everything snapped into focus.

"Rankers!" Nikki shouted. She saw Josiah smile slowly and only half-realized that he had been watching her think the whole time. Faces turned to her, blank and questioning.

“What did you say?” an older guy asked, brows raised.

Nikki explained in a rush of words. “The people attacking us call themselves Rankers.”

Faces fell when no one recognized the name. They had at least been hoping to know exactly who was attacking them.

Nikki urgently raised her voice, cold shivers stealing over her skin. “They want to corrupt us! Kill us! It’s what they do. It’s, like, their whole purpose!”

“Nikki?” Tyson murmured, stunned. He craned his head back to stare up at her.

Kitty, sounding worried about her friend’s sanity, asked gently, “How do you know this?”

Nikki clawed her hair away from her face and behind her shoulders impatiently. The words flew from her lips before she had time to process them and take in what she was saying.

“My boyfriend told me.”

Tyson gave a jolt as if he’d been electrified. Vince’s eyes widened. Lia’s hands flew to her mouth, Kitty gasped, and Ben recoiled as if struck, his expression pained.

“What’s a Ranker?” a young woman asked.

“How does your boyfriend know?” asked someone else.

“What do they want?” came a question from the back of the room, and suddenly desperate questions were boiling up from every corner.

“Oh brother, her boyfriend?” A guy in a hoodie near the doors sneered scornfully, his tone angry and abrasive. “Big deal. Everyone knows this is all just some elaborate hoax; terrorists or something. She's making stuff up to get attention!"

Many other youths cast him anxious, disdainful looks, disapproving of his tone.

Furious, Nikki exclaimed, "My boyfriend, *Jonathan He'klarr*, told me!"

At this, a hush crashed down on their heads ominously. Everyone knew Jonathan or had at least heard that he had gone missing.

One younger boy had looked up at Jon's name. It was Carl, the young man whom Jonathan had once saved from being eaten by a bear up in the mountains after Garrett had tempted him into trouble in the first place. His lips twitched in remorse at Jonathan's name, but his dark eyes were expectant. He had experienced first-hand Jonathan's selfless heroism. While nursing a sprained ankle alone on the cold mountain, hungry predators had circled closer. Carl had called for help as the surety of his impending death had crept in upon him. Then Jonathan had appeared like a bright light to pierce shadow. Who better to know the darkness than someone with a light as bright as Jonathan's? So Carl instantly believed Nikki and was ready to learn all he could about this new, unknown enemy.

Ben, however, didn't seem as interested.

He whispered hastily into Kitty's ear, "Bathroom, be back. Tell me everything later."

Nikki overheard him and turned to give him a flustered look. Given what she had to say, she thought that Ben could wait to take a potty break later. But before either she or Kitty could ask questions, Ben slipped out the doors and disappeared.

"I'm *not* lying," Nikki fumed, her face flushed, turning back around to frown at the skeptic glaring by the exit. Josiah's hands were steepled, and he watched her over them, seeming amused by something, encouraging and expectant.

Nikki growled, "You all knew him." There were morose nods. "He was a friend to all of us."

She pointed suddenly at a scruffy girl in a tie-dye beanie, who jumped fretfully.

"Do you remember when he fixed your skateboard and then afterward helped you personalize it? It was the talk of the skate park for weeks!"

The girl bit her lip and nodded.

Nikki redirected her point to a handsome boy her age with curly hair. His face twisted in chagrin when he saw that he would be picked on next.

Voice shaky with suppressed sobs, Nikki said, "When your girlfriend's dog got stuck in a drainage pipe, Jonathan climbed down and got all mucky and soaking to rescue it and let you have the credit for saving it."

Nikki's gaze landed briefly on Carl. The boy sat up straighter, waiting for her to address the great thing that Jonathan had done for him, but Nikki only smiled sadly and looked around her at the attentive faces.

"He wouldn't tell me anything but the truth. Especially about something as serious as these catastrophes."

"She's lying!" rebuked another scowling boy in a black hoodie. He stood with his hands in his pockets in the corner nearest the first malcontent. Nikki hadn't noticed him before. Yet, there was something odd about him. In her startled surprise, it took Nikki a few seconds to realize what it was: though everyone else sat in frustration, anger, or dire dismay, the corners of his mouth fought to smile. He held himself as one who knew a juicy and unpleasant secret.

Josiah leaned forward, frowning at the boy. His knuckles were white on the arms of his chair.

"No!" Nikki objected, voice pitching into tones of desperation. "It's the truth, I swear!"

The hoodie-boy moved forward to lean against the table's edge with the stealthy grace of a cat. Then, sneering across the table challengingly, he said, "The people attacking us only wish for peace. But, as with any great change, there arises opposition, and that opposition must first be annihilated. Such is the way of war. Such is the way of...conquest."

Faces revealed shock. Those nearest to the crazy hoodie-boy scooted away.

All at once, the boy moved aside, out of the way of the doors, Josiah launched to his feet, and a host of people in black robes burst in. Their movements coordinated, precise, as if rehearsed, they surrounded everyone. Their faces were all covered in deep, cavernous hoods. No light reached their faces. Those nearest the door parted, and one more person entered. His hood was down, and he held a large gutting knife. Kids screamed and ducked or threw themselves backward. Those that scrambled for the doors or a window were shoved back.

The newcomer leveled his weapon at Josiah. "Sit down," he ordered smoothly.

Josiah sank obediently into his chair, and from where Nikki stood, it almost seemed as if his eyes were alternately blinking white and red. Terror and adrenaline chewed her heart as the knifeman turned to face her.

"There's a new gang in town," the knifeman grinned. His black hair framed his piercing green hawk-eyes, which were narrowed malevolently.

The boy pointing the knife directly at Nikki's chest...was Garrett.

AT JONATHAN'S HOUSE

Ethan He'klarr teetered on the steps of a rickety, creaky ladder. He smiled to himself, ignoring the burn in the muscles of his arm from holding it up for so long. A drop of green paint splashed onto his upraised cheek, but he simply rubbed it away on his shoulder.

His wife may have passed away long ago, but ever since he had heard her voice telling him that their son Jonathan was alive, Ethan had felt a sense of purpose and focus that he had not possessed in more than ten years. For starters, Ethan had stopped watching the increasingly depressing news, had stopped hanging out with the wrong crowd after work, had gotten rid of all the alcohol in the house, and had started living his life again.

Cleaning up the house had been a lonely but distracting chore, and the company where he had been employed as an electrician was contemplating letting him back on full time at regular hours. Jonathan had tried to do their taxes and pay the bills with the income from his job, but now Ethan was ready to take over and be the parent he was supposed to be. When Jonathan came home, Ethan wanted him to see a new man.

After the initial task of fixing up the house, Ethan had gone out and bought paint for one more job. Now he was in his son's room, doing his best to finish up the fantastic mural that his son had been painting on the ceiling. He was no major artist, but the painting was coming along nicely.

Half paying attention to the local podcast cracking jokes and discussing high school sports from his phone resting on Jon's bed, he almost didn't notice the sudden hush in the hosts' raucous laughter.

Ethan frowned at his phone, waiting, wondering if the Wi-Fi had dropped or if his phone had died, but then he picked up faint voices as if the hosts had leaned away from their microphones to have a low conversation.

After a minute had passed and the podcast still had not resumed, Ethan set down his brush, picked his way down the ladder, and lifted his phone–then abruptly dropped it when one of the men began speaking loudly and dazedly as if he'd just seen something extremely shocking.

"Breaking news, Firestonians. There's been some kind of commotion at the meeting chambers–my daughter just called and-and said that..."

His co-host joined in with a bit more alarm–"Our employees are getting calls from loved ones who attended the meeting tonight, reporting that a small group of armed individuals is holding them hostage. I don't know what's happening, but a cavalcade of patrol cars just raced by, and–with everything else going on, I dunno, something isn't right. I'm going to go check it out, man."

There were more sounds of commotion away from the microphones, a jumble of voices and doors opening and closing.

Ethan stood stock still, holding the phone away and watching it as if it would grow a mouth and start talking to him. After a moment of fighting with himself over what to do, Ethan He'klarr closed the podcast, set his jaw, grabbed his coat, and was out the door.

CHAPTER TWO:

BECOMING A MONSTER

IN A BATHROOM OF THE TOWN MEETING CHAMBERS

Ben stood in front of the bathroom entrance in the meeting chambers; a thick wooden door with the bronze plaque labeled, *Men*.

He had followed Donovan sneakily until the kid had slipped inside here. Now Ben was having second thoughts. Maybe the reason Donovan had left the meeting really *was* that he had to relieve himself. But something about the new boy just nagged at Ben's conscience.

Donovan was too calm in a crisis. Too expressionless. Too cold and indifferent. He treated Kitty like she had the plague, even though Kitty was the kindest person on the planet, and he hovered at Nikki's elbow like she was an invalid and he her crutch. Then there was Donovan's irritating penchant for never using contractions.

Though Ben couldn't quite describe it, even to himself, Donovan had an aura about him: when Ben stood right beside Donovan, he felt uneasy...afraid of something that he couldn't name; something ancient and primal, like the creatures that stalked the shadows before Man had been blessed with fire. And was it only by coincidence that Donovan had shown up at the hospital just in time to save Nikki from falling through a window to her death? Was it a coincidence that he had left right after Nikki had announced that Rankers were behind all the chaos?

Ben frowned and slowly pushed open the door. It was time to get some answers. But he heard Donovan's cultured voice murmuring from a corner of the wide bathroom and hid behind the wall, letting the door close slowly with a careful hand.

The bathroom stalls were vacant; their doors tilted open. There were five mirrors suspended over five pearly sinks. The yellow lights warmed the tiled floor, patterned with different shades of brown. Donovan's skin was marble-white in the comparatively dark room.

An old flip-phone, compact and simple, was pressed to Donovan's ear. He seemed to be wearily defending himself.

"All I am saying is that you must make your entrance now. The hex is wearing off of the girl!"

Ben stiffened.

Donovan paused and, mollified, murmured, "Alright. Good luck... Yes, I will be there soon... Yes, I will, for as long as I am needed to. They don't suspect a thing. I just need to catch my breath. Trying to maintain that hex took it out of me... No, I have not eaten in days. I will not let it happen again... Okay, see you. Make haste." He clapped his phone shut and dragged his feet slowly to a sink. He braced himself over it, both hands on either side of the porcelain, and took a long, shaky breath. Without turning, he said in a carrying voice, "You can come out now, Ben."

Ben's stomach dropped at his name, but he rounded the wall in what he hoped was a steady gait. His eyes dark, he approached Donovan and stood to one side of him. "Who was that?" he asked lightly.

Donovan looked over his left shoulder at Ben, whose eyes widened with shock at how dark the shadows were beneath

Donovan's eyes, how pallid the skin of his face was. He seemed sleep-deprived of a week's worth of nights.

Concerned that Donovan would withhold an answer, Ben contemplated a quick dart for the other boy's cell. He could easily scan his phonebook for the most recent calls. But Donovan blinked and replied, "Garrett."

Ben could not disguise his surprise this time.

"He is the leader of the operation taking place across the globe," Donovan explained readily. "First General over the Rankers."

This meant little to Ben at the moment. However, it confirmed what Nikki and Tyson had speculated–that Garrett was involved in the worldwide mayhem, apparently part of some powerful cult or gang and in possession of a high rank among its members.

"The girl you mentioned," Ben said, "The one who you said was hexed. It was Nikki, huh?"

Donovan frowned, the expression temporarily hampering his good looks. "Yes. I was trying to keep her from remembering what Jonathan had told her. Then she would have given us away before our time was ripe. You see, I have a talent for hypnotizing my prey with my gaze." At this, Ben looked away. Donovan chuckled, as if amused by a useless effort.

"You have treated me like a leper for quite some time now, Benjamin. What was it that aroused your suspicions?"

"You don't use contractions," Ben said with a winning smile. "And you've been treating Kitty strangely for no reason."

Donovan made a pouting face as if disappointed in himself, though his eyes still twinkled like those of a fox sitting just outside a henhouse.

"Ah, I see. I will admit that it is against my nature to speak as... brutishly and monosyllabically as those of your generation do. My kind possesses a pattern of speech that lends us a certain level of... intrigue. And as for Kitty... I profess I do not much like her kind. She is as salt in a fresh wound–her very presence causes me discomfort."

A scary realization struck Ben: Donovan was being quite forthcoming with his information. Perhaps Donovan was telling him all this because he had already heard too much. Were these words the last Ben would hear? That instinctive sense of cold fear for something inexplicable stole over him, and he snapped to reality.

Donovan had shifted to be at a better angle to corner Ben. Ben slipped to the right and around Donovan so that he stood directly facing the boy and the mirror beyond. Ben was so wrapped up in the moment at first that he was only faintly aware of something wrong. The age-old fight-or-flight response coursed in his veins. And then it clicked.

In the mirror behind Donovan, Ben saw himself. His eyebrows furrowed, his teeth bared in a slight grimace.

But Donovan's reflection was not there.

"You–" Ben started to say. An awful chemical stench suddenly offended him. Donovan hissed and stood to his full height. Ben's attention drew back to Donovan. The other boy's eyes were now blood-red, his canines sharper and getting longer, the reeking odor rolling off him.

In a voice like the screaming of hundreds of dying people, Donovan cried, "*Your eyes shall be opened to the horrors of the earth!*" He bent into a poised crouch. "*Try to run. Try to warn your people. This is only the beginning. Your death will be the first of many.*"

Ben was strongly tempted to do as Donovan had suggested; turn and book it out of the vacant lavatory. Sheer terror, confusion, revulsion mixed to make an acidic cloud burning in his chest and throat. But somewhere deep inside, blooming next to that panicky animal instinct of horror for a supernatural creature that was smarter and more powerful than himself, Ben knew his attempt to escape would be futile. An image flashed into his mind of a hare running from the speeding shadow of a hawk overhead, only to feel talons buried in its spine moments before it had reached the shelter of its warren.

And then, for some reason, Ben received an image of Jonathan with his shoulders squared, facing Garrett bravely even though Garrett was stockier than him and held a knife in one hand. There was no time to wonder why his brain had randomly invented such an oddly inspiring image.

Ben stood tall, fists braced. "I don't know what you are. I don't know what you want. But I will kill you before you hurt any of my friends," he said in a deadly murmur.

Donovan sneered, all of his white teeth showing. "*Then this shall be interesting. How can you kill one who is already dead?*"

Ben swung his fist at Donovan's face, hoping to surprise him, but Donovan had vanished–zipped around behind Ben with supernatural speed. The monster twisted one of Ben's arms behind his back and ran him forward into the wall, and the sound of Ben's body colliding with the plaster thundered monstrously through the room. Ben sucked in a breath and kicked out behind him. This time he connected, and Donovan backed away, snarling.

For a few precious seconds, the two stood apart, sizing each other up, searching for gaps in the armor. Ben massaged the shoulder of the arm that Donovan had twisted, flexing the muscles to stretch them out and loosen them.

Ben had been in a total of two fights before in his life. One had been when he was four, and a neighbor boy had taken off with one of his toy dump trucks. The other had been in middle school when he had first met Vince and asked one too many of his innocuous but admittedly personal get-to-know-you questions. Neither fight had been against an undead monster.

But Ben didn't know that Donovan was fighting with his own misgivings: this lean human seemed to be getting strength from somewhere. Jonathan was out of the way, though, floundering around helplessly in the dreamworld, according to Garrett, so *he* couldn't be lending griffin-courage. Was there another griffin nearby?

Not willing to find out, Donovan lashed forward, his cold, slender hands wrapping around Ben's throat. *How slow human reflexes are!* He thought with disgust. With a twirl and a heave, he had thrown Ben against a stall, slamming the stall door open, which caused him to lose his grip around Ben's neck.

Ben shuffled his feet to regain his balance, one hand latched around the side of the stall, gasping for air. Donovan swung his fist into the soft flesh of the boy's stomach, listening to the breath leave his lungs with satisfaction, watching him stumble and drop onto the tiled floor in a fetal position. Grunting, Donovan stomped on Ben's exposed side. Something snapped.

Ben gave a strangled shout of pain, tried to move, but a dagger of agony shot through his body. He coughed. Blood flecked his lips and scattered in a scarlet spray over the floor. He stared at it with a kind of distant wonder. All of that blood was *his*. He shouldn't be coughing it up...that meant that he was...

Valiantly, Ben tried to rise.

Donovan laughed, grabbed Ben by the collar, and threw him mightily into a mirror. The glass shattered, tiny shards sprinkling into Ben's hair and clothes. Ben cursed helplessly, tears starting to his eyes. Whatever Donovan was, Ben couldn't best him. Holding his ribs, he made a last-ditch attempt to flee towards the door, mad with fear, drowning in agony.

With one hand, Donovan grabbed Ben's arm. With the other, he clutched a fist full of Ben's hair, pulling so that Ben's back was pinned against him, and Donovan twisted Ben's head so that his pain-filled eyes squinted up at the ceiling. Then Donovan spread wide his jaws, aimed at Ben's jugular and the rapidly pulsing vein beside it, gave a grotesque animal-hiss, and pierced it with all four of his great fangs.

Warm blood seeped like a delicious elixir into Donovan's eager mouth. He swallowed with gusto, closing his ears to his prey's shrill screams. When he had drunk his fill, Donovan let Ben fall heavily to the ground, fetching a paper towel to daintily clean the corners of his mouth. His teeth were normal-sized, and his eyes had melted into their original midnight-blue shade.

Ben's white face turned up to the fuzzy ceiling. All of his weight rested against a garbage can, and with the hand he could still feel, he kept pressure on his neck. Blood ran from between his fingers. His wound stung and itched like a bug bite, but the searing burning had numbed the more Donovan had quenched his thirst.

"Don't worry, my dear Benjamin," Donovan murmured, placating, a winning grin on his feminine mouth. "We will take good care of Nikki...and Kitty." He patted Ben's shoulder heartily, making the boy wince, and gracefully stepped across the broken glass towards the door, retrieving his cellphone from where it had fallen as he went.

Ben's sight dimmed and winked, and his twitching muscles tensed bit by bit.

And then something strange and alien stole over Ben: death.

CHAPTER THREE:

REUNION

BACK TO JONATHAN

That morning, I walked ahead of the squadron.

The pine-needled forest floor had given way to springy grass. The trees were a mixture of palm, cashew, and other such exotic types, and a variety of thistle and berry bushes guarded their rough-barked trunks. Scrawny little monkeys watched me curiously from the leafy canopy, and they were so darn cute I only barely resisted trying to communicate with monkey sounds.

The land of the Tahtltikis, besides having numerous rivers and streams of mountain-fed snow water, had invigorating hot springs. I heard one boiling from my aimless wandering on the near-overgrown path. Trotting towards the source, I found a round, bubbling pool nestled in a clearing right at the base of a tall, sandy rock. Smiling with pleasure, I made sure no one was watching, not even the embarrassingly curious monkeys, and shed my clothes, throwing them in a pile at the bottom of the rocks. I kept my coral necklace. Every griffin develops a special ability, and the necklace had granted me my unique griffin power of mind-reading. Though I didn't need to be wearing it for my ability to work, it had also been a gift from a mermaid, who had given me much-needed encouragement, and as such, I valued it on a personal level.

It had taken us longer than usual to make it this far. We were pushing ourselves almost to our limits to travel as fast as we could, but Peter, my mentor and friend who could take the form of a big, shaggy, chocolate-brown griffin, had also been drilling and training me as much as possible along our journey. He drove me to strengthen my griffin form's flying muscles, tested my endurance, encouraged me to practice my mind-reading, and of course, engaged in frequent, often surprise, duels in which I'd have to drop my plate of food or stop in the middle of a conversation and draw steel to meet his blade before he could crack my head open.

Because of all the physical exercise, I had changed completely in appearance since first arriving in the dreamworld. Not an ounce of bad fat was left on my bones. Directly beneath my skin was iron-hard muscle. My legs were lean and strong from all the walking I had done. My biceps and triceps had swelled. My back muscles were roped–most likely from flying. My face, I could feel with my calloused fingers, was more defined. My hair was definitely shaggier, and new hair sprouted from my chin in peach fuzz. I would have to find a pair of scissors and a razor sometime soon.

Sucking in a cheerful breath, I jumped feet-first into the spring, letting the hot water massage my skin and open my pores. When I came up again, steam surrounded me, and I leaned back against the grassy wall of the spring, sighing exultantly. The bubbles buoyed me up as if I floated on a very hot cloud.

Yet, there was one person I couldn't prevent from intruding upon the rare moment of peaceful seclusion: myself. As the boiling bubbles gushed and fizzed around my ears, I thought about the events of a few weeks past and turned them over in my mind like my friend Lia would turn over her old Rubik's cube.

I was still wrapping my mind around the fact that I was the next in a line of people destined to protect the Land of Dreams from nightmares. The dreamworld, made of everyone's dreams past, present, and future, was a vast realm that had long been ruled and guarded by the "griffin-hearted–" people who, like myself, could take on the form of a griffin in their sleep. Griffins, symbolic of virtue, chivalry, honor, and other such knightly qualities, were the antithesis of Rankers–nightmares given physical form.

After washing up on the shores of the dreamworld, Peter had taken me underwing and told me that on the way to the capital city, where I would become king and be granted all the authority and power that I needed to command an army against the amassing Rankers, we would be intercepting "clues."

I snorted, absently scrubbing at my hands to wash off the grime of travel, thinking of the confusion and obstinance I'd felt at Peter's words. The clues had been tainted with a dark spell, meant to summon Ranker reinforcements from afar in secret, right under the griffins' noses–a siren call as deadly as the actual sirens that had been guarding the first clues in the ocean shallows right there at Pebble Embark. No one knew the precise location of the Ranker base, and Peter had suspected, correctly, it seemed, that the clues were meant to summon Ranker reinforcements and then lead them to the next clue, and so on until they were ultimately guided to the Ranker fortress.

The first clues had led us to a swamp, where I had helped rescue a village from a gargoyle Ranker and bring peace to its inhabitants. I had inspired some of them to join our cause and vow to aid in stopping the Rankers from bringing ruin to the waking world. We had found the next set of Ranker clues, and I'd discovered my griffin ability. Each of these events had been monumental successes and morale boosts in themselves. However, I still considered the greater victories to have come afterward: first, I had befriended Kayle, the surliest member of my squadron of bodyguards and specialists, and I had learned of how he had come to be in the dreamworld. Then, something he had said had brought a powerful, terrifying realization crashing down on my shoulders: Garrett, leader of the Rankers, my arch-nemesis since childhood who had disguised himself as a human and bullied my friends and me relentlessly growing up; Garret, who had stabbed me in the back and left me bleeding out in reality–the waking world–in hopes of sending me to the dreamworld where he and his kind could keep me out of their way and continue to manipulate me; *Garrett* wanted to take my place as the king and protector of the Land of Dreams.

My limbs tingled with restless, nervous energy, and I paddled a few laps around the hot spring, fretting at the concerns and questions that had been circling my mind of late. Were my friends okay? How was I going to get back home? How was I supposed to defeat the Rankers, and now, foremost among them, a simple and piercing *why*?

If Garrett meant to take my place, why had he sent me here instead of just killing me? Why keep me alive? Was it because he wanted to turn me into a "Dark Griffin," a creature of pure evil and viciousness? Peter had said that such was their intention for my predecessor, King Brody. But Peter had also said that it was very difficult to corrupt a griffin into becoming such a loathsome monster. I vaguely remembered the gargoyle Ranker saying something about Garrett possibly needing my blood. Still, I couldn't figure out if that was out of spite, for some dark spell, for a sacrifice to their god that they called "liege master," or, heck, maybe Garrett was just runnin' low on some good ol' AB positive.

I sighed. If there was one thing I knew, it was that there was a lot I didn't know.

I soaked until the dirt was scoured from my body, then reluctantly climbed out, red-skinned, and threw on my clothes. The squadron was probably caught-up by now. The clues we had found in the swamp had directed us towards the Tahtltiki tribe, and there was no time to waste. We had to find them as fast as we could and see why they had caught the Rankers' attention. I lifted a foot to take a step but froze before I could put it down.

Something had crashed in the bushes and then cursed violently.

Slowly, I put my foot down and revolved to face the crashing underbrush, my hand on the hilt of my sword. It struck me that a Ranker wouldn't give away his whereabouts, swearing like a liquored pirate. Unless it was a trap...a pretty *lame* trap...

"Who's there?" I called. "Come out!" The clumsy noises stopped, then grew louder as a shadowy figure stumbled towards me. I pulled out my sword and stepped back, ready for a fight.

But a large animal emerged from the thorn bushes, burs and smears of berries mixed into his blue-colored coat. He shook himself and looked up at me. His face was blank, but then his eyes became round.

"Are you a griffin of some sort?" I asked.

The animal frowned.

He did indeed look like a griffin, but in a different way. His wings were cavernous, handsome bat wings with a transparent, light-blue membrane stretched between the supple, bony digits. The beak was more wickedly curved, with jagged points along the sides like teeth. His proud collar spread up his neck to make a sleek, feathered mane. His hind lion paws were a deeper blue with white toes, and his eyes were a warm hazel flecked with white–which meant that he was currently in a state of fear.

"I am dead," he said blandly. The familiar tone of voice took me aback.

"Why would you say that?" I asked.

"Because *you* are here," the griffin said.

I finally recognized that voice.

"*Ben?*" I cried.

The blue griffin nodded sadly. I paused, waiting for the punch line. He watched my face morosely. His eyes were so familiar, almond-shaped, with a permanent mischievous look even despite the eagle brow. My heart stopped. It *was* Ben, deep inside there. I didn't care why he was here, but just that he was. I burst into laughter, joyful laughter, and Ben's face crumbled into a mild grin. His eyes lost their white and instead became golden with happiness.

"This is great!" I shouted.

Ben tilted his head. "How is this great? We are *dead*. And I left everyone behind with that blood-sucking backstabber..."

I was too happy at the moment to really digest what he was saying, and I chuckled. "We are *not* dead. If you were, you wouldn't be here."

Ben's black talons clenched into the ground hopefully. "Then where are you? Where are we? Why am I this?"

"You're a griffin, I think. Only the bravest of people can shift into a griffin when they come here. Here, try thinking about what makes you *you*. Think of something special that you maybe haven't told anyone else about before. A secret that's a part of you. You should change back. At least, that's how it worked for me."

Ben closed his eyes, concentrating mightily. His outline shimmered, refocused, and hazed out. Within minutes, he had successfully transformed. He was just as I remembered him: tall but wiry with hidden strength. His sleek brown hair and sculpted face were paler than before, but his intelligent, clever eyes were the same. The main difference was the strange aura about him... He radiated gentlemanly civility but also exuded a predator-like hostility. Part of me wanted to run away from him to safety. It sank in, too, that he wasn't using contractions when he spoke. Ben had always been the most eloquent of my friends, but this was something else.

"You might transform off and on," I said, grinning at him so broadly that my face hurt, "But you'll get the hang of it once you adjust." We embraced, overjoyed at our reunion. Then, concerned, I thought of what Ben had said. "What backstabber were you talking about?"

Ben's eyes became fierce and glaring. He told me of the truck crashing and demolishing the hospital where Ty had been staying.

He told me, and my heart ached, about how Nikki had nearly been thrown from a window but then had been rescued by a kid named Donovan. Gratitude swelled in my chest, but it must have shown on my face because Ben growled, "He was not the saint everyone thought he was."

Then he told me about the meeting at town hall; how he followed Donovan into the restroom and heard him plotting with Garrett on the phone. I stiffened, frowned.

Ben said slowly, "He did not have a reflection in the mirror. Jonathan, he was a vampire!"

He waited for me to laugh, but I nodded vaguely and said, "I believe you. What happened next?"

Ben tried to hide his surprise at my reaction and said, "We fought. He bit me." I looked up sharply, and now I could see four deep puncture marks in his throat.

"I think I fainted," he mumbled, staring at the grass thoughtfully. "And I woke up here."

Fury coursed through me. I wanted to bust Garrett's head against a rock.

"Does Nikki know?" I asked, my voice trembling.

Ben's lips tightened, and his eyes lost the natural mischievousness. "I think not. Donovan said he could hypnotize people with his gaze. I do not know what will happen when or if Nikki finds my body."

I was deep in thought and almost didn't hear Ben's question: "But what has happened to you?"

Gathering my memory, I told Ben about how I had been beaten over the head by a rat on steroids and my comatose body was supposedly guarded by something. I told him about Peter and the others and the whole griffin thing. I told him about the Rankers and the swamp and where we were now. I briefly transformed, told him about my special ability, and showed him my sword and the switchblade that popped from a hidden compartment in the hilt when I depressed three talons in the handguard.

Time had passed, though it hadn't seemed we had talked long. The greenish light that shone through the canopy was a deeper color now. My wet hair and skin chilled me as the waning sunlight left the jungle gloomy and cold. Gnats and mosquitoes hovered at our bare faces and hands. I crossed my arms to warm myself, but had to keep uncrossing them to swat at the flying pests.

Ben didn't have any questions. It was my turn to be amazed at how collected he was. Suddenly, he said, "This is all so strange. I keep waiting to wake up!" He ran a hand through his pale brown hair as if to sweep away the overwhelming nature of our conversation and the new world he found himself in, then chewed his lip and went on slowly, carefully choosing his words. "I grew up just like anyone else. I make mistakes like the next person. I take things for granted. But this... I never thought I would have a purpose. Like, that something this crazy would happen to *me*..."

I nodded solemnly. Ben had just summed up my own feelings in words I could never have found. He smiled at me. "I always knew you were different, even when we were kids. You were always so...cool.

You knew what you were doing. I think that is why you are the prince of this place."

A swing of humility pushed through me, and responsibility, and fear, and I didn't know how to respond. Ben, noticing my discomfort, looked away and changed the subject.

"So these Rankers. Are they, like, demons? Is this the Apocalypse?"

"I don't know," I said. "Kitty's the one you should ask. Doesn't it talk about the end of the world in the Bible?"

Ben said sarcastically, "Let me just go ask her real quick."

I pulled a face. "Sorry. Let's go talk to Peter; he'll know what to do. Maybe we can get you back home." Ben tried to hide his excitement, but I could see it plain on his face.

Something shifted in the brush behind him. He turned, and we both faced the sound. A young boy emerged from the bushes and stared owlishly at us. He had three red dots painted beneath each black eye, and his long black hair was tied into a braid. He wore only a leopard-skin loincloth but had a dagger tucked into the waistband and multiple tiny red flowers patterned into his hair.

My fingers twitched at my side, where they were hovering over the hilt of my sword. The boy caught the movement with his gaze and tilted his head to better see the taloned hand-guard. His face brightened.

"You Prince?" he asked in a voice that hadn't broken yet. I nodded warily. The boy took a step closer to me and pointed at Ben with a dark frown. "Devil-man Prince-friend?"

Ben was trying not to smile. I nodded again. Tension leaked out of the boy's shoulders and his stance became more casual and relaxed.

He pointed in the direction he had come from. "Dark eagle-lion waits for you at tree-home."

"Peter?" I asked. The boy nodded.

"Come on," I said to Ben. "Let's join the party."

CHAPTER FOUR:

CHIEFTAINESS OF THE TAHTLTIKI TRIBE

Ben and I trailed after the Tahtltiki boy, slapping at the ferns and fig leaves that were obnoxiously right at face level. The jungle humidity had soaked our clothes, and it was hard to breathe in the muggy heat. Animals wailed to each other, unseen by us.

The boy, who had addressed himself as Pon, flitted coolly ahead of us on a trail only he could traverse without hassle. I exchanged a look with Ben, whose hair was stuck out all over the place from being brushed by a wet fig leaf, then trotted to catch up.

Just when we were about to beg for a rest, the boy led us out into a clearing much larger than the one Ben had met me in. The trees had to be over 100 feet high, with trunks as big around as Olympic swimming pools. The sky exposed above us was deep blue, and the trees were arranged so that their tops formed an image of a flower against the sky. I struggled to breathe and follow Pon. This was a far cry from the malodorous environs of the Reekwood Swamp. Excitement built in my chest as I wondered what surprises this place had in store.

The farther we walked into the clearing, the more we saw. Huge, ornate houses were constructed high in the boughs of the trees. Lanterns made a friendly glow that doused the thatched roofs and bark structures in golden shades. Walkways, their railings twined in ivy, had been carefully built against the trees to form paths, alleys, plazas, and even mini-roads trafficked by rickshaws. Vine-and-wood ladders hung down to the grassy jungle floor, ready to be pulled up at a moment's notice.

Wow, Ben sighed behind me. "It is like looking at a dream..." Then he paused and chuckled at the irony.

I closed my mouth, conscious of the desperate mosquitoes buzzing against my face. Tahtltiki people stared down at us from their high perches, excitement alight on their faces. I subconsciously reached out with my mind and picked up on their thoughts.

It's the prince! was something I heard a lot, and then the odd phrase or so:

He is so young!

He carries an awesome weapon.

The young man with the prince is a cold-man. A devil-man. He wants blood!

I shut my mind and moved closer to Ben so that those above would see that he wasn't dangerous.

From what I could see, the people dressed vividly. The women wore silk dresses and cotton leggings that went down to mid-calf. The colors were bright, even in the diminishing sun. Every girl and woman wore her sleek black hair up away from her face and neck. The only jewelry I saw were anklets and bracelets of painted wood, rings of dyed vines, and earrings of polished bone. The men were either shirtless or in cotton tunics and had either loincloths of animal skin or leggings. They held spears and wore their wavy hair down, though it wasn't as long as the women's. Everyone's face was painted, and they had tied flowers of some sort in their hair.

Pon called to us, and Ben and I followed him dreamily to a ladder dangling down from one of the walkways. I tilted my head back to stare bemusedly at the mossy bottom of the overhead platform. A breeze nudged feebly at the ladder, making it twist and tilt. My stomach churned, just imagining trying to climb it without falling.

Ben started forward, resigned, but I grabbed the sleeve of his jacket. He looked at me curiously. Pon was holding on to the bottom of the ladder, trying to keep it firm against the wind with his weight. I admired his determination, but frankly, he wasn't accomplishing squat.

"Can we transform?" I asked. The boy looked at me uncomprehendingly.

"You know." I flapped my arms. "Fly?"

Pon's expression became one of wonder. He nodded.

"You want to try?" I offered Ben. He looked up at where the villagers waited, their features smudged because of the height.

"I will pass," he mumbled.

I stepped back into the clearing, for more room, and transformed quickly. The spectators gave murmurs of approval.

Pon had started up the ladder, climbing swiftly without even swaying it and pausing at times to look down at Ben. Pon was on about the forty-third rung. Ben was on his like...fifth.

Spreading my wings, I pumped once, got about three feet off the ground, flapped again. My pinions struck the grass jarringly, and I clacked my beak in irritation. There was no wind down here. I was like a wet paper airplane.

I was having an "I-wish-I-could-just-disappear" moment. *Somebody pull the fire alarm,* I thought hysterically, *somebody* start *a fire!* But, as the Tahtltiki villagers watched me teeter like an obese chicken, I tried not to listen in on their thoughts for fear of hearing something like, "If this is the prince, I am going to shoot myself."

My back and wing-shoulder muscles burning and straining, threatening to cramp, I dipped sideways and commenced circling, spiraling higher and higher. It was a slower but just as sure way of ascending, just like walking down a steep hill in zig-zags.

When I was high enough to be level with the huts, I tipped myself out of the spiral. Flapping loudly, I stretched out my paws until I felt smooth, well-worn wood beneath them, pulled in my wings, and touched down, transforming back. Panting and sweating, I swatted at a cloud of mosquitoes with murder on their minds.

The Tahtltiki's pattering footsteps approached. Rolling my shoulders to stretch the muscles, I smiled and turned to them. Some young women and children rushed me and squashed me into a group hug. I choked in surprise, the smells of their floral perfumes overwhelming me. One of them looped a necklace of white flowers with golden-spotted centers over my head to join the coral against my chest. The rest of the Tahtltiki joined them and took turns embracing me, patting my head, greeting me, and touching my clothes. I thanked them and said hello. The young girls bounced up and down on the balls of their feet and clapping their hands gleefully, tittering to each other in their native tongue.

An elder, some frail and bent guy with hooded eyes and a knobby staff, pointed out over the break in the handrails where the ladder was draped.

"Who is the blood-drinker? Why have you brought one who kills here among our children, my liege?" he asked. Some of the people scowled disdainfully at him, as if he were being impolite. But others cast dubious glances at the ladder. One woman crossed herself, something I only expected to see back home. Maybe she was a dreamer from reality, just like Ben and I were.

"That's Ben," I replied. "He *is* a vampire, but a griffin as well, and luckily, our ally. He is my friend, and he's only here because a vampire Ranker in our reality bit him."

The elder still seemed suspicious, so I stepped over to the ledge and sat with my legs hanging over it to wait.

Pon and Ben were about halfway up. Well, Pon was halfway up; Ben was halfway up Pon's halfway. Pon waved cheerfully to me, causing the ladder to tremble a bit, and I returned the gesture in kind. Ben hugged the rungs and clenched his jaw nauseously, his face going the color of sour milk.

Within around ten minutes, Pon scampered up to join me and then held out a hand to assist Ben. As he stretched out his arm and grasped my friend's, his biceps and deltoids flexed–all the climbing that the Tahtltiki had to do had made them beefy as heck. Ben, sweating and panting, allowed himself to be dragged up and over and reclined onto his back, chest heaving and nostrils flared, eyes closed.

"Good, good!" Pon complimented, patting Ben's arm. The girls that had first fawned over me rushed to Ben's side with some sort of drink in half of a coconut shell. They crooned in concern, and one combed his untidy hair with gentle fingers. Ben gulped from the coconut, focused only on quenching his thirst and oblivious to the females trying for his attention. But when one carefully set a loop of flowers identical to mine around his neck, he became aware of his surroundings and sat up and smiled at the women blissfully.

Once we had recovered, Pon led us along the walkways past open-air vendors, huts, and staring people. One man smoked a cigar. A cream-colored monkey with a black face sat on his shoulder eating an apple. It looped its long, fluffy tail around the man's neck. Lime-green parrots with red masks, or rainbow-hued macaws, so bright they were almost painful to look at, bobbed at us from the branches and watched us with beady eyes. A ring-tailed lemur was poised to jump at a fox-like fruit bat, but it got tripped up and ended up clinging upside down on its branch–looking for the entire world like an abashed cat.

People pranced ahead of us and threw petals across our path. Ben kept saying, "wow," and I kept opening my mouth at the sheer wonders I saw so that I looked a little mentally unbalanced. I saw a few kids my age playing some kind of board game that involved colored tiles, dice, and sticks. One of the kids flipped over his tiles and revealed a beautiful painting of a rainbow. He saw me and waved.

The huts were full of life. Torches glowed at the windows, and various flowers grew in clay pots. An older woman stood just outside her door and illustrated a decent picture of a flying griffin with a charcoal pencil. I had to stand back for a parade of toddlers. They wore beaked masks and had fake wings and tails. The child in the rear pulled a wooden toy Eso-grohd on a string. The same black flowers I had obtained in the Reekwood Swamp were strung up everywhere. Peter had said that every flower in the jungle had a purpose to the Tahtltiki, whether medicinal, symbolic or communicating a message. These black flowers meant someone important had died. I wondered who and what had happened. And again, why the Rankers had thought it was important enough to send their army this way.

Something moved above us, and I looked up to see a huge chameleon sticking vertically to a tree. Its eyes rolled, and its pink tongue stuck half out of its toothy mouth. A warrior was strapped in a saddle on the lizard's back. Patches of red paint circled his eyes. He had a necklace of small teeth, and a brown paw print splashed on his chest. In one hand, he held a spear. At his belt was a dart gun, and a row of spiky green flowers ran along the crest of his head. As our procession passed, his steed ambled down the tree to land soundlessly behind us and followed us onward.

We were all slowly coming to a vast tree-hut, bigger than the rest. A mossy awning stretched over the doorway, and a vine-rug in the form of the sun rested below it. By now, it was very dark and cold, but torches were lit all along our path and on either side of the hut. I'm guessing the flames also carried some sort of bug-repellant because the pests left us alone.

A guard stood stiffly on either side of the doorway. Both looked very much like the lizard-cowboy behind us, spears and all. But these fellas had some sort of big cats on tethers sitting at their feet. They were vipercatz; mottled black and burnished gold with a black mask around their glowing, green-slitted eyes. Their claws were several inches long, and their fangs, which curved down over the jaw, were venomous. Each cat watched Ben and I warily but otherwise did not move and wouldn't unless given the command to do so.

The Tahtltiki had stopped behind us, still talking among themselves. One of the guards pointed behind him at the hut entrance. Ben and I stepped inside.

The hut was like something out of *Swiss Family Robinson*. We came into the main room, where vases of plants were set in corners. A blue bird with a long beak slept on a perch with its head craned around on top of its back. A vipercat cub rolled around by a water trough, playing with a ball. It was too fluffy for its own good. There were seeds and petals stuck in its downy, gray cub-fur. When it saw me, it sat up and mewled, bouncing over to bat at the cuffs of my pants.

"You have an admirer," Ben chuckled, watching. I was too busy taking in the people in the room to notice.

On a long couch of matted bamboo and straw, Peter, Kayle, and Mariah–my friends and the other three griffins in my squadron besides myself–sat coolly. Peter's bushy white beard rested against his broad chest, and his dark skin shone in the torchlight. His silver eyes twinkled at me and then sized up Ben curiously.

Kayle sat hunched forward with his elbows on his knees, as pale and freckled and moody as usual. But I knew by now that there was a kind heart beneath his hostile exterior.

Mariah beamed around at everyone and everything. She had pulled her dirty-blonde hair back into a messy bun away from her neck, perhaps to keep cool against the humidity. Her jeweled, dwarf-made necklace, which had given her her griffin ability, gleamed at her collarbone.

Perpendicular to the couch and against the wall was a wooden throne carved in the shape of a tree with two of its branches forming arms, and its roots, a seat. Little golden-green fruits dangled off the tree's "canopy," suspended over the throne like a hood. I remembered from reading in Peter's *Locations* book that every tribe leader of the jungle people had these thrones. The fruits were actually explosive weapons. If someone came in to threaten the tribe leader, he or she could pluck off one of those babies and blow them to kingdom come...in this case, like 100 feet to the ground.

An aged woman stood beside the throne wearing a long red dress and a crown of white feathers atop her gray head. She watched Ben with mild alarm. Ben seemed to have noticed her at the same time and slowly looked at the others in the room, mouth partly open.

"Took you!" Kayle proclaimed in his lilting Irish brogue.

I nodded wryly at him, then asked, "Where are Marcus and Flaherty and them?"

Peter gestured outside. "In the guard-houses." He shot Ben a glance and asked pleasantly, "Who is this?"

"My friend Ben," I answered, and their faces went blank. "I'll tell you later," I said pointedly.

The old woman hobbled over to us. I was ready to reach out and catch her–she was as frail-looking as a wet leaf. Extending a wizened hand, she gently took mine and slowly kneeled to rest her forehead against it. She was quivering with the effort–her trembling shook my whole arm.

"Greetings, Great Prince He'klarr," she croaked in an old granny voice.

I searched for words. "And to you, miss...?"

The woman straightened and said proudly, "Chieftainess. Chieftainess Chalk-talk of the Tahtltiki people."

Oh.

Ben had been uncomfortably watching our exchange. I knew he probably thought it was weird to see his friend treated like royalty. But now his eyes widened, and he looked at me like I had just gotten caught doing something naughty. I fought to get back on even ground.

"Ch-Chieftainess! You have my salutations." I bowed to her. The old woman was smiling faintly.

During the ensuing silence, in which one of the guards outside the door stuck his head in to make sure his Chieftainess hadn't collapsed into a pile of dust, I mentally kicked myself. Trying to remember the discussions I'd had with Kayle, Peter, and Mariah about royal discourse and protocol, I tried to come up with something good to say and pulled the lei and razor-disk out of my pocket.

"We recently obtained these from the Reekwood Swamp, my lady," I said formally. Chieftainess Chalk-talk took the items and observed them curiously. "The Rankers had left them as clues for their followers, instructing them to come this way, but we have intercepted them. Could you please share your thoughts as to their purpose?" I glanced down at the frisky vipercat cub. It had untied the laces of my right boot and was wiggling its haunches in the air to pounce on the other one.

Chalk-talk tenderly put the lei around her neck, setting the razor-disk on a table. "Guard Leelan!" she called.

One of the guards trotted in. The Chieftainess had him arrange the table in front of the couch. Ben and I sat on the ground on the other side of it, declining the offer for chairs. Chalk-talk lowered herself to the throne. Food was set out for us; sliced fruits and veggies and gourds of a really creamy sort of milk that smelled like *Froot Loops* to drink. Only when she had swallowed a green wedge of kiwi did the queen speak. Her voice had become pained and wrung out, hollow.

"My husband was killed not one year ago. There is a monster that prowls these glens and paths. The chimera."

I pursed my lips grimly. The tropical chimera is one bad dude. It has the body, forelimbs, and head of a large cat, the hind legs and second head of a horned goat, and the tail, wings and *third* head of a dragon. Not a nice image. Not a nice place to be. Not a nice beastie.

Chalk-talk ran her hand over the lei.

"After the death of my husband, the women of my people fashioned these flowers and sent them out into the land to lament his passing, hoping and praying that anyone would help us. Little did I know the Rankers must have picked up the news and decided to have their wicked armies stop by on the way to wherever their foul brethren reside." Her words ended in a disgusted snarl. "Luckily, you all got it first!" she added gratefully.

"Exactly what kind of help were you hoping to get?" Peter asked, his hands steepled against the bridge of his nose.

Chalk-talk winced and averted her gaze to the vipercat cub, who was tottering outside to pay a visit to its big-bad parents. In a more subdued voice, she explained, "Naturally, my son, Boyzun, would take the throne in his father's stead. But instead of attending to his responsibilities as ruler, he spends all of his time in the infernal training hut, planning to seek revenge on the chimera for his father's death. I would appreciate it if you could speak with my son, Prince, and help him understand that our people must come first–that they need him and that I..." She gazed down at her feet, forlorn and very tired-looking. "That *we*...cannot lose him, too."

I shrugged and gave her a small, encouraging smile. "I'll try, of course."

Chalk-talk exhaled deeply. "That is all that I ask."

"Tell us more about the chimera," Peter said, leaning forward, his silver eyes intense and shrewd. "I get the sense that this is not your average beast."

"No, it is not. The chimera is an ancient evil that our people have suffered for hundreds of years. Over time, he has killed many of our hunters and those who stray too far beyond our boundaries. Until recently, the power of the griffin kings, and the light that they cast out into the land from the winged throne, have been enough to keep the creature at bay. But...since King Brody's death, it has become bold, encroaching ever further into our territory. Its evil influence has seeped into the very soil and spreads further each day so that our patrols bring back new reports of rot and death. That is why my husband ventured out–to spare our people further suffering. And then he was slain."

I grimaced. My heart went out to the poor old woman. She had kept her tribe together despite all that they were suffering through, and I admired her strength–but I could see by her weary frame that that strength was running out. I wanted to help her.

Peter interlaced his fingers. Even though I wasn't actively trying to read anyone's minds, I still sensed fear and tension emanating from his thoughts like a toxic cloud. I looked at him with concern as he spoke.

"One of the clues that the Rankers had left for their allies was the recipe for a foul concoction that would have given them rabid strength and a vicious temperament. It was being put to use in the Melancholy Bog, poisoning the villagers' minds just as this chimera is poisoning your land.

"I suspect the Rankers hoped to use the chimera to bolster their troops and intensify their dark powers just as they intended their "Bowl of Bemusement" to do in the bog. Doubtless, the chimera would have joined them had they come."

A shudder rippled through everyone present. Mariah's eyes flickered white with fear, and I forcefully shoved away my imaginings of the horror that the Rankers were unleashing on the land.

In a gentle voice, Peter looked straight at Chalk-talk and said, "Your son may not have the welfare of your people at the forefront of his mind right now, but destroying the chimera may very well be the best thing he could do for your people."

Chalk-talk's mouth tightened in a dismayed smile of reluctant agreement. She sighed and cast her gaze over the table.

"Now, I will tell you about your razor-disk." She pointed at the lethal serrated weapon and said, "My warriors use those to fend off wild beasts. But none of the disks are as small as that, with so many teeth.

"There is a legend among my people. We believe a special disk–not like others–is meant to be brought to The Place of the Ancient Totems. It is a key, and the elders say it was created to unlock 'truth' for those who are chosen to receive it. I do not know how the Rankers found this disk; perhaps they've had it all along, and any so-called 'truths' secreted away among the Ancient Totems have long since been plundered by the monsters. But I've a strong feeling that is where you must travel to beat the Rankers to their next clue. Boyzun's mentor at the training hut knows more. He dwells deeper in the trees, in the highest branches."

Peter spoke up. "You have helped us more than you can imagine, chieftainess. Prince Jonathan will indeed help your son and, in so doing, help himself. If your son is determined to fight this chimera, then he shall at least have a strong comrade and guardian with him."

"Am I training too? Why?" I asked, trying to sound cool about it but hearing my voice threaten to break. It had been painful enough to train with Peter. What would training with Boyzun's mentor be like?

Kayle was holding his beanie off his scruffy brown hair and itching his head with the same hand. "Peter doesn't have time to keep training you like he did in the swamp," he said. "You can get the rest done here."

Mariah put her reasoning in. "Just think about how tough you'll be when you're done!"

Yeah, right. I was actually thinking about the times Peter trained me and how I went to bed afterward feeling like a big, walking, talking bruise.

"Take care, Jon," Peter added, tilting his forehead at me in a very serious way. "Learn well. The chimera is likely guarding the Rankers' next clues at this place of Ancient Totems, and it won't give them up without a fight. This won't be like your bout with the gargoyle in the Reekwood Swamp. You cannot do this alone."

"Come on, I'll lead you there," Kayle said with finality as I bobbed my head at Peter in an obedient and slightly nauseous nod.

Ben turned to follow us out, but Peter cleared his throat tersely. Ben revolved slowly to meet Peter's silver eyes.

"I'd rather you stay here and talk to me, young man," Peter said. "We should get to know each other."

CHAPTER FIVE:

IN THE TREE-HUT OF THE CHIEFTAINESS

Peter struggled to his feet from the steep bench and hooked his thumbs around the belt keeping his tunic snug. The Chieftainess had moved outside, and it was only the three of them in the hut.

Mariah watched Ben over her gourd. When it came down, she had a milk mustache and hastily wiped it away with her palm, showing him a small smile. For some reason, the smear across her lip, the flash of her teeth, reminded Ben of Donovan. He shook himself, furious heat washing through his body, and looked back at Peter.

Peter chuckled. "No need to be mad, sonny. I don't bite."

At Ben's look of confusion, Peter pointed at his own eyes. "Griffin eyes change color depending on mood. Yours were red. I'm not going to hurt you–just wanted to chat, is all. Your average dreamer doesn't have the focus required to remain lucid in the dreamworld; not unless he's been badly injured. I want to know what happened to you."

Ben shrugged and said curtly, "I am not angry at you. I was just thinking of a guy named Donovan. He is the one who did this to me."

Mariah choked on her milk and started coughing up a storm, tears pouring down her cheeks and face turning red. Peter didn't have a drink to choke on, but his eyes flashed scarlet, then white with flecks of gray.

Startled by their reactions, Ben stepped back, but Peter snatched his collar and yanked him close, his eyes red again. “Don’t move,” he growled and began examining Ben closely.

Ben felt like a patient under the hands of a doctor who worked as a bouncer part-time. Peter lifted both of Ben’s eyelids and then Ben’s lip, gently pressing his knuckle against the canines. He felt Ben’s chest, placing a hand against his heart. Lastly, Peter checked Ben’s wound.

“Vampire,” Peter mumbled. Mariah took too sharp a breath and started to cough again.

“It’s alright, Mariah; he’s a good one. He doesn’t have the Trance, and his heart isn’t beating.”

Ben was looking from one to the other with mild heat. “Would somebody please explain to me what is going on?”

Peter apologized and said in a much more courteous voice than he had used previously, “If you had had any blood lately, it would circulate through your system, and your heart would beat, at least temporarily.”

“I mean, who is Donovan? How does he know Garrett?” Ben would rather not think about the disturbing nuances of being a blood-drinking vampire.

“Donovan is Garrett’s first-mate,” Peter said, “His lieutenant, if you will. Tell me everything that’s happened to you.”

So Ben did, starting with when Jonathan had left, to Tyson’s hospital stay, to the town meeting, to his own fight.

“It’s as Jonathan told you. You aren’t dead,” Peter reassured him. “Just sort of in a coma while your body adjusts to its new functions.

But when you return home, you will be a vampire yourself–" He frowned thoughtfully and tugged at his beard. "Though...of a kind I've never encountered before. A griffin-hearted vampire...a mix of unwilling Ranker and noble griffin, hmm..."

Ben's beat-less heart dropped into his stomach. "Right. How can that be? How can vampires be a real thing?"

"They aren't," Mariah said, her voice accented French. "Not in the real world, at least. He's a Ranker, and they take the form of all manner of nightmares. They embody people's fears, and now they finally have the power to manifest physically in reality."

Ben absorbed the horror of that explanation, that he was now one of them, and tried to muster the strength to speak.

"And...is there any way to turn me back?"

Peter smiled. "Possibly. I'll look into it. Be strong."

Mariah was pinning her bangs back with a black flower, just like the ones on the lei Jonathan had found. "You said there was a man there who led the meeting named Josiah?" she asked.

Ben nodded miserably. "Yes, he is...like, a counselor."

Peter brightened. "Well, now! Josiah is one of us! He's a messenger for the White Griffin, probably sent to keep an eye on you and your friends."

"If he is a dream, how is he in reality?"

"Dreams come true!" Mariah grinned, her voice cheery.

Peter shook his head, humoring her. "He's very real. He communicates with Michael–the White Griffin–in dreams and relays any messages he wants to be delivered to the recipients in reality."

"If anyone finds you or protects your friends," Mariah added, "It'll be Josiah."

Ben looked up hopefully, his entrancing eyes briefly sparkling yellow-gold.

CHAPTER SIX:

MENTORED BY THE MASTER

I turned a bend in the path, feeling the warmth of a torch against my face before Kayle and I passed on into a break of shadow. Fewer villagers lived around here. Their voices drifted from the main paths behind us.

Kayle held aside a branch overgrown into our path and asked, "Do you like it here?"

"It's okay," I answered, tugging up my hood against the night's coming chill. "Makes a nice change from the Melancholy Bog, am I right?" I let Kayle pass in front of me and studied him as he led us on up the wooden path.

For some reason, I picked that moment to notice that he walked like he had an attitude; like he was going to go break some faces. But there was a cocky don't-mess-with-me bounce in his step, too. And beyond that, he still slunk gracefully with purposeful ease. It was like watching a wolf run or a panther stalking prey–smooth but deadly.

Kayle had quite the tragic backstory. He'd lost his parents and his standard of living in a house fire caused by English bigots. Struggling to survive and deal with his hatred, he joined a Northern Irish gang where he grew up targeting English officials and police officers until one day he'd been shot in the chest and wound up here.

Kayle's long time in the Land of Dreams, becoming a griffin, discovering his abilities, working with my predecessor King Brody, whom he had idolized, until Brody had been killed, had matured and wizened him. He had told me he no longer hated people; he hated the darkness in their hearts, the evil that drove them to commit such terrible acts as burning down a house with a family inside of it. He hated Rankers.

"You know, Kayle," I began, "You told me that your brother was in America. Maybe he'll come back to Ireland and find you, and you'll be–"

Kayle whirled on me, bending me back against the rail with his face inches from mine. "Watch it," he warned threateningly, maroon eyes blazing. But then he sighed and stepped back, walking on.

I silently trailed after him, waiting for him to speak. When he did, his voice was shallow and sad, his melodious Irish accent at odds with the melancholy change in mood. "It's better to think realistically." He paused and added, "I'm never leaving here."

We traversed a small flight of steep, creaky stairs and came to a round landing. The black shape of a hut stood out like a phantom against the white moon. We had to be up very high to see this much sky through the treetops.

I wasn't about to drop the subject, not when I was the one who had brought it up and made Kayle this upset in the first place.

"It's best to be positive," I pressed, starting up the stairs. "You *might* get out of here. I plan to."

Kayle put a hand on his chest and tapped himself with it. "That policeman's bullet hit my heart, Jonathan," he argued. "I felt it. A shot like that can't bring me back. I either stay here for the rest of my life, stuck in a coma, or I die and go to..." He broke off and glanced up at the sky uncomfortably.

It was then that a thick arrow whistled through the air and wedged itself into the railing right beside Kayle's hand.

Kayle only took the time to glance at the quivering arrow before grabbing my scruff and heaving me backward down the stairs. My head and back hit the edges of the steps painfully, but I rolled behind the cover of some overgrowth. Kayle joined me, jumping lightly to my side.

I pulled out my sword, reassured by the grating sound of its blade against the sheath. With all the practice I'd been putting into using it on our travels since the swamp, its weight no longer bothered me as much. Kayle watched me out of the corner of his eye.

"Can you get any thoughts?" he whispered.

I reached my mind out–an intellectual arm–exercising my recently discovered griffin ability to read minds. I nudged Kayle's thoughts but stretched past them. It was quite a distance before I found the mind of another. It belonged to a young boy, a kid only a little older than Pon. I sensed his curiosity, but there was hostility too.

"He's anxious to see who we are," I murmured. "Not a lot of people come up here. But he can tell we aren't much of a threat."

"Yeah, we'll see about that," Kayle hissed, swiftly pulling his lighter from his pocket.

Of all of our griffin abilities, Kayle's impressed me the most. Peter could blend in with his surroundings, and Mariah could instantly grow plant matter directly from the soil or even flesh over a grievous wound. Still, Kayle's power was both beautiful and destructive–a force that seemed to have its own wild personality.

The moon glinted off Kayle's silver lighter, making white sparkles and outlining the engraving of the phoenix in gray lines. I was worried about the attacker catching sight of the flashes and knowing where to aim, but clearly Kayle didn't have the same concerns.

He popped open the lighter, and the tiny cone of fire illuminated a sphere of wood and branches around us. He closed his hand completely around the flame, and when he pulled his fist away, the flame was gone. With a toss of his hand, the fire sprang from his fist, grew to the size of a beach ball, hovered above us, and brightened the ground yards in every direction, churning like a miniature sun.

A form bent low on the leafy roof of the hut, a round three-story-tall building, built right against a wall of trees. The side of it facing away from us was open to the air. Zany designs and shapes made painted whorls on the walls. The sudden light made the figure crouching on the roof reel back, trying in vain to blink away the dots in his blinded eyes.

"You!" the kid cried out and stumbled down from his perch to scamper toward us. The light suspended as a red ball far above us winked out, but the moon was now high enough for us to see by. Kayle was tense as the boy came closer. I kept my sword out, my thumb ready on the talons to eject the knife hidden in the secret compartment in the hilt.

I already knew this was Boyzun, the young Tahtltiki chief. He carried himself regally with his head held high and his arms swinging confidently. A thin band made of crimson petals and beads rested atop his short, dark hair. His eyes, an interesting tawny-gray color like rabbit fur, flashed suspiciously, but he raised a long finger and pointed at us from feet away.

"You are not of my tribe. Who are you, and what are you doing here?" His voice was deep and husky.

Kayle looked as if he would take immense pleasure in setting Boyzun's eyebrows on fire. He stood up stiffly, pulling me with him.

"I'm Kayle, a griffin. And this is the Griffin Prince Jonathan He'klarr. He's here to assist you in finishing up training and then slaying the chimera and collecting whatever secrets it may guard."

Boyzun raked me with his eyes. I sneered at him, loudly sliding my sword back into its scabbard and running my finger along one of the talons. The kid briefly looked at my weapon, then tightened his grip on his longbow. *Yeah, that's right, my sword could take your puny little toothpick any day,* I thought proudly.

Without turning his head, Boyzun shouted, "Master!"

Something moved in the hut, and an old man with bushy white sideburns and lean muscles made his way down to us from the upper platform.

Kayle bumped against me and headed back the way we had come.

"See you," I mumbled.

The old man blinked twitchily at me, tilting his head to one side. Boyzun held out both hands towards me and said, "This is–"

"I know," the Master said, taking my shoulders and looking deep into my eyes. "Welcome."

“Thanks,” I said uncomfortably, wanting to get my hand on my sword again for reassurance. Unfortunately, the Master’s arms were in my way.

“You are here for the mystery of our land,” he declared. He had some kind of accent. It was awkward trying to understand the odd enunciations. “But first, you will train.” He smiled slyly straight white teeth like neon strips. “Then better you will understand what you must know, and better prepared you will be for what you must face.”

CHAPTER SEVEN:

VAMPIRISM

BACK TO BEN

"There is one last thing worth mentioning before you return to reality," Peter said to Ben. "Your powers. You can now transform into a bat at will and have superhuman senses. Your stamina has increased, and you can run faster than any mortal. Even your unique speech pattern is meant to captivate potential prey."

Ben nodded somewhat sorrowfully, staring off into the distance and memorizing the list. Peter put a big hand on the boy's tensed shoulder.

"Son, you now have a major responsibility. Without letting Donovan know, you must somehow communicate to Nikki, Jonathan's father, and your closest, most trustworthy friends how to come here in dreams. Only then will we be able to continue communicating and relaying information."

"And how *do* we get here?" Ben asked softly.

Peter replied, "Because you are now not one of the earth, but of a place in-between, *you* can come here whenever you want. But the others must first go to the culvert by Jonathan's house and speak these words: 'We unite beside Prince Jonathan of the griffins.' Michael has made it so that those words bind them by truth and pledge as leaders of our cause, and they can then visit this realm securely in dreams. This task is important, Ben. It may be what saves others from your fate."

Ben grimaced and sighed shakily. Peter hadn't told him very much about Michael, the enigmatic White Griffin awaiting Jon at the capital city, but he sounded like a force to reckon with. "Okay," he murmured. "I'll remember."

"Good." Peter smiled and sharply tapped Ben's chest. "Wake up!" Ben vanished.

"So," Mariah mused, carrying her empty gourd to a washbasin. "Jonathan's friend..."

"Yes," Peter chuckled, his eyes alight. "And not the last one we'll see."

IN A RESTROOM OF THE FIRESTONE MEETING CHAMBERS

Ben stirred sleepily. His cheek rested on a cold floor and water trickled somewhere nearby. Something was different. At first, lying there in a groggy daze, he couldn't make out what it was. But the more aware he became, the more he realized that what he felt was an *absence* of feeling.

As a regular human, he had always endured a constant if minor discomfort. He was either sleepy, or sore; his clothes were scratchy, his limbs fell asleep, or something was stuck in his eye... These pains were easy enough to endure–like any other human, he had felt them all his life. But now, he was as weightless as a soap bubble and strangely detached from himself. He thought at first that maybe it was because he had become only a brain, floating in the air thinking thoughts. But then he remembered the truth: he was, by mortal standards, "dead."

Ben opened his eyes, raised his head, and pushed himself up into a stand, all with a fluid agility that suggested hidden strength. But at that exact moment, he sensed he wasn't alone. He turned around and saw Donovan squatting beside a sink, watching water drip from its pipe with distaste.

"Took you a while, did it not?" Donovan said when he noticed Ben awakening.

"What are *you* doing here?" Ben spat, baring his neat, white teeth instinctively in an animal snarl.

Donovan stood and frowned. Ben was satisfied to see that they were the same height since his transformation. "Steady... It *is* hard to adjust to the effects..."

Ben shook himself heartily. He remembered Peter telling him that Donovan would assume that Ben was now on the Ranker side. So he would need to set aside his hatred for the Rankers and do his best to play the part.

"Indeed," he agreed and massaged his neck, his cold fingers rubbing against the four, deep puncture wounds. "Must you have bitten me so hard?"

Donovan smiled wickedly. "My apologies. I usually only bite to kill."

Ben thought of how close to a real death he had come and hastily took his hand away from his neck.

The restroom door creaked open, and Ben tensed up, expecting Donovan to launch another hideous attack on an unsuspecting victim. But to his surprise, the boy who came in was Garrett.

Ben had to smother the powerful urge to perform his first act as a vampire and plunge his own fangs into Garrett's neck. According to Jonathan, this was the man who had started it all. This was the leader of the Rankers.

"We have another one, Garrett," Donovan announced proudly.

Garrett looked from Donovan to Ben and his eyebrows raised in surprise. A wicked grin of malicious pleasure stretched across his cheeks. "One of Jonathan's own friends, no less? Excellent work. We can certainly use him."

Ben's stomach fluttered. Though Garrett *looked* the same, short black hair, vivid, green, frowning eyes, he *sounded* different. His voice was deep and growling, like something not of the real world.

Garrett came close and sidled a circle around Ben, studying him like a man admiring a prize horse. "I do not know this one well. I recall the loud one, the pretty one, the one of faith–" Donovan hissed, and Ben wondered if they meant Kitty "–But I don't remember you."

He paced around and around. Ben kept his focus straight ahead on one of the paper towel dispensers.

Garrett poked his head over Ben's shoulder so that his words, that terrible voice, thrummed directly in his ear. "*You* did not leave an impression. A wallflower. A watcher. A listener. An unusual friend for a character like Jonathan... And just the tool that I need."

The Ranker paced to stand beside Donovan and spun on his heel to fix Ben with a brazen, authoritative expression.

"What do you feel?"

Ben thought on the words of advice Peter and Mariah had sent him away with and made sure to wait an uncomfortable length of time–uncomfortable for a human, that is, not an immortal being–before responding.

"I feel nothing."

"You will spy on your old friends for us. You will help us monitor Jonathan's actions in the dreamworld, and you will report to us frequently. Does this bother you?"

"Nothing bothers me anymore," Ben replied, his tone lofty and somewhat dreamy as if the changes that had come over him still dazed and disoriented him.

"Very good," Garrett grinned. He gave Donovan a congratulatory nod, which the vampire accepted with a humble bow of the head. "When the territories are assigned, I will make sure that you can claim the county around Firestone."

Ben didn't quite understand what that meant, but he said in a dull monotone, "I am gratified."

Then, sneering with disgust, Garrett turned to face the door out. "Now come. Let's return to the pitiful creatures in the meeting room."

On the way to the room, Donovan asked Garrett under his breath, "Why is the gargoyle not present? I thought he was to oversee the state?"

Garrett looked troubled. “He’s been out of contact,” he muttered. “And so have the allies we sent for.”

“Would you like for me to dig? Find you answers?” Donovan asked.

“As soon as we’re done here,” Garrett confirmed. He glanced at Ben over his shoulder and gave him what Ben thought was a forced smile, colored at its edges with anxiety.

They know something’s wrong, Ben thought. *Soon they’ll find out that Jonathan’s been to the bog and intercepted their clues...*

The door to the meeting room loomed nearer. The hall stretched between all the meeting rooms in the building, packed with Rankers still in their human disguises, all looking excited, their movements jerky and exuberant.

“You and Donovan are to pretend to be my hostages,” Garrett instructed him. “That way, your old friends will suspect nothing contrary. After our business tonight, our glorious ascension will begin. We will be princes of the earth, Ben, and these worms, our subjects.” He showed his teeth in a wolfish smile, and his teeth seemed to grow more pointed as Ben watched. “After we have broken them, after we have found and killed those determined to oppose us, we will each receive gifts proportionate to our works. So look well, Ben,” a crimson glow burned to life from somewhere deep within his pupils. “This is how you make an entrance.”

Garrett threw wide the doors to the meeting room, dragging Ben and Donovan alongside him. Seeing his friends huddled against the wall on the floor, their expressions concerned, Kitty moving as if to go to him before Nikki pulled her back down, almost broke Ben. Was this the last time he would ever see them?

Deciding to commit to his new role, Ben tried to break free from Garrett and go to his friends, but Garrett threw Donovan to the floor, then gripped Ben's collar and dealt him an unrestrained right-hook across the face.

He may not have felt average human discomforts, but Ben felt that.

Blinking gray fog from his eyes, Ben collapsed to the floor, too dizzy to right himself, pressing his hand over his throbbing cheekbone.

"Ben! Oh, honey, are you alright?" Kitty tried again to crawl over to him, tear streaks running mascara lines down her cheeks. It was all Nikki and Tyson could do to restrain her.

Garrett kicked Donovan against the wall and shouted in his normal voice, "Anyone else feeling brave?"

Ben noticed that Carl, the boy Jonathan had once rescued, avoided the Rankers' eyes, his hands gripping the edge of the table, his entire body twitching with terror. Panic rolled off of him in waves, and he was so tight with tension that he reminded Ben of a rubber band about to snap. If anyone was near the breaking point and about to tip towards the insanity of sheer terror, it was Carl.

Scanning the room, Ben found Josiah at the far end of the conference table. The man was half leaning forward–his face as blank as stone, staring piercingly at Ben. Josiah's knuckles were white, and his jaw muscles clenched. Ben smiled at him; nodded. Josiah's expression became one of surprise. Ben wondered if something like this had ever happened before. *Are there other people who have been turned into monsters by the Rankers and still kept their personality?*

Josiah blinked but sat back and gave Ben a brief, puzzled, and hopeful grin. He knew that Ben was aware of his identity.

"Alright, I'm going to tell you how this is gonna go!" Garrett shouted, looking at every face in the room in turn, meeting every eye, as if he had memorized their faces and would remember who caused trouble and who didn't.

"I am now your leader, your king, your god," Garrett declared, pacing around the room. One of his men took a position by the doors. "You work for us. We tell you what to do, where to go, and who to be–no questions asked. Your laws are now irrelevant. *Our* laws will be enforced. Thou shalt kill when told to kill. Thou shalt lie when told to lie. You are humans no more. You are less than humans. You are insignificant."

Murmured inquiries sprouted up from barely moving lips, and questions appeared upon brows. A few kids actually had the nerve to look indignant.

"They talk like *they* aren't humans," Ben heard Lia whisper fearfully.

"We already knew Garrett wasn't," snarled Vince loudly. He glanced at Ben and said, "It's okay, man, we've got you," to which Garrett threw back his head and laughed derisively.

Pale with pain from sitting for so long on his injured legs, Tyson raised his own voice and said boldly, "What makes you think we will in any way comply with your commands?"

Encouraged by Vince and Tyson's fearlessness, or maybe made courageous at seeing Ben and Donovan mistreated by the person they had always only known as the school bully, other kids in the room began to speak, to gather closer together, eyes flashing defiance, heads turning as if choosing a target.

Garrett stopped pacing and laughed again.

"We *know* you will comply," he said, once he had composed himself, "because we're *not* human. We are Rankers. And, as is your nature, you will succumb to your fears–to our power!"

As Ben had expected, Carl broke. The boy rushed Garrett like a startled hare as if to shove past him to the doors, throwing his chair back in a fit of adrenaline and panic. At the same moment, Garrett unfastened his cloak and tossed it aside.

Carl skidded to a stop with a strangled cry. Ben recoiled. Screams rent the air.

With the shedding of his black cloak, Garrett had also shed his disguise. He wore deep-red leggings, tall, black boots, and black leather gloves. A tunic, regal and blood-red, was stretched tight over his compact body. A heavy, crooked sword rested in a loop at his waist.

But his face could have been a death mask.

His flesh was a grayish-green and pulled over a bony skull. Instead of a nose, he had a gaping hole in the center of his face. His lipless mouth held sharp teeth and a forked tongue. The skin of his cheeks in places was tearing away to reveal his molars and gums. A pair of thick, round, black horns had replaced his ears–one of which had a golden ring studded with a ruby around it. Hornlets covered his bare head, broken in places and non-existent in the areas where white skull showed through.

Worst of all were the eyes. They had vanished into empty, furrowed sockets. Red pinpricks flashed from deep within the holes, like dying stars flickering from the black vacuum of space.

If Garrett had expected his unveiling to cause submission, he was mistaken. Instead, his nightmarish appearance was the last push needed to snap everyone's self-control and cause them to scatter. The other Rankers were showing themselves to be various kinds of monsters that set a chain reaction of screams and shouts. Donovan huddled by the wall, his head in his hands, screaming as if the Rankers revealing themselves had driven him mad. Ben had to admit that the vampire was a wonderful actor.

Ben pressed his back against the wall, trying to stay out of the bedlam. A terrible, long-limbed Ranker revealed its true form and leaped at Carl, grabbing his arms in its pale, bony, spidery fingers. The poor boy squirmed and struggled, trying to yank himself away as if attempting to tear off his own arms in the Ranker's grip if it only meant survival. The Ranker exposed a mouth full of rows of fangs that spun and whirred like the teeth of a chainsaw, lowering its face with cruel slowness down toward Carl's head.

Ben tensed, his instincts crying for him to help, but being a hero would only expose the lie of his Rankerhood to Garrett. He could only watch, despair welling in his breast, nausea churning in his throat.

Then Josiah threw himself chest-down across the polished table in a sliding skid that took him under the swipe of a razor-clawed Ranker. He rolled onto his back and turned as he went, dealing the monster attacking Carl a powerful kick with both of his feet and sending it into the wall. The man helped Carl up and shoved his way to the doors, wrestling them open. Everyone began to pour out.

Nikki and Lia lifted Tyson into his wheelchair, jostled and shoved and then carried out into the hallway like leaves caught in a river current. Kitty tried wrestling through the black cloaks and fleeing youths to get to Ben, but it was no use. With a shout of dismay, she was forced to follow their friends or else fall and get trampled.

Garrett watched the whole spectacle gleefully, his chest heaving as if he were overcome with passion or ecstasy–it was difficult to read his horrific face. His crimson laser-eyes tracked Ben's friends as they departed, as the Rankers out in the hall hollered and snarled in response to the screams of people now stampeding from the building en masse. He looked at Ben, showed his yellowy fangs, and said, "Watch them." Turning his gaze down, he dealt Donovan a kick in the leg and said, "You too."

Outside in the parking lot, people ran everywhere, colliding in heaps and then clawing fiercely at one another to get away from the Rankers that playfully chased them. Babies cried, and adults gathered children up in their arms, screaming for their spouses or older children and then rushing together into the night.

Ben stood there on unsteady legs, shaken by the hysteria that his world had so quickly dissolved into. Next to him, Donovan observed it all with a mad gleam in his eyes and a pink flush in his cheeks. Police cars had pulled in, sirens flashing, and were swarmed by Rankers. One car tried reversing to safety but bottomed out on the curb, engine smoking and one tire blown. Gunfire began to drown out the sounds of screams and roars.

Ben saw his friends vanish into the darkness of a wood across the parking lot and raced after them. Donovan called to him, but Ben lost him in the crowd of mayhem, pretending not to have heard. His new, increased speed brought him to his friends in moments. To his relief, Josiah was with them, as well as Carl.

Josiah's head spun, and he stared hard at Ben, suspicious, slowing to a trot, his eyes glowing white, then red, and then their normal, prismatic, grayish-greenish-brown.

"Stop!" Ben cried, and his friends pulled up, sides heaving.

"Oh, Ben, you got away!" Kitty threw herself at Ben's chest and knocked the wind out of him. He wrapped his arms around her. She trembled against his body. But no tears fell from her eyes. With admiration and wonder, Ben thought again of the fear that Donovan seemed to possess whenever he was around Kitty, about the physical pain he had claimed to feel in her presence.

One of faith, Garrett called her, Ben thought. *This could be something very important...* But there was no time to ponder it now. Donovan would doubtlessly track him down.

"Welcome back, brother," Vince said, panting. "But we can't stop. We've got to hide somewhere!"

"Donovan is still back there... He... he didn't get away... I thought..." Nikki's stare was distant.

"You were hexed, Nikki," Ben blurted, casting a look behind him towards the screams still issuing from the meeting chambers. "Donovan is a Ranker. He attacked me in the bathroom, and now I am…" He stared down into Kitty's wide, loving eyes and couldn't bear to tell her the truth about the monster he'd become. "They think I am one of them. But while I was unconscious, I spoke with Jonathan."

Carl couldn't seem to believe his ears, and Tyson grunted as if he'd been punched.

Nikki's face cleared. "*Jonathan's back there?*" Something fierce entered her eyes, and she made to march past Ben back toward the havoc, calling frantically, "Jon? *Jon!*" But Josiah grabbed her arm and pulled her back. Nikki squealed, growled, and struggled in the young man's bear-hug of a grip. "Let me go! We have to go back and help him!"

Lia gently, kindly, brushed Nikki's hair back from her face and said, "I don't think that's what he meant, honey." Her voice was weary. Nikki deflated and sagged in Josiah's arms, weeping.

Facing Ben, Lia asked, "What *are* you talking about?"

Taking a deep breath, Ben explained as quickly as he could. He told them the words of fealty they were supposed to say, and about Josiah's identity. "Listen; Donovan is a Ranker–a vampire. He bit me, and I entered a world called the Land of Dreams–it is where we all go when we sleep and where the Rankers come from–except Rankers are nightmares. I found Jonathan–he is safe–and when I woke back up, I…" He fell silent, pained. How could he explain he was a monster now, too? How could he tell his childhood friends what he had become? "Well…Garrett and Donovan think I am working undercover for them to spy on all of you."

He looked up; his friends gazed at him with doubt, fear, confusion, and anger. He swallowed the lump of misery in his throat.

"I know it sounds crazy," Ben murmured. Sounds of chaos and violence still echoed from the direction of the Meeting Chambers. "But Jonathan is the protector of our dreams; he is called the Griffin Prince, and he is on his way to his kingdom in the dreamworld, where he will be crowned king and given the authority and power to take his armies and destroy the Rankers."

Nikki had gone pale. It had to be extremely hard on her, on all of them, to wrap their minds around something so bizarre as what was taking place right now.

"Listen," Ben said, looking around him and taking a few steps back. "I need to get back to Garrett and try to figure out more of what's going on–what their plans are. Go to Jonathan's house. Tell his father the words I told you to say and repeat them by the culvert." He stopped and paused, looking at them all as if waiting for goodbyes.

"I don't understand," Tyson finally murmured. "They turned you into one of them? You're a...a Ranker?"

"No!" Kitty cried, clutching Ben close to her protectively. "No, he isn't! How can you say that, Ty?"

"You saw those things disguise themselves," Tyson said. He drooped in his wheelchair as if all of his strength had left him. "We can't know for sure, Kitty. We can't be sure about anything anymore. I need time to think..."

Vince moved forward. His eyes, normally docile and friendly, were fierce, his face twisted into an intimidating scowl. One fist was clenched, but the other hand pointed at Ben with all the intensity of a brandished knife.

"I swear to you, Ben, if you *are* lying to us... If you are working for those *bastards* back there..." Vince let the threat hang.

Ben only smiled sadly and murmured, "I am sorry that it has to come to this. Be careful. Take care of one another. I will keep an eye on you the best I can."

"Ben..." Kitty murmured mournfully, one hand wrapped around the crucifix necklace she wore as if drawing strength from the metal, the other grasping his jacket as if she could hold him in place, keep him from leaving.

"It will be okay, love," Ben assured her. He gave her a swift kiss on the forehead, looked into her face, trying to sear her into his mind's eye in case this was the last time they ever spoke. Then he nodded once and trotted confidently away through the trees.

Pain stabbed through his breast as if he were attached to his friends by a hook that slowly pulled his heart from his chest the further away from them he moved. Lowering his head, he charged forward into the darkness, attempting to lose himself to the new power flooding through him, bracing for the inevitable misery that awaited him, working for the Rankers.

In a blink of movement, so swift that it sent the autumn leaves on the ground whirling away in a flurry, Donovan suddenly appeared in his path, looking thunderous.

Ben skidded to a stop, keeping his features blank. For almost a minute, the two of them stared at each other in silence, neither breaking eye contact nor showing signs of submission.

Finally, Donovan said, "We work together, Benjamin. That way, no one can pick you off."

“I was...overeager,” Ben said, sheepish.

Donovan chuckled, and Ben relaxed somewhat. “I understand. It is easy for those like us to lose ourselves in revelry. But worry not. There will be more great things to come. Did you find your friends?”

“I did. They fled east. What should our next steps be?”

Donovan speculated. “We will watch and wait. Take a Ranker later and remain near their usual haunts, their homes. Report if they do anything unusual. It will be difficult to keep a proper eye and ear open until myself and the rest of Garrett’s lieutenants establish the new order.” He took a deep breath, clasped his hands before him in a gentlemanly way.

“I suspect that something ill has befallen our companion, the gargoyle. I will take you with me to investigate. It will be an opportunity for you to adjust to your new state of being.”

Excitement filled Ben, though he let none of it show on his features. Torturous it would be, to work in such proximity alongside Rankers, but perhaps he would glean some important information that he could share with Jonathan or his other friends.

Donovan opened his mouth wide a few times as if to stretch his jaw, pulling his lips back to expose his pearly teeth. The canines sharpened into fangs and shrank again like a cat extending and retracting its claws. A sick tremble wiggled in Ben’s stomach.

“But first,” Donovan said, examining the black sky through the treetops, sniffing the late-night breeze, favoring Ben with an excited smile, “Let me show you how to hunt.”

CHAPTER EIGHT:

FINDING JONATHAN

Tyson took a deep breath, watching their friend return to the terror and turmoil of the meeting chambers. *Please take care of yourself, Ben,* he thought.

"What do *you* say, Ty?" Lia asked her boyfriend. Tyson had been very quiet through Ben's story. "Was he telling the truth? Did he see Jonathan?"

"*I* remember seeing him," he began, his chin on the knuckles of one hand. "Do you remember? That day in the hospital, I woke up and said I'd seen Jonathan? I'd had a dream and seen him. You didn't believe me."

Nikki sobbed, biting her lip, tears streaming down her pale cheeks. Tyson looked back and up into her face, slowly and softly saying, "This whole time, *you* were the one who knew what they were, Nikki. You've had the Rankers pegged for weeks now. Then you forgot." He snapped his fingers. "Just like that. Maybe Donovan really was hexing you. There's no reason not to trust Ben. Not after all that happened tonight. I think he's being honest. Somehow...dreams and nightmares are coming to life."

Carl puffed out his chest and spoke *his* opinion. Tyson had forgotten he was there and gave a slight jump when the youth started speaking.

"Jonathan He'klarr saved my life–and he didn't even know me. But here you guys are, doubting Ben because of how bizarre his story was? I'll tell you what's bizarre: those freaks at the meeting chamber.

And Jonathan is somewhere out there getting ready to fight them! If you're tearing *Ben* down, you're tearing Jonathan down. *I* believe Ben and *I'm* going to the culvert!" He nodded his head sharply with finality, and a fond, amused smile spread across Josiah's face, his eyes going wide with exaggerated shock.

Squirming guiltily, Jonathan's friends turned to look at Josiah for support. He straightened out the cuffs of his flannel shirt before speaking. "Carl's very right. I would prove the truth to you if I could, but I can't."

Vince growled, "Ben said you're a griffin. If the Rankers can show their true forms, why can't you?"

"The gist of it is that reality has codes and laws upon which it is built. If too many of those laws are broken, then the earth itself would fall apart like wet paper. Therefore, dreams cannot physically manifest unless they are realistically probable. But there are loopholes, such as the Rankers are using. Terrible evil already exists in reality, and that evil has been building swiftly in a way that will poison the earth and render it uninhabitable. The Rankers are just feeding on that preexisting evil, living off of it, using other-worldly power. The Celestials, by contrast, use the power of ultimate good–like, uh, God's, for example... Rankers use someone else's."

"What're Celestials?" Vince asked.

Josiah waved a hand apologetically. "Oh, um...like guardian angels."

"Now there are guardian *angels*?" Tyson's voice was strangled. He pressed his hands against either side of his head as if his brain was close to bursting. Kitty beamed, suddenly looking braver than anyone else felt.

Josiah gave Ty a *don't worry about it* look. "I'll tell you more later, but right now, we need to find Ethan He'klarr."

They skirted the Firestone meeting chambers through the trees and found the road–vacant and bathed in silvery moonlight. The only life for miles around were the nocturnal animals and the silently watching shrubbery. Nikki was still trying to come to terms with all that had just happened. If the Rankers had chosen that evening to rise up all across the world, what would the coming days bring? Garrett had made it sound like the humans would be enslaved, not instantly massacred. But why? What were their ultimate plans?

A pickup truck raced around the turn at the end of the road to their left, driving Nikki back to the present. Its back fish-tailed wildly, but the rear tires gripped, and the vehicle continued its mad approach.

"Gobackgobackgoback!" Tyson hissed. He grabbed his wheelchair wheels and hurriedly pumped them backward.

"No," Josiah said. He tilted his head as if listening to a quiet voice and said, "It's okay."

The driver of the truck seemed to have noticed them. He turned on his brights and slowed down. The brake lights flickered, and the truck jerked to a halt, jouncing forward on its suspensions. The driver's door opened, and Ethan He'klarr climbed out. The kids shouted in recognition and formed a ring around him, speaking in overlapping voices.

Nikki could see some of Jonathan in his father. Although Jonathan had inherited his mother's golden hair and brilliant blue eyes, he possessed his father's sculpted jaw, angled cheekbones, and curving lips. Like his son, Ethan was a man who had once been strikingly handsome before the death of his wife had driven him to drink excessively.

"*What's going on?*" Ethan shouted. "What are you kids doing out here? I heard that something terrible was happening at the meeting chambers!"

"It *was*," Nikki said. "We escaped."

"I will explain everything, sir, but for now, you must take us to your house," Josiah said seriously.

Ethan stared at Josiah cluelessly and spluttered a bit, clearly torn between asking who Josiah was and demanding immediate answers. But the determination in Josiah's eyes must have convinced Ethan that at the moment, actions were more important than words. With a growl of consternation, Ethan shifted some paint cans and garbage bags from the passenger seat to the back of the cab, then nodded at the empty truck bed and said to the kids, "Get in the back."

They clambered from the bumper or top of the tires into the pine-needle-strewn truck-bed, leaning against the sides, while Josiah situated himself in the passenger seat.

Vince and Josiah helped Tyson into the back, hooking their hands beneath his arms and pulling up while his feet floundered for purchase. He cried out only once when his knee collided with the truck. Ethan folded up the wheelchair and put it in back with the kids. Then, getting back into the cab, he gunned the gas, and they were off. Nikki could hear the mumble of Josiah's low, husky voice as he began speaking with Ethan.

The night wind whorled into their ears and tangled its chilly hands into the crevices of their hair and lashes. Lia was shivering, and Tyson hugged her close. Nikki watched them with a mixture of envy, loneliness, and adoration. Thoughtfully, she glanced at the back window of the truck, but she couldn't see through the tinted glass to the men within.

Jonathan had never spoken about the verbal and, very rarely, physical abuse he had endured from his father when Ethan lost himself to fits of drunken depression. It took Jonathan's many stubborn refusals to introduce her to Ethan, and the times he would come to school sporting a fading bruise before Nikki was able to piece together what was happening at home. Soon all of Jon's friends had established a sort of unspoken support group, taking turns inviting Jonathan to their houses, waiting in his driveway whenever they drove him home to make sure his bedroom light turned on as confirmation that he'd slipped past his father without confrontation.

Hot fury simmered in Nikki's chest, then just as quickly died, smothered by a cloud of exhaustion. Ethan may have been a man in pain and a terrible father, but the man who had been racing downtown to see if he could help rescue people from an enemy that he didn't even fully understand had been clear-faced and obviously possessed of good intentions. She huffed a breath through her nose. Many things had changed that night, heralding worse changes soon to come. But maybe not *all* of those changes would be bad. Perhaps it was a silly, fragile hope, but at the moment, hope was something she knew they all desperately needed.

Vince stared up at the fading stars with his head leaned back against the rear window of the truck's cab. Kitty stared into space, letting the wind make knotted curtains of hair over her face. Carl picked up pine needles and broke them into smaller and smaller bits until they were too tiny to snap anymore. Then he tossed them into the wind where they would be flung away into the shadows. Watching them all like a hen keeping an eye on her chicks, Nikki had begun to fall asleep when Ethan turned slowly into his driveway and shut the truck off. Vince launched himself with one hand over the bed and onto the gravel, accepting Tyson's wheelchair from Carl and unfolding it.

Once everyone was out, Ethan led them past his house, into the woods at their right, and along a wide, lengthy path that gradually curved and dipped down towards the culvert and the water that burbled along beside it. *That's odd,* Nikki thought. *Shouldn't the water be going* through *the culvert?*

"There's nothing here," Nikki said sadly. She wasn't sure what she had expected to see: Jonathan standing there waiting? An army of Celestials like Josiah had mentioned, waiting to march out against the Rankers and put things right?

But Josiah paced forward cautiously as if worried he would collide with something. When he was a few steps away from the big metal culvert, he said in a soft and strangely reverent voice, "We unite beside Prince Jonathan of the griffins."

Nikki tensed, looking around her. The words that Ben had told them to say burned in her mind and seemed to ring with some kind of power, the kind that Josiah had described earlier–the kind of power that didn't belong on earth.

Ethan leaned heavily against a tree as if physically depleted. He pinched the bridge of his nose. Nikki couldn't imagine the magnitude of shame, guilt, and pain that the man might be feeling. After Jonathan had vanished, these cold, wintery trees were among the first places the police had searched for a body. For a moment, irrational anger heated Nikki's face and reddened her cheeks. Regardless of whether or not it had been intentional, Jonathan had abandoned his family and friends.

Moments later, something moved from inside the gaping recess of the culvert. A large creature gave a great snort, and then they heard loud and heavy footsteps. A white horse appeared, coming head-first, crawling almost on her belly. She was built more like a deer–at the same height, with long, thin legs, a slight body, and a neck that formed an arch at the crest of the narrow head. She was a breed of her own. Pawing the creek-pebbles with one solid, brassy hoof, she walked to Josiah, nudging her muzzle into his upraised palm. The others made a group around the horse, running their hands over her soft hair and feeling as if they were greeting a lost friend.

"I don't know who she belongs to," Ethan said, joining them. "But she's been wandering around out here for a while now. What use were the words if they only called her to us?" Ethan's voice was heavy and forlorn, but his expression was doubly mystified as he untangled rare knots in the horse's silky mane.

Nikki recalled the reports on the local news: that a stray horse roaming the forest on Jonathan's property caused everyone who came near it to be overcome by a feeling of peace and assurance. Even Ethan had admitted that the beautiful horse brought him comfort.

"Where is he?" Josiah asked. Nikki blinked and faced him, but Josiah hadn't asked any of them.

The mare twitched an ear and gently backed away from their touch. She wandered back down into the culvert, stopping to wait at the entrance. Josiah withdrew a small red flashlight from his pants pocket and aimed it ahead of him as he traversed the dip towards the wide, dark, tunnel mouth. Staring into the gloom, he grinned and looked to the others. "Come here," he said happily. "There's something you need to see."

Curious and apprehensive, not sure if they should heed the invitation of the strange young man, the others skidded down the mulchy brown carpet of dead leaves to him, following that golden beam of electric light.

Nikki moaned and rushed into the culvert. She bashed her back sharply against the jagged edge of the metal pipe's rim, but if there was any pain or injury, she ignored it.

Jonathan's body sat against the curving wall within, partially covered with a thick blanket.

Cinder blocks and leaves stopped up the creek water that should have been trickling through the tunnel, causing it to redirect around the culvert in a frigid, sinuous ribbon. Jonathan's arms were folded across his stomach, the hands at the opposite hips, unnatural-looking, as if someone else had arranged his body this way. His eyes and mouth were closed, his head against the culvert and tilted sideways.

Gently, Nikki touched his cold cheek; checked the strong pulse beating in his neck. His eyes flickered beneath their lids, and when she once more ventured her fingers into Jonathan's hair, she found a clotted mass of blood over a healing lump of a bruise. By now, the others had joined her, and Ethan, crawling desperately on his hands and knees, cradled his son, sobs choking from his chest.

For one terrible moment, Nikki had considered the possibility that Ethan had done this to his son: injured him and then stuffed the unconscious body into this tunnel. But seeing him now, wracked with heaving sobs, the accusation dissipated from her mind.

Tyson sat helplessly at the entrance, his wheelchair unable to move along the uneven terrain. His eyes were wet at the sight of his best friend, and he looked demandingly up at Josiah. One by one, the others all turned to face Josiah, waiting.

Without turning his gaze down, Josiah said, "Don't despair. You will all bear witness to miracles."

A weasel–or something weasel-like–stuck its head up from over Jonathan's shoulder. Lia squeaked and moved closer against the opposite wall. The weasel bounced outside, into Tyson's lap, and from there to the white horse's back, seemingly using her mane for handholds as it climbed.

"Ah, you're back," Josiah said warmly, taking a red-white-and-blue marble from his pocket and giving it to the animal. The weasel rubbed its paws around the marble, nodded, and yawned.

"You can't rest just yet. We have work to do!" Josiah admonished wearily with a fond smile.

Carl tripped out of the culvert, caught himself, and straightened. "What Ben told us," he said breathlessly, "It *is* true? All of it? About Jonathan and–and everything?"

Josiah cocked an eyebrow. "What do *you* think?" He called into the tunnel. "Come out, guys. Jonathan is well-guarded, and we have to begin the search for allies."

Nikki lifted her head from where it rested against Jon's chest, and the sight of her, curled up beside her love, her eyes, lackluster and hollow, seemed to stir something in Josiah. Nikki didn't know it, but the grief and joy mingling on her face reminded Josiah poignantly of the previous Griffin-King. When he had marched from the fortresses with his army stretched out behind him to go skirmish the Rankers, the kith and kin of the men prepared to die to save their lives had all possessed Nikki's same lonesome and lost look.

The last words that the White Griffin, the magnificent Celestial being who awaited Jonathan at the capital city, had told Josiah rang through his ears: "The rules have changed. The laws of the earth have become bent. Everything that once was is undone, and this will be an Age of Miracles."

CHAPTER NINE:

DUAL-WIELDER

BACK TO JONATHAN

The next few weeks were terrible. I would be grateful for it later, but at the time, I was frustrated enough to stomp my feet and cry like a child.

The Master divided mine and Boyzun's training into two phases: weaponry and exercise. Since the Master deemed me a shrimpy little squirt, I had to struggle with tedious *Karate Kid* chores. His high-pitched, accented voice became a bane to my ears.

It started out easily enough. At first, all we did were some yoga-like stretches in the middle of the Master's hut. Shuttered windows were open to the crisp early morning outside, and the cool breezes and various bird songs relaxed and soothed us. As I raised my arms over my head to go through another stance, my thoughts jumped to Ben.

It was clear to me now, thanks to Ben's arrival, that Garrett was moving his attacks towards my friends and possibly family. Peter had said that's how Rankers worked. My eyes opened, and I stared at the wooden floor, thinking up horrors that Garrett could be inflicting on anyone back home while I stood stretching in some tree-hut.

My tense vibes must have been stinking up the room because the Master murmured, "Clear your mind, Great Prince..."

I wiped all my worries from my thoughts with difficulty. Boyzun pretended not to notice me except to frown, as if an annoying bug buzzed at his ear. The little twit. I wanted so badly to knock him off his high horse. It would be satisfying, seeing as the fall would be a long drop to the ground.

After the yoga exercises, we would all do tons of various push-ups and sit-ups that increased in amount day by day. My arms and stomach became incredibly sore. But that was the easy part.

After a while, the Master leveled us up to do harder things. Boyzun and I would dangle off the side of the hut in vine harnesses, the slick, green ropes suspending us over a mesh net tied to the trees below. Using only our arms, our task was to pull ourselves up to the ledge protruding from the Master's hut. If we even tried to use our legs, the Master would chop the vine, and the one who broke the rule would plummet to the net. That in itself wasn't so bad, but the net was old and the climb back up to the hut precarious. One moment you could be like, "Oh, phew! The net caught me again!" and the next, "Er–what's that snapping sound? Aaaaaaahhhh!!!!" So, Boyzun and I both dutifully strained our biceps to carry our weight up to the Master and were rewarded with tea and apple cakes covered in a syrupy glaze.

A few times, the Master had me transform and fly around the hut while he and Boyzun chucked stones at me to test my flying and reflexes. He even threw weighted saddlebags over my back to strengthen my wings.

Occasionally, the Master would make like he was going to lead us through some stretches or take us on a walk along the bridges wrapping around the nearby tree canopy, only to jump us. Unfortunately, fist-fighting had never quite been my forte. I could hold my own for a time, as I had with Garrett, but unless my opponent went down after the first two or three haymakers, they would eventually wrap me up and toss me aside. My instinct was to charge in, as I had with Garrett, and the Master proved with reprimand, open hand, knobbly fist, a chokehold, or a couple of kicks that this was a stupid idea. He taught me the basics, enough that, were I ever disarmed, I could fight my way free and get away, but the press of time forced us to move on.

I was dismayed at my lack of excessive skill, but then we moved on to the weaponry part of the training, where I finally showed some promise. I was surprised at all that I had retained from my training bouts with Peter.

The Master decided to build on what I already knew rather than try to pack my head full of a bunch of new skills and fighting styles that would take years to perfect. On my first day working with the blade, he took up a sword himself, and we dueled in slow motion. It was strange, and at first, I had to keep from laughing, but it helped the Master observe the extent of my knowledge about blocks, parries, and strikes.

Taking a step back and bobbing his head, the Master said, "Peter Griffin-Scholar taught you well, Prince. You show promise as an offensive swordsman. Let us drill."

We coated our sword-edges in the oil of the brother's hand carnation to temporarily dull the blades, and the old man gave me just enough time to drop into a loose, defensive crouch before attacking. We moved fast, fierce, and I had to spin, dodge, and duck to keep him in sight, startled by the mobility he possessed despite his advanced age. Within seconds, he jumped spryly back out of range and cried, “Stop!”

I froze, my sword still out and horizontal to block what had been a descending blow to my head. My sides heaved as I panted for breath; my arms shook a little with exertion. The Master studied me, frowning, then shook his head and said, “There is something here... Again!”

We launched toward each other, our swords clanged mightily. Boyzun trotted upstairs with a mouth full of mango slices in time to see the Master grab me by the front of the tunic, spin me around, and slam me against the wall so hard that it shook, trapping my sword above my head. He turned right around and went back downstairs.

I shoved the old man away, sliding my sword down towards the base of his own where I could better control it, but he jumped nimbly back, raised his sword in preparation for another hacking assault aimed at the side of my neck, and shouted again, “Stop!”

I froze once more–and this time noticed what the Master had: my sword was up, ready to deflect his weapon...and so was my left hand. A spike of alarm zapped through my fingers, and I lowered my hand, staring at it, mystified.

“Whoa... Weird, I didn’t even know I was doing that...”

“You intend to catch your opponent’s blade with your hand, sire?” The Master grinned playfully. “That would not serve you well.”

“It’s never happened before,” I replied, a little defensive. “In all my bouts with Peter, that hasn’t happened.”

The Master nodded gravely and returned his sword to the weapon rack, dabbing at his sweaty forehead with a sponge of moss from a bowl of cool water. "As your skills develop, so too does your body. It is becoming aware of its strength, even if your mind is not aware of that strength yet, and it is trying to communicate them to you. Let us rest... I need to think."

The next day, the Master had me fight with a sword and shield. He fastened the heavy wooden buckler to my left arm and said brightly, "This will give your free hand something to do other than be cut in twain!"

But when we dueled, we both noticed in tandem that, while at first I instinctively knew to use the shield to block certain attacks, once our speed increased, I turned the shield aside and once more drove my open hand up as if to catch his descending blade and stop it with my own flesh and bone.

"Maybe it's just a bad habit," Boyzun commented lazily from where he lifted weighted wooden disks by the far wall.

"Thanks, peanut gallery," I snapped.

"No," the Master said, squinting in thought at my suicidal left arm. "It is a habit and a bad one, but this is not one to be broken. This is one to be developed." He went to the weapon rack and returned with another sword.

I unstrapped the shield and held the second sword in my left hand. Though that arm wasn't as developed as my right and shook the longer I held the heavy blade, it felt...*right.*

We resumed our duel, and this time, though I by no means won, we were both satisfied that we had discovered my strength.

"You are a dual-wielder," the Master said after our bout when we sipped refreshingly cool milk from coconuts. "It is interesting. We haven't had a ruler so clearly gifted at the art in many decades. But, of course, you will have to mind yourself more carefully as yours is an aggressive style more than a defensive style. You will need to practice and strengthen your arm for much longer than the time you will spend with me before you are ready to truly wield a pair of blades, but this is indeed your calling, Great Prince."

I smiled, content, feeling like I had discovered another piece of my identity. I was a griffin, and now I was shaping up to be a pretty decent swordsman. The Land of Dreams was seeming less like a scary place where nightmares were born, nightmares I was apparently obligated to defeat, and more like a world of adventure, a challenge in which I could prove to myself once and for all who I was and what I was capable of.

CHAPTER TEN:

WHEEL OF FATE

As the days passed, I continued to pick up a few tricks, like how to disarm an assailant, and use my environment, even something as innocuous as a bit of string, to defend myself with. The Master also had Boyzun and I battle in hand-to-hand combat, which certainly wasn't my strong suit. My only saving grace was that I could read Boyzun's thoughts. I don't think he knew that.

One day during our weapons training, Boyzun became frustrated. With an easy roll of the wrist that was stronger than I'd expected, he ripped my sword from my hands. I expected him to let me pick up my weapon, but instead, he socked me in the mouth.

My head shot to one side, my hand flew up to my cheek. Massaging my face, I tested out my jaw, rolling it around. My tongue brushed against my teeth, and I tasted some blood.

"Take it easy!" I admonished angrily.

Boyzun crossed his arms like an impudent child and shot back, "Would a Ranker take it easy? Man up."

I don't know where he learned that line, but it made me mad.

The Master came upstairs with a tray of tea and saw Boyzun and me rolling around on the floor like rabid wolverines. He set the tray aside and ran at us, flapping his arms. I was bigger and older than Boyzun and was able to twist his arm behind him and pin it. He yelled resentfully.

"*Take it back!*" I roared.

"*No!*" Boyzun squealed, his voice breaking.

I twisted harder. "*Now!*"

But Boyzun just thrashed around beneath me. The Master took up his staff and conked me with it. I flopped back on my butt, glaring up at him. Boyzun scrambled to his feet, stretching the kinks out of his arm.

"Do you not see yourselves?" the Master scolded. "You act more like misbehaved youngsters than mature princelings!" He faced Boyzun, who winced as if struck.

"Boyzun! You are now the chieftain of our people! We look to you for answers to our problems. We need your guidance and, above all, your patience."

It became suddenly apparent to me how much responsibility Boyzun had on his shoulders. He was so young, and coping with the death of his father. In fact, I could really relate to him.

"I'm sorry," I apologized after a moment. "It was my fault. You're right. I guess I do have some manning-up to do."

Boyzun grimaced and shook his head. "No. It's *my* fault... I know I've been giving you a lot of attitude lately, but...you..." He groped at the air with one hand as if searching for words. I brushed against the edge of his mind, and to my astonishment, I detected anxiety, fear, and envy. Boyzun was *envious* of me.

"Mother thinks that I'm being brash. She thinks I care more about avenging my father than I do about taking care of my people. But that's not so." Boyzun unwound the flower stem that kept his tar-black, shoulder-length hair away from his face and started to pull it back again into a neater bun, his eyes unfocused. "I grew up hearing stories about the chimera's wrath. I have friends who've lost relatives to its appetite. I've *always* wanted to kill it; I've dreamed of sitting on my throne, knowing that my people could roam our territory finally safe and free from the monster. But now that my father is gone... Now that my coronation awaits and the prospect of slaying the chimera is...is *tangible*..."

He took a shallow, shaky breath, dropping his arms. "You're so confident," he said, "and such a quick learner and...I'm just so stressed out about the chimera–about what's coming."

"Kid, I am not confident," I grinned. "I'm just good at faking like I am."

Boyzun tried to return the smile, but his mouth only trembled, as if he were fighting not to cry.

"The chimera... How do you plan on killing it?" I asked, standing and returning my hand to my jaw.

Boyzun pointed to where his bow leaned against a wall. "With that. It's never failed me. It will be difficult, but I am ready."

"And it isn't like you're alone," I pointed out, putting my hands in my pockets loftily.

"Those like you are never alone," the Master said, smiling. I was puzzled, but he clapped his hands and said, "Come. Again!"

So, the Master taught us how to be deadly. I learned about the areas of the body that had great veins and arteries that, when slashed, would bring quick death. I learned how to get behind someone and use them as a shield or how to apply just the right amount of torque to break their neck. I learned high and low kicks and punches, blocks, and stances that would guarantee me superb maneuverability.

Once I had taken in all I could on fighting with weapon and fist, the Master briefly schooled me griffin-wise. It was the same basic idea. If I bit a person in the tops of the shoulders, I could cleanly cut all nerves to the arm. I learned to use my talons systematically, as if I were wielding ten knives. My wings were like aluminum bats. If I hit something right with the bony joints, I could break it. When I asked, during one of my rare respites, what a griffin suit of armor looked like, the Master informed me that, though it wasn't unheard of, griffins normally *didn't* wear armor.

"Your griffin form is symbolic," the Master explained while I guzzled some water and poured some down my sweaty face. "It represents your best attributes as a human, as a dreamer. As such, it possesses berserker-strength and considerable power. It is incredibly difficult to mortally wound a griffin with a single thrust of a sword or even a slash from an axe. Additional armor will protect you further, yes, but it will also weigh you down and impede the very thing that makes griffins so uniquely resilient: your reflexes, endurance, and grace. Now come—transform and show me how you pounce!"

The last thing that Boyzun and I were taught in those final weeks of difficult training were the powers of the mind. We were given situations we had to plot our way out of. We learned how to ambush and plan battles. We learned how to hold still and silent for hours at a time in the underbrush while at the same time remaining alert to our surroundings. And finally, one day, when Boyzun and I had completed our exercises and settled down some for a light lunch, the Master folded his hands and declared us done with training.

His words were a shock to me. An apple cake was halfway to my mouth and doomed to remain there until it sank in. Done with a few months' worth of training. He may as well have said that I was done in The Land of Dreams and could go on home. Boyzun, who had already stuffed a cake in his mouth, gave a muffled humming sound of pleasure. The sticky apple-cake glaze was running down my fingers, so I took a bite and dried my hands on a napkin made of watered moss.

The master said somberly, "You are both ready for whatever shall come next. And so now, I will tell you of the secret, priceless treasure of the Tahtltiki Tribe, one that I suspect the Rankers have only ever gleaned rumors of, and that is likely one of the reasons why their clues would have led them here. Listen well, for this is the tale of the Mystery of our people...

"Long ago, the ancients made a mosaic of beautifully colored ceramic tiles. If you deciphered its pictures correctly, you would get answers to your most secret questions. It is divided into sections relating to every part and time of our Land of Dreams. Just recently, I interpreted the meaning of a section referring to the Tahtltiki Tribe. Come, I will show you."

We all moved downstairs to an area neither Boyzun nor I had ever come to before. As we rounded the bend in the stairwell, we found ourselves in what seemed to be the Master's bedroom. But across the round room and somehow suspended on the wall, as if built into the wood, was a circular mosaic about as big as a large Jacuzzi. At first, I thought it was all just a mish-mash of different colors and wondered how the Master had been able to decipher anything at all. But when we came closer, I saw bajillions of minute pictures covering the mosaic. It was also divided into a hundred rings that could be turned around, with tiles forming images that stretched from the center of the mosaic to the outer edges like spokes on a wagon wheel. I tried hard to settle my eyes on one picture, but they kept sliding to the next.

The Master pointed to a part of the mosaic that appeared to match up.

"I realized that by aligning certain pictures, I could glean knowledge." He moved his finger across a long item that stretched from the center of the mosaic to the very outer ring. "I thought to myself, what sort of connection would represent the Tahtltiki? A vine, perhaps! So, I found all sections of the mosaic that had a vine running through them and lined them up. I got answers, but only ones I already knew. I discovered that if you match only the main symbol for any region of the Land of Dreams, such as the vine, you will only get that region's past and present."

The Master winked knowingly. The vine that lined up the rings involving the Tahtltiki people was evenly divided to alternate with another image: a bow. The two formed a pattern: vine-bow-vine-bow, all the way to the end.

The Master explained. "I tried mixing the central connections. I knew Boyzun wanted to avenge his father's death, so I tried splitting the bow and the vine. I found my answers." He pointed to a few of the little random pictures, five or six in each ring, and slowly moved outwards.

"Many of these icons are impossible for me to understand. But a considerable few can be deciphered. This crown in the center must represent Boyzun. The bow lying across the dark flower means Boyzun would try to avenge a death. From there, it gets more difficult. Here is a verse of the old language that can be translated to mean 'Mystery.' In other words, Boyzun would have to solve our people's mystery."

The Master looked at me and said quietly, "From the time we are children, we are taught that the great chieftains of past ages were instructed by the Celestials to build four totems that would keep a secret truth safe until the pre-destined one was ready to discover it. Look," he put his finger on the next image, a feather, "The sky totem," then on the picture of a stone, "The earth totem," next on a pink seashell, "The water totem," and on the second to last picture, a tree, "The heart totem. The last picture is of a bow and a sword crossed beside a twisted black heart. No doubt, this is the fight to be had between the chimera, Boyzun, and you, Prince Jonathan. The mosaic explains no more beyond this."

Boyzun touched the tiles reverently, his eyes wandering up and down its bizarre surface.

"Can it show the fate of...well, me?" I asked carefully. "Can it show what's going to happen to the world?"

The Master gravely raised his bushy brow. He watched me for a long moment, inscrutable, his thoughts impenetrable.

"It is not my place to tell. And it is not your place to know. Come now; let me help you prepare for your hunt."

CHAPTER ELEVEN:

BONDING TIME WITH BOYZUN

"Well, there's something you don't see every day."

"Something *you* don't see every day."

"Good point. That category is rapidly filling." I crossed my arms and tapped my elbows. Boyzun strung an arrow and squinted down the shaft with uncertainty, aiming to shoot the totem down.

We stood on a grassy slope in the middle of the jungle. One of the totems that we had searched hours for hovered above us. It took the form of a sort of dream-catcher: rings criss-crossed with zany designs by nets of black string. Colorful feathers dangled and twitched from the rings, and something was suspended in a little wooden platform beneath the totem. The strings webbing the center of the rings formed an image of the three heads of the chimera. Boyzun's ancestors apparently had a dark sense of humor.

Seeming to be satisfied with where his arrow was aimed, Boyzun mumbled, "Sun?"

I looked at him curiously. "Maybe ten seconds behind cover."

"Wind?" Boyzun continued, squinting along the shaft.

I rolled my eyes. Quickly transforming, I lunged into the air, beat my wings once, snatched the totem in my talons, and was back on the ground in my normal form, staring at Boyzun pointedly. His hair was badly tousled from the gust of wind my wings had washed him in.

"Don't," he said, pointing at me and slinging his bow across his shoulders.

"What?" I chuckled, innocently spreading my arms.

"Just don't."

"I didn't even *say* anything."

"Your look did."

"Sorry that I can fly."

"You cheated."

"Sore loser much?"

"Give me the totem before I kill something."

Setting our playful banter aside, we studied our trophy. There was a ratty old pile of thick, rubbery leaves on the platform. They were a deep black–so black that they shone white in the sun that beamed on their shiny skins. Minute holes that didn't seem to serve a purpose covered four of the leaves. The last leaf had a sort of list of instructions on it. Markings on it corresponded to markings on the edges of the other leaves.

"These are star-gazing leaves," Boyzun declared with surprise. "Our shamans use them to read our fortunes. We'll need to wait until the stars come out."

Without further ado, we spread our blankets and settled in to wait for night with a meager meal of bread and the all-too-familiar mango. The night came upon us chill and swift. One moment the sky was an electric blue, the next duller tones of gray and midnight slate. At dusk, there were admirable streaks of gold and blush, and these melted into a baby-blue, speckled with one or two white, staring stars.

I was trying to figure out the meaning of the charts when Boyzun elbowed me in the ribs. He pointed up, silent. The stars had now accumulated together from their foggy veils and made numerous patterns in the heavens. It was an unfathomable array, much clearer and more colorful than any night in reality on earth. Stars and planets twinkled in every shade, and astral clouds glowed as if lit from within, embracing their own distant suns. I could've stared at them forever. But it was time for some star-gazing.

"The symbols on these instructions and the other perforated leaves look to me like an eye," I said, holding out the leaves for Boyzun to see.

"Yes," he agreed. "An eye in the sequence of opening and closing. Then there's an arrow on the directions too. It's parallel to the eyes and pointing up."

"Any idea what we do?" I tugged on my coral necklace and yawned.

Boyzun stood and carefully kicked ashes over the last embers of the fire we'd been using for warmth. Without the extra light, my predator pupils dilated and zoomed in on the sky above. I could faintly distinguish rings around some of the planets, and the many-colored gaseous clouds of the stars' surfaces. Boyzun squinted and held up the leaves so that the stars made little bright dots on his face through the holes.

"The Master told me of the ancient ones who perfected the art of fortune-telling. They watched the stars on a nightly basis," Boyzun said in a strained voice as he tipped his head as far back as it could go without popping off his neck and rolling away. "They could use them to tell time and stories and directions."

"Some people, in reality, can do the same thing," I said in a hushed and reverent voice.

"Let's lay these leaves one on top of the other in the order the instructions go," Boyzun suggested.

"And then hold them to the sky!" I added.

Boyzun stacked the leaves in the proper fashion beginning with the eye symbol open and then in the process of shutting and opening again. Some of the perforations in the first leaf were covered up, and some were open–they formed a shape, and Boyzun raised them upwards, holding his breath. To our delight, it revealed an arrow, pointing behind us to the east. After that, Boyzun repeated the process but backward, and this time five letters were punched into existence before our uplifted and star-reflecting eyes that spelled "stone."

It occurred to me then how easy it would have been if some nice person had just *told* us, "Oh, hey! The stone totem is to the east! Good luck, have fun!" But then...that's not how things work in the Land of Dreams. The human mind is too complex and marvelous to cut corners–our thoughts, emotions, fears, hopes all combine to become dreams, those dreams shape who we are and the world around us, and really, I wouldn't change that for the world.

I just wished I could take my time and enjoy it all instead of constantly wrestling with the pressure of protecting it and making sure the Rankers didn't tear it all apart.

I chewed and fretted at my circling thoughts and came to wonder about something. Rolling over to see that Boyzun was staring skyward–no doubt chewing on his own thoughts–I awkwardly framed a question.

"Boyzun...are you a real person? I mean, did you come from my reality, and now you're living here because something happened to your body?"

Boyzun studied me as one would scrutinize a confusing computer screen. "I was born here. My parents died, and the good chieftain and his wife took me in as their son."

A strange feeling came to me then; a sense of loneliness. If Boyzun was a dream-creation, he wasn't "real" in the sense that I was. He resulted from his creator's consciousness–an amalgamation of their experiences and the personalities of the people they were closest to. I felt, briefly, like I was hanging out with a mannequin–a doll imbued with a false life.

"You know what that means, right?" I risked asking. Boyzun blinked cluelessly, and I explained gently in my best bedside manner, "You aren't real. You're a figment of someone's imagination."

Boyzun reacted as if I'd told him some unimportant morsel of information. He stretched with an exaggerated, satisfied sigh, taking care to flex his arms as he propped them behind his dark head.

"Well, whoever it is, they have a fantastic imagination," he remarked. We both chuckled.

"That really doesn't bother you?" I pressed, astonished.

Boyzun frowned. "No. Maybe it should, but as far as things go, I *feel* real. I've lived a life here, so I believe I've grown up like any other person. It's just that someone else shaped my thoughts and personality." He smiled, and irony raised one of his eyebrows. "But didn't everything, even real things, start out as thought? Isn't the person you are today the result of the influence of others? Aren't you Someone's creation too?"

I had to concede his point. The guy I was at that moment, the person talking to Boyzun, was the result of my father's abuse, my mother's death, my friends' love, Garrett's bullying, and thousands upon thousands of other influences. As far as being a created being...

I was reminded of Kitty and her belief in a Creator. Thinking of my friends hurt, but thinking about someone as powerful as God, someone who was closely watching and guiding everything, including my fate, hurt too.

"I don't know," I admitted. "I haven't really thought much about it. It sounds right, though... It feels right." *Just because it doesn't feel good doesn't mean it isn't right,* I thought pensively.

Boyzun settled deeper into the nest of grass he'd made for himself, and I rolled over onto my stomach to better keep the night's chill out of the core of my body.

"You know, mother chieftainess is of your world," Boyzun said unexpectedly. "She told me once. She said that she's a sick old woman who had always dreamed of having a child but was barren. I think she's the one who "made" me. She wants me to lead the people because she knows soon she will pass."

I creased my brow. "What do you think will happen to you when...she does?"

For once, he looked disturbed. His lips clenched, and his eyes grew vacant. "I think I shall live on. Mother chieftainess told me that dreams never die."

I turned down a corner of my mouth, pondering the cosmic statement.

"No. I suppose they don't," I murmured.

"What of you? What's your story?" Boyzun asked, going up on his elbows.

The conversation turned, and we talked long into the night.

CHAPTER TWELVE:

TERRIBLE TOTEMS

At around noon on the second day of our mission, we had forsaken the jungle for a white-sanded beach. It was a small one, close to the uniform trunks of the tropical trees, but it breathed upon me a freedom from restraint all the same.

Pebbles, driftwood, an assortment of cracked shells emptied of their contents by the circling seagulls, and the occasional dead jellyfish or clump of seaweed festooned the upper part of the beach where the sand was crusted and dry. Lower down by the blue waves, the sand was moist, gray, and clean. It was here where Boyzun and I took a reprieve, depositing our bags by the empty shell of a giant crab and splashing in along the shore with wild vivacity, taking to the lukewarm water.

Sand gathered in my ears and hair. The biting wind, bringing with it a scent of salt and the distant roaring of ocean breakers, dried us with its chill. Shivering and laughing, we returned to our bags and let the sun dry our skin before unrolling our pant legs, pulling on our shoes, and replacing our shirts.

We couldn't put off the mystery of the next totem any longer. With shifting gazes that slid longingly towards the sea, we made our approach to the stone totem. The great boulders were huge and bleached bone-white. They were stacked, I don't know how or by what powers, to resemble the head of a roaring vipercat. A stout column made the neck; there were two hollows for eyes and two fanned-out bunches of gingko leaves for ears feebly fluttering in the wind. The chasm formed as the totem's mouth stretched tall before us with jagged stakes of wood serving as ominous teeth.

The cave itself was shallow, with room enough for three people to stand side-to-side and take several long strides to where the sun's rays just barely touched the back wall. The sand here beneath our shoes was cooler and free of beach debris. The pale-cream walls were peppered with holes–I assumed from the eroding wind and salt. A thin chute, emerging from above us somewhere in the head, curved into a trough at the "throat" of the totem. And below the trough was a button, convex and square and built into the rock by long-dead hands.

I started to hum the famous *Indiana Jones* theme but stopped when Boyzun shot me an irritated glare. I cleared my throat and placed my hand against the button, leaning my weight slowly, bit by bit against it, feeling an uncharacteristic knot of worry standing the hair on my neck on end. But no pit opened beneath us to a treacherous fall. No acid spewed from the dark nooks and crannies. A musical "clink" sound–like glass-on-glass–rang out from above us, from within the stone ceiling, and then something slid into the trough.

It was a vial corked with wood and full to the brim with sand. I couldn't be positive, but I thought there was something else in the sand. I kneeled to better observe the contents in the light.

Absorbed in our findings, I only half heard a dry, hollow, "poof" sound and assumed that some bird had alighted atop the cave. But immediately after this minuscule and unimportant sound, there was an odd, pinging, ricochet-type noise, a sickening *thwack,* and Boyzun gave out a sharp wail.

I whirled, drawing my sword just as another airy note sounded, and something small and made of wood shattered into slivers against the metal blade. Pressing the button had given us our next clue, but it had also triggered a booby trap–not a wall of spikes or a giant rolling boulder, but a sudden deluge of tiny darts.

Boyzun collapsed to his side. He grasped his elbow, moaning and rocking side to side.

In quicker repetition, the darts ejected from the other holes in the cave walls, crashing into each other or being crushed against the stones.

"I thought the chieftains of the past were friendly!" I cried. Boyzun only growled painfully through his teeth, the horrible sound dwindling to a whimper at the end.

Crouching low over Boyzun, I considered our options. The darts were shooting in waves, one narrow column at a time, and would soon reach us at the back and punch us full of golf-ball-sized holes. The only thing we could do was time it, and to do that, I would need to rely on my griffin reflexes more than I ever had before.

Roughly forcing Boyzun up to his feet, I ducked low, shouted something that I couldn't remember saying later but that Boyzun told me had not been very pleasant, and rushed forward. The next-to-last wave of darts sprang from the wall ahead of us. Pressure built in my eyes like it did when the irises changed color, and the world seemed to plunge into slow motion.

A tardy dart flashed by my face after the next-to-last barrage now shattering against the opposite wall ahead of us, and I tilted Boyzun out of harm's way, arcing my blade over my head and down along the side of my body. A few darts were demolished against it.

The last wave was about to launch. We passed the holes in the wall. I turned as the heads of the wickedly-pointed darts emerged. Sheathing my sword, I let griffin-instincts take over and grabbed Boyzun even tighter. Time seemed to speed back up, and the breeze from the darts whisked against the back of my tunic as they shot past. Cloth tore as one grazed my back, and shattered splinters bounced off the stone walls and showered down on us.

With a final heave of effort, I dragged Boyzun out into the open. Within seconds, the sounds of the darts died off, and all that remained of them was a battlefield of splinters and white scrapes on the cave's interior.

A few scarlet runnels of blood coursed sinuous trails down Boyzun's forearm and dripped off the clenched knuckles. We were both drenched in sweat from our close encounter, and the sun was making new beads on Boyzun's pale forehead. His black hair, so fine and clean, was shaggy. His teeth were bared, his eyes squeezed shut.

"Oh, help! It stings!" he cried. I was glad he couldn't see how worried I was, tearing off some of my sleeve to mop up the blood and make a bandage. How much damage had the booby-trap done? Were the barbs poison-tipped?

The dart had buried itself into the soft flesh right above the bone of Boyzun's elbow. I would have to dig a little to get it out. *Crimeny, why can't people dream of hospitals?* I poured some of the drinking water we had on my hands to clean them and then some on the wound.

Some muscle tissue had lifted away from the ligaments, and a white crescent of bone flashed from a corner of the wound. At least I had taken enough anatomy classes in school to be able to identify bloody mushy things from other bloody mushy things, thank God, or else I would have been lost to helplessness. But the damage was severe enough that I worried whether or not Boyzun would lose his lower arm.

"It'll be fine, buddy, hold tight!" I soothed. I hooked my forefinger into the wound and pulled the dart out as quickly as I could amidst a new sheeting curtain of blood and a shrill keen of anguish from Boyzun. I chucked the soggy dart back towards the cave and swore under my breath. This thing was going to take more than a tourniquet; it was going to take a miracle.

"Green...flowers," Boyzun gasped out through his teeth.

"Say what?" I leaned closer.

"Get...green flowers. Put in wound..." he repeated.

"Right," I said. Then, casting a worried look up at the circling sea-birds, as if I expected to see vultures waiting for Boyzun to drop dead, I made for the trees. Growing in the shadows were bunches of tiny, lime-green flowers. Each had around eight triangular petals and a yellow circular center with a filmy sheen. I picked a fistful and rushed back, scaring a curious cormorant higher into the sky.

"What now, Boyzun?" I panted. His eyes had slipped closed, and the skin under them had turned an ugly shade of mauve. At first, he didn't answer me. I shouted and nudged him, and he opened his eyes wearily.

"Peel off centers and...put in..."

Surprised and dubious, I removed the filmy covers on the flowers' centers. When my thumb brushed against one, I found it was sticky. Carefully, I fit three of the blooms into Boyzun's wound. The bleeding slowed to a trickle. I tied my torn sleeve snugly around the laceration and helped Boyzun sit up. He blinked dazedly, winced, and thanked me. I said nothing but helped him drag himself over to the pony-sized empty crab shell and propped him up against it.

"What'd we get?" he asked, trying to sound nonchalant even though his teeth were clenched in pain. I was glad he was no longer wheezing in agony, and his eyes were clearer, his face less pasty, but how was he supposed to visit vengeance upon the chimera with one arm?

"Um," I had for a moment forgotten the item that had fallen into the stone totem's throat. Reaching into my pocket, I removed the vial of sand and held it up to him. He rolled his eyes, looking pointedly, spitefully, at the acres of sand all around us.

Smiling, I uncorked the vial and emptied it into my hand. The sand spilled through my fingers in soft curtains, some of it dancing away on the wind. But something else landed solidly in my palm: the ancient, dry, and shriveled body of a small fish.

As one, our gazes moved to the innocently lapping ocean.

"The water totem must be in there somewhere," I pondered to myself.

"At least it won't be deep," Boyzun reassured me. "The Old Ones who made the totems couldn't have swum too far." That wasn't what I was entirely worried about. The last time I had dared to swim in the ocean, a Siren had tried to eat me alive.

I extended my thoughts to see if I could "hear" some attractive woman making devious dinner plans, but all I got was a multitude of simple sea life.

"I'll be back," I said.

The deeper into the water I went, the colder I became.

The shore gave way to a steep drop-off that I discovered the hard way. One moment I was wading in a waist-high tide and the next, slipping into oblivion. Coming up, I took a breath and dove with more grace. When my stinging eyes opened, it was to a new world.

The sun shone through the clean, blue water to beam light on silver walls of mackerel schools and the back of a mottled sea turtle. He bumped into me with his beaky snout, and I moved aside to let him paddle steadily on with his scaly flippers. A quartet of translucent jellyfish floated below me, their deadly tentacles tinged varying shades of pastel pinks and purples. Beyond me in the deeper waters were vague outlines of sharks. I went up for another breath and then kicked down towards where the coral grew.

Orange clownfish darted amidst the anemones. Long-finned angelfish, the royalty of the fish world, haughtily moved on their way. A quilled lionfish found itself face to face with a saurian moray eel, sizing it up before swimming on. An octopus, jetting away from me and only slightly encumbered by its sack-like head, crossed the path of a timid hermit crab who hastily withdrew into its barnacled shell.

It was by this little critter that I found the water totem–a colorful *something* the size and shape of a soccer ball. I was fast running out of air. I only had time to grab it and swim upwards to the sun where I belonged.

"Did you get it?" Boyzun shouted excitedly, watching me tramp through the shallow waters. I held my prize up and shook it in triumph.

Now that I had my breath back, I studied the totem. It was an air-tight ball of shells molded with thick, dry clay. We chipped at it with stones until Boyzun grew too weak, and then I carried on alone. Finally, the ball cracked neatly in half, part of it rolling away down the beach. I watched it go and then blinked in surprise at the roll of parchment that lingered in the half I held in my lap, tied shut with a leather string. I unrolled it and positioned myself beside Boyzun to read the contents.

We beheld a crude map. There were no lines of longitude or latitude, no key corresponding to points, no names of locations... Just a solid line leading to different landmarks in a zany path, like something a child would've drawn.

"Well, obviously, this is us," Boyzun pointed to an illustration of the stone totem in the middle of the left-hand side of the page. With his finger, he traced the trail that led straight back from it into the jungle, around a curve, and to a tree that split into three forks. Two seemed to be healthy, leafy boughs, but the third appeared to be made entirely of roots stretching the wrong way–towards the sky.

When Boyzun had rested long enough, we set off into the trees. It was hard to judge distance by the map. We had to make our own scale. By trial and error, we estimated that one inch on the map was around one mile in actuality. By early evening, we found the tree.

It had wizened considerably compared to the illustration, but the third bough did indeed extend gnarly roots instead of leaves. We made camp up in the wide branches (large enough to build a house on) and started fresh at the chilled bite of dawn.

From there, we traveled to the next landmark: an old pirate ship skewered on some rocky crags. We passed close enough by it to see the individual planks of wood and chipped paint. A mast burst through the canopy, now nothing more than a resting place for birds.

There were ragged gray sails like deflated clouds and a shredded black flag with remnants of the notorious skull and crossbones. Rusty cannons were smashed against the once fine rails. The glory of the once-powerful ship was gone.

"A tidal wave must have thrown it here, and here it stays," Boyzun said grimly. Still, I felt like an insignificant ant in comparison to the ship's once majestic bulk.

Over the next few days, we beheld so many other wonders according to the map's directions. We found a waterfall that somehow flowed uphill. We came upon one of those hot-tub pools I had soaked in before, but it was covered with vines, and we had to pick our way across it. There was much falling and bouncing and crawling.

We stopped briefly by a lush oasis. A clear stream of mountain water ran into a lake packed with teeming life. Birds flocked into the trees. Jaguars and vipercatz drank, watching us with lazy curiosity.

The huge chameleons bathed in the water, splashing some over their backs with thick tails.

The last landmark we came to before reaching our destination was a tunnel of painted cave-rock. The ancient images splashed across the stone depicted game hunts, children playing, women making the numerous flower necklaces, and men stalking the shrewdly elusive chimera. The last picture showed the little stick-figure chimera with a little stick-figure man in its mouth, flailing his limbs madly. Charming.

"Apparently, the chimera's been around for a while," I said, my voice low.

"Maybe centuries," Boyzun replied, just as softly. "Since the ancients were alive." He trembled, perhaps with nerves or fear now that we were so close to the end, to avenging his father. But his grip on his bow was strong. His injured arm had healed well over the past few days.

The tunnel opened into a grassy clearing strewn with piles of dark wood. At first, we were worried: the map showed the final totem at the end in the form of the chimera. But then we realized that the wood around us *was* the totem, and we had to build it.

The totem's trunk, a rectangular block projecting from a rock, was partially built into the stone. Leaving it alone, Boyzun and I set to work.

The dragon head took us almost two hours to construct. We had to find each individual scale that locked into place and then connect the horns, and place ivory teeth into the spread jaws. According to what was strewn in the clearing, we had to kindle a fire in the mouth so that smoke billowed out from an iron cage that contained the flames and tinder.

The whole final effect was spooky. A fifteen-foot tall version of the very monster that had slaughtered Boyzun's father and haunted the jungle for possibly hundreds of years glittered and smoked before us. But nothing happened.

"Oh, hey, look!" Boyzun hissed, pointing. Embedded in the totem's chest was a recessed engraving that seemed vaguely familiar.

I took a wad of cloth from my pocket and unwrapped it to expose the razor-disk that I had found in the Reekwood Swamp and thoughtfully touched the serrated spikes. Striding forward, I pressed the disk concisely into place...

And a compartment beneath the totem fell open with an ejection of dust and a small pile of objects.

CHAPTER THIRTEEN:

MEANWHILE, FOUR DAYS PREVIOUS

ON A BALCONY BACK AMONGST THE TAHTLTIKI TRIBE

The Tahtltiki people knew how to party. It was one of their harvest days, and also the day they had learned that their young Chieftain Boyzun and the High Prince Jonathan had finally set out for the chimera and hopefully their next clue as to how to intercept the Ranker plans.

Kayle watched the goings-on from where he sat atop an empty cart, trying to eat a plum without getting messy. Chieftainess Chalk-Talk had awakened everyone early with the sound of a brassy gong. Peter had then led the squadron, Kayle, and Mariah through the trees to where the Tahtltiki had built a wide wooden plaza, supported by tree branches below and vines above. Tossing his plum pit over the balcony where it would decompose on the ground, Kayle stood and mindlessly moved to dry his hands on his shirt. But he stopped himself just in time and groaned.

Everyone had dressed up for the occasion. The men in the squadron had polished their gear and worn their military outfits. The Amazons had braided feathers into their sleek, long hair and painted elaborate symbols on their faces and arms. The Tahtltiki donned hats with fake fruit, feathers, or flowers on top and clothes embroidered with golden thread to form snarling vipercatz, flowers, or random designs. The outfits that the Tahtltiki had tailored for their griffin-guests were more down-to-earth.

At Mariah's encouragement and Peter's insistence, Kayle had forced himself to forsake his comfortable sweatshirt for a more presentable blue tunic. Still, he'd popped the collar and rolled the sleeves up to his elbows. Mariah had also convinced him to remove his hat, and Kayle's brown-red hair had refused to be combed down. He knew that dressing up was the right sort of thing to do on special occasions and that it brought out the gentleman in him. After all, he had once *been* a gentleman, groomed to spend his life attending special events and representing his family name proudly.

But that was before a mob had burned his home to the ground, taking his family and inheritance with it. Now he would much rather settle into the airy comfort of one of his sweatshirts where he could feel invulnerable, all to himself, and *not* be reminded of everything he had lost, everything he had once been.

Kayle found something to clean his hands on and took a walk around the plaza, trying to enjoy the festive cheer hanging over him like a contagious disease. People were walking around with bags and handing out toys and noise-makers. The warriors were letting the younger children take turns riding with them atop the docile chameleons. Percussion music from a band to one side was enchanting the young adults. Women were teaching some youths how to make flower leis; men were keeping a close eye on those they were teaching to use the bow and arrow. There was the popular tile game and a swing suspended over the ground far below.

Kayle paused to scratch a lemur behind its ear. All of the animals had been festooned with leis or paint for the occasion. This creature had red dots all around its mask and blue rings around the white parts of its tail. It reared up to nibble at the lei around its neck and scampered off to investigate a fallen slice of honeydew.

A booth stood nearby, displaying buckets full of fake flowers, and a chart above them displayed what flower was dedicated to each day of each month. Kayle found that *his* flower was a deep mauve one whose poisonous nectar ensured a slow death. Shrugging, he found a secluded balcony between two quiet huts and looked down at the mesh of branches that extended towards the grass, unseen, below. Shuffling movement behind him caused him to turn reluctantly.

Marine Sergeant Flaherty, looking as sharp as a sword-point in his dress-blues, came around the corner and stopped. One hand was on top of the tasseled sword at his hip, and the other grasped a gourd of wine. Marcus the gladiator and a knight by the name of Sir Tobias came up behind the marine, their gold and silver armor polished to perfection. Marcus's helmet, made of engraved gold with an impressive nose-guard and Roman crest of sweeping horse-hair dyed red, was studded with the flowers tossed by admiring young Tahtltiki women. Sir Tobias's helmet visor was up to reveal his twinkling brown eyes and a blond mustache. A parrot perched on his shoulder sometimes rubbed its head along his neck in a friendly way.

"Kayle lookit yerself, m' boy, all alone in a dark alley! Come and enjoy the grub!" the knight invited merrily.

Kayle smiled at how close to being intoxicated the Scotsman was. "Maybe later, mate. Save a spot for me by a few of the local women, okay?"

Marcus, a robust and fair-faced young man, raised his drink in the affirmative and teased, "That we will, Kayle, but if you're lookin' for them to turn their big doe eyes on *you*, you'll have to get rid of the competition first!" he gestured at himself with his thumb.

Flaherty pulled a face behind Marcus and pantomimed knocking his helmet off. Kayle chuckled and waved them off. They moved on, and Kayle returned to his private thoughts with cheeks slightly dimpled. The Land of Dreams had been his home for years now, and he appreciated the friends he had made along the journey, even if at times they intruded upon his thoughts.

Kayle wondered about things: what Jonathan was doing, how Michael, the White Griffin, was handling the capital city in their absence, and above all, as always, what the Rankers were up to. Had Garrett yet discovered the death of his gargoyle or the information given to Ben?

And though he had come to respect Jonathan and regard him as a friend, would Jonathan be ready in time to defeat the Rankers? He possessed none of his predecessor's regality, poise, and fearlessness, though Kayle would say that Jonathan had an enviable amount of perseverance, confidence, and...kindness wasn't the right word. Jonathan was a watcher and a learner in a way that King Brody had not been–he absorbed Peter's lessons readily, remembered them clearly, and could apply them almost instantly.

But would that be enough?

A throb of pain pulsed in Kayle's heart, and he leaned over the railing so that the wood pressed close against his chest as if to crush the pain behind his ribs.

I can't watch another friend die.

One of the people throwing out toys and trinkets passed the alleyway and threw something to Kayle with mute kindness, slipping on towards the louder quarters. Bending, Kayle picked up what had been tossed his way and saw that it was a small flute.

With a strange, reminiscent look on his face, Kayle put the instrument to his lips, placed his fingers on the holes, and blew. A high, trilling note curled into the air and echoed away into the jungle's depths. It sounded painfully similar to the tin whistles of his homeland. Rearranging his fingers, Kayle struck another note, this one more familiar to him than the first.

Ever since the fire that had destroyed his past, Kayle had tried to forget this song, but it returned now, and the melody, so lilting and familiar, rattled the chains over his heart.

After playing the song through once, Kayle set aside the flute and lifted his voice into the cadence, singing softly and sorrowfully.

"Night's an unforgiving dark; it's a burden to a traveler's heart.
But he must fight on if he wants to rise with the dawn.
The traveler's far away from home; he is used to the cold of being alone.
But a new love bears fire and brings him a feeling unknown.
'Come along to see,' she calls out to me, 'My heart it aches for love!
Don't you see, boy, come to me, for the stars sing up above,'
But I cannot break, I know what's at stake, I'm my own man's man;

I tear away, although shame-faced, and leave that gentle hand.
And—yet, I still don't believe it, my young heart just won't receive it,
Can't ignore those sparkling eyes, my tongue cannot tell my heart more lies,
I return—but love is a myth!—Did she wait? What of that one kiss?
She's been taken, trapped by a beast; her life—is—forfeit.
Gone the traveler's cloak, leave the open road, open my heart and let the lion roar!
Time to win her heart again, her tormentor feel the bite of my sword!
'I can finally see, love is for me,' I deal a mighty blow,
When she is free, she turns to me and shouts, I'm her hero...
But I am hurt, death-white with pallor, at least I shall die with some valor,
Watching her in all her beauty, her own tears she sheds upon me...
With my last breath, I tell her softly, 'Twas your love that has set me free,'
That's why there's war, for men to learn of things worth dying for..."

Kayle ended the song abruptly, distinctly remembering the last notes he had played with the chubby fingers of a younger child on his piano. His chest hurt with a pain that almost felt good–like a muscle sore after a good workout. His eyes were wet, and this time, he didn't hesitate to dry his tears on his shirt. When he twisted his face into his arm, he saw a flash of pink behind him and turned to face Mariah, assorting his features into a blank expression.

"Kayle, that was beautiful," Mariah said a little hesitantly, seemingly worried about setting him off. Kayle said nothing.

Mariah came a little closer. "Did you come up with it?"

"Yes," Kayle replied, his voice flat.

"What inspired it?"

"I...don't know."

Mariah lost all hesitation, annoyance flickered across her features at how cold he was being, and her accent became stronger as she needled, "Strong and silent, huh?" She joined him on the balcony and tried to see his eyes. When he still refused to meet her face, she grew a vine out of the railing and used it to gently take his chin in its tendrils and turn him towards her. She laughed at his indignant frown.

The vine shrank away, and Kayle mumbled, "Strong 'n silent, that's me."

"Are you the traveler in the song?" Mariah questioned.

Now Kayle squirmed. "Mariah, I was only, like, ten when I made that."

Mariah touched the back of her hand to his cheek. "A child with a big mind, big feelings." She nodded confidently. "Maybe you weren't once. But I think the traveler is you, now."

Kayle turned his gaze to hers, eyes timid with wonderment.

She murmured softly, "Because, like the traveler, you don't let anyone into your life. You experience everything in a foolish headlong rush as if you want nothing more than a good brawl. You poke and tease and aggravate like you did with Jonathan when he first got here, but at the same time, you watched over him; prayed for him. You're a good friend. You're a good man."

Unexpectedly, Mariah leaned forward to kiss Kayle full on the lips.

Kayle only had time to brush the fingers of one hand through her curled hair and breathe in her scent like fresh autumn air and actually acknowledge the softness of her mouth at his before she broke away. She stood there, flushed and breathless, her eyes sparkling.

"You're *my* hero, Kayle."

Turning, she ran gracefully back into the light and noise. After a moment's lull, Kayle smiled ear to ear, his reddish eyes coming alive as they hadn't in a long while. Then, humming his song to himself, he followed Mariah into the light.

CHAPTER FOURTEEN:

LIES ARE UNTOLD

BACK TO JONATHAN, FOUR DAYS LATER

Coughing the dust from our lungs, Boyzun and I bent over and shuffled beneath the totem.

A small pile of items had fallen from the open compartment in the trunk, but they were so half-buried in dust that it had seemed like more. One was a golden crown. Metal wires twined around each other like twigs to form a circle, and bronze leaves stuck out here and there. In the front was a tear-drop-shaped diamond set into the gold and surrounded by flecks of emerald.

"This was my father's," Boyzun said in a tremulous voice, lifting the crown as if it were made of spun glass and tilting it wonderingly in his hands.

The other item was a greenish-gray globe about the size of an orange. Its surface was smooth and glassy, and the contents swirled like a ceaseless fog. I was surprised to see one here of all places: an Oracle in the guts of a totem in the middle of the jungle.

Oracles, I remembered reading in the journals Peter had written to help prepare me for the dreamworld, were beings that usually took the form of a young woman in swirling robes. Despite popular myth, Oracles aren't all-knowing; they are the mouthpieces of the Powers-That-Be–God, or Celestials like Michael, the White Griffin–and can only answer a few questions at a time about one's present or past, or give vague hints about the future. There are two "breeds" of Oracle as well. One type is human, and they will answer questions for anyone–they often dwell on the outskirts of communities near a sacred cave or tree. The other, much rarer and more powerful type is crafted by unknown powers for one person exclusively, and *that* Oracle usually takes on attributes or the likeness of that person. They dwell in foggy globes rumored to contain the most powerful type of magic, and if destroyed, they are said to bring a curse on the destroyer and his family that will last generations.

Boyzun picked up the globe, studied it, and gave it to me. As soon as the glass touched my hands, it came alive, letting off a bright light that started at the center of it and spread out until I had to shut my eyes.

When I opened them again, the heavy ball was as light as if it were hollow plastic, and a dark-skinned woman with glitter on her face, garbed in a white dress and silky scarves, hovered over the globe. The scarves danced along her arms and neck and billowed in an invisible breeze. She smiled, baring perfect teeth. Her eyes twinkled–the dark green irises held slitted griffin pupils. Her long, black hair was tied up in a bun and plated by a shimmering amber griffin head. She held a staff, the top of which closely resembled the globe I held and was crowned by the likeness of a venerable talon. She spoke with cool purpose, her voice slow and deep.

"Prince Jonathan...greetings. I am the Oracle of Destiny, crafted long ago by ancient hands to speak truths unto you this day. The Rankers did not see me when they hid their items within the totem, for my revelations are not theirs. Long have I awaited your arrival, stored safely away at the command of the Celestials who foretold the

Griffin King's prophecy; by seers who saw that you would arrive here, and be ready to receive undisclosed knowledge. I have answers to your questions. You have only to ask them."

Finally! Some answers! So this *must be the truth that the ancients were told to hide–an Oracle!*

I opened my mouth but I couldn't find words to express what I wanted to know. My questions were too...*big*. And there were so many.

"Are my friends safe?" I said feebly.

The Oracle slowly turned her head side to side, and my heart took a plunge into an icy ocean of worry.

"Not now," she explained. "None are safe now that the Rankers are establishing their order on the earth. But they are alive."

I breathed out in relief. Boyzun smiled at me, fiddling with the crown in his lap.

"So, it's started, huh? They're making themselves known?" I asked grimly.

The Oracle closed her eyes. "Sadly, yes. They have shed their disguises and are even now imposing their reign upon the earth. Resistance is little and easily crushed, for your people were taken by surprise. At the moment, the Rankers focus on establishing their rule, and they govern with an iron fist.

"My time is limited here, Prince. I will answer three questions that I know are disturbing you to unrest within yourself. And then you must take the Rankers' clues and continue your quest to the capital city."

I nodded and waited expectantly, occasionally looking at the holes of sky in the canopy for the chimera. Finally, the woman clasped her hands before her and began.

"You wonder about your purpose; if, all your life, you were born to do this, if it is the only reason you are alive."

I blinked and my cheeks grew hotter. This was never a question I had voiced, nor one that had ever fully been realized in my mind, but as she spoke, the truth of her words hit me like a sucker punch. Such was the price of an Oracle's knowledge. All my feelings would be exposed to her, and all my thoughts laid bare. She went on.

"Everyone has a destiny, of course. Your paths toward fulfilling that destiny are always changing, but there is one outcome that will stay constant no matter what: death. Life is a sort of test that will decide what comes after death, and everyone must take it. So, Prince Jonathan, in a way, you are no different from other humans, for all humans who live must die. But also, in a way, you are different." She tilted her head to one side to watch Boyzun scoot closer to me and resumed speaking.

"The trails you have decided to walk in life, unbeknownst by you, have ensured your arrival here to the Land of Dreams. If you hadn't followed Garrett into that house, been critically injured, and then found and cared for by the Charlatan–" 'cared for' was a pretty fond term for being knocked into a coma and sent to the Land of Dreams, but I wasn't going to argue, "–then you would have somehow arrived here all the same because of the sort of decisions you make and because of who you are. Yes, Prince, you *were* born to do this. You are possibly one of the only people on earth capable of the task."

"How?" I asked. I could imagine so many other people better suited for my position. Someone like Peter. Or Kayle, who would just light all the Rankers on fire and be done with it.

The Oracle leaned casually against her staff. "Think, Jonathan. You enjoy football because you like stretching your mind by coming up with clever strategies. You enjoy the heat of the game when you are surrounded by the enemy with no choice but to battle your way out. Your mother died, and your father was an unfit one. So you learned empathy, independence, how to handle pain and sorrow... You are curious but cautious. You have a sense of justice, displayed so when you saved that young man's life on the mountain. And I know that every time you gazed upon the griffin murals at your school, you felt a sense of belonging and mystification. In short, Prince, you are not a griffin by chance but by design. By destiny."

To think that I was *meant* to be anything at all! I never wanted to forget that feeling: that sense of a higher calling–that someone was governing all this and keeping it in control and that I was helping them; I was an integral piece in the game. Just a few months ago, I had bristled at the thought that I was a pawn, that I was a tool to be pushed around by complete strangers in a war that I had no business fighting.

But now I saw the truth. Pawn or not, I was helping people, and if I tried to resist the great events taking place, tried to escape or pawn my responsibilities off on someone else, then I'd still wind up doing exactly what I was trying to avoid because of the man my destiny was shaping me out to be. It might be unpleasant at times, but I couldn't fight who I was, as Peter had once told me. There was comfort in such knowledge.

The Oracle went on. "You secondly wonder about Peter, attendant to the White Griffin. You wonder at who he is and where he has come from."

I jolted–this was too good to be true! I nodded slowly, and she answered my second un-asked question.

"Peter is a wise man. As a child, he enjoyed writing snippets of things here and there. He had quite a talent. In his early teens, he was gaining literary attention among his peers. But before he could begin any career as an author, World War II hit. At age 16, Peter lied about his age and joined the fighting with patriotic relish."

I was aghast. World War II? That would mean that... I did some quick math. Peter was at least in his late eighties or early nineties now!

"What happened to him?" I asked, half to myself. How had Peter arrived here in the Land of Dreams?

The Oracle tilted her chin down to look at me contemplatively through her lashes. "Later on in the war, Peter and his squadron were separated from the rest of their unit during an intense firefight with the Nazi Germans. In the morning, Peter and his companions were completely alone and surrounded by dead men from both sides. Their radio had been peppered with bullets, but before it failed completely, the radioman was just able to get a message to their distant comrades that they were isolated but alive. They were told of a small German village nearby and that they would be retrieved from there in about a week.

"That night, the squadron, starved and thirsty and very cold, went into the silent, sleeping community. Peter was about to knock on the first door he saw and ask for a place to stay, but luckily a German woman, in the early months of pregnancy, had seen their approach from her front windows and stopped them. She took them to her home, and once they were well-fed and comfortably settled in her secluded sitting-room, she explained that out of the whole village, she and a few other small, soft-spoken families were anti-Hitler.

"Her husband had been a Nazi draftee against his will and had been killed not three weeks earlier. If anyone else had seen the wandering Americans, it is quite possible that they would have been shot on sight or handed over to the enemy and faced a worse fate. The woman promised to care for them until their rescue, hiding them in a secret space with a Jewish family beneath her house.

"That young woman was your grandmother, Jonathan."

I choked on my tonsils. Peter had known my family! Mother hadn't lived long enough to tell me *that* story, and maybe she hadn't told father either.

The Oracle accepted my shock with a sympathetic smile. But as her time was running out, she continued, leaving me to handle my bewilderment on my own.

"Peter remained safe in your grandmother's hands. Until their rescue came. This time the unsuspecting American soldiers marched into the village in broad daylight, expecting the people of the village to be friendly as Peter and his men had first assumed.

"Peter's hostess saw them shouting to the furious Germans, but she saw too late. Shots were fired, a young soldier killed, and the fighting began. Your grandmother rushed outside, trying to calm her neighbors to no avail. Peter heard the fighting from where he was hidden. He broke out, and he and his men rushed outside into the melee.

"Once the villagers saw the hidden Americans rushing from one of their neighbor's houses, they turned their fire on them and her. Peter saved her life, pulling her to the ground beside him. A Molotov cocktail exploded beside his head. Despite the dangerous wound, Peter picked the woman up and, shielding her with his own body, carried her to safety. Not only did he save her life, but he went back to rescue the Jewish family, one of whom had been shot in the arm when he had tried covering Peter with a pistol.

"Later, when the American soldiers had detained the villagers and put them under military arrest and when the war was won, your grandmother gave birth to your mother, Esther. Sadly, Esther's mother died in labor, but not before naming Peter her godfather."

I choked again, feeling a knife of hurt and anger gouge at my heart. Why would Peter keep this from me? The Oracle wrapped up her story with a few sad sentences.

"Peter loved your mother and took her in as his own daughter until she grew old enough to make her own life. But Esther didn't know that a deadly lesion was growing in Peter's brain, growing since that cocktail had detonated beside his head.

"A worried neighbor looked in on Peter when she hadn't seen him outside for a while, and she found him collapsed in the hall in a bad way. He was taken to a hospital, and there he still rests, under medical care but growing weaker by the day in a deep coma." The Oracle looked away, picking at invisible specks of dust on her staff to give me some time to compose myself.

Boyzun stared at the Oracle, his mouth wide. I gave a start when I noticed how ragged my breathing had become, and put a hand on my chest as if I could close the aching hole growing there. Peter knew my mother. He had *known* her! But why hadn't he told me in all of this time we had traveled together? He had to have known that I was her son! Had something happened between them? Was he disappointed that I was her son?

The Oracle looked concerned for my sanity. "That is a lot to take in. Maybe I should stop at that."

"No!" I barked desperately. "If there's just one more answer, I... I'd like to hear it."

Searching my eyes, the Oracle puckered her lips in deliberation. "As you command, Prince. Thirdly, you wonder about the White Griffin and your future here as guardian of the dreamworld. I was told to deliver this letter to you." With a wave of her staff, a scroll of pale pink paper sealed with violet wax appeared from nowhere over my head. I took it and caressed it wonderingly with my thumb. What words were concealed inside? The ever-observant Oracle explained.

"That note contains very valuable words, instructions, and assurance from Michael, the Celestial White Griffin, and your–"

"What does that mean?" I blurted, my tone a tad harsher than I meant it to be, but the realization that Peter had a connection to my family had tossed up all kinds of emotions. "I keep hearing that word. What's a Celestial? Who is Michael?"

The Oracle appeared to deliberate how to answer or whether or not to answer at all. But when I made an involuntary whimper-growl of frustration, she took a deep breath and said, "Celestials are ancient, angelic beings that obey the will of the Golden Griffin, He who created the line of griffin rulers and appointed them the post of nightmare-slayers. They have watched over these realms from a time before they were even entrusted to griffins. I know very little about their kind, but the little I *do* know I will not share with you, for I cannot. You, in your mortal state of being, would not be able to comprehend."

I opened my mouth to snap an argument, but she lifted one hand sharply, and I quieted with a sullen frown.

"Suffice to say, Prince, that Michael has long assisted the griffin-rulers, and he is here to help you as well. It is because of Michael that I am here. The Golden Griffin foresees all and, centuries ago, instructed that I be crafted for this very moment in time and given to Michael, who gave me to Boyzun's ancestors, who created the trial of the totems to ensure that should anyone other than yourself attempt to find me, they would pay dearly."

Boyzun and I exchanged tense looks, and he absently rubbed at the bandage around his injured arm. What would have happened if Boyzun had gone alone to try and slay the chimera? But, according to the Oracle, he wouldn't have gone alone because it was my destiny to have gone with him. It was all quite confusing, and I thought of the Master's wheel of fate, the thousands of tiny images on its spinning rings that could tell a person's future. I had to grudgingly agree with the Oracle: this was all beyond my comprehension.

"Michael will guide you along your journey for as long as he is told to. Though he cannot interfere in your destiny and destroy the Rankers on his own, he is a powerful warrior. You should consider yourself extremely fortunate to have such power at your back."

"He sent me this letter?" I asked, lifting the scroll and turning it in my fingers.

"Yes. It is a gift, for Michael knows of your experiences and the wounds in your heart. The words within should comfort you, for they have been written by Esther...your mother..."

She stopped speaking and watched me closely, trying to gauge my reaction, but actually, my first response was to laugh. It was loud and harsh, and I rocked back on my heels with the force of it. Boyzun fixed me with a somewhat frightened stare. Still, the Oracle's words hit home. My hands shook, and I dropped her into the grass. She stared calmly upwards, parallel to the sky.

After the laugh died, I pasted a fake smile on my mouth and picked her back up. She was tapping her nails against her staff.

"I'm expected to believe that?" I groused sarcastically, not having the strength to say the words repeating themselves in my mind: *My mother's dead, remember? My mother's dead...*

The Oracle replied smoothly, "You already do."

I gulped hard. This couldn't be happening. Any second now, the Oracle was going to be like, "Hah, J.K. Gotcha! Okay, cue the chimera!" But instead, she said, "Your mother *is* dead, Jonathan, but not in the sense you think. In her time on earth, she performed great acts of charity and brought hope to the suffering with her words and actions. She was a griffin-hearted woman, though she never came to realize the full power of being such in the manner that you have. But because of her connection to this place, her connection to *you*, her spirit claims greater ken of the events occurring than other spirits do. Thus, the letter."

I looked around with desperate thirst, wondering wildly if my mother's "spirit" was hovering nearby wearing a halo and strumming a harp, but as I'd expected, all I could see was the surrounding jungle. Boyzun was watching me with new respect. It irritated me.

The Oracle's speech faltered as she tried her best to find words to explain. "Esther and the White Griffin each have parts to play in the ancient plot that is unraveling, just as you do. They are here to help you."

I scowled and shot, "I don't need her or Peter's or the White Griffin's help! They've never helped me! They *never* came to me! Where were they when I was..." *Suffering, alone, hurting, screaming for a sign, a purpose?* I couldn't say any of those things in front of Boyzun or the Oracle's penetrating gaze.

The Oracle narrowed her eyes dangerously, the vertical slits menacing.

"Think twice," she warned, "Before letting your sword replace your tongue. You have never been alone, Prince Jonathan. And you never will be."

I grimaced at the chiding. With a sweep of her staff, the dust and dirt from the totem billowed away to reveal two more items that'd been buried in the detritus.

"These are the clues that the Rankers hid that will reveal to you the next step on your journey," she said shortly, sore at me.

I half-heartedly ripped my attention away from family matters and towards the clues. One was a weighty red scarab-beetle made of interlocking pieces of metal painted scarlet. The other clue was a leather drawstring pouch full of strange money and a list of random items. I stuffed them and the letter into my pack with a forceful shove.

I only half-heard the Oracle say, "This is it, Prince Jonathan He'klarr. After this last journey, you will go to the capital city and engage in war. Adventures await you still, but you must keep control and clarity through them. And heed my warning, Prince," her voice had turned sharp. I looked peevishly down at her.

"Do not use the paint chariot-horse."

My mental record player screeched off its track. That hadn't made any sense. I knew what a paint horse was, but where would I get one? They were about as common around here as indoor plumbing. I was about to ask for more information on the subject, but it was then, at that moment, that Boyzun absent-mindedly set his crown on his head.

A sudden shock-wave of air blasted outwards in a wide radius from the crown. The veins burst in my and Boyzun's noses from the wave's pressure, and blood trickled from our nostrils and ears. The Oracle's globe developed a great crack that split through it. Her image flickered but didn't die. Boyzun clutched his head and winced. I wiped the blood from beneath my nose with a sleeve.

"It has been called," the Oracle said in a faint voice.

I tried to shake the dizziness from my head, and the effect was a sudden barrage of black dots that refused to wink out of my vision. *The crown...the Rankers must have hexed it,* I thought.

"Goodbye and good luck, princes," the Oracle whispered. She turned her eyes to mine and, in a quiet voice, said, "And remember; you are never alone." Then she vanished, and the globe went dark. I picked it up. It was heavy again and cold as a Coloradan winter.

"You're wrong," I murmured, thinking of my abusive childhood, of Garrett's incessant bullying, of my mother's violent death. "I've always been alone."

CHAPTER FIFTEEN:

THE CHIMERA

Something pulled at my shirt–Boyzun was attempting to drag me beneath the wooden totem. I went willingly, my thoughts a tumultuous mess of questions and emotions. We cowered in the totem's gloomy shadow, awaiting the chimera. Its distant wing beats foretold its approach. My head snapped up, eyes searching, senses straining. The cyclone going on in my mind subsided to a whisper as all the training I'd received from Peter and the Master took over.

Boyzun drew an arrow, keeping it relaxed but ready atop his left fist. I drew my sword and kept it close to my body so it wouldn't catch any sunlight. Boyzun was shivering. Or maybe I was. But I didn't have time to ask.

A thick red tail, covered in smooth, overlapping scales, smashed into the totem, ripping it violently sideways in a shower of wood chips and dust. We were exposed.

Boyzun went down with a bark of pain; one of the totem's column-like legs had collided with his injured arm. Then, through the confusing whirlwind of grass and dirt, I saw a flash of three pairs of ruby-red eyes and stabbed blindly upward with my sword. There came a twisted scream of shocked pain, a shower of warm beads of black blood, and then light was upon us to reveal that Boyzun and I were alone in the clearing. I circled in place, breathing heavily, sword ready. The blood in my ears made every noise seem hollow, far-off, and meager.

Something like a brick wall smashed into me from behind, dragging me to the ground and knocking the wind out of my lungs. The chimera swooped up and curved around in front of me, and I got a good view of it.

It actually looked a lot like the demolished totem. The body was covered in a thin, spotted pelt that stretched over bunched muscles and distorted bones. The central head was the same way–golden-furred, covered in rosettes, a cat head, a jaguar's in this case, complete with powerful whiskered jaws full of sharp teeth. The head to the left of the jaguar's was a hideous goat's with curving, stunted horns, vacant, glassy eyes, and a protrusion of chiseled lower teeth. The crimson-colored tail and cavernous bat wings belonged to the last head–the dragon's. Smoke wisped from the slitted nostrils at the end of its narrow snout and needle-teeth fenced in a forked tongue. A crest of spines followed the neckline and rough ridges of gold scales shadowed the malevolent eyes. This head seemed the most intelligent–it watched us keenly.

Touching down on all fours, its wings half-open, the chimera stood tense and poised, like a cat watching a mouse readying for the pounce. I had to admire the wild, vicious beauty of the colorful rosettes in the golden fur, the sparkle of the red scales.

A voice wriggled into my head, unwelcome. It was a faint murmur, as smooth and subtle as sin. I blinked at the staring heads, my gaze lingering on the dragon's focused ruby-red eyes, wondering if the chimera spoke as one, or if the faintly mocking tones came from the dragon alone.

The Dark Ones put a curse upon the crown of the corpse-king. When the Dark Ones' soldiers arrived, it was to summon me so that I could raze the villages in my jungle and rid it of any loyal to your kind. My power would have become the Dark Ones' own and filled the hearts of their followers. We would have taken the Wheel of Fate for ourselves, that all knowledge and foresight would be ours, and then set these trees alight in a conflagration of woe. We would have forever left a scar in this domain and in the minds of all dreaming humans.

Guess you didn't count on Boyzun and me showing up to ruin the surprise? I replied mentally, a sneer pulling at my face.

Nay. The fires shall still come. In tandem, all six pupils in the eyes of the three heads contracted eerily, and its muscles tightened as if it were about to leap forward. *Only now, you shall bear witness!*

Boyzun shot an arrow into the monster's flank. The dragon head locked us in its gaze and pulled fiercely against the other two writhing heads to turn back to us, though it was now scarred by two wounds. With an unexpectedly sinuous grace, the chimera darted back into the trees.

"This thing is fast!" Boyzun moaned. I didn't say anything. We went back to back, rotating, eyes on every detail.

The chimera burst out of the trees behind where the totem had been, snapping wide its wings when it reached the apex of its leap and gliding around us. I raised my sword, dancing lightly on my toes. The goat's head came nearest to me–the others snapping at a dodgy Boyzun. Its teeth ground hideously together, and I was washed in its foul breath.

I twirled dancer-like to the side and arced my sword sideways against the creature's snowy white cheek. Its blood slicked my blade, and I stumbled. The goat bleated in pain and fury.

In the time it took for the chimera to shake itself and rock away, I hastily cleaned my blade on the grass and stood. The goat's tongue lolled bloody, but it narrowed its eyes at me and butted me in the chest with its horns. I went sailing a few feet away and hit the ground again, gasping for air. I really wasn't making a good impression so far.

The chimera made for me; the jaguar snarled. The goat weakly wobbled its head; the dragon seemed to wear a mocking grin. But an arrow whistled from nowhere and embedded its deadly point into the side of the goat's neck. It gave a strangled cry, flopped sideways, and was no more. At the same time that its brain shut down, the hoofed hind legs gave out, and the chimera's back half collapsed. Then, straining its wings, the beast lifted its mismatched bulk and soared into the trees to try again.

I took note of how exhausted I was already becoming. The Oracle's information overload had really drained my energy. On top of that, my chest had been bruised from my fall, and the muscles of my arms and hand ached from gripping my sword so tightly and from being jostled around like a maraca. Boyzun, if anything, had to be faring worse.

The birds were silent and watchful. If we were to die, it would be alone. It was a chilling realization that made me shudder from head to foot. *No,* I thought, with a glimmer of defiance, of hope. *It isn't my destiny to die yet.*

"We can't beat it from the ground," I declared, sort of casually moving to prop Boyzun up with my shoulder without him knowing I was helping.

"What are you suggesting?" Boyzun panted. He twitched his arms towards the sound of a twig snapping in the jungle. The arrow he had strung wobbled dangerously.

"I need to transform," I said forcefully. "But keep the arrows coming."

"Jonathan, that thing is going to chew you up and spit you out," Boyzun said, grabbing my arm.

I gave him a fierce, manic kind of smile. As the Master had said, my griffin form worked like a suit of mail. It wasn't impervious to injury, but the berserker-strength, avian reflexes, and feline endurance of my transformed body would give the injured chimera more to consider than my feeble, unarmored human form would.

Boyzun reacted to my expression with a start of concern and looked ready to protest, saying something about how small my griffin form was compared to the monster, but I picked up dark and hungry blood-thirsty thoughts from somewhere behind us and shoved Boyzun aside.

The chimera leaped into thin air. Its wing grazed my hair. I cut out and chopped off a piece of the tail. It twisted, and the dragon opened its jaws impossibly wide, arched its tongue, and spat fire at me.

I ducked the molten heat and shouted, *"Is that the worst you can do? I hang out with an Irish pyro-maniac with burning stuff on the brain, and you think* that *will stop me?"*

Boyzun sent me a worried look.

The jaguar gave a throaty growl and crouched to pounce, its paws splayed. Its furrowed eyes were fastened on me like fishhooks. I heard the stretch of a string and the whoosh of sliced air, and the fletching of an arrow appeared stuck in its forehead. The creature howled, falling forward onto its chest. One wing became pinched beneath it, and with the other, the dragon tried in vain to make an escape. In frustration, it nipped at the jaguar's ear, and with one last effort, the cat stood, shook furiously, nudged aside the useless goat head, and tried to crawl to us.

Boyzun and I exchanged grim but victorious looks. Boyzun slowly drew another arrow, aiming at the chimera's broad chest. But to our surprise, the dragon suddenly reared up and wrapped its jaws around the jaguar's neck, shaking it hard. The jaguar hissed and yowled, but it was too weak to fight back. It was dead in seconds. No longer hindered by the other two heads, the dragon struggled to fly its dead bulk into the air, gurgling and coughing, obviously suffering from the deaths of the other two heads in ways that Boyzun and I couldn't see. The monster was indeed dying, but it sure wasn't dead yet.

I stabbed my sword into its sheath and transformed. With a glorious and unexpected feeling of strength, I spread my wings to their extent, letting the breeze flutter my pinions, letting the muscles quiver with anticipation. I turned the soil with my talons, filled the air with my piercing shriek. The dragon backed off a bit and succeeded in making it into the sky. I pounced upward and flapped my wings furiously until I, too, caught wind.

Warm air cushioned under me. My wings filled with it, my lungs sucked it in, my heart came alive as a jungle panorama filled my vision in a carpet of a hundred different shades of green with the sun blazing golden above. I pulled the feathers at the end of my tail together and closed my wings, swinging myself into a backward flip so that my feet pointed up at the chimera. With one paw, I kicked aside its tail, and with the other, I landed a hard kick into its chest. The dragon lost its breath in a scalding wave. Using its distraction to my advantage, I toyed with the wind, arced into a sharp curve, and smashed into it. I had to try to stay close to avoid its fiery breath. Peter's flying lessons raced through my memories.

For countless minutes we were locked in a mindless battle that involved feverish pain, shrugged away and ignored. Fangs like steak knives snapped above my ears, claws raked at my wings, shimmering clouds of heat washed across me in waves smelling of burnt hair. But all that mattered to me was landing my own strikes. One primitive goal had settled in my mind: to defeat the other first. Geysers of fire chased me. My beak scraped scales. My talons dragged through coarse fur. Our wings beat against each other with jarring force. Our calls thundered across the heavens as we ascended higher and higher.

The chimera dodged a swipe of my talons that probably would've taken one of its eyes, ducked beneath a follow-up beak-jab, and suddenly its teeth were fixed in my chest. It watched me with one ruby eye, excited. Eager to see my life leave me. Warm blood began to mat my feathers. Numerous tooth-inflicted cuts blazed with stinging pain. An agonized mewling pierced the air and the shock that came with the realization that *I* was making that noise was enough to clam me up.

The chimera growled, my blood mixing with its saliva to create a bubbling froth, and gave me a shake like a dog with a rat, forcing a high, gasping shriek of pain from my throat. It was nearly twice as big as me–if it wanted to, the chimera could've forced its jaws together and broken my back. I tried to flap my wings, but one of them was stuck in its mouth. The chimera made a stuttering, grunting sound of what could only be cruel laughter.

In a disjointed and bleary way, I thought about how many times I had seen the look that the chimera was giving me. That look of loathing and hatred as the jerk who wore it knew that they were in control and that they had me at their mercy.

I had seen it on the gargoyle when I had been his captive, tied into a chair and awaiting death at his claws, but mostly I had seen it on Garrett: whenever my team and I won a football game; whenever I would pass him in the halls at school, smiling with my friends; whenever I would succeed in getting the student body pumped at pep assemblies; when, years ago, he had insulted Nikki in the middle of the school cafeteria during lunch, remarking lewdly, lustfully, about her beauty, baiting me into a reaction even as Nikki had wept in embarrassment behind me.

A new sound came to me. I roared–a pure lion's roar of fury and defiance. As the chimera ground its teeth together, I curled up, dug my hind claws into the monster's snout like a cat curling around a toy mouse, and ripped up towards the sky. The chimera yelped, and its grip on me loosened. I curled up and kicked again, again, until, shaking its head, the beast released me. I let myself roll out from between its teeth, then spread my wings and swatted aside the dragon's head with open talons. I could've sworn I saw some of its teeth go airborne.

Recovering with a jolt, the chimera spat fire at me. I dodged the full brunt of the blow, but some secondary feathers still sizzled. With the agility of a starling, I tipped sideways and clipped a hole in one of the translucent webbings of the wings. The chimera sank lower, circling beneath me, trying to angle itself back toward the clearing we had taken off from, tilting into a dive and slowly increasing speed. We were both aware that it was weakening, and it couldn't last for much longer up here, where the wind currents were powerful and sweeping.

I followed behind at a distance, fighting off my weariness, content to take advantage of the lull in combat while I waited for the dying monster to make a move. Dark thoughts from the chimera beat my consciousness; sinister promises formed coherent words in my mind.

I am owed! that malicious voice snarled. *I was to feast on your flesh and sharpen my teeth on your bones! You're mine*! *The dark one promised! Mineminemineminine!!!*

"Well, somebody lied!" I shouted. I spun in a tight circle and, as if tackling an opponent in football, threw myself against its wing. With a loud *snap,* it shattered at the "wrist" joint. The wing became a piece of canvas flapping and convulsing in the air. The chimera began to freefall.

At the last second, it grabbed one of my forelimbs in its teeth, and my wings trembled and collapsed–unable to handle both of our weights. My third eyelids slid over my eyes to keep away debris, but still, the wind tore at my face. We fell at an incredibly fast rate, and the wind caused the chimera's broken wing to snap and flail, buffeting against me like a demolished tent. The meaty "arm" of the wing struck me in the stomach, and I was thrown back over its head, my forelimb wrenched painfully in the beast's molars. It twisted its neck and tried to rotate so that I would be crushed between its body and the ground. But *my* wings weren't broken.

Taking deep, relaxing breaths, I tested the wind currents with my tail-fan, absorbed the speed, power, and direction of the rushing air as it teased through my fur and feathers. Yes, my new position under the beast gave me an advantage; the chimera's body blocked most of the vicious, chaotic wind above, leaving an aerodynamic cone beneath me. If I timed everything right, I could ride the beast's slipstream past it to safety.

I forced my wings open, twisted, and tilted them around until I found the cone of carefully-shaped, carefully-controlled air. The wind flowed along my contours like grasping fingers, shaped into something useful by my pinions and secondaries, and it sent me shooting gracefully sideways and upwards, ripping my arm from its vice in a flurry of copper feathers and scarlet beads of blood.

As I ascended above the shocked chimera, I closed my wings slightly and planted my lion paws into the beast's chest, essentially riding it like a snowboard as the ground swelled to fill my vision.

Smacking away its head with my talons whenever it came too close, the other two heads flopping grotesquely, I bellowed, "*Now, Boyzun!*"

Boyzun aimed and released his next arrow. It soared through the air, a deadly missile... and stuck into the dragon's neck just beside the huge crest. I shoved down with my hind legs, letting myself drift above and away, and the chimera crashed into the ground with a grim thud that rang with finality.

I floated to land beside Boyzun and shifted back into my human form. Blood soaked my arm, and the front of my shirt was likewise drenched and shredded, but the deed was done.

The chimera turned its last head to us and blew out smoke and sparks, but no fire. Accepting that with a weak sigh, it instead maneuvered its tongue to the bottom of its mouth and gave an ear-splitting roar of defiance. Boyzun whooped back, but I frowned into the dragon's eyes. It was speaking to me again, sending its thoughts into my mind.

The Dark One told me you were mine, it thought contemptuously. *He promised... I was to feast on your blessed blood...*

I had no doubt of whom it spoke and thought back, *You shouldn't believe everything you hear. Dear, sweet Garrett wants me alive, don'cha know? You were duped, buddy.*

The chimera gave a choking cough that could've been a laugh. *You, Great Prince, are cocky, but you hate the Dark One. I tasted your hatred, even before the crown summoned me. You think yourself better? You think yourself...worthy? You hate like every other human...and every other Dark One...*

Yes, I do. I scowled, swallowing the needle of shame and self-doubt that the beast's words pricked into my heart. *Anything else you want to share with me?*

The chimera wheezed, grasping at life, but managed its final words.

This territory has been mine since before you could walk, Great Prince. I have watched from the long shadows as your predecessors fumbled about this land and claimed to protect it. I smell the fear and uncertainty upon you. You are right to feel such things. The Dark One allows you to live, yes. But there are others alive, too, others you care about. And their lives belong to him.

A wicked smile crawled up the dragon's toothy, blood-streaked mouth. *But you are stuck here, Prince, so-called Guardian of Dreams; here, alone, where you cannot guard the ones you love most. And here... you will forever remain...*

The chimera dropped its head, body relaxing in death, and I stared straight into the dilated pupils of its dead eyes, feeling helplessness, anger, and, yes, hate.

CHAPTER SIXTEEN:

CHIEF BOYZUN

We arrived back at the village in the afternoon two and a half days later.

By the end of the first day, my lacerations had scabbed over somewhat since the fight, and none of them had been deep enough to warrant the use of the sticky flowers that had saved Boyzun's arm, but though they were shallow, they were long, messy, and blistered in places from the dragon's hot breath. At the end of the second day, Boyzun was in the middle of helping me to change my bandages when a Tahtltiki warrior sitting astride his trusty chameleon scrambled down a kapok tree and offered to give us a lift back up into the branches.

The man babbled the whole way about how there would be a grand celebratory feast and spoke proudly of how much Boyzun's crown suited him. He kept trying to get us to describe the fight in detail, pestering me eagerly to tell him the story behind my jagged wounds, but a combination of the Oracle's revelations, the chimera's final words, weariness, pain, and blood loss made me despondent.

I let Boyzun narrate our tale while I mused over what I would say to Peter. Or if I was going to say anything. Not only had he known my mother, he had been her *godfather* and essentially raised her. Yet, he had said nothing at all about it to me, and I still couldn't figure out why.

The clamor of cheering shook me from a stupor. I looked up and found myself instantly bombarded by a wave of smiling, relieved, happy faces. The sudden swarm of back-slaps and hugs and handshakes caused me to slide back down the chameleon's tail, but Boyzun and I were lifted into the air and crowd-surfed upon hundreds of hands to who-knows-where.

My wounds had started to burn pretty badly, especially the one on my arm, and I asked several times for aid, but no one heard over the loud voices and fluting music. All around were twinkling eyes, painted faces, goggling lemurs, and parading children.

Soon we were gently deposited onto our feet before a crowd of young women. One with waist-length black hair and bright red lips put a lei around my neck, and she and her friends coated my cheeks and forehead with kisses, brushing aside my lengthening bangs. The flowers were big and golden, with honey-colored speckles in the center. They gave off a citrusy scent and attracted minute hummingbirds that would boldly flitter up to my neck to extract nectar. I fingered the lei, smiling politely. Boyzun was basically getting the same treatment, except he was trying to get kissed on the mouth. His new crown glimmered in the torchlight.

The crowd hushed. Chieftainess Chalk-talk was threading her way towards us through the crowd, smiling proudly. She placed her hands along the sides of her son's face and declared, "Today will be remembered as the dawning of not only a new generation but a new empire for our people!" There were tumultuous cheers.

"Life, as we know, is a great adventure, and it carries with it numerous smaller adventures, such as the significant enterprise from boy to man. My son has left behind the obstacle of childhood and will sit upon the throne of warriors! Of leaders! Golden Griffin be praised!"

It was funny because as that old woman spoke, her voice grew stronger until she seemed to be a pillar of strength, not to be trifled with. I could finally see through her ancient features to the generous woman within who had created Boyzun, turning him from a weak and vague idea into a full-blown...vision. A perfect dream.

This, I thought, *is the true beauty of the Land of Dreams.* A hot bolt made from a potent mixture of terror and excitement zapped through me. *This is my kingdom.*

Boyzun raised his hand authoritatively for silence, and the thunderous applause receded.

"Yes, I have learned many things on my journey. Some from my wise Master," he waved at a face in the crowd that no doubt belonged to our hairy old mentor, "But also much from Great Prince Jonathan."

Eyes gazed merrily my way, and I shifted uncomfortably with a surprised look in Boyzun's direction. He thumped the shoulder of my uninjured arm and said, "I couldn't have made it without him. Because of him, I'm alive. Through him, I've learned that though the body may be beaten nearly to death, the heart still fights, pumping its life-giving blood. The mind still works, concocts, feels, and dreams. And the soul of the dreamer still breathes. The soul of the dreamer lives ever on. Thanks to the prince, I have avenged my father!"

Then, Boyzun bowed to me and announced in a carrying voice, "Long live the Great Griffin Prince...Jonathan He'klarr!"

My mouth dropped open. The words saluting me echoed all around. Dazed, I watched every person, young and old, bow down to me.

"I... I didn't really do anything," I stuttered out, and for some reason, that made everyone laugh.

Chieftainess Chalk-talk thankfully squeezed my right hand. Then she raised Boyzun's arm into the air.

"My people!" she called, smiling, tears brimming in her eyes, "Boyzun, your Crowned Chieftain!"

I grinned and clapped along with everyone else. Boyzun grinned back, and the procession moved forward until we soon found ourselves in front of the Chieftainess's hut. The two guards at the entrance shifted aside, and Boyzun entered timidly, staring at the vacant tree-throne. I, too, was allowed entry, standing against the far wall and crossing my arms–but that hurt too much, so instead, I looped my thumbs around the belt of my scabbard.

I couldn't remove the smile from my face, though my cheeks were hurting. The Tahtltiki people crowded outside, trying to catch everything going on through the doorway. The vipercat cub bounded over to rub against Boyzun's ankles. *It's so small,* I thought, *so small and defenseless. But just like Boyzun, it'll grow.*

A big, long line of gifts started being transferred from the crowd outside to Boyzun and even some to me. There were various little knick-knacks that I would have to somehow find room for in my bags or sadly do without, some yummy-looking foods, and the warriors gave Boyzun a little red chameleon that would grow up and become his steed. It climbed up his arm and perched on his shoulder.

Chalk-talk noticed the tourniquet wrapped around her son's arm and connected it with the missing sleeve on my shirt. She rushed to his side, hands out, eyes wild, and exclaimed, "You are hurt!"

Boyzun blinked uncomprehendingly at her. She tugged on his arm. He looked down at his old wound, and all he said was, "Oh." He untied the makeshift bandage and let it fall to the floor.

At first, I wanted to go and grab a nurse. Boyzun's dart-inflicted laceration looked nasty. But Chalk-talk and I released breaths of relief after a few seconds of closely studying the wound. The generous amount of crusty black blood was dry, and once Boyzun had scrubbed it all off, we saw that the cut that I had stuffed the green flowers into was sealed. In its place was a whitish-green scar in the shape of a star and about the size of a silver dollar. Boyzun examined it with mild interest. "I'm fine," he said, and looked at me. "But our friend needs help. The chimera gave him a tougher time than it did me."

Chalk-talk seemed to absorb the blood on my arm and chest for the first time. She instantly sent for a nurse, and I was taken away from the reveling through a back door, up some stairs to a smaller hut filled with empty hammocks. Here, the noise from the celebration was filtered out. The nurse, a petite woman with silver-streaked black hair and small, beaver-brown eyes, felt how warm my forehead was with her lips and stepped back, concerned. Her small, pensive frame swam in my vision. My wounds burned, and my head hurt. Nausea churned in my gut. When I told the nurse this, she nodded.

"Loss of blood, Prince. All you need is a pint of it back, a good cleaning, and a refreshing rest."

She helped me peel off the ragged remains of my tunic and threw it into a fire burning in an iron cauldron outside, transferring the clues from my pocket to a small side table. With smooth, careful strokes, she used a wet wad of fabric to clean the injuries. The scabs cracked and bled anew, but as the cloth scrubbed and turned steadily pink, I was better able to assess the extent of the wounds.

My forearm had been peppered with many small but jagged holes from the chimera's teeth. None of these were too deep, but a shiny peeling burn from the monster's hot breath surrounded them. The nurse coated it in some sort of creamy salve and sprinkled seeds from some tan-colored flowers into the cuts. After wrapping the arm in a stretchy white cast that smelled like rubber, she moved to my pectorals. The teeth marks here were dragged along my chest jaggedly. Some required stitches. Using a needle and some thread, the nurse sewed me closed and wrapped more of the rubbery stuff around my torso.

"There you go," she said tiredly, giving me a sip of some sweet-tasting medicine and holding a large, mossy pouch. "Good as new."

I was too tired to even thank her. I fell back into the hammock and slept.

When I opened my eyes, it was to a familiar face.

"Kayle!" I cried groggily and sat up, swaying dangerously in my hammock. Kayle steadied it gently and threw me the sort of smile I expected from a more vivacious man than he. His eyes were bright, and he had dimples. It was like someone had cracked open what was supposed to be a hard-boiled egg, and a fresh, sunny yolk had spilled out. I squinted at the corner of his mouth.

"Is that lipstick?"

Kayle hastily turned away and rubbed at his lips with a horrified expression.

"Did I get it?" He tilted his chin toward me.

I smirked playfully. "Kayle? Have you been struck by Cupid?"

Kayle frowned and took a breath to say something smart, but instead, he took on a vague look and smiled. It was sort of creepy. I fiddled with the bandage on my arm and poked at the mossy pouch by my hip that must have been full of the blood the nurse said I needed–it was warm and connected to the crook of my elbow by a stiff, yellow tube.

I peered mischievously up at him. "What, did Cupid have to corner you and *stab* you with an arrow?" I faked a scared look. "I'd hate to see what the *girl* looks like!"

Kayle stuck his tongue out at me and said something in Gaelic that I knew wasn't a get-well tiding. I blocked some faux punches he aimed at my stomach and said, "No, seriously, who is she? One of the Tahtltikis?"

Kayle inclined his chin haughtily and smiled crookedly. "Mariah."

"Nuh-uh!" I cried, splitting into a smile. Kayle's beam confirmed all. "Wow, congrats!" I sat up and gripped Kayle's left arm with my good right hand. We embraced, me still chuckling in disbelief and Kayle still wearing that uncharacteristically happy expression.

I was so overjoyed for Kayle. He and Mariah had been friends for years, traveling the dreamworld together and serving King Brody before me, whom they had quickly come to respect and admire. Now, their bond had transformed into something even stronger. Mariah was definitely a special girl if she could make Kayle this happy. I had a burning desire to know the details, but I also knew it would take a million years before Kayle would indulge me.

He even *dressed* better! He had on a white, silk long-sleeved shirt with the sleeves rolled up to his elbows and a black vest over that. It was the first time I had seen his arms. They were pale but knotted with imposing muscle that cast deep lines up and down his limbs. One detail hadn't changed, though: there was the telltale protrusion of his lighter showing in the pocket of his white pants. He ran a hand uncomfortably through his unkempt gingery hair, no doubt subconsciously reaching for the beanie that usually perched there.

I found a pile of clean clothes beneath my hammock and got dressed after the nurse came in and removed the blood-pouch, and gave me the all-clear. There were some pants that were baggy around my legs but tucked into some knee-high cloth boots. The long-sleeved tunic was an off-white embroidered in gold. The thin leather belt that cinched it snug at the waist had a clip that allowed me to attach my scabbard. I liked the feel of the fresh outfit. It was wonderful to be clean and rested again.

I already knew the answer, but I asked anyway, "Where's Ben?"

"He's gone." Kayle made a motion with his hand as if sweeping something away. "Peter briefed him on what to do, and he went back home some time ago."

I flinched at Peter's name and, avoiding Kayle's eyes, asked where he was. Kayle noticed the cold tones in my voice and raised his eyebrows but tried to act unconcerned, swinging on the hammock across from mine. "Back at the celebration with everyone else. You've been out for a long while–almost an entire day."

Silence permeated the room, an unwelcome and awkward fog. Kayle took out his lighter. He made pictures with the flames, dancing his fingers like the director of an orchestra. He worked on a romantic vision of Mariah with fiery hair that licked her face and two glowing orbs of molten yellow for intense and burning eyes, and I found myself suddenly missing Nikki with a longing that was more painfully intense than usual.

Finally, Kale asked for a detailed narration of my fight with the chimera, making me reenact some parts and asking questions about the battle's finer points. I think he could tell that I had a lot on my mind and was trying to cheer me up. But then I told him about the chimera's final words.

"It told me that the lives of my loved ones belong to Garrett and that I'll never leave the Land of Dreams."

Kayle's eyes flashed, and he lifted his lip in a sneer. Staring out an open window into the deepening night, he let out his breath in a hiss and swore, "*Mallacht iad*!" Then he took a deep, loud, gusty breath and said, "It was dying, Jonathan. Those were just bitter threats, meant to frighten you. Your friends are under Ben's watch now. They'll be okay." The loathing in his voice was at odds with the forced reassurance in his words.

“That’s not all,” I added, feeling rotten for bursting Kayle’s number-nine cloud, but he did have to know. He shot me a concerned glance. I took a breath and told him how Peter had rescued my grandmother and been dubbed my mother’s godfather. I didn’t mention the letter from my mother’s ghost or spirit or whatever. That was something personal that I wanted to muse on alone for a while.

Kayle looked shocked. So Peter hadn’t told him the truth, either. That made me feel a little better. He closed his mouth, swallowed, and raked the floor uncertainly with his eyes, as if an answer would be there.

“What do I do?” I asked helplessly.

Kayle pursed his lips sympathetically. “Peter isn’t a bad guy, Jon. Go find him and talk to him.”

That idea made me shudder. “I don’t know…”

Kayle put a hand on my shoulder. “If you don’t get this off your chest, you could screw up the war for us all. Don’t harbor your feelings. Grudges and bitterness have brought great men down.” Kayle’s words may have seemed harsh, but he was just telling me the blunt truth, like a good friend would. Though the thought of talking to Peter about something so personal made me want to retch, I had to do it.

“Okay,” I relented. “Thanks, man.” I shuffled for the door. “See you later.”

“Good luck,” Kayle said.

CHAPTER SEVENTEEN:

NEVER ALONE

Peter stood alone, pouring himself some lemonade at an open table.

I skirted the crowd of merry villagers and stomped to Peter's side, glowering into his silver eyes.

"Hello, Jonathan," he rumbled jovially in his deep voice. His eyes twinkled, and I sensed the relief and joy he felt at seeing me safe and whole. My anger faltered a bit–I was unaccustomed to receiving such fatherly concern–but I clung to it tenaciously. "I didn't get a chance to welcome you back earlier. You were whisked away too–"

"Why didn't you tell me about my grandmother?" I growled. Yeah, that was rude, but this wasn't a conversation I could begin with a cheery "hello."

Peter knew what I meant. He averted his gaze and tapped his fingers against his cup, searching for words.

Finally, he said, "I want you to know that I *did* try to stay in contact with your mother, Jonathan. I went to her wedding, helped her move into her new home, and then we had to resort to writing one another letters because this was right around when the Rankers began to act up, and we both had our hands full. Esther's last letter told me she was pregnant with a son and that she and her husband were doing fine. Then, a few years later, she was killed."

Peter frowned, clenched his jaw, and shook his head as if attempting to shake away tears.

"Your mother and I were sort of working undercover–trying to understand why there were random acts of violence suddenly taking place–and almost it seemed, systematically against influential people: politicians, mayors, even young adults who showed promise as future leaders or great contributors to society. Main targets were the faithful, the compassionate, the innocents. As an essayist and counselor, your mother focused on doing what she could to mend and inspire those victims, and she was constantly traveling, writing, speaking. I worked on the other end, doing research, asking questions, trying to prove that there was a pattern to the mayhem erupting in the quiet corners of the country. We were both always so busy…"

He gave a bitter laugh. "We thought that perhaps we'd discovered a complex terrorist cell or perhaps some government-level conspiracy… We never would've guessed…"

I wanted to speak, to protest, to argue, but my jaws felt cemented shut. Instead, I drank in Peter's revelation about my mother's character with pride and pain. Had she truly seen the bad times coming from a mile away? If she were still alive, would we have worked together in seeking an answer? Would we have discovered the Rankers as a family, and would I still have been sent to the Land of Dreams?

"When I learned it was you who was coming here," Peter continued, "I hit my knees in prayer. I could finally meet you! What a blessing! But when I saw you… I couldn't find the right words. And the moment didn't seem right–you were so confused and angry. I thought I'd teach you up a bit, help you adjust, get to know you, and then maybe… But…"

I fought with myself, trying to choose whether to listen to my logical side that empathized with Peter or my stubborn side that was adamant that Peter was a jerk and still should have told me. I kinda met both sides in the middle.

"... I get it...but I need to be alone for a bit..." I brushed past him and hurried away. The image of Peter standing there looking awkward, trying to explain himself to me, lingered in my mind, and I felt a pang of pity for him. I knew he had fallen into a coma soon after mom's death and that it was a fantasy to think that he could have swept in and rescued me from my miserable life, but I didn't want to be rational at the moment. I wanted to pout.

While standing by a balcony, trying to distract myself from my feelings by counting as many leaves below me as I could, my Master joined me.

He looked me up and down and said in a half-satisfied way, "You are alive. I taught you well."

"Yes, you did," I admitted gratefully. "Your training saved my life."

"Good, good." He leaned to one side as if I reeked. "You are radiating emotion, Prince. What offends you so?"

Dang it! I couldn't keep anything from that guy. I decided to sort of summarize all my issues into one statement-slash-question.

"It's just, sometimes I wonder what's going to happen to me... And if this war will ever end."

"All wars end," the Master said.

"Yes," I acknowledged and sighed, resting my head in my hands. "But I wonder about the outcome of this one."

"Ah, you seek answers to the future, Jonathan. But, as I have said before...that is something none should know."

I jolted, snapping my head up to look at him. "*You* did," I said. "You used that wheel thing in your house to find out about the future of your tribe."

The Master winced, as if hoping I wouldn't have thought of that. He nodded. "Yes, Jonathan. In desperation, I Looked. And I almost Saw too much."

I cocked my head quizzically.

With great reluctance, the Master continued: "If you wish to see your future, Great Prince, I will not stop you. But I say again that it is not your place to know your fate, and those who are wise do not wish to."

"Why?"

"Oh, many reasons. For one, life is a surprise. Though certain events are predestined to happen, like marriage, or death, the little choices you make and the little words you say that lead up to a predestined event can change the details of its outcome. Sometimes knowing answers to the big questions can warp one's entire life. You'll find yourself incomplete, your life a ruin of its potential. There will be no joy in it, for every terrible thing that you attempt to prevent will only happen in another way. You will be as a man laboring to stop the course of a river by pushing a boulder into its path–the river will only diverge, resume its course, and erode that boulder away to nothing. No, Prince, life is meant to be lived one day at a time."

He took a deep breath.

"So, do you really want to see?"

I really thought of saying yes, but then I considered the answers I'd find, some of which I really didn't want to know. On the upside, I would find out the outcome of this war, whether or not I would see my friends again. If I went back home. If we defeated Garrett... But I would also find out when and how I died. When and how my father, Nikki, and anyone else close to me died. I'd find out whether they died because of the war and if their deaths were due to my failure as a king.

"No," I said, putting my head back in my hands. "One day at a time."

The Master leaned against the railing beside me, his arm pressing against mine. His voice was hesitant and faltering. "I did not tell you before... You were not ready... There is a... prophecy about you, Prince. One written long ago."

I looked up at him. A thrill of astonishment, or maybe fear, flitted up my backbone as if I had seen something predatory flit past in the corner of my eye, from the shadows of the tree boughs. Oracles and all-knowing mosaics were one thing–prophecies another. Prophecies weren't real–prophecies were things from books and movies with mermaids and dragons and knights and...oh, wait.

"Would you like to hear it?" The Master's face was solemn. I hadn't noticed before how very deeply lined it was-like a raisin or very old suede that was about to start crumbling and falling apart.

"Why are you so scared?" I murmured.

"Because prophecies can leave one with more questions than answers. They have caused men to despair and break." He looked down at his bony fingers, twining together in agitation. "They can give men false hope."

Maybe it was my mind-reading ability or maybe just a suspicion I had, but I said, "Are you talking about King Brody?" Peter had mentioned a prophecy before–that everyone in the dreamworld had thought Brody would be the one to fulfill it.

He shut his eyes tight. Gave his head a sad shake. "We all thought it was about him. We all felt such joy when he was crowned. But then he..." The Master fell silent. I thought I heard a tear or two plip down onto a few gingko leaves below us.

I considered a moment. Was this like knowing the future? Was it something I was truly *meant* to know? I thought of Peter, and my heart stung. No. There were already too many secrets. Too many unanswered questions.

I put my hand on the Master's shoulder, and he blinked at me with bloodshot, watery eyes.

"Tell me," I said softly. "Please."

He took a deep breath. Nodded. Collecting himself, he clenched his jaw a few times and then spoke in a low, rhythmic voice that seemed to pulsate through the trees and thud into the jungle depths like some primal drum.

"From darkest night, in dark, the light, the Griffin King shall rise to fight.
Come nightmare shadows, darkest might, the King shall prove himself a knight.
Eclipsed the sun, corrupted all, a King shall rise, a King shall fall.
Millions rally to his call, the bane of many, a King of all.

Foes from memory, heart, and mind, he shall set free, and he shall bind.
To purge the world, to end the blight, the King is coming with the night."

"'A King shall fall,'" I said, after digesting the haunting words for a few moments. "Does that mean Brody?"

The Master shrugged. "Kings rise and fall every day."

"Well...what about ending the blight? Is it the Ranker blight?"

"Perhaps..."

I understood his bitter, noncommittal tone. "But...am I the one to end it?" I said, speaking for him.

The Master faced me, and his voice rasped desperately as if he were begging *me* for answers and reassurance–not the other way around. "What are your thoughts, Prince? Is knowing futility? Or are you the subject of this prophecy? One that was written thousands upon thousands of years ago, carved into the very bones of this land?"

The weight of the onus was a new, aching burden on my shoulders. It dug into me, pressed against my mind. But a flicker of defiance kindled deep inside me–the kind I used to feel whenever we were behind in a football game or whenever Garrett and his pack of mouth-breathing idiots leered at me in the hallways, their cruelty and hatred leaking from them like an oil spill.

"I don't know if the prophecy is mine or not," I said. I was pleased to hear how steady and bold my voice was. "But I *am* here. And I *will* fight."

A very gentle, fond expression suffused the Master's features. His chin trembled as if he were about to weep again. Then, speechless, he smiled and bobbed his head a few times in silent nods of support. To preserve his dignity, and because my own eyes were a little wet, I peered away into the trees. The Master patted my back with his bony hand, and when I next looked up, he was gone.

The nurse who had burned my clothes had put the clues and letter that the Oracle had given me into the pockets of my new trousers. They bulged against my hip bone when I leaned back over the railing. "'*The Griffin King shall rise to fight,*'" I said.

With an electric shock, I remembered the precious value of one of the items I had obtained–how it had made my heart ache like it was being torn in two when the Oracle had given it to me. I fumbled in my pockets until I found the pink scroll, then broke the seal and opened it up, using the flickering torchlight behind me to see the loopy script. The parchment carried within it a scent I never thought would brush my nose again. Vanilla. My mother's perfume.

Tears came to my eyes and spilled over in thick rivulets down my cheeks, running onto my neck. I put a hand over my mouth. My body shook, and my heart ached, and it only got worse as I read and re-read the words. Somehow, by some kind of wonderful magic, this *had* to be from my mother. I had long ago forgotten the sound of her voice and the way she spoke. Still, as I scanned and re-scanned the words, even though there was something...*otherworldly* about her writing, as if she were in possession of great knowledge and wisdom, I imagined I could hear her voice again now, as soft and warm as an embrace.

The fifth time I read the words, I let them sink into my heart and ring in my mind.

"Dear Jonathan, my wonderful son.

Even on earth, I always knew that you were special—and not just because you were my son. But it was not until I forsook my mortal form and the earthly realm for the glorious reality of True Life that I learned of your destiny, and the very moment I understood was a moment of great joy and sorrow.

I wish I could take your burdens. I wish you could live a healthy, normal life. But it was not meant to be so, and my motherly fear swiftly became pride, for yours is a noble and righteous fate—one that will echo across all realms and remind the Dark of the Greater Power that oversees all. Let us take this moment to exchange just a few words, mother to son, before you face your task.

Know this: Ethan loves you so, but for years he was blinded by my death. Can you find it in your heart to forgive him, Jon? Forgiveness is a powerful tool, and a Prince's mercy is a sweet medicine. Even as you read this letter, he is trying to help our cause in reality to the best of his abilities.

You have done so well in school, and the friends you have chosen are honest and true. I have seen how Tyson's good humor has carried you through trials that I was not there to prevent, and Ben's loyalty is a priceless and powerful gift. They each and every one have something to teach, son. Listen to Kitty, for her words are true and precious. Watch Lia, for though she may care too much for the opinion of others, she will soon exemplify what it is to emerge from the crucible of hardship refined. Vince... He is a solid rock of selflessness and courage. Honor him by remembering all he has ever done for you, Jonathan. And I very much approve of dear, young Nikki. The love in her heart is limitless, and she is such a boon to you. Someday she will grow into a lioness among griffins.

As you may be beginning to realize, I have been with you ever since my departure. I have cheered for you at your games. I have cradled you when you had a bad day and desperately tried to shield you from your father's bitterness. I've watched you and Nikki grow together, and I was so proud when you rescued that boy on the mountain. Believe me, many of us were there with you that day, and it took Great Power to keep both of you boys safe from harm.

I was there when you tried to learn to cook your own meals at age eight and when you painted your mural and sang yourself to sleep and learned how to drive in Tyson's van. I was even there when you fought Garrett. By God's grace, you weren't killed—but it was a near thing.

Michael, that is, the White Griffin, is telling me I must turn my topic now to what you must do, and sadly, I must heed him. There is one more place you must go before you meet with Michael: the desert oasis of Tencina-Ahrroc. It is there that you will find knowledge and truth. After the desert, you will see the White Griffin, sit your throne, and march out to battle.

That is all, my son. I look forward to seeing you once more in safety.

Undying love and God bless.

Mother

I stared at the last word. I felt more whole than I had in, well, ever! But my heart also hurt more than it had in a very long time. It was hard to smell her, see her penmanship, and yet not see her. I looked up and around me, smiling widely. Was she watching me, even then?

I closed the letter and slipped it tenderly into my pocket. So I was to see the White Griffin, this Michael character, soon. The more I learned of the guy, the spookier he sounded, but I still looked forward to it. He had met with my mother, somehow. Maybe he could bring me to her or summon her ghost, or however it worked.

I dried my tears, spirits lifting with my thoughts, and turned towards the rejoicing shouts behind me. The Master and the Oracle had both been right. No matter how I felt about the past, no matter how I feared the unknowns of the future, I wouldn't face them alone. Now, I could truly enjoy a party.

CHAPTER EIGHTEEN:

MEANWHILE, BACK IN REALITY

IN THE RUINS OF ST. PAUL'S HOSPITAL...

Carl peeked around the corner. The hallway stretched ahead, vacant. He nodded reassuringly at the kids behind him and led the way forward.

The hospital had been abandoned after a truck packed with explosives had driven into it and detonated. Piles of rubble made unmovable barriers, and the glass in places made a glittering carpet. Sections of ceiling were gone to reveal the sky or rooms above where one could see dangerously tilting beds and destroyed equipment.

The hospital patients who had survived the violent ordeal, and anyone else who needed medical attention, were taken to ramshackle shelters or housed by compassionate families with medicine and room to share.

Carl checked another hall and moved forward tentatively. A chill went down his spine. Nikki had almost been thrown to her death out a window when the explosion had rocked the building. But Donovan had saved her. Donovan, who, according to Ben, was a bloodthirsty, vampiric Ranker in disguise. It was a marvel that Tyson, his family, Lia, and Nikki had made it out of the hospital alive.

The Rankers could now be found in every town, in almost every neighborhood. Garrett had established a sort of system, assigning Rankers to manage neighborhoods, towns, and city sections. They patrolled the streets and chose to settle in large buildings with plenty of open space to house them. Derelict areas like the hospital, which they assumed no one would be crazy enough to hang out in, were ignored for the most part. They instead preferred to materialize from the shadows and confront passersby on the main streets, taunting them, resorting to near-violence until their poor victim had amused them enough to be allowed to hurry away.

Life for Firestone, life for the whole world according to the news, had been turned upside-down. Just last Friday, the Rankers had demanded that everyone turn in their cellphones, laptops, iPads and such to the Rankers that managed their town. Carl had heard of one old man in Boulder who had refused. The Rankers had dragged him out into the street and literally torn him to pieces in front of everyone.

Unless they were performing a vital task such as fetching food or going to a job that the Rankers deemed essential, everyone was forcibly quarantined until, Carl assumed, they were ready to enact the next phase of their plan; whatever that was.

However, every evening, local kids would sneak away from their families and past the Rankers to gather at the abandoned hospital for what they called "secret meets." They had been doing so undiscovered for about three weeks, despite the risk, despite the fact that wandering Rankers would snatch up anyone they found who broke curfew, who ignored the quarantine, and they would never be seen again.

Oppressive though the monsters were, terrifying and demanding, they had not yet managed to snuff out these minor acts of defiance. Carl thought it a significant flaw on the Rankers' behalf that they didn't understand this finer point of human nature: the more you told a human teenager "no," the less likely they were to comply.

Nikki had told them everything she knew about the Rankers and the things Jonathan had discussed with her before he had vanished. She wouldn't tell them why he had gone or where he was. Tonight, though, that would change. Tonight, Carl told his followers that Nikki would tell them a *real* secret.

Carl exchanged grim nods with the scouts in charge of patrolling this floor, both of them older siblings of one of the meeting attendees, approached the door to room 214, and entered, standing aside for the new recruits.

Those gathered within automatically drew in a collective gasp and gave startled flinches in response to Carl's arrival. He closed the door and gazed, astounded, at the sheer number of kids packed into the room. Had they really collected that many more in one night? Then he saw Tyson. Tyson and Nikki each had one room that they talked to split groups in. Every night they'd come together after meetings and exchange news and ideas. Tonight they had combined the groups, and it was a full house.

"Hey, Carl," Nikki greeted softly from where she sat amidst jumpy, wide-eyed kids. "Is that the last of them?"

Carl pulled his hood tighter to his face to fight the cold. "I checked names, and this is everyone who responded to Ty's message, so it should be." Kitty had saved her laptop from being absconded–the Rankers had not intruded as far into her home as they had with most everyone else in Firestone, and she had tucked it beneath the mattress of her bed. She had given it to Tyson, who had used his hacking skills to send a private message the Rankers wouldn't see to other friends from school who'd secreted away their electronics, encouraging them to spread the word and attend the secret meetings.

Carl, Kitty, and Vince had volunteered for the unenviable task of personally vetting all who had responded in favor to make sure that no one was a Ranker in disguise or someone being coerced by one. So far, they had been lucky.

But, Carl thought, *Luck eventually runs out.*

He took a position near the door. "Did we miss anything?"

"We were just about to start talking." Nikki forced a tired smile.

A girl raised her hand, and Tyson pointed at her from his wheelchair.

"Has anybody watched the news lately?"

Many had not. They had been too busy fetching food and other much-needed supplies from stores prowled by Rankers. They had been too caught up with the disturbing information at secret meets, too emotionally exhausted from worrying about missing loved ones, friends they could no longer contact with text or email. But some had found time to check the television, the youngsters or those with disabilities keeping them home. Tyson was one of the few who nodded his head grimly.

Nikki said, "No, I haven't. What are they saying?"

"Well," the girl answered bitterly, "Rankers have spread throughout the world. They've stopped all global trade and obliterated our economy. We're not getting any food or supplies from other countries. The Rankers are forcing factories and companies to revert to self-management, but only for things like steel, leather, and cloth. We're on our own for things like medical care and fresh food."

There was a collective murmur. A boy with cropped brown hair whose brother had served in the Middle East added angrily, "The Rankers even sent all troops stationed overseas back to their home countries. But they aren't letting 'em return to their families. They're keeping 'em all bunched together along the coast."

Tyson pitched in, and they all turned towards him. "Guess who the new president is? Our very own Garrett. A Ranker has filled in the spot of every head of every country. Those they replaced were kicked to the bottom of the food chain if they were allowed to live at all.

"In Australia, they've put together a labor force of humans and forced them to start construction on a building of some sort. Those they don't consider able-bodied are used to burn textbooks, Bibles, encyclopedias, CDs, archival records, churches, synagogues... How long before they do the same here in America?"

The cropped-hair boy mused, "There won't be any oil soon since we can't import or export, so we won't be able to drive anywhere. We're gonna have to give up the rich diet we're used to. Most of our technology, our weapons, have been confiscated, destroyed, or given to the head Rankers. We're prisoners in our own world."

It soon came to everyone's attention that a slightly creepy grin was spreading on Tyson's face.

"What's so funny, Ty?" Vince asked from where he sat beside a thin blond girl known for having random panic attacks.

Tyson's grin turned into a smirk. "They don't know what they're doing. They're uniting us!" There were some blank stares struggling to melt into understanding nods.

Tyson went on. "Do you know what the most resilient, strongest element is? It's not iron. It's not titanium. It's the human spirit. No matter how many hundreds of people the Rankers enslave, there will always be at least one crazy fool who will rise up against them, especially in America. So we can't drive anywhere–we were riding horses long before we had cars! So they've taken away our places of worship–we'll have fellowship in secret, just like this! They took away our technology? We'll just start talking to each other. They confiscate our weapons? We'll make our own. We *will* fight back in the end, just like humans do anytime someone tries to break them!" Now there were happy smiles, aggressive murmurs, back slaps of camaraderie.

In a steady but quieter voice, wearing his smirk, Tyson said, "The Rankers don't understand human nature. They're giving us all something to fight for, and fighting is in our blood. We will rebel. We will revolt. And in the end, we *will* make the Rankers regret ever setting foot in *our* world." Then came some cheers, a smattering of clapping hands.

A tiny voice brought the noise to dwindle–the panic-attack girl.

"Well, we still have a long way to go. The people on the news have Rankers standing right behind them to make sure that they only say what they're told. Garrett is apparently preparing to enact his 'phase two' and is searching for bodies–they didn't say much more than that. But why he's looking and who he's looking for is a mystery. We don't know anything about their plans."

Through the murmurs that swept the room, Nikki, Tyson, Vince, Lia, Carl, and Kitty exchanged brief knowing looks.

"Actually," Nikki said, "*We* know."

A hush descended. Nikki was the one who had first told them about the Rankers. She was the one who had come up with the idea of secret meets. If anyone had more information, she had to.

From the large, green backpack at her feet, Nikki slowly pulled out three handmade books. The first she held up was thin with a yellow cover.

"We found these three books at Jonathan's place," she said slowly. "One of them, this one, is about places that none of us have heard of." She passed the book around and held up a red one covered in feathers. "This one is all about griffins. And this one," she gave the second book to Lia and reverently displayed a thick blue book plastered with pictures, "is about every mythical creature thought up by man-kind."

Kids were looking doubtful. Why was this so important? As if reading minds, Tyson took up Nikki's thread and explained in an important voice, "*Every* creature... Including Rankers."

There were delighted shouts, kids jumping up, hands reaching and pointing at the book. Once Vince got everyone to settle down, Nikki opened to the proper page and read the very words that Jonathan had read to himself months ago.

"Rankers are creatures born of nightmares and sinister thoughts, and they are the eternal foe of the griffin. They fight using an arsenal of dark powers; they can vanish into and control darkness, turn invisible, and anything else that will intimidate and cow their foe, for Rankers are

essentially spirits that have no moral conscience, appetite, or heart, but a cunning disposition.

Rankers can only be vanquished by brave and determined hearts, but they are hard to find: each has its own "other self," a disguise used to spy on their victims without taking on their mysterious and frightful cloaked form."

Once the last mysterious words had passed her lips, no one looked any wiser. In fact, any excitement or curiosity seemed to have been swallowed up by bewilderment.

"So someone knew about the Rankers before all of this started? Who?" An older guy asked.

"That's where this gets confusing," Kitty said mildly, blushing at the frustrated looks in her direction.

"The man who wrote this is what you'd call a griffin," Nikki said.

"Like our school mascot?" a freshman girl asked.

"Yes," Tyson smiled. Some of Carl's tension eased away, replaced with relief that everyone was trying to understand what Nikki and Tyson were talking about. "But this man, and others like him, are regular people who are unusually noble and brave, which lets them change at will into griffins in their dreams... Jonathan is a griffin."

There were astounded looks but not disbelieving ones. Everyone was way past waving off impossible news as a myth. Were they finally going to discover the secret of where Jonathan was?

"Go on," someone encouraged.

"We can't tell you where Jonathan is, but he's safe," Nikki said to a few upset grumbles. "But you have to believe me when I say that there is an entire world that we travel to in our dreams. That's where the Rankers come from. If they take control of that dream land, they control our minds–the most important part of our minds that lets us grow, flourish, and create. That's what Jonathan and many others are trying to prevent. They are the ones who the Rankers are searching for."

"Is there a way we can help them?" someone called, and voices echoed enthusiastically.

"Well," Tyson said slyly. "Do you guys want to see Jonathan?"

This was met with silence.

"I thought you just said we couldn't," the girl who watched the news reminded him.

"Not his *physical* body," Nikki said, her tone betraying her own mounting excitement.

Carl beamed at her. Was this really happening? He rolled onto his back, hands behind his head, his cap pushed down over his eyes. Tyson began answering questions and giving instructions, and Carl tried to listen around the anticipation that made his heart race.

Yes. This is really happening, he thought. *We're going to see Jonathan again. And together, we'll make Garrett and all the other Rankers pay...*

CHAPTER NINETEEN:

LOVE AND LOYALTY

When Vince told everyone they would have to go to sleep to see Jon, they started getting comfortable, curling up on the floor, legs tucked up to make room for others, eyes shut tight, snorers and droolers burying their faces in their arms. Nikki moved equipment aside to make room, and once she was sure that everyone was moderately comfortable and that Tyson was secure and safe by the wall, she slipped outside. She heard a few final questions and Tyson relaying the oath of fealty that they themselves had had to repeat by the culvert–the words that would supposedly help them to focus their dreams and secure their sleep.

There was a spot Nikki had found that she went to for alone time before or after their secret meetings. It was on a middle floor. Part of a wall was gone, and the floor looked out over the town, almost hanging out in space since the floor below it had come off worse after the explosion and been almost entirely obliterated. No cars traversed the roads anymore, and the only lights were those that lined the sidewalks and those that controlled invisible traffic. But the stars were luminous and the world broad and beautiful.

She couldn't believe what she was going to do! She was going to see Jonathan again! Would he be different? Would he remember her? Would he even be there? Lately, Nikki had slept deep, dreamless sleeps, even after having spoken the oath by the culvert. Apparently, the words themselves didn't guarantee dreams, even if they were supposed to help focus them. But something about tonight just felt right. After seeing all the tired, hopeful faces of people relying on her and her friends to give them answers, it felt as if a door in her mind had opened.

It was still difficult for her to swallow everything Ben and Josiah had told her about Jonathan and what he was going through. That Jonathan, handsome, charismatic, sometimes obnoxiously arrogant Jonathan, was going to save them all from the Rankers was overwhelming. But that night in the meeting chambers, when her memories had come flooding back after Donovan's hex had broken, was still a chilling blot in her memories. Rankers were monstrous and powerful. How could Jonathan stand against them? She had believed in Jonathan more than he had believed in himself, but perhaps he was capable of more than even Nikki knew. She couldn't wait to find out.

Nikki straightened, cold sweat chilling her as if she were about to leap off of a cliff.

Okay. I'm ready.

She took a rejuvenating breath of air and turned around.

Donovan stood behind her.

The vampire looked as handsome as ever, though his face was dirty and his clothes torn. Nikki lost her breath in a painful gasp and choked. She stepped back, stuttering fearfully.

"I-I-I w-well I was just–I um..."

Donovan blinked, concerned.

"Are you frightened, dear friend?" he asked in his lilting voice. "I had no intention of startling you..."

Nikki couldn't help but stare at his innocent, white teeth–at the very canines that had plunged into Ben's neck to suck the blood. When she said nothing, Donovan asked her what she was doing.

Now Nikki was pulling together. She needed to pretend that he was a selfless young man who had saved her life at great risk to his own–not a blood-drinking monster. He didn't know that *she* knew he was a double-crosser.

"I was walking," she replied coolly and looked him up and down. "How did you get away from Garrett? Are you okay?"

Donovan sighed a sigh that almost sounded as if he were really exhausted. "That beast is terrible. He tortured me in ways that I shudder to remember and spoke vile threats I recoil to repeat. But one day, I overheard someone say that they found one of the bodies he was looking for–you have surely heard about the bodies, Nikki?"

Nikki nodded slowly.

Donovan swallowed and said, "While everyone was captivated at the news, I escaped and, through whispered rumors, discovered that there were rebel meetings taking place. I pressed many for directions to yours, and here I am." He smiled weakly, attempting to look mildly pleased with himself.

But Nikki could act too. She pulled her features into a tearfully proud gaze and simpered, "I am so happy that you're back. You have no idea how much we've missed you. Was Ben with you? We haven't seen him since the incident in town, and we're worried Garrett might have..."

Donovan threw his arms around her for a brief embrace that made her shiver and then held her at arm's length. "I am terribly sorry, dear one, but I have not seen your friend since the horror that unfolded at the meeting chambers. I fear he is lost. But do not weep—he may very well show himself soon. For all their attempts at control, at suppressing us, the Rankers are not omniscient. They cannot be everywhere and know everything. Perhaps he is merely hiding himself."

Donovan looked around them, letting eagerness slip into his visage. "I would very much like to attend the meeting... Where is it?"

Nikki smiled and led the way inside—in the opposite direction from her sleeping friends. They roamed the corridors and halls, navigating rubble, with Nikki careful not to lead them in circles but always going for the staircases, going down and down and farther from the actual meeting room.

They spoke in hushed murmurs as they went, about the Rankers, about Ben, just like casual friends who hadn't seen one another in weeks, and Nikki was surprised at how easy it was. Her heart pounded fit to burst, but even she was surprised at the defiance in her breast. If she could just keep him walking, maybe a plan would come to her to send him away somewhere, or maybe someone would come looking for her, and they could fight him off together. If not, then she had read the passage about vampires in Peter's bestiary—and she had a Hail Mary.

After long minutes of walking, Donovan asked curtly, "Nikki, where is the meeting?"

Nikki kept looking straight ahead, drops of sweat rolling down her spine. "It's... around here somewhere."

With a sudden sidestep, Donovan had blocked her path. Nikki bumped into him, and he walked her backward against a wall.

"I would really like to be at this meeting," he said darkly. He shook his head at her. "Oh, Nikki. Dear one. I could smell it on you the moment you became aware of my presence... Fear. No more pretending. Do not treat me as a plaything. This is not a game, and I do not wish to show you how very...unsportsmanlike I can be."

Nikki emitted a whimper, then collected herself and murmured, "Okay. It's just down the next hall. I'll need to get the key out."

Donovan sneered and stepped back to give her room. Nikki reached for the thin silver chain of a necklace that Kitty had given her the day after they had separated from Ben, when he had mentioned that Donovan seemed to be sickened, pained, by Kitty's presence. They had put their heads together, made their best guesses as to why, and realized one glaring certainty: if Rankers were creatures of fear, wickedness, sin, and despair, then how cowed they must be in the presence of fearlessness, hope, faith, and joy.

Donovan, too late, seemed to know what Nikki was doing and lunged at her. She pulled at the pendant tucked beneath her shirt and held it out, her thumb securely wound around the chain.

It was a simple stainless-steel crucifix. Her Hail Mary.

Donovan howled, clawing at his eyes. He seemed to be snarling gutturally, but then Nikki interpreted vengeful words in his speech.

"I am supposed to keep you alive until the end," he growled, as if trying to also remind himself of the fact. He reared back and bared his teeth at her, red eyes wild, his voice echoing as if his words came wailing from multiple throats. "But I will make your life a living *hell!*"

A stocky body hurled itself at the vampire from nowhere. A fist made contact with Donovan's face. He made a pained whimper but ended it with a seething snarl of rage.

"*Go... a... way*!" Vince bellowed, fists clenched for another swing. A group of other young adults who had been patrolling the hospital ran toward them, raising bats, knives, and a pair of antique rifles.

Donovan sized up the two defiant friends, the support they were about to receive, his bloodshot eyes glowing, steam wafting from the flaking flesh of his face, and he grinned.

"I allow you two to live with the knowledge that the end is near. *Let the shadows eclipse the light. The Griffin Prince will die one night.*" He bowed mockingly and fled down the hall with sinister grace.

Vince gave his retreating back the bird and then turned to Nikki with a softer expression. "You alright?"

"Yes, I think so," Nikki replied and fell into her friend's arms, suddenly drained of all her former courage. "Thank you so much! I was so scared..."

"Shhh..." Vince soothed, stroking her head. "You did just fine. He wasn't as powerful as we thought..."

The other kids slowed to a panting stop nearby, ensuring that Donovan kept retreating. Nikki pulled away, drying her eyes. "No, he's *more* powerful. For some reason, he let us live, but he'll come back with others, and I doubt that Kitty's faith will prevent a hundred Rankers from... We'll have to move the meeting place."

Vince wasn't sure what to say to that. He was used to being the stronger guy who could handle anything. But now, when he was up against immortal monsters, he hated to realize that he was weak. So he said, "At least now we can see Jonathan."

Nikki's heart fluttered. She removed her crucifix to hang it on the door to their meeting room, Donovan's final words sharp in her mind.

The Griffin Prince will die one night.

"Yes. Let's go see Jonathan..."

AT THE HOUSE OF ETHAN HE'KLARR

The newsman was a balding, sweaty guy in his early forties with lines under his eyes and a trembling lower lip in place of the usual fake trademark smile.

He was sweating because a Ranker had dragged away the man he had just replaced for daring to report, and happily, that people were sneaking into other states right under the Rankers' noses.

"Well, um..." The newsman shuffled his papers in an act of control. The last choked, gurgling coughs of the former reporter finally died away somewhere off-screen. The new reporter read his report in a guarded, measured tone to avoid making a mistake.

"I have here a set of rules that we are meant to follow," he started. His hands were shaking, so he had to set the papers down and read them unprofessionally from the tabletop. "The first reads that 'all shall obey any command given by a Ranker.' The second is that 'all remaining material belongings shall be collected and destroyed at nine o'clock tonight and lasting three days. Report at that time to your local Ranker with your goods. Any discovered disobeying shall be severely punished.' Rule three, 'anyone who sees someone inciting rebellion against the Rankers in any way must report said mutineers or face offensive consequences.' Rule four, 'everyone must accept the medicinal packets distributed to them individually by the Rankers assigned to their street. These pills ensure a restful, dreamless sleep to keep you healthy for work and can even be safely crushed into baby formula.'"

Here the man's brow momentarily creased as if he had an infant of his own that he was thinking about. But, at a soft hiss from a Ranker somewhere to his right, he quickly concluded with the last rule. "'None shall gather in public or communicate with anyone other than household members via proselytizing, the writing of letters, or the use of technology unless said gathering or communication is Ranker-approved.'" An uncomfortable quiet settled during which the reporter habitually stacked his papers, seemingly lost in thought.

In a faltering, distant voice that slowly grew stronger, hinting at defiance, the reporter gave his customary closing words, eyes averted from the camera.

"These rules may seem unfair...but they are for our own safety. The Rankers mean only to help us adjust to the sudden changes in our lives, to this 'new normal,' as comfortably as possible. They mean us no real harm and look forward to our prosperous, united future." His lips abruptly twisted. He looked like he was about to cry.

"That concludes tonight's 11:00 news. I'm Sean Daley. Have a good night–" He looked up suddenly, eyes flickering in the direction of the corpse of the man who had died bravely in front of him. His body relaxed as something like peace and acceptance passed over his face, and his eyes narrowed. "And God bless."

Apparently, this was considered unacceptable proselytizing. There was a chorus of inhuman hissing. A pack of Rankers leaped upon the reporter from all directions, their teeth bared and limbs scything as they clawed him to shreds. The man gave a scream of hatred that pitched into agony, the camera dipped and then flashed, and the screen went blue with an annoying flat-line sound.

Ethan He'klarr turned off the television.

The people crowded in Ethan's living room with him were all adults; scared people, some of whom were parents just like him, who all lived in the neighborhood up the road a way. Nikki's parents were there, and Kitty's.

Hushed discussion bubbled up like a breeze, and for a time, Ethan only sat and listened.

"'Medicinal packets?' You're telling me the Rankers are pharmacists now?" Nikki's father growled.

"No," a woman responded solemnly. "My best friend lives in Norway. She's a scientist. Before the Rankers showed themselves, she was keeping me posted about strange case studies they were having her oversee–test trials for bizarre, new medications. People were getting sick, developing brain tumors, hemorrhaging from the eyes–"

"What's your point?" an elderly man asked abruptly.

"I've heard similar rumors," Kitty's mother said, her voice as gentle and caring as her daughter's. "I think that the Rankers have been working below the radar for quite some time now, using their disguises to worm their way into our lives and get things ready for their plan..."

Ethan considered what he could remember of the world leading up to the Rankers' revelation. Of course, he'd been too inebriated, too wrapped up in his own stupid mind, to have paid much attention to global goings-on. Still, even in his drunken condition, he had been aware of the steady uptick in violent crimes, deaths, disappearances, and other bizarre happenings in their world.

Now they knew the cause.

"I have family in Brazil," one man said, his heavily accented voice bitter. "After the Rankers destroyed Christ the Redeemer, they forced people to begin cutting the stone and transporting it back up Corcovado. They're making a building. If you are not building, you are sewing great panels of cloth, or mixing dye, or smithing, or helping the Rankers to enforce their rules as spies and devotees."

A rumble of disgust and spite rippled through the room.

"What hope do we have?" Someone whimpered in the shadows. "This is the end."

Clearing his throat, Ethan stood up and faced the twenty or so pairs of eyes that blinked at him. It was hard to see much of anything without the TV on, and the curtains were all drawn shut, but Ethan strived to at least seem like he was making eye contact.

"I don't have any reassurance to give you, nor can I make any promises about the future. Things are definitely going to get worse before they get better. But I can certainly offer hope. We are going to fight back." There were blank stares, a current of fear that flickered through tired glassy eyes; but some sat straighter, gave Ethan stiff nods of rapport, and took a few sips of strong black coffee–probably some of the last that anyone would enjoy in a while–to keep their tired, baggy eyes open.

"Our kids are fighting back," Ethan added. His gaze turned inward. "*Jonathan* is fighting back."

"What do you mean?" someone asked. "Has he contacted you?"

"Ethan...he's been missing for months..." Nikki's mother said softly.

Ethan didn't even wince.

"True, but my son still has a vital role to play in all of this." His face brightened. "To play with words, I would say he's like the king in our little game of chess."

People mumbled to one another now–either worried about their host's sanity or excited about what he was getting at. They had been given a tour of the house when they had first arrived–had seen the mural on Jon's ceiling, the mural that Ethan had finished. Had the man snapped?

"I don't understand," someone said.

Ethan grinned. "I can help you there. If you want to understand, then the first thing we have to do is take a little nap..."

CHAPTER TWENTY:

THE FINAL CLUES

BACK TO JONATHAN

We left the day after Boyzun's coronation party. It was a great, touchy-feely moment, except for Kayle, of course, who would have probably knocked the teeth out of anyone who tried to get sappy on him.

Chief Boyzun grasped my forearm with his hand–the one scarred by the white-green star inside the elbow.

"I anticipate the day we battle side by side," he said solemnly.

"As do I," I grinned. "We'll take them down."

We embraced, and I hugged Chalk-talk and patted the vipercat cub's head. Then we departed, and the cheers and chorus of good-byes slowly vanished behind us.

Now, according to Peter, we had almost a month's worth of hard walking ahead of us. The next day, I lifted into the air to get a look at our surroundings.

Below, for miles to the East and West, stretched the bumpy green carpet of the tops of jungle trees. Behind me, I could just barely make out the cloud of fog hovering over the Melancholy Bog swamp-land and a slice of sand lining the beach where I had arrived. But far ahead waited a small meadow of dry yellow grass and small herds of deer, and at the far edge of it, rising into an impressive, jagged, brown-gray pinnacle, towered a mountain that stretched high above a hedge of smaller, less impressive mountains. I couldn't see beyond the range unless I wanted to risk ascending into the oxygen-deprived upper-reaches of the sky, or unless I felt like chancing lengthy flight to either side, and I didn't want to get separated from my buddies, so I dove to ask Kayle why I couldn't see a desert of any kind.

Kayle, however, was deep in conversation with Mariah, his face warm, a gentle smile on his freckled cheeks, and I didn't want to interrupt. With a growl of frustration, I touched down in a nest of ferns and sought out Marcus or Flaherty or one of the other people in the squadron who could give me information.

No, I scolded myself. *You've avoided your dad for not talking to you and treating you like a son your whole life. Don't avoid Peter just because he didn't know* how *to talk to you.*

With a grunt of assent, I remained in griffin form so that it would be harder for Peter to read my discomfort and found him in his usual place at the head of the marching column. As I approached, he watched me like he was afraid I'd come to yell at him, but a kind smile put a twinkle in his silvery eyes. I wrestled with a desire to pretend like nothing had happened and treat him like the mentor and friend he had become.

"Where exactly is the desert? All I saw were mountains."

Peter pulled some leaves out of my feathers. It was hard to make a decent, majestic landing when trees covered the ground. I ignored the griffin-shaped hole in the canopy above me and raised my long brow feathers inquisitively.

Peter answered, "The mountains you saw form a barrier of snow-capped volcanic ridges between us and the desert. We have to cross it. My plan is that we'll reach the Meadow of Time in about three weeks, pass through it in maybe four, five days, and then reach the mountain's base on the night of the fifth day. That taller mountain you saw is known as Boiling Point Mountain—home to the same hospitable dwarves who crafted Mariah's necklace."

"Cool," I said. "Are they our allies? I mean, will they fight with us?"

"They would follow us to the moon and back," Peter assured. "They are enduring survivalists. All bone and muscle and fight. They have what they call the Bedrock—the dwarf elite. They are trained assassins. One of their favorite fighting techniques involves cutting their foe down by the crook of the knee and then finishing them off eye to eye."

I gulped.

Peter said in a lighter tone, "But they're a proud supporter of the crown. They've already sent loads of special dwarven armor made from the minerals they mine to the capital via the native rock pegasi."

He described the plan of passage as much to Sergeant Flaherty as to me. The marine had broken away from twirling his rifle in boredom to ask the same questions I was.

"The dwarves promised us a peek at their armor schematics on our return through their mountain," Peter beamed. "And they have word from the White Griffin on our battle plans."

My innards squeezed and released. Every time I thought about it, the battle was closer. Soon it would be down to Garrett and me, fighting for the fate of the world. I had changed from when I'd first washed up on Pebble Embark: the thought of death, survival, and battle strategies was now constantly on my mind.

"I also wanted to check something in the meadow," Peter added quietly, and when I said I hadn't heard him clearly, he just started whistling a 50s song, and I was left to my own thoughts.

We traveled steadily on, bathed in cool shadow from the leafy jungle trees. We passed a few tree spirits who only had time to smile, wave, and bow to us before roaming imperiously onward in search of water. In the time since I'd first arrived in the dreamworld, many of my questions had been answered. But I still had many more, and these buzzed around in my brain like mosquitoes, stinging and itching. If Celestials were angels and angels were a thing, how come none of them had saved my mother or protected me from my father? If mother could send me letters, how come she hadn't tried to contact me before now? How far had things deteriorated in reality? Were my friends still alive?

And I digested several hard-to-chew thoughts as we went as well, some of which had been nagging me since day one. First of all, of course, why had Garrett left me alive?

Second, the Rankers had some kind of "Liege Master," a god or idol that they worshiped and whose will they claimed to obey. Peter didn't think he was a threat, but could we risk ignorance?

Third, the clues we followed were meant for the Ranker allies. What kind of creatures would pledge an alliance with nightmares? Where were the Ranker allies now? What would the final clue divulge to us?

And finally, how much time had passed in my world? I did a quick mental count. It had been...about four months since I had first arrived in the dreamworld. If time was tracking similarly enough in the waking world, that meant that it would be around early February back home. A lump formed in my throat. I had missed Christmas. I had missed the arrival of the new year. But, really, what kind of celebrations could be had when the Rankers were ripping the world apart?

I cast my gaze about for Kayle, seeking someone I could share my burdened thoughts with, then remembered that he and Mariah were off on a long flight. It was probably for the best that the new couple wasn't around because Marcus and one of the samurai were enjoying themselves teasing the pair.

After a few hours of quick walking, we passed out of the jungle into deciduous woodland, and I was almost shocked out of the air while flying later when a flock of songbirds flew into my slipstream. Many Land of Dreams songbirds don't just tweet and chirp–they make instrumental noises. They weren't much to look at in the beauty department, being sort of shaped like the instruments they imitated and blandly hued, but it was stimulating to hear drums come from one bird's gullet, piano and violin from two others, and a mournful Bing Crosby voice singing a goodbye ditty from the pudgy leader.

I returned to the squadron in the early evening with my feathers letting off wondrous scents of fresh air and free wind, humming the songbirds' tune. Peter was starting a fire, and the squadron was settling. Shifting into a human after a long day of being a griffin, I pulled up a comfy branch and observed the goings-on.

One of the army men was balancing his gun on his nose to cheers from his friends. His eyes flicked nervously to me, and he teetered a bit, but I clapped a few times encouragingly and moved my sights on. Some knights and a sailor were talking with manly indifference about their luck with the Tahtltiki women. *Eew, moving on...* Many of the Amazons were working out–using large tree limbs as weights and doing push-ups and sit-ups. Some of the soldiers were comparing pictures of their families. I heard one guy say, "her first smile," and another say, "his first chin hair." I wondered if their families were real, or dream-creations like Boyzun had been. A samurai loudly told a joke to some marines.

"What did Kayle say to Mariah...? *Will you go out with me*?"

The marines burst into roaring laughter.

Tears streaming into his mustache, the samurai, barely intelligible around his laughter, said, "And what did Mariah say back? *Yes*!"

They all rolled around in a fit of good humor until Kayle himself stepped from the brush behind them like a ghost, leading Mariah by one hand.

"What did Takeo-Kou say when Kayle heard him making fun?" Kayle asked, grinning mischievously at the samurai. The man gaped, unsure of whether to play along or beg forgiveness. Kayle held out one hand, palm up and out. "My arse is on fire!"

Sparks from Peter's campfire bounced toward the joking men, forming into a dragon. The samurai batted at the approaching beast, but Kayle made it vanish just before contact. After a pause, everyone burst into laughter–even Takeo-Kou, despite the nervous sweat on his face.

Mariah grew some veggies, and a knight came back after hunting boar with success. Peter put it on a spit he'd fashioned from a branch, and within minutes we could hear the satisfying sizzling of our cooking dinner.

"Let's take a look at our new clues, shall we, Jonathan?" Peter asked. I had been staring at the fire, grinding my teeth in anticipation, and had to redirect my attention.

"Hm? Oh yeah." I reached into the pants pocket that still held my mother's letter and tugged out the scarab and the money bag. When the spark of gold and scarlet paint caught the firelight, a collective intake of breath rushed down every throat and every eye locked on to the scarab's carapace.

Peter nodded appreciatively at the insectoid gem's craftsmanship.

"This did indeed come from the desert–the desert kingdom of Tencina-Ahrroc. It is a busy metropolis ruled over by a young Pharaoh, and it's a place loaded with fine and exotic pieces such as this. Living so close to the dwarves' jewel-encrusted mountain ensures a frequent supply of riches in exchange for water and crops. As a result, they often display scarabs like this as special items. They decorate wedding gifts, stud the throne...and are a sort of mascot for our desert allies."

I perked up, intrigued. I knew the *Rankers* had allies, I knew I had supporters, and I had assumed that I had an army of knights or something awaiting me somewhere at or near the capital city, but I hadn't considered the thought that *I* might have a metropolis full of allies.

Peter tilted his head and squinted thoughtfully. "They're a clever, covert bunch; they frequently communicate with the 'King's Eyes,' which is a sort of spy ring spread across the land. If memory serves, this red scarab is passed around secretly to other members in times when dire assistance is needed. There is a way to open it, but I have forgotten. We shall have to discover that when we arrive. Hopefully, they're okay."

I took the little fake bug and thumbed its faceted eyes. Secret members? Wasn't the Pharaoh also an ally? If so, why did the members have to be secret? What exactly was goin' on over in the ol' desert?

Peter emptied the money carefully into his palm and counted it out. While he did so, Kayle twitched abruptly. I looked at him, drawn to the sudden, abrupt movement, thinking a mosquito had bitten him. But Kayle met my eyes grimly, his mouth set in a worried pucker, and sent me an eerie thought.

These clues were originally left for the Rankers to follow. We came that close to the Rankers finding our allies first. They could've extracted all kinds of secret information from them.

I grimaced and gave him the double thumbs-down sign by my knees so only he could see.

But, I thought, *How did they get the scarab in the first place? Either they made one of their own or intercepted it from a member. And if they got their hands on a member...*

"This currency amounts to about 700 American dollars," Peter said, speaking mainly to me. "The small gold coins are called 'suns' and are worth the most, hence the image of the ankh, the sign of life, on them. The large silver 'moons' are equal to a fifty-dollar bill, and the bronze 'stars' are twenty dollars' worth.

"Our list here is written in hieroglyphics. We're going to have to wait on deciphering it. The dwarves are excellent multi-linguists. They should be able to translate." He handed me back the clues to keep and talk turned to the desert–how great it would be to get hot instead of cold or drenched in humidity, how bizarre the food was, and so on.

I was sleepily chatting it up with Marcus, discussing the 'King's Eyes,' the new moves I'd picked up in training, and listening to one of the Amazons tell old legends about past griffin rulers when a heavy, white fog began to congeal in the corner of my eye. I blinked and massaged my face distractedly with the heel of my hand. But it didn't go away, and I flinched convulsively when I discovered that the shape wasn't something in my eye but a milky-white figure standing by my feet.

CHAPTER TWENTY-ONE:

REUNION

Marcus yelped, and I shot up and scrambled backward on my butt, drawing my sword. The shape dissipated and drifted a bit, but then shot sharply back to focus at its original location, its outline more rigid.

I had read about ghosts in Peter's book, but this...*being* wasn't eerie or malevolent, just sort of standing there and shifting woozily from one cloudy leg to another. More weapons were drawn. Peter frowned in confusion. More and more ghostly images appeared all around our campsite, featureless and vague.

"Protect the Prince," someone whispered, and bodies that I didn't dare turn my head from the specter to look at inched closer to me. It was a funny thought, but the ghost-like *thing* looked exactly like the familiar form I'd seen across the street back in the Reekwood Swamp–it was the same color and consistency.

The first figure to have arrived had by now lost its cloudiness–it was a slightly translucent young kid. He seemed to be drained of some color–his shirt was a washed-out red and his hair gray instead of black. He stared at his formed fingers and then looked up, squinted, teetered on his feet, and peered intently at me. I leaned back, sword tip out.

The boy's eyes rounded, and he pointed at me, balance suddenly firm, and squealed in an echoing voice, "He's here! He's here! It's Jonathan. We found him!"

The squadron looked at each other. Peter looked at me, I looked at the boy, and the boy was looking around at the fifty or so other people crammed into our small clearing, some standing in the trees or the middle of bushes.

I stood up, sword pointed limply at the boy's chest.

"Who are you?" I croaked.

The boy stared at my sword with fascination rather than fear. I found myself swamped, all of a sudden, by a swarm of happy faces and cold hugs and greetings all mixed with each other into babbling. Through the transparent forms, I saw Kayle reach for his lighter, but Peter raised a hand to halt him, shaking his head with a huge, warm smile.

"How can I be sure this isn't fake?" one of the cloud-people asked her friend.

"What, and we're all having the same dream?" someone scoffed. "No way."

Dream? Holy moly... I took too big of a breath and got dizzy, laughing weakly. These were all people from home...from reality... dreaming about me together!

A hand ruffled my head, another patted my back.

"Look at his hair!" an older woman tutted in a motherly way. "That boy needs a haircut!"

"I just felt his shoulder," one of the freshman football players from school hissed to his friends. "He's a beast! He could be our whole football team!"

"Umm...hello," I said uncertainly. People giggled and murmured to one another, overjoyed that we could actually communicate.

"Hi, Jon!" shouted a girl from my math class.

A chorus of "hi's" made a noise like a strange flock of big, cloudy birds.

"Get out of my way, please! Let me see him, let me see!" A gruff voice came from the midst of the crowd, full of longing and anticipation. I knew who it was long before he squirmed past a knowingly smiling couple and skidded to a stop before me.

Dad.

The man who had punched me across the face the last time I saw him in reality.

Dad, who I'd witnessed caught in the throes of a nightmare in the Reekwood Swamp, wailing for me to come home.

Dad, whom I'd only ever seen drunk, or hungover and crabby and getting ready to go to work. Dad, who, in the deepest stupor of alcohol, would weep for my mother and beg my forgiveness.

But here he stood now, leading a pack of other adults into the dreamworld. Here he was, thin, scruffy, malnourished-looking, but clear-eyed and sober.

His eyes met mine, and tears began dripping off his eyelashes, streaming down his cheeks. Old pain arose within me; anger, bitterness. But with my new griffin ability, I could sense him, feel his emotions in a way I had never been able to before. The shame that rolled off him in burning gusts was powerful enough to rock me on my feet. I felt his guilt, his self-hatred.

And, more than any of that, for the first time in my remembered life, I felt his love. He'd always loved me in his way. But loss and pain of a sort that I couldn't imagine ever surviving had smothered that love. Now, it was the opposite. I sensed all his suffering in one moment, tamped down and shoved away by compassion, joy, and the powerful love of a father for his son.

My eyes stung, and I closed off my mind to force away those tangible emotions. But all I could manage was an awkward twitch of the hands that may have been an invitation for him to come closer, to embrace me. He rushed at me with carefree abandonment and swung his arms around me. I stood almost a head taller than him, and it was *my* chest that Dad leaned *his* head into.

Together, he and I wept. Tears ran down my cheeks into his hair, but Dad was sobbing hoarsely, shaking in my arms.

"My son," he choked between shudders. "My boy!"

There was still a lot of healing to be done between us. And maybe our relationship would never be "normal." But this was a step in the right direction. This was a beginning.

I heard the creak of an approaching wheelchair, and a hand joined mine against my father's arm.

"You knew he was alive, sir, you knew all along," a familiar voice said. Dad moved, and I saw Tyson.

"Hey!" I laughed through my tears. "You got yourself a wheelchair!"

Now Tyson was crying softly as we hugged, me having to kneel and him reaching up. I could feel new muscles in his arms when they gripped my shoulders. Tyson wasn't one to sit back and quit, no matter how bad things seemed to be.

Vince appeared and wrapped us both up in a squeeze, his face alight with joy. He had always been the thoughtful, empathetic one in my group of friends, sensing our emotions before we could name them ourselves, always ready to support us however we needed it. It was because of Vince's encouragement that I had tried out for the football team instead of winding up in juvie.

Kitty and Lia came in for a double hug, and I gently squeezed them. Kitty's faith had been a balm to me growing up; her love for me as a friend was as warm, gentle, and comforting as a blanket. And Lia's sass and can-do attitude pushed us all to persevere, whether it was motivating the school before a game or just getting us all off the couch at Tyson's to go out, explore, and find an adventure. Even Carl–I was surprised to see him again–ran in for a fist bump and a quick hug.

My friends were here. I felt safe, content, brimming with incredible happiness, the likes of which I couldn't remember ever feeling before. I owed them all so much–I owed them my life.

But still, I searched faces, craning my head, glad to see everyone but missing someone.

Then–

"Jonathan?" a quiet and doubtful voice murmured from my right. I waited eagerly as the crowd parted to let one final person through.

Nikki. My Nikki.

We stared into each other's eyes for a split second and then rushed forward. We collided with a force that probably should have hurt, but we were beyond that. I lifted her up and swung her around. She took my hands in hers and danced in place like an ecstatic child, laughing and crying at the same time. And finally, we calmed down enough to kiss long and sweet, her form pressed tightly against my chest, my arms holding her to me, a precious treasure I never wanted to release. Her tears joined mine on our faces; her hands were white-knuckled around my neck. It was a wonderful moment that we both wanted to last forever, but human beings have to breathe.

We broke apart, gasping and smiling and happier than we'd been in months. People were cheering for us as if our reunion had tied reality and the Land of Dreams into one world.

"What is all this?" I chuckled with amusement to Nikki. "How is this happening?"

With a huge smile that was completely at odds with the grim news she had, she told me about the words Ben had told them to speak at the culvert, how the Rankers had begun to lay their rule all over the world, that Donovan now knew that the secret of him being a vampire was blown and that Josiah had started a chain reaction by finding people and helping her to initiate "secret meets." She told me how my friends, my father, and herself were gathering people and telling them the truth of what was going on: the truth that I had told Ben, who was currently undercover as a Ranker, and that Ben had told Josiah and the others. I was gaining a following.

"The Rankers are doing some bad stuff," that was from a skater kid a bit younger than me with blond hair that made fair curls around his ears. He stepped closer, gesturing wildly with splayed fingers poking from a baggy jacket. "Some *wicked* bad shit, bro! They're isolatin' us–we're all jammed together like *sardines,* man!"

The kid's big brother, a young policeman famous for the cliché way he twirled his handcuffs around his finger, joined in. "They've started making us build things like... I don't know, temples, maybe. They're trying to force us to take medication that prevents us from dreaming, and Nikki told us they're searching for your body and others like you."

Peter slipped without a sound to my side, for the first time I'd ever seen looking scared to death. "They're moving too quickly for us," I thought I heard him say.

"Oh, this is Peter," I introduced him. "He's been my guide, mentor, and friend on this crazy ride." Peter gave me a surprised but pleased look and accepted greetings from the dreamers with hearty nods and flicks of his hand.

I pointed to Mariah, who waved feebly, and Kayle, who jerked his head noncommittally, and then introduced the squadron.

"We're all here trying to stop them," I added at the end.

"Well, let *us* bring 'em down too!" said the skater boy.

An Asian-American girl chimed in, "Yeah, we're ready to fight! We won't make it easy for them!"

I thought hard, frowning, vague ideas drifting through my mind along with disjointed words: allies, temples, Rankers...Garrett. If he thought we were down and out, that I was just some scared kid that he could keep here while he hurt my loved ones in reality, then he had another thing coming.

"The battle starts here," I said falteringly.

"What are you thinking, sonny?" Peter said encouragingly.

I looked up, showing him my teeth in a fleeting grin.

"Can you guys transform like this?" I changed into a griffin to gasps of shock and fear. "It's okay," I said hastily, a bit self-conscious when eyes moved to my beak as it formed understandable words. "I–er–don't bite. Just think of a griffin, like our high-school mascot. Think of *being* a griffin, being brave and fierce and valiant."

Perhaps it had something to do with the oath of loyalty that everyone had spoken; the possibly magic words that Ben had relayed to our friends that allowed everyone to dream lucidly and find me here. Whatever the reason, a lot of people transformed into griffins on their first try, and I saw a crayon-box of colorful feathers and sharp eyes, clacking beaks, pacing talons, half-open wings, and puffing crests and frills.

Nikki, a deep yellow in color like a daffodil, ran her dainty talons along the edge of one wing, marveling at her striped pinions. Vince, a big and brawny hulk of sinew and brown, white-striped feathers, shared an astounded laugh with Lia, who had an off-white pelt like a dove coated in dust, sprinkled with lavender specks. Carl, black and white like a cow, sat awkwardly and stared at Tyson, a rich brown with black stockings. Ty could move his legs in this form, and he scrambled out of the wheelchair to stretch them out with youthful glee.

"Yes, you *can* fight," I shouted, getting their attention. "With and beside me, if you're willing. Griffins are the protectors of dreams and defenders of purity." I thought of something Kitty had once told me about my relationship with Garrett–how he represented a kind of crucible, turning me into a better, stronger person–and added, "The Rankers represent everything we don't. They're our foil." I shot Kitty a brief, reminiscent smile. She smiled back, her broad wings half-open, gold and chestnut feathers ruddy in the firelight.

"Being a griffin is like a symbol of your potential, a reflection of who you are on the inside. Because of people like you, we have a chance at winning this war. But you'll need to be careful. I think it's *you* they're looking for in reality."

"What if we get hurt, or...die?" a younger girl dared to ask. I winced. We had come to the speed bump.

"If you die while you are here with me, it's because the Rankers at home found your body while you were sleeping." There were grimaces as the implications sank in.

Peter said helpfully, "Find somewhere safe and secret to sleep, or sleep in a rotation with someone so you can watch one another's backs."

To the self-conscious and sheepish crew who could not transform, I said reassuringly, "It's all good if you can't turn into a griffin. You can keep doing what you're doing in reality–inspire and make strong the ones who have lost hope. Give the Rankers something to keep an eye on without pushing your luck."

Everyone began to fade back into murky smog. They all noticed at about the same time and looked at me, the griffins shifting back into human form with some difficulty. Nikki, no longer a griffess, grabbed my hand in hers. I squeezed it, kissed it. Dad put his arm around my shoulder; Tyson climbed back into his wheelchair and sighed.

"Check in with us," I spoke out. "Come see us whenever you can! But be cautious about it–don't draw attention to yourselves. Meanwhile, keep pushing, *shoving* back at home. Tell others about what's really going on; try to get it out of state, out of the country.

Brace for the worst, but if push comes to shove, don't be afraid to take some names!" I heard faint cheers from the dissolving fog.

My father's arm was no longer around me.

"I love you," a sweet voice whispered into my ear.

"I love you too. I don't ever want to let you go," I whispered, looking at the cloud at my side, trying to peer through it as Nikki struggled to remain, trying to see her eyes.

"Do your best, be brave, be safe," she said.

I hugged her, felt her thinning form.

"I will. Don't do anything stupid, honey," I murmured, tears fresh. "We'll see each other again soon."

And she was gone.

"We've got ourselves an army!" Flaherty whooped, his men whistling sharply and triumphantly.

I rubbed my eyes on my shoulders, trying to act like a hole hadn't been torn out of me with each person that had returned home. Trying to act like I wasn't worried about each and every one of them. Trying to remember the contours of Nikki's hand, of her face, under my touch, hoping no one saw.

But Peter saw.

He patted my back, smiled warmly, proudly, down at me, and suggested that we all get some sleep.

CHAPTER TWENTY-TWO:

MEANWHILE, BACK IN REALITY

ON A DARK, VACANT STREET IN FIRESTONE

Ben stepped from the pitch darkness into a frosty Coloradan evening, stumbling a little as he recovered from the disorienting transition from dreams to reality. He had yet to master many of the nuances of being a vampire, interdimensional travel being one of them.

Donovan followed close, emerging from the shadows beneath the pine behind Ben as gracefully as if he were stepping off the sidewalk. He sneered, eyes flashing, in a foul mood.

Their search for the gargoyle Ranker had been fruitless. They had attempted to track down his "scent," starting at the golden shores of Pebble Embark beach, where Donovan said that the Rankers had planted their first clue and left it as a beacon meant to draw their allies from the dark edges of the dreamworld.

But though they had discerned that the gargoyle had at one point traveled to the beach, weather and time had caused its tracks to vanish. Although seeking the gargoyle had turned up nil, combing the beach for an idea of the missing Ranker's whereabouts had not been entirely without answers. Donovan now knew that the clues had been intercepted.

"Griffin-stench was all over the shore," Donovan spat, walking a furious circle around Ben, eyes flickering side to side thoughtfully. "No doubt Jonathan's personal guard discovered our plans. Oh, those wretches!" A seething hiss boiled in his throat, and he halted mid-step, staring up at a flickering streetlamp nearby.

Ben watched him, nervous.

Still gazing up at the light, Donovan spoke in slow, musing tones. "We shall have to move with greater secrecy now. Any allies we manage to collect will have to be gathered with the utmost care. It will be nowhere near the numbers we could have managed before Jonathan's interference, and the...*collateral damage* shall not be to the extent we had hoped for. But it will be better than nothing."

"What was the point of hiding clues for our troops?" Ben asked, sincerely curious. "Why the secrecy? A great lot of dark creatures tromping across the land would have attracted attention instantly, anyway."

Donovan gave a delicate, scoffing snort at Ben's expense as if the answer were obvious. "The trail of clues had another purpose. Each of the clues was stored in a location that we call a "crux," a place of fairly balanced power where great supporters of the griffin rulers have long strived against powers of nightmare and darkness. The troops were to raze these places as they went, depriving Jonathan of valuable support and gaining power themselves."

Hatred of such vitriolic strength that Ben doubted he would have been physically capable of feeling it before becoming a vampire filled Ben at Donovan's callous words. He turned away to hide the fearsome emotion from Donovan's detection as it passed across his face and leveled his tone before asking, "Our allies gain power from such acts?"

"Acts of murder? Of course!" Donovan's irritation at what he clearly perceived as stupid questions may have been more poignant had he not suddenly been distracted by something he scented on the air. He lifted his head and sniffed once, twice, and Ben fought a chill when he saw Donovan's pupils dilate so that his eyes turned almost entirely black.

Donovan gestured for Ben to follow and began to track the scent along the street, walking as light and graceful as a stalking leopard. He continued to speak, though it was in a soft voice that Ben wouldn't have been able to hear without his heightened senses. "And, in addition, slaying Jonathan's allies would cause him grief, which would drive him ever further into our clutches, where he may become our Dark Griffin."

Garrett had already told Ben that a Dark Griffin was an extremely rare monster created when a griffin-hearted person had been tormented and corrupted enough that they turned completely away from the light. Such a beast was said to possess almost unheard-of power and was a legendary prize among the Rankers.

"As we have already discussed, your old friends know of my true identity now. You must serve in my place and watch them ever more closely and carefully. And the task of finding Jonathan's body now rests wholly in your hands."

"Why do we need his body? Or any of the griffin-hearted's bodies?" One of Garrett's demands had been that every Ranker overseeing a town kept its eyes out for the sleeping bodies of the griffin-hearted—especially any that might be comatose as Jonathan was. Ben had yet to witness it himself, but from what he'd gleaned from other Rankers they'd met, the griffin-hearted were instantly killed and their bodies sent away. He had managed to secretly tell Nikki as much the last time he'd seen her, during one of his patrols through Firestone, and he hoped to glean more information that he could pass on–though the tasks Donovan kept assigning him were claiming more and more of his time.

Donovan abruptly turned, stepped over a low row of hedges, and began striding across someone's back lawn toward a large garage that towered, dark and empty-looking, near the treeline.

"Control," the vampire replied. "Incentive." He peered back at Ben, his dilated eyes almost as dark as if the sockets were empty, unreadable. "A backup plan. Perhaps we can discover something unique about a griffin's chemistry–something that will allow us to detect them in the future by scent or sight or...taste...alone."

Ben suppressed another shudder, reaching up to touch the scars on his throat from Donovan's fangs.

Donovan held up one hand, indicating that Ben should wait and be still, and silently opened the garage side door. Though it was pitch black inside, Ben could see as clearly as if it were moonlit dusk. There were no vehicles parked within, but an assortment of shop tools were suspended neatly on the walls, and empty gasoline cans and vehicle maintenance equipment were arranged atop a table.

"So...we are experimenting on them?" Ben pressed. He finally suspected why they were there, and he wanted to distract Donovan as long as possible.

Donovan flashed Ben a slightly affronted look. "We are as scientifically minded as any *human*. We have questions we want answered–things that we want to understand. And if, say, Jonathan or Peter's bodies were in our possession, it would be that much easier to break their sleeping minds, for as you know–what affects you here, in reality, affects you there in the dreamworld." He began to search cupboards and cabinets, sniffing some more, wrinkling his nose at the stench of gasoline and oil.

"And...why not kill Nikki? Why did you let her live when you saw her?"

"Many reasons. She was armed with a crucifix for one; dear, sweet *Kitty* was nearby for another–her faith is strong. Even being near it is like staring into the light of the sun. You'll need to practice caution with that one."

Ben's heart clenched at the mention of Kitty's name, and he could only grunt affirmation. Even after becoming vampiric, Kitty did not affect him like she affected Donovan–a fact Ben was grateful for. But he would need to remember to pretend.

"But mostly, while Jonathan's friends are alive, they can be used to manipulate Jonathan or followed to reveal knowledge to our gain." Donovan bent and flipped back a large, patchy rug on the floor in front of the workbench. A trapdoor was revealed beneath.

Donovan's eyes flicked up to Ben's, and the two stared at each other in silence for a few moments as if to gauge one another's reactions, reading one another's emotions.

In an even lower voice, his eyes gleaming wickedly, Donovan said, "At the moment, they are expensive toys, but make no mistake–they are expendable as needed. Nikki, especially, is a fine prize." He licked his lips. "A delightful treat."

Ben lifted a corner of his lip to reveal one canine in what could be interpreted as either a sneer of rapport or disgust. Donovan seemed to take it, incorrectly, as the former. He nodded and crouched, resting his hand on the trapdoor. "All must be orchestrated carefully, Benjamin. A surgeon does not hack at bone like a butcher but practices finesse and treats the body with precision and patience. When Jonathan is right where we want him...when he has been pushed beyond his limits and is naught but a shattered puppet, then he will kill his friends for us."

Ben abruptly dropped into a squat and pressed his own hand against the trapdoor to keep Donovan from opening it. Donovan's eyes slowly crawled up Ben's arm to focus intently on his face, as sharp as arrows.

"Do you really think he will break?" Ben asked, his voice hopeful though his insides writhed with dismay.

"Trust me. He will break. And if not, then he will be a sacrifice that will forever corrupt the winged throne. Now silence. And follow. There is something you must do."

Questions still swarmed in Ben's mind, but he had already amassed a trove of information about the Rankers' intentions–info that he could share with Nikki the next time he saw her and Jonathan the next time he saw him. Donovan had been particularly generous with his answers this evening, and Ben didn't want to push his luck. So, he suppressed the wonderings fluttering around his thoughts and followed Donovan down a flight of creaky stairs to a cramped landing that opened on their right onto a dark room slightly smaller than the garage above.

Suddenly, from out of the darkness, swarmed a small group of people armed with hatchets, hammers, and kitchen knives. Ben, who hadn't expected anything in the way of prepared resistance, drew back against the wall, but Donovan gave a vicious growl and lunged into the fray.

The commotion that followed was a blur of movement and a blend of sounds: screams, metal clattering on the floor, the thud of a fist striking flesh, cloth ripping, and finally silence broken only by two voices–one growling with each breath and the other gasping and grunting in pain.

Ben reached out and flipped the light switch.

With a buzz, a fluorescent tube light flickered on overhead, illuminating a scene of carnage. Four dead bodies lie strewn around the room, the remains of what had perhaps been a family. The eldest present, Ben assumed the father, lay behind a couch, impaled with his own weapon. A woman in her thirties, perhaps the man's daughter, had had her neck broken when Donovan had thrown her against the wall. The two other bodies, both of them boys a few years older than Ben, had bled out almost instantly in different corners of the room, their throats missing.

Ben swallowed hard, pressing the back of his hand against his mouth–not out of nausea, but because the odor of so much blood called out to him in a powerful and perverse way, like water to a man lost in the desert.

Donovan held one survivor, a boy no older than 16, by the shirt front, pressed against a wall. Shattered picture frames lay at their feet. A crimson mess of flesh and blood not his own stained

Donovan's chin and chest. He ran his tongue along one elongated canine, eyes gleaming on the boy's. Tears ran trails down the boy's cheeks, and he held one hand against a grisly laceration above his hip.

"What is your name, child?" Donovan asked wetly. The boy cursed at him. Donovan tossed back his head and gave a harsh, echoing laugh. "Oh, how I cherish the feisty ones! Very well. Ben," he looked over one shoulder, and Ben approached, carefully stepping over the dead woman's legs. "We have just rid ourselves of a nest of brave rebels–plotters whose insolent whispers have finally reached our ears." He gave the boy a shake and leaned closer. "You should be careful what you say to your neighbors, child... You never know who could be a Ranker supporter..." The boy gave a gasp of pain, blood trickling over his fingers to drip on the floor. Ben's throat burned at the smell, and his stomach cramped at the sight. He drifted closer as if in a trance.

Donovan showed his gore-smeared teeth at the boy and said triumphantly to Ben, "This one is griffin-hearted. He is the reason you are here today, Ben."

Without preamble, Donovan shifted one hand to wrap it around the boy's neck and then cruelly dug his free thumb into the wound in the boy's side.

The boy shrieked, squirming and kicking, his voice breaking into sobs of pain and fear.

"Where is Jonathan's body?" Donovan asked calmly over the screams.

The boy didn't answer–his grip on sanity was fraying beneath his pain and terror, his eyes going wild as they rolled, unseeing, in their sockets. Coldly, as if he held a manikin rather than a human being, Donovan said, "Look around you, child. You are going to die alone. Abandon hope and share your knowledge. Where is Jonathan's body?"

"W-who? I don't know!"

Ben looked away. Whether the boy knew Jonathan or not, Ben doubted he could remember his own name in his current state.

Donovan tsked and asked boredly, "Where is Jonathan in the dream world?" He gave the wound another jab.

"I don't know what you're talking about!" The boy writhed and gave a squeal of gut-wrenching agony.

"Enough!" Ben whirled around, and his eyes flashed. Donovan blinked at him, cocking his head, and Ben added, "... I find his cries irksome."

Donovan blinked again, then shrugged. "Oh well, we tried." He let the boy drop heavily, licking his stained fingers with relish as he turned away. He stood aside and waved Ben forward with a dramatic, formal bow. "Kill him."

"What?" Ben blinked. The boy tried to stand but sagged back down onto the carpet of fragmented glass, nursing his injury, sniffling, staring around at the secret room and the bodies stiffening around him with eyes that betrayed total despair and a broken spirit.

Kneeling to dry his hands in the hair of the dead woman, Donovan said, "Just as our allies, you must defy any light in your soul and embrace darkness to access our isles. You must commit to an act of evil."

He tilted his head toward the boy. His pupils and canines returned to their normal size, handsome and winsome as ever. "Kill him, Benjamin, and let us be off."

Ben turned his eyes upon the boy, fighting within himself. How could he do this? How could he be expected to end a life? Taking slow steps toward the boy, Ben scrambled for a way out of his predicament, but none came. To refuse would mean blowing his cover and very likely dying for real. But the alternative was monstrous.

Ben stopped with the toes of his hiking boots mere inches from the boy's. He gazed down at him, drinking him in, knowing that he would forever remember this moment–that he would be scarred by it, shaped by it. He tried to send a wordless communication to the boy, some kind of reassurance, a secret admission that he was doing this against his will, that they were comrades forced against one another in an unfortunate circumstance. But the boy was finally succumbing to shock. His eyes wandered, bloodshot and bleary, the skin of his face was milky white, and he kept twitching sharply and violently–almost convulsing. Whimpers squeaked from his throat, and his head lolled.

This is a mercy. Here, you are alone. But I will return you to your loved ones now, Ben thought the words, but they were for himself–a pitiful attempt at logic to justify this, the vilest thing he had ever done.

Feeling Donovan's eyes burrowing into his back, Ben reached out, took the boy by the jaw close to the jugular, and, with a burst of his new, supernatural strength, gave a violent flick. A nauseating *crack* burst through the air as the boy's neck broke, and he slid sideways to collapse on the floor.

It was Ben's turn to grapple with shock. It had been so easy, so *effortless*. He stared at the corpse, clenching and unclenching his hands, feeling oddly fuzzy, as if each of his nerves had suddenly fallen asleep. Dizziness caused his vision to waver, and suddenly, more intensely than ever before, the urge to indulge in the feast of blood before him arose in his breast. His canines lengthened over his lips, and every thread in the boy's shirt jumped into incredible detail as the lenses of Ben's eyes flexed–but he defied the urges of his appetite, struggling as if he were attempting to roll a boulder up a hill.

Donovan laughed joyously, but Ben barely heard. The foul energy that suddenly and inexplicably flooded through him as the boy breathed his last was both a dazzling elixir...and a crippling poison.

CHAPTER TWENTY-THREE:

THE EPICNESS OF DWARVES

The following few weeks passed in a mixture of anguish and bliss. We marched along through woodland and glade, the distance between us and those brooding mountains shrinking with each step. On my midday flights, sometimes accompanied by Peter, or Kayle and Mariah, who all seemed to think I needed to be on a 24/7 watch for my protection, I beheld the sight of unicorns running through distant vales, clouds of fairies dancing in the treetops below, and once, even a giant sea monster breaching out in the ocean far to our left.

Despite the ever-present wonder and beauty of the dream-world, none of it captivated me so much as the evenings when my friends and fellow Firestone-ians managed to sleep deeply enough to focus their dreams and track us down. They arrived sporadically, sometimes interrupting sword practice with Peter, sometimes stumbling out of the bushes at mealtime and causing us all to leap for our weapons. Those first few days after our initial meeting, fewer people showed up because they were so exhausted that they sank into a deep slumber over which they had no control. Sometimes there were missing people that no one could account for–they had vanished in reality as well.

And the news my friends brought with them, some of it information that Ben had sneaked them, was always grim: construction of one of the Rankers' strange buildings had begun in Denver. People were going hungry as food rotted in the grocery stores. Those suspected of rebellious activity, proven or not, were denied the use of electricity to heat their homes, and some began to freeze to death as deep winter settled in. The griffin-hearted were being rooted out, killed, or kidnapped for experimental purposes or torture–questioned brutally and ineffectively about the locations of my body, Peter's body, or the bodies of other high-profile griffins like Kayle and Mariah. News reports remained detached, serving only to remind the world of the Rankers' rules, what punishments awaited rebels, and what rewards would be showered upon the obedient. But word spread of violence in the cities and rebel groups in the countryside. Because the Rankers operated under the belief that they'd collected everyone's tech, Tyson had been able to create an obscure blog where he explained the truth of events to those lucky enough to still possess a computer and savvy enough to track his site down. As word got out and more and more people discovered Ty's trove of information, stories came pouring in from across the world of efforts to fight back, some ending in triumph and some in tragedy.

It was difficult for me to picture what my friends described here, away from the brutality, the misery, the cold, where the Land of Dreams seemed locked in springtime. But with every story, my anger and frustration at my ignorance grew. Garrett was having little trouble in establishing a kingdom atop the ruins of my home. I couldn't let him do the same here. It amused me to think that, only months ago, I wanted to leave this place, no matter what the Rankers were or what they had planned.

As Peter had calculated, we reached the Meadow of Time two days shy of three weeks. Our feet left the packed dirt path of the forest and crunched onto acres of dry, yellow grass. The grass was pretty short, mowed down by herds of deer and antelope and the like. It was almost barren to the point of creepiness, which only made the fact that I recalled the dream I'd had about the place all the spookier.

It was here where I had technically first met Peter. I had fallen asleep while reading one of the books he'd made for me, and in my dream, he had come to me and given me a somewhat vague head's up about what was going to happen. Next, Peter had handed me a pill and told me to focus on its taste and texture to help me remain lucid and clear-minded. Then he had told me that I had been chosen by Michael the Celestial to take the throne.

He hadn't mentioned anything at the time about Rankers being real, or the fact that my ticket to my throne was getting concussed by a rat with a frying pan, but in his defense, the guy had been pressed for time and had to prioritize.

Around dusk of the third day crossing the meadow, I was startled when a stag lifted his head from where he grazed a few paces out. His antlers held an immense, impossible span–around six feet across. He was a hunter's dream–maybe literally. The stag's brawny haunches bunched, and he sprang off. We watched him bound majestically towards the trees, stumble over something that nearly tangled up his long legs, and vanish.

Peter pointed, and we followed the path of the deer to where he had tripped up. There, on the ground, was a perfect circle of dry, golden grass. Where most of the green-yellow grass around us reached up to our knees or shins, here it was as short as if it had been cropped by a lawnmower. Heat radiated from it. I stayed well back.

“This is where I was standing when you and I met for the very first time,” Peter said quietly. “Do you remember?”

I made a small sound of confirmation, then frowned and asked, “How did you find me? Or...how did I find you?”

“I owe it all to Michael,” Peter said. “The Meadow of Time is one of the oldest places in the Land of Dreams. A different kind of magic runs through it. Michael told me where to go, and all I had to do was wait. Sure enough, after a day or two, you showed up.” He shrugged one shoulder as if the complicated minor details were beyond the effort he was willing to make to try and understand or explain them.

“What’s that?” I pointed to a section of the circle that had darkened until it was a crispy-brown, taking up maybe a fourth, almost half, of the shape.

Grimly, Peter crouched down and examined the grass. “The power Michael possesses is pure and good–so much so that humans, let alone Rankers, can’t withstand the brunt of even a whisper of it. The dreamworld survives and thrives on such ancient, otherworldly power. That–” he indicated the burnt grass “–is contamination.”

I bent over with my hands on my knees. “Rankers?”

“Mm-hmm. If their presence, their actions, have spoiled even this small sliver of Michael’s power, then they’re doing too well for my liking.” He looked up at me, and his eyes were grave as they searched my face. I sensed his concern and a fierce protectiveness that left me taken aback and speechless. I couldn’t quite put a name to the emotion because I’d never felt it before or been on the receiving end of it before. But whatever it was, it was strong, kind, and filled with a kind of pain that made my heart ache.

Peter stood up, dusting off his knees. "We'd better get moving," he said.

I let the others pass me, staring down at the warm, glowing circle, a small representation of something much grander and beyond my comprehension, and took up the rear.

The meadow widened into plains that took another day to cut across, and then our journey to the base of the dwarves' volcanic mountain lasted a few hours more. We stumbled out of the scrub and sparse clusters of birch trees on exhausted feet at eleven at night, almost colliding with the rough, gray-black boulders that ringed the mountain's base. As if out of habit, Kayle wearily removed his lighter, held it up, and flicked it open and closed three times.

"Who goes there?" a gruff voice called down to us from a great height. It reminded me of the revving grate of a motorcycle engine.

"Peter Malone!" Peter shouted back. "I'm making the return journey with my squadron and the Griffin Prince!"

There followed a few beats of silence.

"I need proof!" the voice finally answered. "Show me your powers if four griffins there be!"

Kayle once more popped open his lighter, bathing us in red-orange firelight. The moon's glow became comparatively dim beside the flames, casting its wan, blue aura upon the ground around us and away from the flickering sun-brightness. I had never actually seen Kayle use his power of griffin fire, only when he had already applied it, such as the day of the battle in the Melancholy Bog. He tipped his lighter upside-down and cupped the flame into his other hand. The tongue of flame vacated the lighter, which Kayle slipped back into his pocket, and he put the bite-sized fireball into his mouth!

I flinched, waited for him to howl in pain, but he swallowed the fire as calm as you please, like it had been nothing but cake. A hellish glow emanated from his face. His neck and cheeks were lit yellow from within. Sparks danced into the air from his eyelashes, which rimmed eyes with irises like red rings of glowing phosphorescence. His hair curled, the ends wisping into licks of smoke. Kayle transformed into a griffin, but it was not the burly black one with midnight speckles and shaggy feathers that wreathed his neck. This was a griffin made entirely of fire.

Kayle lifted into the air, leaving four rings of dwindling flame where his feet had been. Blanketing us with gusts of hot air from his wings, his fiery form made a circle of light that shed fully upon us down on the ground. He turned his burning head up towards the side of Boiling Point Mountain, circling us like a giant, four-legged phoenix, and I knew he could see the dwarf-scout that surveyed us from his high perch.

Using Kayle's glow, Mariah knelt and grew a small apple tree up from the ground. Peter stepped forward and camouflaged into his surroundings. I grinned up at the small shadow sticking from a cave in the mountain and opened my mind.

"We just crossed the Meadow of Time...my name is Jonathan He'klarr...and yes, I *am* reading your mind."

Kayle's wing-beats made crackling, whump-ing concussions–the only sound in the night until the dwarf above shouted in a voice only a notch below hysteria, "*Hold on a moment*!"

I raised an eyebrow at the squadron and said, "He's going to get you guys a couple of Pegasi." They moaned. They would've rather kept their feet planted.

There are a few types of pegasi; the Rock pegasus is small and stocky like a shetland pony, with shaggy hair, a bristly mane, and sturdy wings capable of short flights. Due to living in high elevations, their lungs can take in a minimal amount of air, and their hearts still have enough oxygen to pump blood normally. They're as spry as mountain goats and can sense where precious gems are buried.

About two dozen dark and rounded shapes soared down to us, crunching rocks beneath iron hooves, snorting, and pawing. I and the other griffins guided the militia toward the winged horses–their hands were out in front of them to feel for the coarse manes and pull themselves onto the barrel backs. We griffins spread our wings and followed the Pegasis' spiraling ascent, listening to their deep whickers and the squadron's anxious whimpers.

A crooked square of light became bigger and bigger above us, and soon I had carefully pulled close my wings, ducked my head, stretched out my talons, and skidded onto harsh, cracked, stony dirt lit by torches. Peter was in front of me and Mariah and Kayle, who was no longer on fire, were behind. The squadron was shakily being helped down from their sturdy mineral-hued steeds by the dwarf scout.

The dwarf was about as tall as a large wallaby–bald, with a short, scrubby, blond beard. He was stocky in frame, but his ominous muscles were made up for by his merry, black eyes and the way his feminine lips made dimples at the corners even when he wasn't smiling. He wore a black velvet cloak clasped with a round obsidian stone, and his tunic and breeches were just as dark, blending into the night. After counting out the Pegasi to make sure each had returned, the dwarf rushed me as I was shifting into a human and grabbed my hand in both of his.

It was like shoving my hand beneath a pile driver. My knuckles popped. Before I could try to escape the vice, the dwarf shouted, "Greetings, Great Prince!" in his motorcycle-engine voice. He knelt to kiss my hand and bowed his head. It was completely embarrassing.

"Whoa, chill!" I said, trying to lift him back to his feet by the hands he clasped over mine. "Call me Jonathan."

The dwarf found his feet unsteadily and released my hand, which was probably about half of the size it had been before.

"I am Magnus," he said shyly, and may have said more had he not seen the sword at my hip. He sucked in a breath and pointed sharply, making the rest of us jump and spin around, expecting an enemy. "May I see that under closer examination, your esteemed highness?" Magnus nearly swooned.

"Oh, sure." Slowly, I removed the sword from its scabbard and held it out, balanced flat on my palms. Magnus traced the talons at the handguard in respectful silence.

"These belonged to the departed griffin-king, rest his soul, if I am not mistaken?"

"Nope, you're not," I said sadly.

The dwarf popped open the hatch at the sword's hilt and examined the hidden dagger with nimble fingers. When he gave the sword back, all he said was, "A trustworthy weapon. We worked its spirit well," and smiled.

As if seeing everyone else for the first time, Magnus blinked and turned in a circle, peering into every face.

"Ah, Flaherty," he said warmly to the marine. "I trust your men have served you well?"

Flaherty was still nauseously clutching his stomach, taking deep breaths from where he leaned against a nonplussed pegasus. He looked up when Magnus spoke to him and swallowed hard before responding.

"They don't serve me, buddy. They serve God, King, and country." He removed his hat from his scruffy hair–no longer really a crewcut–and fanned his face with it. "But yes, everyone has proven their worth."

Magnus nodded appreciatively and went to Peter, wrapping him in a crushing, waist-high hug. I grimaced at the brute force the dwarf unknowingly put into it, but Peter stood firm and patted the dwarf's shoulders. "Good to see you again, my friend."

The dwarf shook hands with Kayle and asked Mariah if she was enjoying her necklace, which the dwarves had crafted for her. Once the pleasantries had been exchanged and the squadron looked recovered, Peter asked, "How goes production?"

Magnus bounced happily on his feet. "Oh, it's booming! The Golden One's blessings are many. I would be honored to show you our progress!" He glanced up at me, looking like he didn't know whether to smile or kiss my hand again.

I folded my arms safely out of reach and said, "Lead the way."

We were taken down the rocky tunnel, deeper into the mountain's crust. Magnus babbled good-naturedly about how the dwarf elite would react when they saw us and that new and stronger jewels were being discovered every day in the mines.

We should have been getting wickedly hot the closer we got to the volcanic core of the mountain, but the dwarves had built air lines through the tunnels–minute holes that led outside and let in steady currents of air. The Pegasi followed us until they came to a side tunnel that led to their "stables," and they all turned down it for fresh hay and rest.

After around 20 minutes, I could pick out distant echoes of metal against rock and shouts and burning fires threading around Magnus's voice. Finally, we rounded a bend and came to a rocky catwalk carved out of the side of the mountain and lined by a railing of wood posts tied with rope. Yawning below us, in a wide cavern lit by hundreds of torches, was a gem mine.

Dwarves chiseled away at pockets of jagged stone encasing glittering jewels. Depending on the type of rock and its heat, there were different gems. Each team of dwarves wore a different color of helmet according to their work. The helmets were made of jewels, form-fitted to a dwarf's head and covering everything but their eyes and mouths.

I watched a group of yellow-helmeted dwarf men extract a sheet of gold an inch thick but six feet square and heavy enough that the whole team needed to maneuver it to one side. Kayle pointed, and I watched a big whiskery dwarf apply a coating of some kind to a sword with careful turns of the blade and measured strokes. The blade wasn't metal but a long and sharp diamond. Four pegasi pulled a cart of green and purple chips of crushed emerald and amethyst. Red-helmed dwarves chiseled rubies and garnets into wood boards... and his co-miner tried to stab through it without being confused and dazzled by the reflective surface. When dwarves say hi-ho, they really mean it.

The others had already seen this on their way from the capital to Pebble Embark, but the beauty of the glittering mine overpowered me. I couldn't stop blinking and looking and leaning forward to catch every detail of everything going on.

Some of the working dwarves looked up at us, glancing back and forth between their work and their new visitors. A few waved at Magnus, who returned the gesture and then rang a small gong suspended over his head. The brass plate clashed and turned into a throbbing thrum that made every helmeted dwarven head below turn up. Hammers were laid down, voices stifled, pulleys silenced as the miners heeded the call that beckoned them from their work.

"My kith and kin!" Magnus bellowed. "Fellow dwarves of Boiling Point! I gladly introduce you to the splendorous and mighty–" he pointed to me where I stood staring down at everyone with my mouth open– "Great Griffin Prince, Jonathan!"

Disbelieving whispers swelled from mouths twisted into doubting scowls. I blinked, remembering myself, shut my mouth, and raised my sword with the same dramatic split-second thinking that had given me the words to speak to the tree spirits on our way to the swamp. I stuck it high over my head. Its weight, so long ago a heavy burden, was now almost non-existent.

The dwarves saw the taloned hilt and the unique grip. The whispers built like a wave first from one corner of the room and then joined by some in the center until the uncertain murmurs had turned into a slamming cheer ripe with applause. They all rushed forward, crowding together to stand beneath us with arms upstretched. Magnus urged them on, clapping his own shovel-sized hands and pointing at me with a proud grin. I was wishing the ground would open up and swallow me.

A loud, gurgling snore rumbled from behind us. Marcus was slumped against the shoulder of a bemused-looking knight, sound asleep and moving on into the drooling stage.

"Oh my!" Magnus exclaimed, looking as if he were in trouble. "How rude I am! Come, you've no doubt traveled far! You must all rest, and when you awaken, you shall meet with the Bedrock."

After shaking Marcus awake, we were taken along the wall and away from the cheering dwarf miners.

Our beds were just gallons of bead-sized gravel stuffed into pegasus-wool mattresses. Our pillows were similar, and no one needed blankets because no one would get cold this far into the volcano. Our rooms were rectangular caverns dug into the sides of the mountain tunnels, and each included a very dim lantern, a bed, a washbasin the size of a bathtub, barrels of water to drink from or pour into the basin, a mirror of burnished quartz, a shelf for storing things, and a curtain of silver beads to draw across the doorway.

All I remembered was being directed by a nudge toward a vacant room, stumbling through the clicking beaded curtain, kicking off my boots, unbuckling my sword and laying it at the head of the bed, and then collapsing on the mattress. I couldn't have budged, even if Garrett had snuck in and started yodeling while dancing the can-can. It was my first blissfully deep sleep in weeks.

CHAPTER TWENTY-FOUR:

GUARDIAN OF DREAMS

It was still totally dark when I woke up–it's not like volcanoes have windows, and dwarves have almost perfect night vision. My coral necklace was under my cheek, and it had left a red mark. I massaged the spot and sat up. Since the bed wasn't up on a box-spring, I sat with my knees up by my chin and examined the plate of food at my feet.

There was some yummy-looking roasted mountain-bird, two slices of bread, a bunch of pink berries that tasted like cold strawberry yogurt, and a cup of pegasus milk. It was a strange meal for kicking off the day with, but it had all the essential food groups except for veggies–unless you counted the scraps of onion and basil seasoning the bird. I scarfed everything down–it was a nice change from boar and squash and the occasional apple or mango. I burped and wiped away my milk mustache and washed out the plate and cup in one of the barrels.

I walked to the mirror as I buckled my sword belt back on, but halted when I saw my reflection.

I touched my hand to an alien face, slowly creeping closer to the glass. My eyebrows looked like they were positioned differently–lower over my eyes so that I looked more intense, more like I was trying to concentrate really hard on something or trying to see something far away. It was kind of mean and rugged looking, a natural sign of stress, of wearing my feelings. My lips were more set, my jaw and cheekbones more defined. My neck had grown wider due to flying and using my sword, adding on muscle. I had been given the clean-cut genes of my family, and so I hardly ever had to shave, but time and stress had sprouted a shadow of blond stubble lightly on my chin–light enough so far that I wouldn't have to worry about checking around for razors yet. And my hair... It used to be a dark shade of brownish blond, and the ends would flip up around my face. But now, it was more blond than brown, bleached by the sun. It was longer–almost long enough to tie back–and a curtain of wavy bangs that swept across one side of my forehead had replaced the ends that turned up.

At first, I was upset that I had changed so much. I for sure wasn't a soft little boy anymore. But then a spark of defiance and pride wriggled in my chest. The change in my appearance was just a physical manifestation that I was becoming a man the difficult way. I'd been hardened, honed, refined, hopefully into someone who could shoulder the burden of defeating the Rankers...hopefully, into someone worthy of being called Griffin Prince.

I jumped when the beaded entryway clattered. A stout dwarf woman came in, bearing a load of clothes. Her dark hair was tied into a bun, and she had a long, spirited face, a round nose, and smiling eyes. She wore an apron across her red dress–making her look like a sweet little granny. Without a word, just a little motherly smile and a noise that was part adoring, part speculative, she bustled to me and started plucking at my clothes.

I backed away, hugging myself.

"Um, excuse me? What are you doing?" I yelped. She sighed and put her hands on her hips.

"I'm gettin' you outta them travel-stained clothes, Boy-Prince! You got a nice new load here," she nudged the new clothes with her foot, her drawl something like "deep South meets gruff shrimp-boat captain."

"I can undress myself," I pointed out.

She raised an eyebrow and said, "Put them dirty linens in one of the barrels when you're done, and I'll wash them proper while you're out."

"Out?" I asked as she headed for the beads.

Giving me a friendly smirk, the dwarf woman said, "What, choo gonna stay in 'ere all day?"

I silently watched her leave and then poked my head out through the beads to make sure that she wasn't waiting to jump me while I was naked. I sank my old clothes into one of the barrels and took a cold bath, enjoying feeling clean. Then I put on the new outfit–simple brown cloth leggings and a long brown tunic with cream-white sleeves. I looked like a pirate. I was buckling on my scabbard when the dwarf woman crashed back into the room.

Her sudden, unexpected arrival once again startled me, but once I saw who it was, I righted myself and got busy tying on some knee-high leather boots that were determined to remain floppy and uncooperative.

Once she was done getting my old outfit scrubbed against a washboard, the dwarf wrung out my sopping clothes and laid them on a bed of heated lavender-scented stones to dry.

"Come on now," she said, straightening a wrinkle in the hem of my tunic and yanking me down to pat down my hair. "The

Bedrock're ready to see ya. We should get there at the same time them others do."

She led me by one hand up a maze of stone halls lit either by torches, phosphorescent mushrooms and rocks, or distant arteries of streaming lava. The caverns that led to mines and caves that housed dwarf families became fewer, and finally, we reached a chasm that spanned at least 200 feet to the wall across from us. Bubbling magma boiled far below.

"Uhhhh... Wrong turn?" I asked, looking through my bottom lashes at the deadly lava. I could feel the heat baking my face even from my very distant height.

The dwarf woman giggled and patted the back of my leg.

"Silly prince. Kin you imagine how dangerous it ud be fer the Bedrock if everyone could get to their door? Golden talons! These er important people whose decisions ain't popular to all. You gotta fly. This is as fer as I goes."

I thanked her, and she waddled cheerfully away.

After casting one more glance at the carpet of writhing liquid-fire far below, hoping that no geysers would erupt and consume me or that the fumes shimmering over the chasm weren't noxious, I transformed and soared across the chasm. I found a warm thermal to ride across to a cave without having to flap. When I dug my claws into sulfuric rocks, I twisted to straighten out some secondaries and pluck a dead feather out of the bunch at my tail. Kayle was gliding over to join me, his crown feathers mussed with bedhead. He yawned and scratched his neck ruff with a hind paw when he landed. Together we climbed a shallow rise into a cave lit blue with ropes of lichen.

The rise dipped down and out into a cavern. And in this cavern were great heaps of precious items.

Armor, maybe commissioned from across the land, was displayed on stands–silver armor inscribed with calligraphic lines and ninja blades forming fins along the arms, legs, and helmet; gold armor with diamond-knuckled gauntlets and a scaled helmet that made a terrifying, scowling mask; simple metal armor set with blue sapphires to make an extra jagged layer; onyx and iron plates set with amber and bronze and pearl to form a heraldic crest on the heavy breastplate. There were mining tools scattered around the room and half-finished weapons and the like. It was a beautiful, fascinating sight.

The squadron was just dismounting from their Pegasi over by a wall where their reins were tied around brass hooks. In the center of the room, Peter and Mariah were gathered at a table, looking at charts with five dwarves. Kayle and I transformed and joined them.

When the Bedrock saw me, they thumped their fists over their hearts, snapped to attention, and bowed. There were three men and two women. All seemed carved out of stone–they were heavily scarred and stiff and rough-looking. Each of them had short, scruffy hair, wiry muscles, and stood with feet apart and arms slightly out, like they were ready to fight. They all wore chainmail and small, golden circlets on their heads.

"Heya," I said. "Nice to meet you, too."

Kayle rolled his eyes exasperatedly at my informal tone, rubbing his brow like he had a headache. Mariah stifled a giggle.

"We hope you are well, sir," one of the women said. Her voice wheezed like something had happened long ago to her throat, and she kept swallowing as if she couldn't get something down.

"What are we looking at?" I asked. The charts showed the illustrated figures of everyone in our group–the griffins and the squadron members. Arrows pointed to different parts of our sketched bodies and listed measurements. In some cases, there were mini drawings beside the main ones of parts of armor or weapons.

"These are our plans, Master Jonathan," said one of the Bedrock. "We have made items for you and your warriors that will surely guarantee your safety for the rest of your journey. Armor we have sent along, for it is too heavy and harrying for you to don and carry through the blistering desert. But we have also invented trifles here and there."

Kayle looked excited, picking up the picture of himself and leaning sideways to show it to a sailor.

"Our efforts have been fruitful," a dwarf man said grandly, striding over to a small pile of glittering objects. "We now present you with your gifts."

For the next few hours, we all tried out the gifts that the dwarves had made. The knights and samurai hadn't been focused on much because of how well-protected they were already, but their armor was touched up, and they were allowed to exchange their old weapons for new or add another to their individual arsenals.

The gladiators were fierce and brutal never-give-up fighters. But they also knew how to defend themselves. So, they were presented with small, square shields of black stone painted with a stylized roaring golden griffin, and each was given a sling with chunks of diamond as throwing stones.

The Amazons were given light, leather armor, and fresh javelins to use. The army men, sailors, and marines were re-supplied with precious bullets and were each given a belt with little experimental bombs on it–they had to have a tag pulled and a button pressed before they would explode with enough force to blow an arm off.

We griffins weren't as spoiled as our companions, but it was like Christmas all the same. Kayle's lighter was fitted into a harness around his wrist so that he could slide it down into his hand and use it without having to look like he was conspicuously reaching for a weapon.

Mariah admitted that she would have a hard time with a weapon, so she instead got a pendant added to her necklace that looked like a crystal of some sort. It strengthened her powers, so that she didn't have to touch the ground to grow something and didn't lose as much energy.

Peter's sword was polished and tuned up–he requested nothing else.

And I got a crown.

I told them it would be like a 'shoot me' sign to enemies, but they promised the crown had another function: it would disguise me in the eyes of my foes; make me look like someone else entirely. Even in griffin form, they said it would make me less noticeable as the prince of griffins.

The crown was a white porcelain band in-laid with triangular rubies. It was a great gift that rendered me speechless. The squadron smiled respectfully as I placed it on my head, nodding as if satisfied with how the crown looked. It wasn't heavy and sat low on my brow so it wouldn't fall off.

"I hope you are pleased?" a dwarf asked hopefully.

There was a chorus of loud, sincere yeses.

"We have prepared a feast in honor of your passing among us, Prince," the tough dwarf woman said. "It begins at sunset. Feel free to explore while you await it. We will have a pegasus sent to find you when it begins."

I took her advice and transformed into a griffin to fly across the chasm, still dazed and humbled at the beauty of the gift.

As I meandered, I considered all that I'd learned about the legacy that I was meant to inherit. The Oracle's words, the ambiguous lines of the prophecy, the way my allies treated me like I was some kind of saint didn't help to boost my confidence–in fact, it did the opposite.

How can I do this? I thought, trailing my hand along the smooth, dusty wall. *How can I* be *this? How can I be the person everyone thinks I am–that everyone thinks I can be?... How will I know when I'm ready?* The chimera's taunting words that my hatred made me no better than a Ranker ghosted back to join the crowded merry-go-round of anxiety spinning in my brain.

I rounded a corner, lost in thought, wandering along a corridor that I hadn't explored yet. And there in the wall, bizarrely, unexpectedly, I saw two very tall wooden doors. They were arched like you'd see at the entrance to a church, reverent and ancient, judging by the dust that filled the doors' natural crevices and furrows. There were no handles, just the imprints of hands in either door like a mighty man had pushed against the wood and left indentations. They didn't seem to belong in the dwarven mountain–in fact, I had the eerie sensation that they had manifested in response to my anguished thoughts.

There was nobody around but me, so I didn't know what to do when a voice that might've come from the doors themselves whispered, *"Place your hands against the wood, stranger, that we may judge thy worth."*

I looked around and tapped my sword hilt, wondering if I should pull the weapon out. But then I thought about how stupid and strange it would be to attack a door, so instead, I rubbed my thumbs against my fingers as if getting any dirt off of them would better protect me from unexpected calamities. I put my hands into the indentations and pressed in. They fit perfectly. A million whispers came from a million unseen mouths.

"Griffin Prince! Thou needest no permission to enter here... You have doubts... Let us speak to them..." and the doors opened inward.

I took a breath of musty air. Light entered the cave I stepped into by fist-sized openings dug sideways into the slanting walls. That yellow, midday sunlight shone upon dozens of statues.

I looked up at the first–a tall and proud young man with round, somber stone eyes. He wore lavish robes draped in folds around his muscled form, and he held a glorious sword out to one side. He had to be as tall as a two-story house. A plaque at his feet read:

GREAT KING DAVID

THE FIRST

A young man materialized beside me, glowing faintly white. He kind of resembled the dream forms of my friends, only less drained and more glowy.

His hair was dark, brown-black, and curly. He had greenish-yellow eyes and a few scars that started at his neck and vanished under his red tunic. The tunic he wore was bright and fine, almost martial-looking. But what caught my eye most was the ornate crown on his head, large and jeweled and trimmed at the bottom with white feathers. He was averagely handsome, but very noble-looking.

"Tell me, boy," he said to me like I was so much younger than he was. "What do you see?"

I didn't say anything, looking back at the statue of David the First. The spirit-boy's question required something more than a practical, obvious answer. There was something deeper that I felt but couldn't put into words. I was totally weirded out by what was going on, yet I was at ease and comfortable at the same moment. I went on down the grand aisle of statues, followed by the stately spirit-boy.

Finally, something fell into place, and I said, "They're all griffins! People just like me!" My voice should have echoed, but it did not. I was in a bubble of space, a bubble of time. Now I stared at the statue of a Viking-looking boy called Great King Fjor the 22nd. The spirit boy hanging close to me sighed audibly, smiling with pleasure.

There were a lot of statues in the room. Some strayed from the aisle-way to the space beyond. I looked at as many as I could, the empty eyes, the chiseled stares. As we passed each statue, a new ghostly form, spirits of past kings and queens that gleamed yellow-orange joined us, murmuring to one another.

We came to the end of the room, and a wider-than-normal shaft of sun illuminated a face–a young face that seemed lost in thought. This statue was half-smiling. He sat in a rocky chair, draped in a heavy robe and balancing a long stave across his lap. A gleaming gold-and-copper griffin sat justly at his side, beak open and wings forward as if to spread. The plaque at this behemoth's feet read:

GREAT KING BRODY

THE 75TH

Here he was.

My predecessor. The very image of the spirit-boy beside me staring up at himself.

The other spirits gathered had stopped and were shifting together, pacing, talking mutedly.

"What are you thinking about?" King Brody asked, turning his firm, focused stare on me.

Here in this hallowed room, I could say what was on my heart and say what I really wanted to, and I wouldn't be judged. I answered, "I've seen a lot of people willing to die for me. Helping me, trusting me, and believing in me."

"And?" Brody urged.

My insides twisted a little, like they were under pressure, like my heart was being squeezed. "I've never believed in myself. I wanted more, sure, I wanted a brighter future, but I never thought that I could be someone worthy of being called...*prince,* you know?

And now there are so many people out there counting on *me.* I don't know if I'm really capable of all the things people think I am."

"But?" Brody pressed.

I smiled and said, "I... I think I'm ready. Ready to find out what I *am* capable of. I want to prove myself to...*myself,* if that makes sense. But most of all, I want to stop the Rankers and put everything back to what it's supposed to be."

The glowing spirit-kings and queens talked in loud, blending mumbles to each other, and King Brody laughed, baring his teeth in an open smile.

"I *knew* you were ready!" he exclaimed. "Your uncertainty called to us. In this time of prophecy, in this Age of Miracles, we have come to speak comfort unto you. There comes a time in the life of every griffin ruler when they doubt their destiny, for our legacy is an ancient and powerful one. Just as I did, you fail to comprehend the great plan you are but a small part of. You fail to fathom the forces beyond your ken that are working through you. Yes, many people will want you to be many different things. Such is life. But as long as you try to be what they want, you will fail, for you can only be yourself–and though you may not be what they want, you will become who they *need.*"

Brody reached out his hand and said in a softer voice, "Give me our sword."

I handed it to him hilt-first with expectantly-held breath. Under his instruction, I knelt on one knee and bowed my head, feeling the sword's weight on first one shoulder, then the other.

In an intimidating and serious tone, King Brody said, “I, King Brody the 75th, pronounce you Sir Jonathan, guardian of the Land of Dreams and the 76th ruler of our ancient line. May your talons stay as sharp as your wits and your heart be filled with wisdom.”

I had read about adages like this in Peter’s book on griffins–they could be kind or rude, or something as simple as, “may your hunts go well today.” The other griffin was expected to respond because it would be considered impersonal or a challenge if he didn’t. What Brody had said to me was a greeting only used between equals–close friends or brothers. I didn’t know *what* to say.

So I just choked out, “You were a wise leader, King Brody. I only hope that my footsteps will not stray from your path. Long live the griffins.” I paused, then said this last part again, more defiantly. That’s how prepared I had become to kick any butt that stood in my way. The other faceless spirits took up the declaration, turning it into a chant.

Brody and I locked eyes, and I saw a promise in his–a sad promise that bad things were coming; terrible things. But also a vow that in the end, there would be good. He closed his eyes and smiled as the chant thundered around us.

“Jonathan?”

I jumped. Colors whirled and blended around me, and sounds that I didn’t understand intensified and vanished. I rocked back on my heels and stood staring at the closed doors to the statue-chamber. The hand-shaped indentations were gone, and the arched doors were now two simple slabs of wood without handles shutting in something that I may have just hallucinated took place but knew had actually happened. My sword was back in its scabbard, but the taloned hilt was warm.

My name was called again–this time in a voice edged with concern. I turned around, shoving aside my mounting disorientation.

Marine Sergeant Flaherty sat astride a palomino pegasus with pearly hooves. It was funny to see such a big guy on such a round, short-legged horse. He stared at me uncertainly and chuckled a bit.

"You look like my daughter does when she's had a strange dream."

He had no idea how close to the mark he'd come. I accepted the hand he held out to help me onto the back of his pegasus, but offered no explanation. Instead, I asked, as bluntly as I had with Boyzun, "Are you real or a figment of imagination?"

"I'm very real," the Sergeant said in a quiet voice. "Took a shot to the head in Iraq. Now I'm here." He said nothing more, and I didn't press, content to wander the dark halls until dinner was ready with a man as brave as any griffin I've ever met.

CHAPTER TWENTY-FIVE:

CLUES AND PUZZLES

The feast that night was...intriguing, to say the least.

Every dwarf man, woman, and child showed up, and I took so many backslaps and generous greetings and bows and stares that it took me at least an hour after everyone else, and some insistence from Peter, to start eating.

Pegasi flew over our heads and ate from great troughs of greens behind us. The feast table stretched long and was packed with guests and food. I sat at the head of the table. At my right were Peter, Kayle, Mariah, and beyond them, the squadron. To my left were the Bedrock.

I took my first-ever sip of ale, spat it out, blinked, and then tried again–this time keeping the liquid down. I limited myself to one goblet before accepting some sweet, light, pegasus milk. The food was excellent–sprinkled with unknown spices and glistening in exotic sauces. I picked up snippets of conversation about how mining had gone for the day and how families were and such. Dwarf children, short, stubby, not altogether attractive creatures, waited for the elders to be seated before they squeezed in beside their parents. A dwarf baby the size of a brick squealed. The Bedrock were unused to being out in public among their people, and their gazes frequently wandered to faces and hands and shadows.

Mariah scarfed down a pheasant leg, realized it had been the last, and grew another one from the finished one's bones. Kayle was telling a descriptive story of a fight he'd had, his goblet of ale sloshing down his front until a rickety rock pegasus foal wandered from its mother and ran its tongue up the back of his head.

The squadron stuffed their faces and got a little tipsy, and a few exclaimed, many times over, what good brewers the dwarves were. The dwarves toasted every time they heard this and joined in falteringly with some loud, old military tunes one of the army men struck up.

A broad, content smile spread across my face. I felt like a new guy, especially after the strange meeting with Brody and my other predecessors. These were my friends and subjects in a kingdom existing only in the human mind. How many people can say that? In a way, I guess it was the closest I had ever come to counting my blessings, to truly feeling that I belonged somewhere. Even if it was all, technically, a dream, it was a very good one. The best I'd ever had.

The next morning the kindly dwarf woman led me to the Bedrock once more. It was our last day with the dwarves, and we were to discuss plans. Kayle had a hangover, so he was cranky the whole time.

The dwarves had helped supply my army with armor and weapons and sent them on to the elves, whom we would meet on the way to the capital. The Bedrock had more news: apparently, the carpenter Joshua, a friendly man we had met in the Melancholy Bog, had already started supervising the construction of catapults and other machines that I hadn't even heard of. Already there had been reported sightings of mermaids, Tree-spirits, Tahtltiki tribes-folk, and bog-dwellers on the move towards the capital.

According to the Bedrock, in his time in The Land of Dreams, Brody had been such an inspiration that the royal army's ranks had swollen with volunteers within a year. At his death, war with the Rankers had officially been declared, and the number of loyal enlistees had increased again by the thousands. Many of the warriors were at the moment dispersed throughout the land, stationed at fortresses and protecting cities still recovering from damages done in Brody's time–I didn't know where the rest were. Still, I assumed they were waiting for me in the capital city.

I thought of my encounter with Brody's...ghost? Spirit?... the previous day. He had worked so very hard in his time as king and done well. Because of his efforts, I wasn't left alone in the dust scrambling to cobble together a plan of attack. This heartened me. Pride for my kingdom and for Brody filled my chest so that, for a moment, I felt unstoppable.

Then came the bad news: it would take at least three days of non-stop walking to reach civilization in the desert, and the dwarves had packed us with gallons of water in jug-like wineskins. We had all been given thin jackets with hoods for the sizzling day sun and warm cloaks for the chill nights. At the last moment, Peter remembered the beetle and the slip of paper in our money pouch. One of the Bedrock–a man with a wolf's face tattooed over his own like a grim mask–pinched the paper in his fingers, scanning it closely.

"These are clues, you said?" he asked in an articulate, cultured voice. "Originally meant for the Ranker allies?" Peter nodded, and the dwarf's eyes became tight, grim. "It is instructions and a list," he said. "Like a...shopping list of sorts. It says here that you must find civilian clothes to blend in and purchase something called fish pods...and a basket... The Rankers must have had some plan in mind involving capturing an animal. It instructs their allies to wait by the royal pyramids and only send a small contingent into the city proper to confer with the Pharaoh."

The dwarf translated the list from whatever written language the Rankers used to English (or whatever passed in the dream-world for a written language I could understand) on some scrolls that we made room for in one of our emptier bags.

"Why would they want to confer with the Pharaoh?" I asked Peter, shouldering my bag. "Do you think they wanted to hurt him?"

Peter helped me to situate the bag and said, "King Brody had his suspicions that the Pharaoh is a malcontent; that he may even support the Rankers. He was kind enough when King Brody met with him on his campaign, but he wouldn't pledge his allegiance or supply any troops to the cause."

"Said it was because he needed them to protect his own lands, and he had none to spare," Kayle scoffed in passing. "The arse."

I hadn't told anyone about seeing Brody's spirit. That was a secret I wanted to keep to myself. But I remembered his noble face and stern gaze, and I couldn't imagine anyone saying "no" to him, whether politics were involved or not.

"This beetle," the dwarf said, frowning at it with an excited gleam in his eyes, "Is a conundrum. I cannot quite figure it out...the Scarab Society has not shared the details of this mechanism with me... However, it appears that the pieces separate somehow, and I could probably force them open…but it may be at risk to whatever contents remain locked within."

Peter took it back, crestfallen. He tugged his white beard thoughtfully and said, "We'll see what we can find out in Tencina-Ahrroc. Thank you."

We bid the Bedrock farewell and departed. I looked up at Peter.

"If the Pharaoh's a lost cause, then is that why my supporters have to be secret? Will the Pharaoh hurt them?"

Peter's mouth became tense, and his jaw set. "Better safe than sorry. They were formed during Brody's time when he found a way to communicate with people in reality. They know that Rankers are everywhere–hiding behind even the kindest of smiles. You can never be too careful."

His tone was bitter, and his silver eyes grave. I looked sideways at him as we walked along a tunnel studded with fanciful tilework and wondered if he was thinking about the time my grandmother had sheltered him from the hatred of her own neighbors.

The dwarf Magnus awaited us at the exit tunnel on the desert-facing side of the mountain. We arrived there in the afternoon and were gusted with hot winds sent up from a sea of golden sand stretching almost to the horizon. An off-white dot, miles off into the dunes, could have been the desert city. As griffins, the flight would have taken a day and a half, but we were confined to walking with the squadron.

Magnus grasped my forearm, and I his. His bald pate gleamed in the sun bursting savagely in from outside. It illuminated how pale he was. When you live in the dark bowels of a volcano, you don't get a natural tan.

"Good luck," he said solemnly.

"Your people are good friends," I said. "Thank you for all you have done."

"See you in the capital city," Magnus smiled, and we set off into the oven of the desert.

CHAPTER TWENTY-SIX:

NOT A FAN OF DESERTS

If you like getting blinded by white-hot sand, or getting your fingers sliced up trying to extract water from prickly desert plants, or sweating so much it feels like it rained, or getting so sun-burned you scab, I'd recommend you either go to a shrink or dream about the Tencina-Ahrroc desert.

The three days it took to get to the city weren't the worst situations I'd been in, but they were up there. As soon as we left the mountains and hit the sand, the sun walloped us a sweaty, red welcome. The heat was a crisping furnace you couldn't escape. We all regretted thinking that we wouldn't miss the damp humidity of the jungle or the swamp. This was everyone's first crossing. Peter said that they had avoided the desert on their way to Pebble Embark from the capital, going around it.

Our food became moist and nasty, but it was edible and kept us going. Griffins can go for a long while without nourishment, but we would need all of our strength for our arrival. We all got major tans. Mariah and Kayle looked like different people. Kayle's freckles were only barely visible against his bronze skin. Mariah's hair was bleached a lighter gold, and mine was a bright blond. It was easier on Peter and the other darker-skinned people in the squadron, but not by much.

The animals native here were your usual lizards and bugs and occasionally camels. But there were also mini-herds of antelope with bizarre horns and blue birds with huge wings that sometimes flew low over our heads and offered shade.

Kayle's hands blistered, and I got red-black burns on my nose and chin, but by Wednesday afternoon, our troubles were at an end. Civilization was in sight.

I crawled weakly up another dune, felt a hand reaching for mine, took it, and let one of the soldiers pull me up. I sat down mechanically and slid down the other side of the dune. Robotically, using the same movements I had for days, I stood up, brushed sand from my clothes and eyes, pulled my hood tighter, coughed up a tumbleweed, and turned to help others scramble down. Finally, half-awake, I reached the summit of another dune and tripped over the crest. I curled into a ball and skidded bodily down, too exhausted to right myself. As I felt myself level out somewhat, I prepared to stand but instead crashed shoulder-first into a solid, white wall. I grunted, registered an aching bruise along one side of my body, and frowned accusingly at the mudbricks.

The sun made a bright halo off the far upper edge of the wall. It sank in that we had found civilization and that it was late afternoon. I sat up and pulled up my hood just as Mariah half-fell half-slid into the wall as I had. Our group gathered silently together, and we stumbled along, following the wall to two open ivory gates. A pair of beefy guards with spears and Ancient-Egyptian-style headdresses lazily rounded the gates, gave us all quick once-overs, saw that we were no threat, and had a big, ol' sack of money, and let us by.

The walls had not only separated us from shelter and a chance to relax but also a bustle of activity. Whiny reed pipes twiddled in the corners where snake-charmers called serpents from wicker baskets. Wiry men danced on coals or breathed fire. Women dressed in scanty scarves danced fluidly amidst claps and flying coins. Millions of wares were sold at ramshackle booths: colorful rugs, clay pots, incense, glass jars, beads, idols, jewelry, and instruments. I had never seen so many sandals and faces and white robes in my life.

Stretching far beyond the crowded bazaar were the great gleaming towers of a mighty palace. Each onion-shaped dome had to be big enough to house the Hindenburg.

An alabaster fountain rested at an intersection that split like the spokes of a wheel down different alley paths. The fountain formed a majestic dog with large ears and a slim build. It bayed upward, and sparkling clear water spewed from its muzzle into a pool below it. Everyone but Peter and I rushed for the fountain and buried their faces into the basin, gulping the fresh water. I stared at the statue. My throat ached for its thirst to be quenched, but something was off about the alabaster dog. I looked closely at it. Upturned at its paws was a scarab beetle, which I thought was an odd detail.

"These people behave culturally almost the same way as the Ancient Egyptians did in reality," Peter said with an ironic arch of his eyebrow. "Except that instead of Ra or Amun-Ra being their dominant deity, it is Setmenrajzda, the Tencinian idol of death and triumph."

"Oh yeah, them beetles can be tough cookies," I said sarcastically, indicating the little stone bug.

Peter sighed at my naïveté and added, "Remember, the scarab is the sign of your allies. The Pharaoh would never openly show his defiance against you, say, by having the Setmenrajzda attacking a griffin, but by displaying animosity, even inadvertently, against your loyal subjects, he snubs his nose all the same."

For a time, I stared silently up at the morbid statue.

"Sheesh," I murmured. "What did we ever do to him?"

Peter led me over to the others splashing in the pool.

"He must like the whole Ranker idea of taking over the world and becoming the ultimate ruler. Like many corrupt men, his weakness is a thirst for power and comfort–even if it's at the expense of multitudes."

I gave Peter a sidelong look, and bent to stick my mouth in the water, even though passersby stared and muttered to one another about our barbarism.

"Does he like the sound of that enough to want to fight against me in the war?"

Peter's mouth turned down.

"At this point, I'm afraid so. It has to be why the Rankers were going to send their allies here–they were going to collect him as well as whatever the final clues led them to. That's why we have to get your allies, get the final answers as to where the Rankers reside, and get out of here."

"What do you suggest we do?" Marcus gasped, water running down his face and chest.

"Split up," Peter said readily. "We'll each go down an alley and explore the parts of this populace individually. Meet up here by nightfall. We're looking for any sign that pertains to the Scarab Society. Look for beetle and griffin icons or themes."

Peter put a huge hand on my shoulder and said in an undertone as the others split their own ways, "Can you do this alone?"

I shrugged. "I have to be independent at some time or another. May as well start now."

Peter patted the side of my face and wandered away back towards the crowded bazaar. I took one last look at the Setmenrajzda statue and then turned away down a shady side street. My crown was tucked under my hood so it wouldn't attract attention. I didn't feel like testing the dwarven enchantment upon it now, on my own. By keeping my face low and my money bag apparent, I could just be a rich tourist with bad sunburns.

I scoured every inch of everything, looking for anything that might have sheltered my allies. The only things that were remotely close to what may have been Scarab Society shelters were a few shops: one that had some scarab-shell incense holders and one that had a stuffed griffin head that I dearly hoped wasn't real.

Hours later, I decided to take a break before finding my way back to Peter and the others. A building made of clay, wood, and straw looked like a promising place to find a drink. Older men sat outside with bowls of wine, and a stone sign over the red cloth awning said a bunch of gibberish in hieroglyphics, but below in gold letters, it translated to *Sweet Oasis*.

I stepped through the open doorway to a breezy room peppered with windows and crowded with people in loose-fitting robes. Instead of tables or chairs, everyone sat on rugs and pillows with numerous patches. The wealthier upper-class occupied the cleaner, cushioned lounge beds stationed under umbrellas outside on a patio. I stood watching one woman open her mouth for a meek servant girl to drop in a fat grape until a wide-girthed man bustled up to me, breaking my fascination.

His ample stomach shoved into mine, and I had to step back to give the beast room. He reached forward around his massive paunch and took one of my hands. Lowering his eyes, he kissed my knuckles and rested his head on them since bowing would be like trying to bend a beach ball in half. At first, I was afraid that I had forgotten to put away my crown, that maybe he'd figured out that I was royalty or even recognized me as the griffin prince, but then I remembered the fat money pouch at my belt beside my sword.

"Oh, marvelous day! That your fine sandals have graced my humble floors!"

So this was the bartender. At least he wasn't a werewolf.

I didn't know what to do, so I smiled, trying to ignore stares from the other customers. I didn't know what to do, so I smiled, trying to ignore stares from the other customers. The man brushed his fingertips against mine, seemingly unaware of how much he was creeping me out. He brushed his fingertips against mine, seemingly unaware of how much he was creeping me out.

"But, such dirty clothes and calloused hands, my lord. Have you no servants to do your bidding and manual labor?"

I was quiet for a beat. This was my chance to test these people and see just how much their ideals matched their Pharaoh's. I replied in my airiest, upper-crusty voice, "Mostly, my good man, but sometimes I work beside my servants so that I may partially share their burden. After all, I am no better than they."

There was a tide of admiring croons from the poorer folks inside and then fast-talking hushed voices. The people outside on the patio shooed away their own servants and leaned in to converse.

"Admirable, my liege, quite generous for a young man with your social standings," the large man shouted, bowing his head again. He pointed me outside towards the patio where a vacant lounge bed awaited under an umbrella. The people outside twisted around, not even trying to hide their open stares.

"Please relax yourself, sire, and I will be at your side shortly," the bartender said.

I made my stately way towards the lounge. It was narrow and long with red velvet cushions. Its wooden frame was made of polished bamboo, and the umbrella was thin red silk that cast a pale pinkish light down on my bare arms as I sat back and put an ankle on my knee. I took in the half-dozen or so faces glued on mine.

All the women had sleek black hair. Some wore their hair down. Some had it braided or tucked under jeweled plates. Their complexions were perfect, their teeth and nails glossy, and make-up caked their dark eyes and lips. They wore silky white dresses with as much skin exposed as possible without seeming too sleazy. The men were bare-chested no matter their weight or musculature, with white skirts and knee-high sandals. They, too, had eye make-up, but also fake goatees and boxy headdresses. Jewels and amulets were on every finger and around every neck. The only thing that fit me in with them was my money and possibly my finely crafted sword.

One of the guys there stood out because he was around my age. He wore a gleaming white tunic and a long headdress accented with golden wings that arched down to frame his face. Great tendons wreathed wiry muscles along his arms. At each wrist were thick, gold cuffs. A blue ornament against his collarbone displayed two outstretched wings.

"What sort of man bends his knee to work beside slaves?" the boy drawled from where he draped on his pillows.

"Me," I said simply, studying my nails arrogantly even though they were filthy.

The boy chuckled. "But...why?"

I gave him my best you're-not-worth-my-time look.

"As I said inside, they're as human as the rest of us, present company excluded. They should be honored and respected. And *we* should be humble." My new friend looked insulted, some of the other rich chums seemed taken aback, but most nodded as if they appreciated my point.

The overweight bartender came and offered me a variety of drinks on a tray. I took a fizzy goblet of what tasted like root beer with a shot of vanilla, and he left the tray on the ground by my feet. He returned briefly with numerous small bowls of various snacks and set those down before leaving. I tentatively examined what resembled a curled-up millipede, set it down, and drank.

"Are you not going to recline?" a woman asked.

"Why should I?" I cocked my head.

"Well, it is better for digestion, of course," she replied as if that was common knowledge. I gave her a dubious look but rolled onto my side, staring down at the food and keeping my sword in hands-reach. I instantly regretted my decision when the carbonated liquid in my stomach sloshed around, mixing with the water I'd recently guzzled and the scraps of cactus flesh I'd nibbled at that morning.

One of the women slid down my hood and started to comb my hair with her fingers. I recoiled, worried about my crown, but she only took it off and set it aside. One of the men reached forward to greedily stroke the jewels set into the porcelain. I felt my disguise vanish like I was slowly emerging from water. I hoped that whatever form my disguise took was not too drastically different from my real appearance, or else everyone would notice the changes. But the woman only twirled a lock of my hair and murmured, "Such a strange color. Such strange words and accent and posture. Are you a prince of another land?"

"You could say that," I said evasively.

"What's this?" another girl asked. I looked down towards my feet. One of the women had somehow removed the red scarab from my pocket without my knowledge and was rolling it around in her hands, her eyes wide. She exchanged strained looks with the others present and then stared awkwardly at me.

"Oh yeah," I said, on instant alert. I didn't know who I could trust, and if the scarab was the sign of my secret supporters, then I had to tread carefully. I'd already established that I was a foreigner; however, I could continue playing like I was ignorant of local tensions. "One of my officials happened upon that in the market. It appears to open. Does anyone know how?"

"I might." One of the men approached, eyeballing the scarab with a mixture of curiosity and alarm like sirens would go off if he so much as touched it. "I'm widely known for my inventions," he bragged a little hesitantly, but I saw his long, dexterous fingers and curious eyes and didn't doubt him. The woman handed him the beetle, allowing a servant girl to come from nowhere and brush off her knees made dusty from squatting.

The tinkerer turned the beetle over and over and pried at its legs and carapace. Looking at minute details barely visible to the naked eye, the man finally and proudly declared, "I have it. Judging by the unique set of the detailed hairs on the scarab's legs, its red hue, and how its antennae are directed towards the sun, heat is the only force that can coax it open. Here..." The man set the bug on the ground beyond the shade of the umbrellas.

Soaking in the late afternoon sun and the day's heat absorbed in the ground, the bug's wings popped out to either side within moments. The women surrounding me clapped gleefully at the solved puzzle. I about joined them.

The tinkerer had one of his poor servants retrieve the insect. The little guy had to use the hem of his tunic to pick up the scalding bug and held it beneath my nose to see. The others crowded around and leaned in as I plucked it up and dropped it on the ground by the hardly-touched food. The kid who had first challenged my ideals was distancing himself, and I should have been more concerned by the frosty look on his face, but the scarab was open, and that took up all my attention.

Tucked inside the bug was a palm-sized picture of a black and brown cat with a round head and big eyes. Rings were in its large ears and rested on top of each other around its neck.

"Awww, such a gorgeous, petite creature," one of the women crooned.

"Why a picture of a cat?" I pondered aloud. What kind of clue was that?

"Why not? Cats are lucky," replied one of the men indignantly.

"How many animals do you *worship*?" I exclaimed, aghast.

"You *must* be a foreigner," the tinkerer shook his head. "Go study the tablets in the Temple of Heaven. Listen to the stories. The Pharaoh is holding a great party at his palace, and if you beat him at his own game, Dominant Deity, you'll get a prize." He exchanged another serious look with one of the other gentlemen present, and I could read confusion and panic warring in their minds, despite their cool exteriors. According to their thoughts, both suspected that my allies were planning something nefarious, which I found ironic considering that the Rankers were in actuality the ones causing trouble.

"A prize, huh? ...Sounds good." *Color me intrigued*. I wondered if the prize was the last clue to the Ranker's location. I wondered how I would get into the party. I also wondered what the stupid cat had to do with anything.

One of the men gasped in surprise, and something sharp poked my stomach. I looked down and followed the sword eager to eat my intestines up the arm, to the furious face of the arrogant kid who'd started our whole conversation.

"*What are you doing*?" squealed one of the girls, gripping me in what she thought was a protective choke-hold.

"You ask too many questions, foreigner," the boy spat, "And you know little of our customs. Either take yourself back to where you came from or take up your sword and let me silence you like a respectable man."

Well, I wasn't much for either of those choices, but I was pissed enough for the second one.

I pulled the woman's arms from around my throat, and she released me easily–probably eager for a fight. Sitting up slowly, I stood and pulled out my sword.

"Honorable," scoffed the boy. "But foolish." He shifted his stance to a cat-like crouch. I copied him, unlocking my knees.

"What, no evil laugh?" I mocked.

Everyone in the vicinity cleared away into a wide circle, and those inside the building were rushing to the doorway to watch. My opponent watched me seriously, malevolently. What had I done or said to upset him this badly? *Who is this guy? A Ranker supporter? Does he recognize the scarab as one of the clues that the Rankers left behind?*

I flushed all thoughts away and charted the boy's weight and figure, gauging his experience. By his stance and muscle tone, I guessed we were evenly matched. But I had superior griffin reflexes in reserve as well. I removed my pack, letting it fall on the lounge.

We lunged at each other. Metal screamed on metal, and we grunted on impact. Together, oblivious to the watching faces, we danced a deadly ballet of arcs and blocks and ducks and stabs.

I shoved the guy back and twirled my blade around his, trying to nudge it from his grip. But instead, I just forced his blade up and into the canvas of an umbrella. The kid tried to tug his weapon down, and I aimed to injure him while he was distracted, but he ripped viciously, and the umbrella collapsed down onto me.

The wooden pole of the umbrella knocked me down, and I strived to get up and protect myself. The boy's sword cut through the cloth and pinned my sleeve to the ground, slicing into a part of my arm. I yelled, and the boy exclaimed triumphantly, thinking he'd done major damage.

I waited, still, for him to pull away the umbrella, and then, my fingers scrabbling out, I grasped the stem of someone's goblet and splashed it at the boy's face. He rubbed at his eyes, cursing. Warm blood ran down my arm, soaking into my sleeve, and I repaid the favor by taking my sword and slicing up at the boy's cheek. A thin stripe of crimson glowed on his face and ran down his chin. I expected this to at least slow him down, but instead, he dropped into a crouch before I could find my feet, pinned my chest beneath his knee, grabbed my hair, and stared deep into my eyes, which I felt flooding red with fury.

"You!" he shouted after a moment, his expression revealing a mixture of grief and shame.

Before he could blab about how "my eyes were giving me away" and all that, I shoved his arm away with my sword hilt and clocked him in the temple. The boy's eyes rolled up, and he collapsed sideways. His head dress went all askew over his forehead and revealed short, scruffy black hair.

"He just bested a sheik!" someone hissed.

I checked the cut on my arm and saw that it wasn't bad. Picking him up by his armpits, I dragged the boy inside the building and out the door, where I slung him up into a fireman's carry. The bartender didn't even ask me to pay for my drink.

CHAPTER TWENTY-SEVEN:

MY SECRET SOCIETY

Everyone else was waiting for me by the fountain. It had cooled considerably, and stars were just winking out from the tarry-black desert sky. I carried the boy's body into view, whistling to myself and occasionally bumping his head against inanimate objects.

"What the–?" a knight belted and turned to Peter. "He's killed someone!"

Peter made his way to me slowly and sighed. "Dare I ask what happened?"

I took that as an invitation and relayed the story with the kid in question sprawled at our feet.

"And you offended him just like that?" Peter asked, concerned.

"Yep," I confirmed.

"Um," Mariah kneeled by the boy's body and held out his winged necklace. "This guy is a member of the Scarab Society."

"He *is*?" My stomach plummeted.

"The wings symbolize griffin wings," Mariah explained. "It's a display they've adapted after the Pharaoh came to recognize their scarab emblem. Judging by the collar's size, you beat cold one of the higher members."

"Why'd he think I was an enemy?" I asked, groping at very slippery straws.

"Well," Peter said, also trying not to laugh, "He saw you with the scarab. He probably thought you were a Ranker."

"Oh, yeah, I'm sure!" I said, insulted. "I'm not butt-ugly."

Kayle gave a harsh laugh and then blinked at me.

"Oh, sorry, you were serious?"

We took the scarab member somewhere out of the public eye: a deep maze-like alley cluttered with boxes. No one would find us unless they were psychotically determined. The squadron had stationed themselves strategically behind piles of crates, guarding us griffins while we waited for the mysterious kid to wake up.

Eventually, he stirred and sat up, groaning and rubbing his head. He picked up his headdress, dusted it off, and settled it back in place. I thought he couldn't see us standing there until he leaned against a box and scowled at us.

"Well, this is cliché."

We all blinked. The boy yawned and even added the extra patting of his mouth to show us how supremely bored he was.

"Why'd you bring me here?" he asked.

I growled under my breath and situated the crown back on my head, trying to think of a scathing retort. He looked me up and down and half-smiled.

"I knew it. You *are* the Great Prince. Have you come to take my people and me with you to the capital city?"

"Affirmative," Peter nodded. "It's time."

I was a tad bemused; I had expected at least some shouting and trying to get away.

"And who are you?" I asked, getting back in gear.

"My name is Amenophis. I am a first-class spy for the Society."

"What about the whole sheik thing going on?" I asked, swatting at a locust on a box by my head and watching it glide off.

"My cover," Amenophis replied. "I play the part of a wealthy, foreign sheik attending the Pharaoh's party to discuss business. It was my assigned duty to spy for you and find out what I could about the Pharaoh's political affiliations before your arrival, but you came sooner than we judged you would."

"Not excited easily, are you?" Peter asked, rolling up his sleeves to the elbows.

"No," Amenophis grunted, getting to his feet and stumbling back dizzily with a hand at his head. "Not easily. But I am relieved." He blinked hard and said, "Come. I'll take you to the others."

We followed him down streets dead-silent now that the vendors were asleep and turned down another quaint alley set fairly close to the palace gates. We all took turns climbing through the gaping window of an abandoned house. Under a moth-eaten rug was a trap-door that opened to steeply descending stairs and into a chilly cellar.

"It's Amenophis; I'm coming down with some guests!" our host called, and we slipped underground, groping at the rough walls for balance. Oil lamps lit up a low-ceilinged, musty room that was large enough for the thirty or so people within to move about comfortably. After the squadron squeezed in, it was snug.

The members of the Scarab Society were a people that looked like they were constantly suspicious and never relaxed. Their dark, round eyes searched relentlessly, and they were always tense. As I watched, people were vanishing and others appearing. Most didn't, and after a while, the disappearing stopped. This came as a surprise to me. I had assumed that the Scarab Society was composed of dream-creations. But no–these were allies from reality that Brody had somehow collected. The people vanishing were the ones waking up from dreaming. It was a cool feeling–a reassurance. It reminded me that Brody, and the rulers before him, had played a part in making sure their successors wouldn't be completely helpless.

They all wore winged or scarab-decorated jewelry–some less conspicuous than others. An older lady had winged earrings and someone else, a pale pink-gemmed ring with a scarab engraved within it.

Amenophis grasped arms with a kid that could've been his clone except that his cheek bones were more prominent, and he was a head taller. He stated the obvious, shoulder-jockeying with the other boy, "This is–stop it, Manu! This is my twin brother Manu."

Manu was about to greet us when he did a double-take on his brother's face and saw the purple bruises on the sides of his head, the swollen lip, and cut cheek.

"*Who did this to you*?" he bellowed in a deep, thunderous voice. Amenophis pointed at me. Manu marched in my direction, his face furious, one fist raised, but what his brother next said halted him instantly.

"The Great Prince, Jonathan."

Manu's countenance withered, and he fell to one knee mid-stride with the others in the room.

"Sire! I am sure you have an understandable reason for laying a hand on my brother, but...I wish to know it?"

"Just a misunderstanding." I shrugged, feeling the dull sting from the cut on my arm.

"Have you come to bring us with you to the capital?" someone asked hopefully.

"Yes," I said. "But it isn't as easy as that."

"It never is," Manu mumbled. "We pray consistently, but we still overcome trials."

"Ol' Setmenrajzda is slacking on the job, huh?" Kayle shot a little scornfully.

"We do not pledge our lives to Tencinian idols, let alone the black jackal of violent death," Amenophis replied calmly.

"Oh. Cool," Kayle said, chastened.

I brought us back on track.

"On our way to the capital city, we have been finding and following clues originally left for Ranker allies that would've led them to their base of operations. Our interceptions have slowed them down and stopped them from gathering their recruits and slaughtering my allies. We suspect we're on our last clue, but it's a toughie." I told them about the cat's picture, and the brothers switched looks. Amenophis looked like a kid in a toy store.

"That was a photo of Pharaoh's favorite pet cat," he said. "Cats are sacred here as bringers of light. We had put together a heist to find out more information on Pharaoh's loyalties had your arrival not been so unexpected, but it looks as if we may have to put it in action after all."

"I love a good heist. Tell us about it," I said, leaning against a giant reed basket.

Amenophis pressed his fingers together into a point resembling the tip of a pyramid and explained.

"In the royal pyramid, a beast is said to guard a great treasure. We of the Society planned to infiltrate the pyramid and study the treasure, destroying it if it was dangerous, selling it if it was of value–the Pharaoh's not an ally, and it could help fund our undercover work. But to get into the pyramid requires a key in the form of a personalized pressure pad. We did not expect to solve that puzzle until that cat picture solved it for us. The Pharaoh has been dispersing them throughout the city to advertise his upcoming party."

"And," Mariah added, tapping one nail against her chin, her eyes distant and thoughtful, "Either Garrett established one of the pictures as a clue inviting his allies to the desert, or the Pharaoh sent it out, meaning for the Rankers to pick it up. Perhaps whatever's in the pyramid will help them."

"Maybe it's whatever the clues have been leading toward," I added. *And maybe Garrett wanted his allies to take out some of my allies while they were here...*

Manu continued his brother's thread. "We have a feeling that Pharaoh's prize cat opens the pyramid. Which works out, because the rough draft of the heist involved going to Pharaoh's palace anyway and beating him at his own game, Dominant Deity, winning the prize in case it too was dangerous or valuable. Now all signs point to the prize being that cat. If you plan on going on with the heist, I suggest you go to the Temple of Heaven and study for the game."

"That's the second time I've heard that today," I grumbled. "What's a temple have to do with playing a game?"

"Dominant Deity is like..." Manu rotated his hands, searching for words, "Like...a mix between a role-playing game and chess. First, you choose a game piece, one of the Tencinian idols, and you collect tokens relevant to that idol's myths. And then, at the end, when you duel your opponent on the board, your game piece is restricted to making specific movements. You're expected to know everything about each idol because your progression depends on your knowledge and understanding of their minutiae. That's a summary; anything else?"

I removed the translated hieroglyph-covered list of things to buy and held it up.

"Yeah, know any good places to shop?"

CHAPTER TWENTY-EIGHT:

MEANWHILE, IN REALITY

AT NIKKI'S HOUSE

Tyson and Vince slouched in a pair of Nikki's comfy easy chairs in her cozy living room. They watched their friend's spunky parents re-decorate. Despite the Ranker's order to burn useless belongings, Nikki's mother and father still managed to keep up the tradition of doing so once every few weeks to keep the atmosphere cheery.

Though no one had been able to prove it, and none of them had thought to ask Ben the last time they had seen him, the friends all suspected that he was the Ranker in charge of their town. It would make sense if Garrett was truly convinced that Ben was a full-fledged Ranker to have someone close to Jonathan keeping an eye on his closest friends. It would also explain the more lax restrictions that the Firestonians enjoyed compared to the poor people in other towns and cities: none of them had been assigned a menial task more laborious than tending to the massive street bonfires or carting the ashes to a dump site in the woods; they were allowed to use their electricity for cooking and cleaning; a toasty fire even burned in the fireplace, but it was small–for some reason, the light and warmth seemed to attract minor Rankers, and it was unnerving to turn and suddenly see a pair of glowing eyes pressed against the window and shining through the curtains, especially when there was a fifty percent chance they would enter and find some bogus reason to cause trouble. It was cold–winter had started to settle in. But Vince thought the decorations made it just a little warmer.

He looked at Tyson, trying to evaluate how he was feeling. Just like before this war, if it could be called that, Vince was trying to be the emotional support, the anchor that his friends could rest their worries on.

Tyson had forced himself to move on to crutches–probably a little earlier than he should have, but there was no convincing him otherwise–and Vince had admired the appreciation in Ty's face as they had watched the woman at the makeshift clinic roll his wheelchair away to someone who needed it more.

Vince watched Nikki's Mom set up a collection of porcelain animals touching noses–an ode to Valentine's Day. She dusted off a pair of penguins making a heart with their beaks and settled them on a puff of cotton resembling snow. Nikki's father replaced a winter painting of otters sliding down a snow bank with a collection of old valentines cards Nikki had made for her parents as a child. After a moment's hesitation, he plopped a pink, sequined hat displaying a silhouette of Cupid on Vince's head.

Vince chuckled and pushed the hat up above his eyes. "Thanks!"

Nikki came in with five cups of cocoa decorated with pastel-colored bumble bees and passed them around. Her parents left to give the teens privacy.

Vince sipped the creamy drink and then looked at Nikki and murmured, "Are you *sure* about this?"

Nikki nodded over her cup, meeting his eyes. Ever since they had seen Jonathan in the Land of Dreams, the idea had sparked in her brain. She had recognized the man that Jonathan had introduced warmly as Peter, the author of the books Josiah had given Jon, and she had used Tyson's laptop once she woke up to do some research.

And there he had been. Peter Malone–a heroic war vet. She recalled her teacher mentioning him once in her AP history class when they'd discussed military heroes from their state. His whole story was there, typed on the website, the whole rescue of a woman named Gracie Knapp. Nikki knew Knapp had been Jonathan's mother's maiden name. And sure enough, at the story's end, there was a happy note about how Gracie had christened Peter her daughter Esther's godfather. Unfortunately, according to information on the website, Peter had suffered a massive cranial hemorrhage and had been moved to a hospital a few counties south of Firestone.

"We need to go find him," Nikki had said, "And make sure he's well protected."

"So, you wanted to do this...tonight?" Tyson asked.

Vince's cocoa suddenly became cold in his stomach. He wanted to take action as much as anyone else, but the other evening while going into town to find food, he had witnessed a huge dog-like Ranker pounce on someone and start eating them alive. He didn't know what the poor person had done or said to warrant such a fate, but without Garrett or Ben or another superior hovering constantly over their shoulders, the monsters seemed to like taking liberties and breaking the rules a little. They wouldn't be avoided easily. Sneaking out of town would be hard and most definitely deadly.

Nikki looked sharply at Tyson, cup shivering halfway to her mouth. She smiled weakly.

"Heck no!" She set her cup on a heart-shaped coaster. "I brought you two here 'cause I got another idea."

Tyson snuggled deeper into the red and pink yarn blanket over his lap. "Goodie."

"Oh, it's simple. Vince, you know a lot of people. I want you to get the word out to avoid taking the sleeping pills the Rankers are giving out–they might not know that it's just to prevent us from having dreams and to keep griffin-hearted people from helping Jonathan. And ask people if they know whether or not the Rankers moved the patients at Peter's hospital anywhere, and if so, where to."

"Okay, will do," Vince said, though he couldn't yet fathom Nikki's plan.

Nikki turned to Tyson next. "Ty, I was wondering if you could post a message on your blog directed at the people of France and Ireland."

Tyson sighed, mystified by his friend's question. He wasn't the only person to have "borrowed" a few battery packs from the local tech store before the Rankers had made the time to destroy it, but there was always a risk in using Kitty's laptop. What if the Rankers had the tech and know-how to track down the real faces behind the fake accounts people were making? Tyson's hacking skills could only take him so far for so long without repercussions.

"I suppose," he answered. "If the Rankers don't catch me and if they still have a working internet over there. Why?"

Nikki proudly raised her chin.

"The two kids traveling with Jonathan, Mariah and Kayle? Right?"

"Right...?"

"They were French and Irish. I recognized their accents. We need to get a message to their home countries, telling them that wherever Kayle and Mariah's bodies are, they need to be protected. Just like the messages you've sent out so far about Jonathan and how the Rankers are looking for griffins."

"I'm on it," Tyson grinned, his fingers clenching and unclenching as if they itched to type.

CHAPTER TWENTY-NINE:

THE GOLDEN GRIFFIN

IN THE CROWDED BAZAAR OF TENCINA-AHRROC

We got some sleep while Amenophis and Manu woke up to reality for a day and then stepped into the crowded bazaar the next morning.

It was time to get some shopping done.

Amenophis took me, Peter, Kayle, and Mariah while Manu remained behind with the Society and the squadron. It was decided that we would be the only five partaking in the heist besides a few disguised backup personnel who would act as servants or waiters.

Being shoved into Kayle once again by some eager-to-get-somewhere busybody made me check that I still had the money and list at my belt. Amenophis told us it was a common technique for pickpockets to use on tourists–bumping innocently into them while taking one of their sparkly possessions.

The Pharaoh's party was the next day, and we all had to hurry up and get our game on. First, we stopped at a stall that sold random tools and homemade items. We got a sturdy basket to hold Pharaoh's cat in when we captured it, and some teeny figurines to study with for the Deity game. Next, we went to an expensive-looking clothing stall and got decked out in some fancy new threads. For the first time ever, I actually looked like royalty in my white, satiny robes. Lastly, we got some food to bring along with us, primarily some oily orange fish pods that Amenophis said every cat in the palace but Pharaoh's despised. Hopefully, they would keep it calm while we had it.

That afternoon we were standing on the steps that led up into an open, columned temple. At either side of the temple sat Setmenrajzda statues, gazing emptily ahead. We stood outside in the shade to take lunch and to wait for the crowds to clear out of the temple a bit. I stretched my neck, craning my head back to look at the chin of one of the massive jackal statues.

"Why did King Brody speak to your father?" I asked Amenophis.

Amenophis looked caught off guard by my random question, but I wanted to hear more about Brody. I wondered if I could ever emulate him as a ruler.

Amenophis thought a bit and then said, "He didn't, really. He entered Father's mind to warn him of a Ranker attack in Cairo. Father's an important official, so if anyone could put a stop to anything that could cause political unrest, it's him. He's also extremely perceptive. Father pieced together on his own what was really going on in the world just based on the dream the King gave him. After that, Father discovered the ability to become a griffin in his dreams, and his dreams started to clarify until he could actually talk to dream creations as lucidly as you and I are talking now. He formed the Society, hoping to join the King's volunteer forces, but then the King died before anyone in the capital even had a chance to summon us, and in the chaos, we had to go underground."

"Where's your dad now? I'd like to meet him." I washed down a mouthful of something really dry and crunchy that the locals considered edible with a gulp of water.

Concern flickered over Amenophis's face. "I don't know. Before the Rankers rose up, he was in Cairo. We haven't heard from each other since. Manu and I fear the worst." He peered within the temple, shading his eyes and perhaps hiding tears. "Looks less crowded now. Come on."

Inside, the walls were covered in paintings displaying the dozen or so animals worshiped in this desert and their associated myths. Amenophis pointed up at the first, and we took off studying 'till my brain hurt. There was Setmenrajzda, worshiped for death and triumph, and Mek-Mhet, the cat of light, and Val-Korr, the falcon of war... The information was endless! I started feeling resentment towards the painted critters for reminding me so much of the minutiae I had to cram into my head before every history test at school. But it took me by surprise when I found out that one of the idols was a griffin.

On the lowest part of the wall, chipped, crumbling, ancient paint faded, a honey-yellow griffin's story was illustrated: healing cripples with his talons, giving food to his followers, standing high above others, wings outstretched, and telling them something that made them dance with joy. He seemed even older than any of the past princes I had seen in the dwarf mountain.

"Guys," I called softly, unable to look away, "Who is this?"

Amenophis approached, his sandals flapping, and kneeled with one arm braced between his knees, the other hand brushing the shadowed stone wall. He made a mournful moaning sound and said, "The Lost Deity... I had forgotten..."

"Say what?"

While Peter and the others joined us, Amenophis told me something that would change my life forever.

"Long ago, everyone worshiped only one God. Here, He was known as the Golden Griffin, creator of the dreamworld, Emperor of Griffinkind. But as time went on, humanity turned from him to worship idols of power, money, and flesh... Things are easier to worship when they are seen, when they can be...brandished. Do you understand what I'm saying?"

I grunted dubiously but couldn't put a finger on the reason why a bitter sort of rage suddenly filled me.

Peter noted my doubt and said, "In reality, Jonathan, the griffin represents Christ in many ways. With our lion blood, we are kings of the earth. But with our eagle blood, we are also rulers of the heavens. It is no coincidence that this is the form brave individuals take in the Land of Dreams. To hold the title of griffin is an honor and responsibility."

I brushed a fingertip against the amber griffin, thinking of Kitty and her unyielding faith. I wondered what she would say if she were there. "But I've never really been religious, so why am I a griffin?"

Peter had an answer for that too. "This isn't about religion, Jonathan. This is about something bigger than all of us and everything, truths that mankind have wrestled with since the dawn of time. Believe in Him or not... He believes in *you*. It's been millennia since He's walked this land, but it bears the mark of His hand still. Though He made it, this is not His kingdom. He's left it for kings and queens who stand for the same ideals that He does; ideals that shape and direct the course of everything in the dreamworld."

I mulled over memories of Kitty singing gentle, comforting hymns to herself on car rides, of the Sunday school stories about love and sacrifice and happy endings that she and Nikki discussed, and the debates she had with Ben about the existence of a Greater Good and an Ultimate Truth. Those memories burst and blistered as my rage returned, smoldering with intensity, contorting into memories of me barely being able to sit in a chair at school after enduring an alcohol-induced belting that had left raised welts on my back; listening to the school nurse tell me a rib was fractured, and then lying that it wasn't because of my drunk father, who had accidentally hit me with a branch while I'd tried to help him make a brushfire, but one of Garrett's goons; a memory of me walking home late from an after-game party and finding myself locked out of the house...not daring to knock on the door and wake up Father, but trudging wearily up to Nikki's and spending the night on her couch.

My lip turned up in a sneer, and I muttered contemptuously, "And? Look at my messed-up family. Look at what happened to you and Mariah and Kayle!" But something halted my words.

It was the pity in Kayle's expression.

"Aye. Our lives were full of suffering, Jonathan, but look at us now!" He gestured in an arc at Peter, standing tall as always with huge arms crossed and a sentimental expression, Mariah with her honest smile and eyes that twinkled ever since Kayle and her had became an item, Amenophis, still crouched on the other side of me, rocking back and forth on his heels.

"You and your Pa are finally beginning a relationship. You have a devoted friend in Nikki and loyal companions. You have an education and popularity. Our suffering didn't damage us, it refined us–it prepared us for facing the truth."

"What truth?" I blinked up at him. He pointed at my sword and the claws at the hilt.

"The truth that there is darkness in this world; true, tangible evil to destroy. The truth that we were chosen to recognize its forms so as to fight it. And the truth that you've been given exceptional strength to carry out the will of the Golden Griffin."

"What does this whole Ranker mess have to do with Him?" I asked, astonished.

Peter chuckled tenderly.

"He wants them gone just as much as we do. Rankers go against everything He stands for–everything *we* stand for: peace, harmony, redemption..."

I looked at the Golden Griffin on the wall, my brain arguing with itself over whether to believe the nice things I had heard or to continue to live in agnostic carelessness. Of course, seeing as I was in a land of dreams about to pull a heist on a Pharaoh and could turn into a griffin at will, the list of things to discard as fairy tales was shortening fast.

"Everyone believes in something bigger, something great," Mariah said softly. "And, well... He's as big and great as it gets."

A tough seed shell in my heart cracked, and a fresh tendril of curiosity and longing writhed out. I knew that this wasn't everything–I knew there were commandments to observe and faith I had to start trusting in, but I was, tentatively, ready. I wanted to be one of those happy people painted on the wall. I wanted some of His light. I wanted peace and hope.

Do you feel brave, little griffin?

The gargoyle Ranker's words floated back to me from the Reekwood Swamp. I wanted the kind of bravery that he had taunted me about–to live my life so passionately, bravely, and wisely that even death lost its sting.

CHAPTER THIRTY:

SOME RISKY BUSINESS

The next night, we all had butterflies.

Peter had let us sleep in so that we would be well-rested for the party. Mariah set the fish pods in the basket and then overlaid them with gifts for the Pharaoh and his Lady: bouquets of rich-colored flowers, beaded scarves, a jade ring–and it had taken the Society since before I'd arrived to barter some silk and a sheet of stained glass.

The desert people loved new things. Trading–export–was a major part of their lives and making everyday necessities out of sturdier, glitzy, new material was a hobby of theirs; thus, the silk and glass. We had to get on the Pharaoh's good side and to do that, we had to bring the best gifts. So we added a golden sphinx figurine (the Tencina-Ahrroc people's symbol for royalty) and...chocolate. Gooey, warm, milky chocolate. One of the Society members had made it himself. As I wrapped the treat in some wax paper, I knew we had it in the bag.

I re-read my mother's letter (though I knew it by heart now) and slipped it into my sword sheath. We weren't supposed to seem threatening at the party, but we weren't stupid enough to go unarmed either.

I placed my crown and looked myself over. I was fetching. At least for a wealthy Tencinian businessman. I wore a knee-length tunic with leather sandals, the crisscrossing straps of which ran up to the hem of the tunic. I wore a light, deep-blue hood that cinched at the neck with a pendant shaped like a scorpion. The blue of my hood faded into brighter and more pronounced colors the farther it got to the hem: blue to green to yellow to orange and finally to a hot melon-red. It was supposed to psychologically remind one of sunrises, i.e., new beginnings, i.e., business opportunities, i.e., a discussion with the interested Pharaoh.

Kayle had gold wrist cuffs; one hid his lighter. He wore a fierce bronze mask that only covered his forehead and ringed his eyes, and his deep-red tunic was more of a toga that draped in dozens of eye-teasing folds over his buff frame.

Mariah was stunning in a black dress sparkling with diamond shards. A blue and silver ornament, painted with an image of the ever-important papyrus plant, covered her bun.

Amenophis wore the same outfit from when we'd fought at the café, and Peter wore a black hooded cape over an iridescent, scaled shirt and loose white leggings.

"You ready?" Mariah asked me, wiping her hands in anxious, jerky strokes down her thighs until Kayle took them and kissed them.

"Yeeeeaaaaa-no," I admitted.

Mariah came over and fiddled with my coral necklace, pulling it down so that it was snugger around my neck.

"Here," she handed me a small, violet drawstring bag. "In case the Pharaoh seems to have lost his own."

Within rested the small, glazed figurine of a Dominant Deity game-piece.

"The Golden Griffin," I said, running my thumb over its painted details. It had gentle eyes, feathers the color of sunlit honey, and brilliant, gleaming-yellow, half-open wings.

"He'll give us strength tonight," Mariah assured me.

"I hope so," I replied, thinking of Kitty and her special brand of fearlessness. My fingers curled over the small figure. "Heaven knows we'll need it."

AT THE PHARAOH'S PALACE

Flaherty, nondescript in his servant's garms, lugged the basket of gifts up alabaster stairs broad enough to fit a couple of football fields across them. I and the others moved ahead of him, merging with excitedly conversing guests and warily approaching a vast, lit doorway. Two behemoth-sized guards gazed stonily at everyone coming in. I tried to look unconcerned and bored and passed into a vast throne room without incident.

The floor was made of more cold, white alabaster shot with blue-gray veins, and reflected everything into an upside-down world. Columns of sculpted deities flushed of color and made of soft, white marble wrapped in different-colored tapestries separated tables piled with food from the rest of the room. The room echoed with thousands of conversations. A long red rug ran the room's length–ending at a short rectangle of stairs that led up to three thrones. Candles flickered all over the place–chasing off any hopeful shadows. I found that ironic.

The others and I slowly followed a procession of new guests toward the thrones. In no time at all, we were staring up, eye to eye, with the young Pharaoh. He occupied the more ornate central throne, staring down his nose at us. He had a black beard on the tip of his chin and long, thin, black lines that swept from the corners of his black eyes to his ears. He wore the typical, trendy Tencinian headdress with twin tassels that rested on his chest. A kid that I could only guess to be Pharaoh Junior (though his papa was, like, *my* age) slumped deeply in the smallest throne, flipping his one lock of hair back and forth across his face. A pretty, snooty lookin' chick I assumed was the wife occupied the last throne. Her eyes kept flitting from us to the basket of goodies with greed. A jackal puppy snoozed in her lap.

A cloaked figure just beyond the kid's throne shifted, and I glanced at him. He and his likewise-cloaked companion, standing just behind him, were dressed in such dark colors that they could have been a shadow that even the hundreds of candles couldn't penetrate. Rankers.

Mariah sucked in her breath and touched Kayle's arm. Kayle had gone rigid–staring straight ahead. Amenophis glanced back at expressionless Marcus, and Peter's breathing sped up. One of the Rankers slowly turned and tilted its head at us. It reached up and pulled its hood back. The other Ranker did the same.

Garrett scrutinized our party with something like arrogance or derision. I didn't recognize the dashing fellow beside him–he was unnaturally charming like he could replace Tyson as my best buddy. But he also sent out weird vibes that gave me chills and made me want to hide somewhere.

I fought off a shiver. *Garrett.* The last time I'd seen those green shark-eyes, that earring with the ruby stud, had been when he stuck a knife in my back...the day I first arrived in the Land of Dreams.

My hood mercifully hid my necklace–if Garrett knew the gargoyle Ranker was dead, then he may have heard a description of the necklace by now, and who knew if the enchantment in the dwarven crown included accessories?

Garrett's brow twitched. He looked at us more full-on. The dude beside him retained his genteel mien, but he too was obviously more aware of us. Flaherty kept his head and set the basket heavy with gifts down on the floor in front of me.

I spread my arms over the loot and proclaimed in my best upper-crust voice, "Greetings to the royal family. We come from distant...distant lands bearing peaceful tidings and gifts. May they satisfy you, and may my company and I please you."

Mariah and Kayle displayed the gifts one by one. After observing them with trained eyes, the Pharaoh passed them around to his family. We saved the chocolate for last, and Flaherty took the now-empty (except for the fish pods) basket. The Pharaoh had his high priests scour the food for any detection of poisons. After the third minute during which one of the pudgy priests held a crumb millimeters from his eye, Garrett made a throaty growling sound and said in a voice full of barely concealed contempt, "It is chocolate, your Highness. I assure you it is quite safe." The Pharaoh sent Garrett a permissive look and took the candy.

It was then that I knew we had lost the Pharaoh. He, Garrett, and the creepy, cold-vibe Ranker at Garrett's flank, were a team. Tencina-Ahrroc belonged to the Rankers.

Pharaoh bit into the chocolate, and his eyes rolled back a bit. He shared half-heartedly with his equally satisfied family.

"This is very nice," the Pharaoh cracked a warm smile. "You are welcome here tonight."

We bowed low, and I murmured thanks. Taking my eyes off Garrett long enough to perform a respectful dip of the head didn't agree with me.

"And have you come only to be frivolous and enjoy the grace of my kingdom?" The Pharaoh asked, looking like what he really wanted was a recipe for chocolate.

"Actually, your Exquisiteness, I would like to discuss business," I said.

The Pharaoh's wife looked eagerly at her husband. He sharply stared her down into submission but then chuckled at me and said slyly, "Perhaps over a game of Dominant Deity? My pleasure...?"

Score.

"I anticipate it, your Stupendousness." I smiled back, ignoring the subtle, scolding nudge that Kayle put in my side, telling me without words to quit playing with honorifics.

Our identities still unknown by the Rankers, we stepped away and moseyed over to the buffet tables, splitting up to look unobtrusively for the cat in case we could nab it before even having to risk betting on winning the game. Mariah had tagged along with me, and Kayle trailed after her, making a bee-line when the scent of spiced venison hooked his nose.

I took a pure-gold plate and twirled it in my hands, making it throw out spinning circles of light. Mariah danced at my elbow, and I was beginning to feel like a parent with a kid that urgently needed to go to the restroom. I put some salads and meats on my plate and balanced it on one hand, leaning against a wall. Taking a bite of roast pheasant, I watched Mariah anxiously bite her lip. I looked down at my food, at a loss as to what she wanted, and held out my pheasant leg.

"Want some?"

She blinked and blurted under her breath, "Garrett's already here! This changes everything!"

I swallowed my meat. "Well, yeah, he's always been a party crasher, but he doesn't recognize us. We can go on as planned."

Mariah shook her head.

"No, no! Nobody has used the Lost Deity figurine in anything since Setmenrajzda! If Garrett sees you playing the game with one, our cover could be annihilated!"

Startled by her conclusion, I started to hand her the little drawstring pouch housing my griffin play-piece.

Relieved at my compliance, she reached for it, murmuring, "Garrett and Donovan are very keen. They would have been able to put two and two together soon enough."

My hand stopped moving of its own accord. That name had hit my ears funny and now I was trying to match it to a face.

"Who?" I asked.

Mariah tugged at the pouch once, realized I wasn't letting go, and frowned. "What do you mean?"

"What's that other guy's name?"

"Donovan."

Hot acid bubbled up my veins, turning on a cauldron in my stomach and making my hands shake. I could almost *feel* my irises turning red with Griffin-rage. In a sizzling undertone, one hand white-knuckled around my sword pommel, I snarled, "That's the guy who *bit* Ben and tried to attack...Nikki?"

"Yes," Mariah squeaked in a small voice, anticipating my next moves and standing like a shield in front of me. I burned mad, so hot-flushed with fury that I probably could have surpassed Kayle in manipulating fire right then.

"Let me have it," Mariah said smoothly, once more trying to get the figurine. I held it tighter.

"No."

"*Jonathan*!"

"I'm tired of hiding," I said fiercely, my voice quivering. "It's like Kayle said; Griffins need a cause. I have to stand for something, or I'm not worth anything. So that's what I'll do. I'll stand for my friends, for my supporters, for my kingdom–for what I believe in. And that is anything that the Rankers hate." *I don't know if I'm ready to believe in a Golden Griffin yet. But perhaps there* is *a reason and a purpose for everything that's happened, good and bad. Maybe I really* can *change things.* I looked at the pouch, speaking to the piece inside of it. "I guess me and You are together from here on out, Big Guy."

Mariah still shifted her weight, fidgeting on the spot, worried.

"It's okay," I comforted her, reading the distress in her head and feeling it thunder tensely against my mind. "If we just keep our poker faces, we'll be fine."

CHAPTER THIRTY-ONE:

PLAYING GAMES WITH A PHARAOH

It was literally game on. After an hour or so, after we'd made small talk with other guests and ate and exchanged secretive looks with one another, Pharaoh had a trumpet blown, and everyone looked to where a table and two chairs were being set in the room's center. Pharaoh strode regally over and sat in the chair that was a bit taller than the other. He cradled a small basket in his lap, and I knew it was the Dominant Deity game prize: the cat that would open the tomb and reveal to us whatever the Rankers had secreted away inside.

Pharaoh announced, "It is time for any to test their ruler's wit at his own game! Who thinks themself brave enough? Let them step forward!"

I could hear the overflowing confidence in his tone. Silently, I slipped through the muttering, parting crowd, listening to the ongoing boasts of the young desert ruler. Finally, I made it to the table. The Pharaoh sized me up, recognized me, and smiled cruelly.

"My friend! I was hoping you would come!"

I just gave a weak twitch of the mouth and looked at the game, studying it. I barely felt one of the burly guards pull back my chair, push me into it, and scoot me in. I hardly saw Garrett and Donovan swoop in on either side to flank the Pharaoh. They looked at me with boredom as if I were a common dandelion.

The game board was made up of ornate, painted tiles. The tiles were built into a square depression with side flaps that acted as a lid and opened out to form two smaller, shallower panels. The right panel resembled a chessboard. Painted porcelain animals were strapped into the left panel. Beside them were the game cards, each with gold-tipped corners, and the die. Without pause, Pharaoh reached forward and unstrapped a little jet-black jackal–sculpted to sit imposingly erect and powerful. He set the Setmenrajzda on the red tile at my right corner of the board where we were supposed to start. I scoured the pieces for a griffin, but as we had all expected, there were none. That would make what I was about to do even more important...and risky.

I pulled up my drawstring pouch. Opened it. One of the guards came menacingly up behind me, but I deposited the Golden Griffin into my palm, dropped the empty pouch, and set it beside the jackal.

The Rankers leaned forward, hissing. Even perfect-patooty Donovan seemed a bit put-out. The Pharaoh and his family were all shocked. The crowd gasped and shifted. I tried to stolidly meet Pharaoh's eyes while at the same time ignoring the two Rankers leaning in to search my face closer.

"V-very...odd, uh, choice, young master," the Pharaoh said, composing himself. "I trust, though, that you know the Lost Deity is no longer..."

"I know," I said and smiled, throwing him off again. He had a choice to make: play or throw me out of the game and look like a petty fool.

"Very well. It is unorthodox and archaic, but I will allow it to slide," he sniffed. He shook the die and rolled it across the chessboard. Everyone got closer. The game began.

The questions were a little one-sided at my expense. They all had to do with Tencinian history or deities or royalty. I was perspiring Niagara Falls by the time I collected my first game token.

"Ah, the brazen Ankh of Everlasting Life," scoffed Pharaoh as I set the minute gold cross onto my tray. "Not as impressive as my Ceremonial Death Mask, I fear."

"Death is only a beginning," I mumbled, old words floating annoyingly through my skull.

Are you brave, little griffin?

One of the questions I asked Pharaoh from a trivia card was how many people he had thought I'd killed. He said none. Without thinking, I shook my head.

"Really?" Since he got the answer wrong he didn't get to move, but he wasn't upset. He interlaced his fingers and leaned forward, raising his eyebrows. "How many?"

"Well, not exactly *people*, per se," I blundered, watching Garrett frown, his black eyebrows like incoming storm clouds. "More like... One... Two monsters and a bird."

"What is a businessman like you doing hunting big game?" the Pharaoh asked suspiciously.

"All work and no play makes Jack a dull Pharaoh," I said, flashing one of my most charming smiles. Pharaoh cocked his head, as though confused by the saying, but frowned, shook his head as if to get rid of a fly, and we moved on.

Pharaoh was three spaces ahead of me. I was an unlucky roller and still in last place by the time we hit what looked like the chessboard. This part of the game was, in fact, a lot like chess, but with fewer pieces and more complicated moves. The Pharaoh took out my pieces left and right. My figurine's half-splayed wings no longer made it look as if eager for a victory but instead ready to fly away and escape. The room had compressed into a sphere of heat and voices and jeering. I felt the pressure on me like cinder blocks were digging into my shoulders. I was losing breath. All I knew was the flash of Pharaoh's laughing teeth. The loud hum of the crowd. Garrett staring down at the chessboard.

The Ranker's chest swelled with a strong breath, and his eyes zeroed in on my griffin. His hands twitched.

I followed his gaze. What had he seen?

My griffin was just a move away from the Pharaoh's jackal.

My senses returned, and I dared to hope. I dragged my piece along, its talons squeaking against the polished tiles.

"Submit," I said. I don't know how it happened. The Pharaoh stopped laughing and moved his jackal one space away in the traditional maneuver of a king. I moved around, swooping to ring his right side, detecting a pattern in my favor. "Submit," I said, more strongly. The room fell silent. This time, the jackal moved into a right dodge, but the griffin advanced. Ever nearer. Ever inescapable. My spirits fluttered. I dared to say the magic words, smug, triumphant. "Submit. To the Dominant Deity."

The Pharaoh summed up his moves, and I saw in his face the moment he realized that none were beyond my reach and that he could no longer evade, but only avoid temporarily what was an inevitable outcome. His wife went pale. His son put a finger in his mouth and made a comical baby-gibberish noise that made his father flinch. Donovan, now more preoccupied than dazzling, scanned faces in the crowd.

"Impossible. I have never lost before," the Pharaoh said in a daze. His shoulders were limp. Garrett locked eyes with me, and he squinted shrewdly.

"Well, *I* have never played against such a worthy opponent, sir," I said truthfully, watching the basket clenched tightly in his hands. He glared hotly at me.

Nervously, I registered the uncomfortable mutters of the crowd and asked, "Perhaps now is proper to discuss business?"

The Pharaoh swept the game to the floor where it shattered, and he stood with such velocity that he knocked over his chair. Red in the face and spitting, the young ruler roared, "You are not here to talk about enterprises! You are here to make a fool of me!" He ripped the top off the basket and yanked out an apple-sized brownish-red kitten. It mewled in protest, screwing up its green eyes. The Pharaoh waved it in front of me and growled, "You are not worthy of my prized feline's brood, foreign filth!"

I staggered out of my seat. That was the prize? A purebred kitten? Our guesses had been wrong all along. The prize was a bust, and now the Pharaoh was ticked, and there was nowhere to run.

"Take him!" the Pharaoh bellowed. The crowd boiled in a frenzy. A muscle-clad guard grabbed my hood, which twisted my crown so that it tilted down to my ear. But then Marcus burst from between a young couple frantically waving their hands. Looking for all the world like an ancient, heroic Spartan, Marcus viciously backhanded the guard, sending him sprawling.

I reset my crown, looking for a face I knew. Peter beckoned to me over everyone's heads. I fought to get to him. He grabbed my wrist and dragged me the rest of the way to his side, making me ricochet off running bodies like a pinball.

"We have to find the cat we're looking for and run!" Peter managed to somehow shout quietly.

We sprinted out of the chaotic throne room through an archway and followed the curving hall in a spiral that gradually descended. Slipping and skidding zanily around the dwindling turn, we came out into a well-tended courtyard full of bountiful fruit trees and fountains and pools and plants. It was way too orderly compared to the overgrown garden in the Reekwood Swamp.

Peter and I turned the heads of worried gardeners as we sprinted down a path that divided the open courtyard into two halves. We jumped up the stairs of a building with two cat statues flanking the doorway, exchanging looks. I wished I could transform—have the assurance that nothing could stand before my talons and sinew and not break.

The cat temple broke into chambers, and the loud sounds of meowing felines led us to the last and largest room, which had an open ceiling and was filled with shrubbery, trees, and half-eaten sparrows and rodents.

Our jaws dropped, and our breath left our lungs like expelled air from blown tires. Hundreds of cats wandered before us, fighting, climbing, eating, sleeping, and going off into darker corners to multiply and add to the multitude of frolicking kittens wrestling playfully under the eye of a pair of frazzled-looking servants that bustled about tending to the felines and paid us no mind.

"*Which one*?" I shouted uselessly, making a nearby trio of cats arch their spines and bounce away. Flaherty appeared beside us, not even breathing heavily. He held out a fish pod.

"Here."

"Your timing is something to admire, kid," Peter chuckled, relieved. "I must say."

"Ditto," I said breathlessly. I set the oily liver-shaped thing down on the grass. A few cats warily approached to sniff and lick the fish, but then they would shake their muzzles and slink away. I kept turning to look behind us to ensure we hadn't yet been found. Marcus and the few other Society members we had taken with us to the party joined us gradually–after being driven outside by the panicked crowd they'd had to sneak their way back in. Amenophis bore a cut nose from a violent brush with a frantic partygoer who "had way too many rings."

Finally, a russet-colored tom strolled leisurely over to the drying fish pod. It had smokey-black ears and legs and a white-tipped tail. Like the other cats, it was long-limbed and skinny with a small round head, large ears, and green eyes. But it had rings in its ears and a collar around its neck that you would more likely see on display in a museum. It reclined and started nibbling at the fish. Marcus swooped in and carefully but quickly shoved the cat into our basket, where it yowled piercingly and started beating at the sides from within. As we rushed back through the courtyard and into the hall, the tom realized it wasn't getting out anytime soon and started to tear away the wax paper we had used to separate the Pharaoh's gifts from the fish pods. The sound of resigned munching became a backdrop to the loud slaps of our anxious footsteps.

We turned right and ran down this new hall opposite from the way we'd arrived. The sounds of an army of clicking metal and shouted orders followed us as we ran. Mariah caught up to us, red and sweaty. Kayle was still missing.

We burst into a round, spacious room with black marble walls and small doors at its opposite curve that led to the back alleys and into the acres of royal desert. Cutting off our chances of a straight sprint to freedom was a huge bonfire set up in a gold grate in the room's middle. Animal bones (at least I *hoped* they were animal) and pale ashes spilled in a dusty radius around the crackling flames that reached almost to the ceiling. Robed priests had halted on their way to the fire, dragging a bull on a rope behind them for a sacrifice.

"Stop them!" a guard behind us shouted, and without even a questioning tilt of the old, bald head, the priests surrounded us. We all drew our weapons. I pointed my sword tip at the bobbing Adam's apple of one of the priests.

"Unwise choice, friend," a commanding voice that could only belong to Pharaoh called disdainfully.

Mariah gasped and moaned in one breath. I glanced over my shoulder. One of the Pharaoh's burly guards had Kayle by the hair and held the edge of a sword to his neck. The blade had cut Kayle's flesh, and blood wept from various thin slices. His mouth was red with blood. His nostrils flared with each breath. And yet, he smiled in defiance. Kayle's captor twisted his arm hard behind him, and he grunted in pain, snarling something in Gaelic. Mariah stepped forward, and a griffin's growl gurgled up from her chest, her fingers tucking in to make fists. I could tell she wanted to transform terribly, but we couldn't know if Garrett or Donovan were nearby and *really* risk blowing our covers.

Pharaoh looked over at us through narrow eyes gleaming with victory.

"Give me my cat," he said. "I know what you wish to use him for, but you will find more than treasure in the secret tunnels of my father's pyramid. Why risk your lives by tempting fate? Or me? Give me my feline, and you will live."

Marcus dug his fingers deeper into the basket's wickerwork and turned partially away. Pharaoh stepped forward into a half-crouch and bared his teeth.

"You do not know who you are fooling with!"

The sacrificial bonfire roared in front of me, beyond the priest blocking my path who was looking like he desperately wanted a raise. I looked from those flickering flames back to Kayle. He caught my eye, his crimson-smeared grin widened, and he gave me a slow nod.

"*Oh,*" I said to myself. Mariah, then Peter, and the others glanced at me, then at the fire. Knowing flared to life in their eyes.

"You don't know who *you're* fooling with," I called back to the Pharaoh. "I'd let that kid go if I were you."

Pharaoh tossed Kayle a wary glance, confused about the implied warning in my voice.

"He's powerful," Mariah cautioned.

"He holds a mean grudge," Peter added.

"And," I grinned, "He *really* likes fire."

Kayle hooked his leg back around the guard's and tripped him to one side. He shook the man off, ran at the bonfire, around the priests trying to reach out and snatch him, and dove straight into the billowing, gusting flames.

"Oh!" one of Pharaoh's men gasped and then looked at us to gauge our reactions. We were all trying to stop beaming and look like hard asses.

A shock wave of blue-green liquid fire rolled up the bonfire. Then, unexpectedly, even to us good guys, a giant human foot and leg composed of a column of dancing flame stepped out from the fire and onto the floor; then hips swathed in a constantly swirling coalition of ash and fire. The muscled torso burned red–dancing–always shifting–and two arms crossed in front of the chest, fists closed against opposite shoulders. But most eerie was the jackal head, a skull of black smoke with eyes that pulsed scarlet like a heartbeat.

Stretching as if newly awakened, Kayle/Setmenrajzda focused on the shuddering Pharaoh and roared. It was an unsettling, echoing, howling bellow that made Mariah and me fidget uncomfortably. The Pharaoh squealed and turned tail, taking his guards and priests with him.

Kayle looked down at us with his massive, black dog-head.

"Go!" he said. "I can't hold this much longer!"

We didn't have to be told twice. We high-tailed it away and into the desert.

CHAPTER THIRTY-TWO:

FALLING FOR A TRICK

"In the pyramid," Amenophis said, "There is rumored to be a beast that guards Pharaoh's treasures–most important of which is an all-telling scroll bearing a riddle. A riddle that unlocks the beginning of the end of the Griffin-King prophecy."

"Ah, yes, the unfathomable prophecy," I said, not bothering to keep the wry tone out of my voice.

"Of course–everyone is at least a part of some prophecy or other," Amenophis said with a dismissive wave of his hand. "But these are rumors we have accumulated over the years. Who knows what truly resides within? Whatever it is, it was placed there in King Brody's time for Ranker allies to find. They've been planning this for a while."

I had shared the prophecy with Kayle, Peter, and Mariah on our travels and all of them had exhibited a mix of surprise and dismissiveness. They had all thought that the prophecy had referred to Brody and had died with him. Mariah had been the most concerned, wondering why the Master had brought it up now, wondering what the implications were if the prophecy truly referred to me. Still, Kayle had retained his stubborn disinterest.

"Where I come from," he grumbled, "you make your own destiny."

"Well, that's not entirely true," Amenophis argued, his tone as mild as if they were disagreeing over whether the pyramid was made of limestone or sandstone. "You cannot stop rain or storm by willing it so. But you can prepare against it and choose how to adapt."

I chewed on that as we made our way slowly through a musty tunnel with Kayle leading us, bathing our travel with firelight that wavered like it was about to go out. He was still weak from the stunt he'd pulled with the bonfire but trying not to show it.

We had been unhindered on our scamper through the section of royal desert that yawned toward three distant pyramids. The largest one was the one we had entered, through a doorway the Scarab Society had once bashed out of a section of old mud blocks.

"So there's a beast in this pyramid? Who'd a thunk?" *Maybe this monster is like the chimera–maybe it was going to give power to the Ranker allies somehow.* I breathed thickly and tried not to taste the dusty air, constantly reminded by it that tons of mummies of Pharaoh's ancestors were rotting away behind the thick walls around us.

Amenophis replied in a haunting voice, "Yes–a monster that guards the bodies of the royal lineage. It was called forth from the dark realms at the dawn of your prophecy–in anticipation of Griffin Prince Blood to quench its thirst and plunge the world into oblivion."

We were all quiet. The air seemed suddenly colder. I was finding it hard to swallow all of a sudden, like my throat had seized up.

"Sounds great, but I'll wait for the reviews," Flaherty grunted, losing his balance on a brick. Mariah chuckled, hand-in-hand with Kayle.

We stopped at the end of the twisting cavern, grouped into a box-alley. But at chest level to our left, Amenophis indicated a dirt-covered indentation that could have fit a small paw. I touched the mark. It felt like smooth clay. Marcus lifted the lid of the basket slowly. Kayle suspended the ball of fire over his head so that we could see the royal cat's sleeping form within, its stomach distended with fish pods. Gently, Mariah lifted the feline out. It stretched sleepily in her grasp and opened its large eyes, gazing around with docile curiosity. Mariah lifted one of the tom's paws and pressed it into the indented paw print.

A loud, echoing mechanism ratcheted around behind the wall, and something fell into place. Mariah dropped the cat when it squirmed frantically and scratched her hand. It raced away down the tunnel, and the ground beneath us caved inward into a ramp that sent us all sliding, yelling and reaching for a hold, into shadows.

My back slammed against a sandy chute, and by the time I hit it, I was already sliding away steeply. It was like a roller-coaster without a harness–almost straight down. I couldn't see but for random flickers of light that had to be Kayle's fire somewhere below or above me. Everyone screamed and flailed. I was thrown into a turn, and my velocity slammed me against one side of my chute–ripping into my shoulder and burning against my face and hip. Kayle's fire vanished behind what I guessed was a partition or a wall. It blinked when he zoomed past, briefly revealing gaping sections of the crumbling walls and supports that held us up. I came to the distant conclusion that we had all branched into different slides. We had fallen into an intricate but ancient trap.

Kayle arced overhead, yelling. His fire lit the area around me. For a split second, I saw Peter on his side in a chute, about to pass beneath me. We reached for each other. Our fingers touched. But then I fell into empty air. I twisted and writhed into nothingness–searching for a foothold that didn't exist, waiting to hit a rack of spikes or a vat of acid. Just when I struggled to gather my thoughts and transform so that I could at least float to the ground, I smashed into cold, hard dirt. Something in my back cracked loudly, flooding me with a burning, electric alarm of pain–and then I didn't feel anything.

CHAPTER THIRTY-THREE:

MEANWHILE, IN PHARAOH'S PRIVATE CHAMBERS

"You are positive that you saw him enter my family's pyramid?"

The Pharaoh was sheathed in a nervous sweat. He sat on a chair carved so that it seemed he was sitting in the lap of a jackal. Garrett and Donovan, still in human guises, stood before him. One, the blood-sucker, was staring into space somewhere near Pharaoh's knee, running a thumb up one of his pearly canines. Garrett had his hands in his robe pockets in the manner of any typical teenage boy, except that he hissed on every exhale like a snake, part angry and part excited.

"Yes. We watched him and his party flee off into the dunes. Your cat returned to us not moments ago with blood on its claws that Donovan identified as belonging to a French female–a companion of Prince Jonathan. A griffin."

Pharaoh launched to his feet as if zapped by lightning.

"Setmenrajzda's black heart! You tell me that the boy who challenged me is the *Great Prince*?"

Donovan laughed derisively. Garrett explained. He was as enthusiastic as a scientist who had discovered a new butterfly species...and wanted to pin it dead beneath a glass case.

"In the melee of your throne room, just after the game, a guard jostled the boy, and his crown slipped to one side. It was as if, in that instant, I was seeing two faces–one a transparent mask suspended over another, more familiar one."

"He was disguised?" the Pharaoh asked, shocked.

Garrett grinned maliciously.

"His cloaking power is centered around that crown–no doubt dwarf-made. Where before he seemed an average, albeit wealthy, young man, he changed drastically. His short brown hair became lighter and longer. His brown eyes became blue. His pale, round face was tanned–sunburned even–with a sharper chin and prouder nose. Before he was whisked away into the crowd, I knew I had seen the Griffin Prince."

Garrett spun on the spot, carelessly examining a decorative urn, turning it in his hand like it was a jar of pickles and making the Pharaoh fret. "He's gotten further than I would have expected. And if his ability is indeed mind-reading, as the Liege Master says, then he will become formidable indeed..." Garrett sounded more excited than worried, and there was a sly, perhaps even proud, glimmer in his holly-green eyes.

The Pharaoh cringed away like a kicked dog.

"He mustn't steal from me! The ultimate disgrace will be if the boy robs me! A Pharaoh!"

"You remember the legends," Donovan said calmly. "There is a beast that dwells in those catacombs." He looked at Garrett and chuckled as he said, "It will slaughter his friends like ants!"

Pharaoh let them laugh while he calmed his nerves, but asked, "What about the prince? Will it not slay him as well?"

"No." Garrett smiled in a murderous way. "It has been told that the Prince's blood is taboo. If anyone gets to spill his *precious* blood, it will be me."

Donovan grasped his superior's arm and said in an eager undertone, "He will lead his friends into the chamber of the monster. Seconds before it attacks, he will read its thoughts and escape it in time to watch his comrades die."

Pharaoh was halfway smiling now. "Then what are you going to do?"

Donovan laughed harshly. "Then he will come to us. Eventually."

"No," Garrett objected. The others looked at him. He had his hands clasped at his chest as if an idea had just come into his head. His eyes were wild and hungry; his body hunched over an invisible victim. He stared down at his feet into an invisible face. "*We* will go to *him*. We will destroy the prince. His stability has already begun to chip away, even if he doesn't know it yet." In a voice directed more at himself, he said, "Soon... I can watch that light dwindle from his eyes–white with terror–and relish the crumbling of his resistance.

"It is people like him." He was louder now, moving towards the doorway that led outside. "Children like him that influence the world. Every child is born with a spark inside them. As they age, the spark grows brighter or dimmer or stronger or hotter depending on what sort of kindling is added. They are instinctively rebellious in their teenage years. The griffins inside them are spreading their wings–making themselves known and heard. At this age, they are most dangerous; because people listen to them! People know that the future rests on these young shoulders!"

Garrett whipped about in the doorway, and the Pharaoh and Donovan, following close to listen to his ranting, almost ran into him. He jabbed himself forcefully in the chest with a thumb. "But then comes *our* chance! Because every teenager has to win or lose a war at this stage in life. A war with the world. If this war is lost, then the griffin in the teenager will die. If the war is won...then the person is a threat to us. The prince is the sort of human that we must destroy. He is one of the rare brats that will not only win his world battle but help others win theirs! Can you imagine how valuable that power would be if *we* could harness it? If *we* controlled it? That is why I want his blood on my hands. I want that spark of his to be extinguished."

Cherry-red points of light glowed from deep within Garrett's pupils. "I'm going to take the initiative and strike a blow. It will break Jonathan enough to make him more malleable for us tonight."

As if suspecting what Garrett meant, Donovan's eyes gleamed, and spots of color flushed his cheeks. "The Liege Master has permitted it?" he asked.

Garrett gave him a crooked grin. "I will kill each of Jonathan's friends this night–except for Nikki. We must have at least one survivor that Ben can follow to Jonathan's body and other griffin supporters in reality. And then I must hear Ben's latest report." He grunted and frowned, clearly frustrated that he was going to miss out on the fun. "Take care of this, Donovan. Keep them from taking the final clue. Kill the griffins except for Jonathan and join me when it is done."

Garrett whirled around and departed, followed by Donovan, who was oddly silenced by his commander's speech. The Pharaoh stayed put.

He had started to develop an unnerving feeling toward the griffin-boy ever since he had been beaten at his own game; Garrett's unintentionally complimentary words toward Jonathan had strengthened that feeling, and Pharaoh now recognized it to be respect.

"You are not remorseful, I hope?" Donovan reappeared, stone-faced.

"No!" Pharaoh snapped. He wasn't foolish.

Donovan narrowed his eyes.

"Then come along."

CHAPTER THIRTY-FOUR:

THE PAIN OF DEATH

"Help!" I yelled, my voice pitched with terror.

Tears squeezed from the corners of my eyes. My breath came in shuddering gasps. I was more in shock and afraid than in pain because I couldn't feel or move most of my body. I couldn't even transform.

I heard a rustling whoosh of wings and smelled a gust of perfumed air. Mariah. At least one of us had had the right state of mind and transformed in time.

"Jonathan," she murmured. Her beak clicked by my ear.

"Mar-Mariah," I sobbed brokenly. "I can't–can't... H-help–me..."

"Sshhh," she soothed. She rolled me over gently, and something shifted awkwardly beneath the skin near the top of my back where I could still feel.

Kayle's voice came from somewhere across the ground in the darkness.

"Need help?"

"Broken back. Severed clean in two at the thoracic vertebrae. I got it," Mariah said. I choked on the dirt.

"Well, me next," Kayle said lightly. "And I'm pretty sure Flaherty's ribs are in a bad way."

"No," I moaned then, feeling Mariah's scaly talon press against my lower neck. Her claws were needle-sharp at my skin. "Help them first."

"Shut up," Mariah ordered. I bit my lip, listened uncomfortably to my broken bones grind into place and lock, and heard the wet sound of painfully re-massing muscles and tendons. Finally, the nerves finished connecting, and I stood up, sniffling. Before I could thank her, Mariah rushed on to the others groaning their anguish around us.

It took us a few hours to recuperate, but after we'd rested a bit and nibbled on the rations we'd bought in the market the previous day, we all felt spectacular and showered Mariah with thanks. It had been a close call–too close. If Mariah hadn't been there to save us with her griffin ability...the war would've been over before we'd had a chance to make our mark.

Peter pointed up at the cavern ceiling. Our griffin eyes had adjusted quickly, and I could see the holes the size of soccer balls far above that we had fallen from.

"I suspect it was a booby trap that only Pharaoh and select others knew how to avoid," Peter said. "This must be an antechamber." He turned to face a back wall where crude steps led up somewhere. "And *that* is our destination."

"What if we–" I started to say, but someone said, "Oh, Jon..." It was a sad voice.

"Huh?" I looked at Mariah, whom I thought had spoken. She stared past me. I turned, and there was the gleaming white dream-Nikki, foremost to a mass of more dreamers.

"Nikki!" I ran to her and wrapped my arms around her. She remained limp in my grasp, but I was too ecstatic to see her to wonder why. Tyson stood slumped behind her on crutches. "Hey, man! Look at you! Walking already!"

I waited for him to shoot somethin' back, but he was quiet, swaying side to side. I took in his face. He had wept recently. His eyes were puffy, and his lips trembled. In fact, all my friends looked about the same way–and as if on top of their sadness, they had been in fights with bulldozers.

"What's going on?" I asked.

Nikki pulled me in close.

"Oh, Jonathan..."

I cradled her, filled with dread.

Her next words made me feel like my backbone had re-broken and pierced my heart.

"Jon... Vince is dead."

CHAPTER THIRTY-FIVE:

WAR IS HELL

AT THE WOLFHILL HOME CLINIC, HOURS EARLIER

"But how did you get here?"

The old, frail doctor held open the doors to one of the many makeshift hospitals of Wolfhill—a town a few counties away from Firestone. The sound of a car engine outside in the black night and torrential rain had given her the swift fear that the Rankers had arrived for one of their random reasons. She was astonished that the minivan haphazardly thrown into park half-on the sidewalk had been full of kids. More injured? There was hardly room anymore in the old woman's large home, and a shortage of caretakers.

Watching a young girl rush towards her with her hood up against the rain, the woman had asked her question in response to a thick-shouldered boy's plea that they see one of her patients. One of her tired-looking orderlies shuffled in from the kitchen and wordlessly began removing the kids' wet coats and hanging them up.

"We drove right out of town. We didn't see anyone patrolling the border," said another boy, one with crutches and a backpack.

"You risked your lives to see someone here?" the old doctor asked, astonished. That had never happened with visitors from out of town. At least not for a while.

"It's important, ma'am," said another young woman with curly dark hair.

The boy with crutches introduced himself as Tyson, and then everyone else stated their name. Kitty, Lia, Carl, Vince, and Nikki.

"You're the ones on the internet," the nurse gasped. "Is what you say true? Are you the rebels?"

"Rebels..." Tyson tasted the word. Lia wrapped her arm around his and put her head against his shoulder. The doctor thought she looked like a preppy, popular sort of girl. Or, better said, she looked like she *had* fallen into that category. Now she was washed out, and her hair was dry and limp at her collarbone.

"Yes," Nikki promised. "We are who you said."

"We need to know if you're housing Peter Malone," Vince said.

The doctor's face fell. She had been hoping to give good news.

"Yes, but he's in a coma. His condition baffled his doctors: he does not, perhaps cannot, wake despite bursts of vivid brain activity. Life support is all he has left. That and his strong will. If the Rankers let my generator go out, and the machines shut off..." But the kids were obviously very relieved. So they had already known of his condition somehow. "Follow me." The doctor clasped her hands at her waist and turned down the hall, passing the kitchen and a sitting room with a fire blazing in the grate.

They came into a grand living room speckled with warm velveteen furniture and expensive tasseled rugs. They climbed up a staircase to a landing and then up another flight. Now they were passing silent, closed doors at either flank. The doctor took up a mini flashlight and shined it on the ground as they walked. In a hushed voice, she said mournfully, "Some people from upstate moved down here. Things were utterly awful..." She briefly checked a card suspended on a patient's door and moved on. "The old hospital had an epidemic of influenza. The situation deteriorated to where we begged the Rankers for help. People were slipping into fevers and dying." Her voice developed a frail quality.

Tyson looked at her. He lost his balance and teetered to one side. Getting his crutch beneath him without conscious effort, he hopped on.

The doctor had unshed tears in her eyes. One escaped down her fatigued cheekbone. She sniffed noisily, but her voice was steady. "The Rankers came in and went into the rooms of the ill. The hospital staff–we were all huddled downstairs. Listening. We heard weak shouts...and moaning... And then flat lines on the monitors echoed all around us, and we were helpless. They slaughtered the sick, the helpless, everyone in a fever, a coma, or everyone who had just come out of one. There was nothing we could do with the bodies–there were too many. So we were allowed to come here and tend to new patients. We are supposed to tell them if anyone falls into a coma, probably so they can come in and... But of course, I try my best to keep them from finding out... It's as if the people they killed at the hospital were people they knew–enemies they had been searching for."

"I don't doubt that," Vince said.

In a tragic murmur that the doctor almost didn't hear, Nikki said to Tyson, "They probably didn't want to take chances and killed those poor people in case they were griffins."

The old woman stopped at a door and reached into a bag beside it, pulling out anti-contamination masks and situating one around her own mouth and nose. "Peter was one of the first patients brought to us here in the early days. He is one of the few who survived a similar massacre at his hospital–some of the staff were able to smuggle him and a few others out once they understood the Rankers' intentions." She carefully opened the door.

A shadow of a man lay upon a bed. The nurse turned up a dull orange lamp beside the bed, and the light threw harsh shadows into the crevices and sockets of Peter's sunken face. His jaw was narrow–his beard scanty. His nose was pinched. Through the fleece blanket draped over the body of someone who had once been strong, Nikki noted a dished-in ribcage and frail arms and legs as wide as her pointer finger was long.

"This isn't how it's supposed to be," Carl whispered. The nurse studied the boy pityingly, his shock of black hair, his average features.

"Look...at–I mean, anything can happen to him," Vince hissed.

"We have to hurry," Tyson agreed. He said to the nurse, "Do not allow any Rankers to enter your home. This man plays an important part in getting us out of this mess." The nurse's eyes widened, and she nodded, one hand at her mask as if to steady it from a stray breeze.

At that moment, something made a muffled "bah-doop" sound in Tyson's backpack. Nikki looked warily at him, and Kitty held open the door, ushering everyone out. Once the nurse shut the door safely behind her, she turned and looked down to see Tyson sitting on the floor with his injured legs stretched out and a laptop open between them. He placed a finger on the keypad and twirled it around, tapping occasionally.

“Phshew,” he sighed, his eyes reflecting the white screen filled with new emails from all over the world and notifications that his social-media profiles were packed with fresh comments and messages as well. His friends squeezed in to read over his shoulders, and the nurse leaned around to see. Italy. Virginia. New Zealand. China. Kenya. All were places where Tyson’s posts and emails had been sent or forwarded in a chain. Tyson clicked on the first, from someone who lived in Istanbul. He scanned it and moved thoroughly on to the next. All were similar: words of encouragement, promises of prayer, newcomers asking what to do and what was going on, youngsters asking how they could help... Tyson would type briefly back to each person, answering their questions shorthand. He gave most of his attention to the emails that told of the situations in other places.

Temples were still being built. If those too ill or weak to perform construction did not recover within three days, they were killed, as were people in comas. The rebels were being tortured. All personal items were burned; humans were being made into slaves. There was still an ongoing search for certain people that Tyson and many others now knew were griffins.

“Oh, one from Josiah,” Tyson said, opening a semi-recent letter. He read it aloud. “Ben says nightmares plan on tracking down K and M. RX and I have your ticket out of here.”

“Who are K and M? And RX?” the doctor ventured to ask. Tyson jumped a bit as if he had forgotten she was there.

“Kayle and Mariah are people we know. RX is Rexus–another of our friends,” Tyson explained, neglecting to mention that the last was a charlatan. "Josiah sends his mail under the code name of Scarlet because he says that's what color his griffin feathers...um...are..."

The nurse was confused, but Nikki didn't give her time to ponder, tying her hair back away from her face and saying, "Josiah wants us to travel to Ireland and France to find two of Jonathan's closest allies so we can protect them. He's at our homes now, telling our parents."

"But all ships and flights have been grounded, dears," the doctor said, her face crestfallen. "How are you going to travel?"

"Long story," Carl said.

"It's a bit past 1:30 now," Tyson observed, squinting at the tiny clock in the corner of his screen. "We should be going before it gets light."

Nikki stood and put a hand on the kind doctor's shoulder.

"Thank you for your help and hospitality. What you do here, caring so selflessly for these people, is very heroic."

The woman blushed and followed her guests downstairs, watching them trot back into the rain and dive inside the van, Vince at the wheel. As it drove away, headlights off and tail lights concealed with duct tape, one of the doctor's orderlies trudged in and asked who the teenagers had been.

"Little heroes, Donna," the woman replied and thought back to Tyson's worldwide emails and when he had mentioned Josiah's feathers.

"Little griffins."

Vince drove slowly, ignoring traffic lights and stop signs.

It was another cold night and their warm breath continuously fogged up the windshield, but no one turned on the heater for fear of adding extra noise to the engine. Nikki texted Ethan He'klarr with her mother's phone, having never gotten hers back from the Rankers at the meeting chambers. Everyone was aware that the Rankers could tap into actual calls, but they doubted that Rankers had the resources to intercept texts or decipher the slang, shorthand, and codes that people had come up with.

"He looks bad," said Nikki's message in translation. She asked Ethan how the parents were taking Josiah's news of the tickets, if anyone had dreamed yet, or if any new ideas for rebellion had been discussed. Ethan's response, though choppy and imperfect, mentioned that the parents were, of course, worried about their kids and that no one had fallen asleep–they had all agreed to wait for the kids' return. A few plans had developed, all involving ransacking stores for needed groceries or somehow traveling to neighboring towns to spread the word and strengthen ties of unity and resolve among the people.

"Good," Nikki texted back. "Be there soon." She added a smiley-face for assurance and shut the phone off, slipping it into her pocket and wondering if she could get away with charging the battery once she returned home or whether the Rankers would somehow sense it.

Nikki heaved a sigh, thumping her head back against the seat.

"What's up?" Vince murmured, not taking his eyes off the dim street ahead.

Nikki tilted her head at him, smiling fondly. "How do you do that? How can you tell when I need to vent?"

Vince shrugged and gave her a playful smile. "It's a gift."

"Or a curse," Nikki snorted. She looked closer at him. He was tired; she could see that. His arms sagged like he'd just latched his hands to the steering wheel and let them rest there. His back drooped, and his head was lowered. At that moment, she couldn't remember if, out of all the times he'd checked in on them, any of them had asked Vince how *he* was doing.

"What do you miss the most about how things were before?" Nikki asked, turning in her seat a little.

Vince squinted at the windshield in thought.

"Fast food," Tyson said in a small voice from the back, and Lia told him to shush.

"Hanging out with you guys," Vince chuckled. The cheer left his face a little. "Hanging out with Jonathan. Back before he was supposed to save the world."

"Yeah, *Jonathan*, who'd a thunk?" Tyson piped up again. He paused and added in a quieter voice, "It's kind of cool, actually..."

Thinking about Jonathan made her insides clench with anxiety, so Nikki said to Vince, "When all of this is over with, I want to ride horses at your place again. You're so good with them."

Vince beamed and gave a short, sharp laugh. "If we don't have to eat any of them to survive, that sounds like a plan."

Carl speculated what horse tasted like with Tyson while Lia and Kitty reminisced about the last time they had been out to Vince's family ranch to ride. Nikki and Vince joked about the time Jonathan and Tyson had spent the whole day riding, pretending to be Tonto and the Lone Ranger.

She was so caught up in the rare joy of reliving happy memories that Nikki was surprised when Vince leaned forward and said, "What's that?"

Dark shadows flitted ahead of the van under a dim street light. They made no noises–only danced in confusing darts, hemming them in. Something hit the side of the van and broke. Carl jumped, and Lia whimpered.

"Hold on!" Vince hit the gas, speeding up.

Now came riotous shouts and yells. More stuff crashed into their vehicle. Someone threw something onto the road, and Vince swerved. But the right tires went up and over a chain of road spikes. With a whine and a banshee scream, they veered in a precariously sharp J to the left. The fender bounced onto the sidewalk and hit the ditch on the other side at such an angle and speed that it flipped forward, smashed onto its roof, and skidded into two trees where it stuck. Some of the lower branches punched through the driver's side of the van.

Nikki's seat belt pressed a furrow in her torso, suspending her upside down; her head had been forced against the roof of the van at such an angle that her neck had been twisted to almost the breaking point. Had she been jarred any rougher, it would've snapped. She gingerly unbuckled and collapsed on her arms and knees on the dashboard and airbag, which was smeared with blood from her nose. Her hips, shoulders, head all hurt. She had minor cuts from the windshield and one long cut at the back of her arm from the jagged passenger-side window.

Vince groaned in shock and pain. He was crunched into a U-shape between his upside-down seat and the steering wheel. His seat belt had snapped, and he gave her a slow, uncomprehending blink. One eye was bloody, and one hand clearly broken. The front of his shirt was so dark and shiny with clumps of blood that Nikki thought–with a rise of bile–that perhaps ribs had punctured his skin.

"Vince?" she choked out.

Vince only blinked again, slowly and blankly. He opened his mouth slightly for a shaky breath–an odd, broken series of senseless groaning sounds came out. Nikki let her tears fall and stared into the shadows at the rear of the van.

Tyson reached pathetically for his crutches, his hands shaking. Carl and Kitty were unconscious, Kitty slumped sideways against the roof (now the floor), and Carl bent forward half-out of his seat. Lia stared out a side window at approaching feet, her breath fogging up the frosted glass.

The doors opened. Hands, gloved to ward off the night's chill, reached in and dragged them out.

They were all bundled into a pile and for minutes their unknown molesters barraged them with kicks and punches. Nikki curled up, her back pressed against Vince's, and tried to protect her head and internal organs, absorbing the fresh pain with muffled mewls of anger, confusion, and misery.

Finally, a voice laden with hate called for an end to their suffering, and the laughing mob backed off into a wide ring. Tyson, hands still wrapped around his crutches, managed to sit up. He spat blood to one side, and Nikki heard Vince retch behind her.

"*Who the hell are you jerks*?" Tyson asked, sounding angrier than he'd ever been. The group around them all wore leather jackets and hoods. Many had red-studded rings in their noses, lips, ears, or brows, as if they were badges symbolizing their affiliation with a gang or a club. Some had black robes, just like the ones the Rankers wore.

"We are worshippers and followers of the Rankers," one guy said, so covered in studs and rings that he resembled a human Slinky.

"The Rankers rule us," someone else said, and the rest joined her, repeating some kind of mantra or cult-like pledge of fealty. "We bend our backs to their command and revel in their tidings of blood and destruction, for it heralds a new dawn. We are their loving subjects."

"No, you're not. You're just scared kids," Tyson said.

One of the young women sneered. "We're not alone in our cult, and we aren't deluded. Everything pure rises from the ashes of ruin and chaos. You'll see the truth. You'll see our ranks swell, and you'll recognize our faces."

"On reruns of *America's Most Wanted*?" Carl breathed lowly, getting a laugh from Nikki.

Garrett approached from out of nowhere, and the pile of friends unwound and crawled as far from him as the gang ring allowed. Garrett wasn't disguised. His green skin stretched tight once more over sharp bones. His red pupils glowed like lasers, and his horns curved high.

"Long time..." he snarled in his deep mountain-slide growl. "Sorry for the rude stop. Any broken bones?" He kicked Tyson in the chest, and the boy fell back, the breath gone from his lungs. "No? Good." Garrett smiled, exposing his sharp teeth.

"If you wanted us killed, we'd be dead by now," Lia sobbed, cradling Ty protectively against her. "What do you want?"

Garrett crouched over them.

"I've been to see the King of Earth, and he told me to pay you a visit. You see, I know exactly where Jonathan and his troop of idiots are in the dreamworld."

"No," Nikki gasped, her own world feeling as if it had collapsed.

"Yes," Garrett argued calmly, as if they were debating something mild, like the economy. "Currently, they are at the mercy of the Pharaoh–a man opposed to Jonathan's cause. Your prince approaches peril in the throat of the Sphinx." He sighed and stood.

"I don't want to explain minute details to you, but I have plans to pay my respects to Jonathan, and I have a proposition to make." He leaned in, and the kids leaned back. "Tell me where Jonathan's body is and what guards it, and I will kill you painlessly."

Crickets chirped in the distance, and an owl hooted tonelessly.

Vince laughed harshly, and after a while, the others joined in.

"Oh, that was good! Tell another one!" Vince chuckled wetly.

"I don't get it," Carl said, hiding a grin. "What's the punchline?" One of the Ranker supporters punched him in the face, and he rocked back, holding his nose. “There it is,” he said in a pinched voice through a welter of fresh blood.

“To get what I want, I see I must first tenderize the meat,” Garrett said, disgustedly. “Know that when all is in place, your defiance will have been for naught, and I will kill the Jonathan you all idolize along with his...entourage. Think carefully about your options.” He flashed Nikki a horrible smile, his forked tongue flickering at her from between his fangs. “I know how much Jonathan hates it when I...touch his girl.”

Kitty shifted suddenly, pulling her legs beneath her to rise up on her knees, leaning close to Garrett. The last time Ben had seen Nikki, he had told her about Kitty’s effect on Donovan, and Nikki, fascinated, had relayed it to the others. Now, Nikki suspected Kitty was testing a theory out of desperation.

“Leave us alone, Garrett.” Kitty’s voice was low and uncharacteristically defiant. Her dark eyes flashed under the nearest streetlight.

To Nikki’s bewilderment, Garrett backed away, his sharp teeth gnashing. He stared fixedly at Kitty, who had jutted out her jaw and stared boldly back, as if she were an unexpected puzzle that he had to solve. Cautiously, like he was testing the range of an angry Doberman’s leash, he stepped to one side, nearer Tyson. Kitty shuffled sideways, mirroring him. Garrett side-stepped the other way, closer to Carl, and Kitty followed.

The Ranker snarled with frustration. As if finally understanding the predicament Kitty posed, one of the followers stepped forward, grabbed a handful of Kitty’s curls, and pulled her savagely back down onto her side.

Nikki reached out to pull Kitty closer, hugging her, feeling her tremble, and marveling at her timid friend's courage. She thought she heard Garrett mutter something like, "I will take what I can."

Lifting his horned head, Garrett gave Nikki one last, hungry glance and ordered his cronies to lay hand to Jonathan's friends. Once more, all became a dancing cloud of shadows and pain. But this time, something in Nikki snapped. A protective instinct overwhelmed her. She had to get to Jonathan.

She heard Tyson grunt and Lia yowl like a cat. Then, struggling beneath the binds of descending fists and shoes, Nikki ripped upward beyond the pain.

She shoved something or someone back and ran free, shouting, "I won't let you hurt him! Long live Great Prince Jonathan!" There was a rap of quiet, then Tyson repeated her words. As one, the rest of Nikki's friends shoved through the mob after her, knocking kids down, landing some departing blows of their own.

But someone caught hold of Vince's shoulder–enough to make him tumble back down. He stood, ran forward, but something was off. He tripped over his own feet, fell, half stood, ran forward into more of a headlong dive. Nikki halted; turned to go back for him. Blood-loss, pulverized ribs, and shock were releasing their deadly toxins into Vince, and the boy had no strength.

"Go!" he yelled to them as the mob rushed to surround him and beat him down, and as Garrett drew his knife and stalked forward. "Get out of here!"

A pair of Ranker supporters lunged forward as if to chase Nikki and her friends down, but Garrett extended one arm to stop them and said quietly, “Let her go.”

One of Nikki’s friends pulled her arm. In her heart thundered a drumbeat of sorrow and loss. Facing the night, she was forced to listen to the mumblings of a last silent exchange of words between Garrett and Vince.

Vince raised his voice in a belligerent “Long live–”

There was a gasp cut short, then raucous cheering and much more subdued weeping.

CHAPTER THIRTY-SIX:

MY FLOCK

BACK TO JONATHAN

I held Nikki but didn't feel her.

I stood in a cavern full of sobbing kids, but I didn't hear them.

Mute warriors surrounded me, but I didn't see them.

I was standing in front of Vince, his body cold on the ground, his body unnaturally still and stiff. Memories of past days I'd shared with him flashed by in my mind in drowning tides of pain. I would never see him again.

Vince, one of my closest friends, was gone forever.

I cried out, a sudden gasp, as the reality of the situation sunk in. No one can ever *imagine* the death of a friend and truly understand its effect on the heart and mind. Only those who *have* lost a friend can understand the hollow shock; the certainty that that person had gone too early–had their whole life ahead of them, had more to do.

Another cry ripped up my throat, and I struck the cold, underground wall with my knuckles hard enough to split one and bruise others. Tyson switched an agitated look with Lia. I sank down, empty, and put my arms on my knees, resting my head in them, trembling. I felt Nikki next to me. She leaned against my shoulder, and for minutes all we did was weep silently in mourning for our brave friend. Eventually, Tyson swung over to us. Though his voice was raw, he tried to comfort us.

"You know, this war or whatever it is... It uh, it makes us into either heroes or villains. Vince was a hero. When he found out that you're the Griffin Prince? He took it in stride because he believed in you that much. But is *this* what he would want? Is this what people depending on you in reality *need*?"

I snapped my head up to him, bristling, but Flaherty came up and defended him.

"He means grief, Jonathan. There's a time to grieve, but this isn't it."

Tyson flinched at how harsh the words sounded. The Marine Sergeant looked at his feet, and his broad shoulders drooped.

"I've lost a lot of friends in battle. And I cried, I got in fights, I drank, I killed... All of us would love to live in an era of peace and harmony, but right now, that isn't the case–it's an unattainable daydream. I've seen grown men get themselves slaughtered in battle because they blamed the deaths of their fellow soldiers on themselves. They lose caution, and their grief drives them to thirst for revenge."

Kitty, brave Kitty who had protected my friends the only way she could, sank down on my other side, rubbing my arm in a motherly way. "'There is a time to be born and a time to die; a time for peace and a time for war.' It was Vince's time to go home, Jonathan. And he went readily. Now he's in a much better place than any of us."

Flaherty crouched and put one hand on my shoulder and the other on Nikki's. "This is not either of your faults. Death is just a part of what we have to face, here in reality, or in The Land of Dreams, so we need to be ready to expect and accept it. Then we'll be strong enough to fight back. And *then* we can grieve and honor the fallen in peace." He winked kindly at Kitty, stood tall. "'There is a time to be silent and a time to act.' And now is the time for action."

"Well-said." Peter put his hand on my shoulder and squeezed.

"And you aren't alone in this, pal," Tyson added, his voice breaking, nudging me with the foot of a crutch. "You have more soldiers in your platoon."

Carl shouted, "Yeah, you have us!"

Cries of agreement came from the other dreamers.

"Here, here," Kayle said.

I couldn't believe how brave my friends were. They were grieving too, yet they comforted *me*. I loved them so much. Vince had died for our cause. Like Tyson had said, he had died because he believed in *me*. He had gone out bravely, readily, as Kitty had pointed out, like so many the Rankers had killed, but this wasn't over yet. There would be a time to mourn, but this was a time for action. We had work to do first. What better way to make the Rankers pay than to bring to fruition plans that had been in place since King Brody? To take the final Ranker clue and deprive them of possible allies?

"Um... Sphinx," I said. "What did Garrett mean when he mentioned a Sphinx?" A plan beat around in my brain. I may not have had it in me for revenge, but to *avenge*...that was very different. I stood up.

"We read up about it before we came here, in your books," a young girl piped. I turned expectantly to Nikki. She smiled at the building mood-change, at the righteous, defiant fury that seemed to buzz in the musty air over our heads.

"Okay," she said. "there was an illustration. It's a big cat thing with the human head."

"Oh! Right, like the one in Egypt," I said, snapping my fingers.

In Tencina-Ahrroc, the sphinx was built as the pyramids were–to honor ancient pharaohs. The lion body, reclining complacently, symbolized power, but the face was modeled after the currently reigning pharaoh's face. In the Land of Dreams, the sphinx held much more magic than any in reality. It was intelligent and could summon dark beings from its mouth. So when Garrett had said so chipperly that I would die in the Sphinx's throat, I wondered if he was being poetically literal...

"Nikki," I said, pulling her around so that we faced each other. Her face settled into a mask of steel–she was trying to block her emotions. "I'm going to ask you to do something. It will be scary and maybe dangerous... Are you up for–"

Before I could even finish asking whether she was willing to join me, fight this battle beside me, Nikki started to smile and nod. She grabbed my coral necklace and yanked me centimeters from her face. Her lips brushed mine as she whispered, "I hear you can read minds. What do you *think* my answer is going to be?"

She kissed me brusquely but lovingly, and before she could break away, I hugged her and murmured, "You're something special, baby." I *could* hear her thoughts. She was almost *shouting* yes.

"We're with you, pal!" Tyson cheered.

"Let's show Garrett we won't back down! Let's show him he just made a big mistake!" I cried. "Sphinx or no Sphinx, we're winning this war!" There was no dramatic thunderous applause as we faced the stairs slanting steeply up towards doom or triumph. But this was action; this was us fighting beyond your pain to dig deep, and finding strength within ourselves–the kind of strength special to humans; the kind that Garrett had woefully underestimated.

The real battle itself, of course, would not take place until much later, but for me, this was when we truly took the first step together, the dream world and reality united. It was under-handed and evil, what Garrett had done; it went against any courtesy and chivalry of a fair battle. But the initial bullet had hit our unsuspecting flanks, and it had cost us a loyal warrior. A brave hero.

A good friend.

The Rankers clearly knew where to hurt us most, and now we were mad and ready for a fight.

Kayle took the lead, transforming into the phoenix-griffin to gasps from the dreamers and securing us the proverbially dramatic entrance that we so deserved.

"So," I whispered into Nikki's ear. "What are all the adults doing? I don't see any here."

Nikki replied in a clipped voice, "Getting his body."

I reached out and took her hand. Her fingers curled tightly around mine. And together, we went to face whatever came next.

CHAPTER THIRTY-SEVEN:

A Time to Mourn; A Time to Kick Butt

We reached level ground. "I'm not picking up any thoughts yet," I said.

"We're right below the pyramid's apex judging by the open air," remarked Flaherty.

"It's a big square room," Mariah said, her eyes shut. "I'm sending a creeper vine around, and I can feel four corners."

Kayle swooped in a wide, burning arc, judging his distance from the walls by an acute sense of Griffin hearing that sent the reverberations of his wing beats off of solid objects back to him. He dove lower and circled around and almost bashed into the face of the stone Sphinx, its features stuck in a silent roar.

"Gah!" he yelped and swooped down to us, landing but still aflame.

"Oh no." I gritted my teeth as another's thoughts pushed up against mine. "It's awake."

Two great, ruby-red sparkling orbs twinkled to life on the monstrous face, bathing the cavern in eerie, ruddy light.

"It's studying us, seeing if we're a threat," I said, standing still in futile hopes that the beast only noticed movement.

"I know *I* react pleasantly when someone shoves fire up *my* eyelids," Amenophis mumbled. Kayle gave him a death glare.

The Sphinx's face was long with high cheekbones and deep-set eyes. The teeth were jagged and the nose sharp. It looked like a corpse's visage. With a grating noise, the head turned and slowly tilted down to stare at us. The stone nostrils flared, and the Sphinx bared its teeth and snarled with enough bass to cause an earthquake.

"Over there!" Nikki pointed. On a pedestal in the room's center lay a scroll made of tightly interwoven links of metal.

Amenophis sprinted to grab the scroll and narrowly avoided being thrown down an endless black gullet when the Sphinx's head shot out to snatch him, making a sound like a landslide.

"What's it say? What's it say?" all of us cried repetitively.

"Um..." Amenophis's hands trembled, and his voice was flustered. "It–there's no words! Just pictures!" I pushed over to his side and took a part of the scroll.

"Okay," he said, pointing to a small column of dark figures in the traditional Ancient-Egyptian art of sideways heads and frontways bodies. His eyes roved in circles, translating the pictographs first in his mind. The Sphinx lowered its head slightly and roared, an inhuman lion-man sound. Amenophis jumped and closed his eyes for a millisecond–lips moving soundlessly and sweat beading on his upper lip. He pointed to the first picture, a dark castle surrounded by thorny ivy.

"This must be their fortress. You see the ivy? It means that they'll sneak up on us unexpectedly and overwhelm us. That's what they started doing in King Brody's time. Here! Seven figures by the fortress... That must represent the seven powerful Rankers they sent out to subtly influence people toward darkness before Brody killed them... I don't believe this! It's their whole plan!"

My heart galloped its beats up a notch. Amenophis pointed to a blood-red field of grass, this time ignoring the Sphinx's warning bellow. "They will gather upon the plains near the capital. That's this white star here surrounded by night. They know the kingdom is defended impenetrably at the gates. I think...this might be a type of Ranker... Peter! What's this?"

Peter trotted over and said, "Shadow Ranker. The stealthiest spies." I noted how the shifty Ranker bodies were approaching the star.

"They mean to spy on us, if they aren't already," I said.

The Sphinx sniffed the air and lowered its head towards the ground. Our time was elapsing.

"At first," Peter agreed. "But I can't pick out any meaning in the other pictures. These strategies are too complexly illustrated. The elves would be the one group of few to understand. And they mean to join us in the Misty Pass before the capital."

While Amenophis and I digested this, Peter pried the map out of our hands and hemmed over the illustration of the black castle.

"This must be the location of the Ranker fortress. One of the dark island keys."

The Sphinx's chin touched the earth with a shockwave of cracking noise and a ripple of dust. Tyson called frantically to me. I was so caught up in the moment that I actually lifted a finger in the "hold on" sign.

"Well, this is good news!" I said. "We know where it is, so we can launch a surprise attack there and end the war, right?"

Peter's face became grave. He rolled up the scroll and looked me level in the eye.

"No man has ever made it out to those keys. They die soon after departure. There is a beast that guards that place, and it is this place where the darkest thoughts and nightmares of the human mind reside. Only King Brody gleaned any information about the Ranker fortress the day before he died: he was on his way back to the castle to tell it when he and his men were attacked. Not a one of his soldiers with him that day lived, and he only had time before he died to tell me the words that would fuel my search for you and to tell me he had found out some terrible truth. He became delirious and passed before he could say clearly what it was."

"A beast guards the key?" I said. "Maybe Brody found out what it was or how to defeat it."

"Perhaps. We may never know. Good dreams are swallowed up by the evil in those isles. It's no wonder that the Rankers chose to nest there, but I wouldn't have thought even *them* capable of withstanding such darkness. In other words, we won't be attacking their fortress directly. Our only option looks to be bracing ourselves for their next move."

But now Tyson grabbed my arm and shoved me around. The Sphinx's mouth was opening. We were staring straight into a throat as big around as a subway tunnel.

"Are you guys ready for this?" I asked, drunk on our success. We had foiled the Ranker plans. We could puzzle out their battle strategies.

"Round one. Ding-ding!" Tyson said, imitating a prize-fighter.

"*Faugh a balagh*!" Kayle said.

"Who is like you, *Adonai*?" Amenophis whispered low. "Nothing compares to Your greatness; no evil can stand in Your presence..."

I tried to pray an awkward, silent prayer, imagining my words written on a letter and squeezing their way up a turbulent tube of thoughts toward the enigmatic, giant figure that was God.

Nikki shifted into her griffin form, shaking out her wings as if stretching, and those of us who could transform followed suit. Tyson abandoned his crutches and gave an eagle scream.

A form approached us from out of the Sphinx's jaws, walking with unearthly poise and grace. Even before he came into the light, I knew it was Donovan. Kitty hissed.

"Do not concern yourselves, children of the light," the vampire said smugly. He paused only once, his eyes going round and flickering around the chamber across the faces of my friends. I got the sense that he hadn't expected to see so many people from reality gathered outside the sphinx.

"You better get your scrawny behind back into that thing before I tear you to pieces, Donovan!" I shouted. My voice echoed, but his didn't–as if his was inside our heads, not yelled into a wide cavern. He floated up to sit upon the Sphinx's broad head.

"I only intrude to observe and pose a riddle: How do you kill one who is already dead?"

"Slowly! Very slowly!" Carl spat.

Donovan's white teeth gleamed as he cackled.

"Well, let us put your theory to the test, boy!" His attention turned wholly from us and instead to the beast beneath him.

"Come forth, my rotting legions. Awaken, dark corpses of the pyramid's sandy tombs. Rid this place of its infestation so that you may resume your timeless sleep!"

A few kids vanished out of the blue. The nightmare had become too much for them, and their brains had saved them by waking them up. But a steady few remained.

Coughs, moans, and squeals called forth from the Sphinx's core. There came shuffling feet and thumping limbs. The approaching monsters had no thoughts; more like animal impulses–like the dolphins I'd frolicked with back by the Reekwood Swamp. They sensed intruders that needed to die.

Amenophis withdrew his sling and inserted a stone into the pouch. When the first silhouette merged from the black, he raised the sling up in a soft arc and twirled it around his head. With a curious flick of the wrist, he sent the stone rocketing forwards, and it collided with the stumbling creature's face. It twirled around with a moan, and something fell and bounced jauntily out into the red light and skidded to a stop at the talons of the skater kid I remembered from our first reunion. He reared up with a dry-heave of disgust, his green, black, and gray-colored feathers fluffing as a decapitated head glared up at him and groaned. A few more people disappeared.

"Zombies," I said, loud enough for the others to hear. "They're stupid–don't worry, they only do as they're told."

"Which in this case is to kill us, dude!" the tri-colored griffin shrieked, his voice breaking.

"Details, details," Tyson said dismissively, venturing to poke the rocking head and tipping it over. Its body, clad in rags and rusted jewelry and rotted skin, ambled out for its head but was incinerated by Kayle.

Donovan acknowledged the confused looks we gave him with a slow wink and a prim yawn concealed with the back of his hand. More groans and more addled steps echoed to us from the Sphinx.

"It's a horde," Peter informed us, and it was then that my brain and heart beat to the tune of battle. I became more alert. My senses sharpened and worries blanked away to make room for instinct. Pain? What was pain? What was fear? This was just business.

They came out in groups of four to six, shuffling with softened bones and nonexistent ligaments. Intermingled with the unsightly zombies were mummies. These were wrapped entirely in yellow-brown gauze except for a strip they had clawed off at the eye sockets. The mummies walked more swiftly and were far more cunning, dirty fighters. They couldn't act independently–they still had to follow a command, but their efficiency in carrying out that command made the zombies look like animated sock puppets. I heard Peter explaining the contrasts breathlessly and without pause to the others.

A raunchy, dead smell permeated the room, and hundreds of groans and moans thundered in our heads. I roared and led the charge, the others bounding behind me.

"Kill them!" Donovan wailed. "Peel their flesh from their bones!"

Flaherty withdrew a gun from beneath his servant's robe and hit a zombie over the head with its butt. Marcus twirled loftily around and chopped sideways at a mummy's neck, chasing after the rolling head. I butted a mummy in the chest and stabbed him through with my talons. Turning, I crouched to leap into the air, but a trio of mismatched zombies grabbed hold of one of my wings. They used brute strength to drag me back down, where I turned into two of them and beat them back hard with the edge of my other wing. I threw the undead corpse I had in my talons at the third. In two cat-like leaps, I made it to clear ground and walked 'round the fight's edge to survey how we were doing.

Donovan jeered and cheered like he was at a football game, the delusional freak-o-path. Nikki pounced at a mummy harassing a smaller griffin, but the mummy hauled back and hit her in the beak. She grunted, her head tossed aside, blood leaking from her nares. Before the undead monster could redouble its attack, I grabbed it by the thin wraps at the back, pulled, and released, and the mummy was thrown forward on its face where it couldn't find the ability to stand. Nikki nuzzled me and twisted clumsily away to battle a scythe-wielding mummy.

Peter landed beside me and said, "We're too big! I've told Kayle—we need to fight this battle as men and save our wings for open air."

"What about the other kids?" I asked. "They can't fight well now as it is..." I watched Nikki kick back at a zombie and take out five others by accident when she opened her wings.

"For their sake, they should stay transformed," Peter said and went to find Mariah. I slipped back into my human shape and withdrew my sword. All the dead seemed suddenly taller and closer, but my brain shifted to awareness of my human form and its abilities.

Familiar, homey muscles stretched like cords in my arms and back. I went for a mummy–slicing up and severing an arm. The beast howled through its wraps and struck me in the chest with its other elbow. I fell back hard and tried to roll away. A pink griffin incapacitated the mummy, but the severed hand clutched my ankle.

"*Ow!*" I cried as the fingers intensified their greedy pressure.

"Someone wanna give me a hand?" Tyson called from where he was surrounded by zombies. Sweat shone on his brown pelt.

"Let me get rid of this one, first!" I blurted and carefully ran the edge of my blade across the tight knuckles, causing the fingers to roll away everywhere. Yeah. Nastiness.

A silvery griffin with white speckles glided clumsily overhead, holding a limp zombie in her talons–she threw it down onto the uplifted faces of its deceased brethren. Tyson's foe was one of the numerous to be knocked silly. He backed away, gasping, his limbs shivering as the muscles burdened with stress. He couldn't take much more, and there were still a few hundred dead left to fight.

I heard a few gunshots from Flaherty and turned just in time to duck beneath the clothesline of a mummy. It twirled around and grabbed me by the hair, pulling my head back as if to rest it on its foul shoulder. It punched me in the throat with its other fist, but on contact, its hand broke at the wrist so that the damage done wasn't deadly. I shoved the mummy away, so focused on the throbbing pain in my neck that I almost didn't notice when another mummy joined the first, took my shoulders, and drove its knee up into my gut. I grunted, breath beaten out of me, but I had the satisfaction of watching the mummy's leg depart the body at the knee on contact. The beast howled in confusion and was felled by a stone from Amenophis's sling. I waved a hand at him in thanks, trying to stand up straight.

A hand-sized rock hurtled out of the air and smashed into the side of Amenophis's skull. He toppled sideways and hit the ground shoulder-first, shouting in pain and with one side of his head red and gleaming with blood. I looked in the direction the rock had come from and found Donovan perched on the Sphinx's head searching for another projectile. So he had finally decided to contribute to the fight. Well. An eye for an eye.

I ran through the maze of tangled bodies until I broke into a relatively clear spot, then jumped and transformed at the same time, flying up along the Sphinx. A single, powerful flap of my wings carried me up over Donovan, and at the apex of the flight, I opened my wings wide, hoping to intimidate him with their span.

The vampire growled at me like a cornered raccoon and shimmied back, crouched so low that he was almost crawling. Without a word, I dove at him, clawing with my talons and slicing his face. He fell back but used his momentum to flip onto his feet–blood leaking from four evenly spaced cuts.

"You realize now I will have to consume more blood?" Donovan smiled savagely. I was beyond witty insults.

"Take mine, then, if you're man enough," I said. I dove to pick him up and drop him on some zombies, but now that he was on alert, he managed to dodge and grab my tail, yanking like it was a bell tassel.

I fell, landed on my back, slid down the slope of the Sphinx's shoulders, and rolled off the stone monster's side to soar back around to its face. Landing atop its head, I glared down at Donovan, the hackles rising in a ridge along my spine like dragon's spikes. My tail hurt from the vampire tugging on it, but I didn't let the pain show, lashing my tail side to side to stretch it out.

"You threatened Nikki," I said flatly, sliding down the back of the sphinx's head like water, keeping Donovan fixed in my vision. "You tricked my friends." I stopped a safe distance away from him, lifting my head, arching my wings. "The only person who's ass I want to kick more right now is Garrett's. You'll have to serve."

Donovan threw back his head and laughed mockingly. "How very...nobly said." He swallowed his mirth, feigning wiping away tears of humor. "Your venom ill-becomes you, Griffin Prince. Hatred has never looked well on griffins."

My fury reached the boiling point. The chimera's similar taunts drifted back to me. Whether it was my own spite or because of something out of my control, I shifted into my human form and spread my arms. "Better?" My eyes still cast a hellish red glow on my surroundings.

Donovan, completely unimpressed, gestured at me and said lowly, "You see? Your hatred is anathema to your supposed role, boy. You cannot be a griffin and be controlled by human passions at the same time."

I looked down at myself. Had my transformation been involuntary? Had I shifted out of griffin form because of hatred? My mind was becoming muddled. I gave my head a sharp shake and reached for my sword. “Stop talking.”

“You have wickedness in your heart, boy,” Donovan continued, coming closer. “Perhaps you will find your own way to our isle. Though by then, you will be more monster than man.”

“Shut up,” I said as quietly as before. I wrapped my hand around the hilt of the sword and half-drew, but Donovan closed the distance between us as quickly as a striking snake and grasped my arm, stilling it. I automatically reached up with my other hand to shove him back, but he spun me around, and now I tilted precariously over open space, fighting to keep my footing on the sphinx’s sloping back.

“There is darkness in you, child,” Donovan said, in a gentle, almost fond murmur.

“We’ve beaten you,” I said, scrabbling for purchase, clawing at Donovan’s robes. If he had a mind to drop me, I’d damn well take him with. “We intercepted all your clues, and now we have your battle plans. Your allies won’t know where to go. They won’t find you.”

Donovan sneered, displaying his canines. I had to admit, they looked quite sharp. Thinking of those teeth meeting in Ben’s neck, I growled and wriggled harder. Donovan had to shift and step back, and I had enough level ground to leverage myself and land a mean right-hook into his handsome face.

The Ranker grunted but didn’t release me. My strike had caused him to jerk to one side, and with a yelp, I went too, nearly face-planting before catching myself on one knee and hand, the other wrist still clenched in his vice-like grip.

"You think the scroll is a simple map?" Donovan spat. His eyes burned with malevolence. He bent over me, took my other arm, and lifted me up like a child. "You think the clues are mere signposts to a destination? You have not begun to perceive even a trifle of our secrets, child. You do not find the fortress of evil with directions; you find it with *action*. Our horde would have followed the clues through places of power, cleansed this land of your precious allies, and in so doing, the gates would have opened to them. This is something a griffin could never understand–this is a working that your kind shall never fathom."

Donovan was interrupted by a breathless voice nearby. We both looked over at the far side of the sphinx and saw a griffin's talon reach up and over to dig its claws into the statue's back–joined in seconds by the second talon–and then a familiar brown head with cat-like ears.

Tyson, not yet knowing how to fly, had managed to claw his way up the side of the sphinx to help me. The sight of him filled me with warmth, washing away the feelings of doubt, fear, confusion, and anger that Donovan's sly words had started to plant.

Heaving himself up and over, sagging a little with weariness, Tyson still managed to glare at the Ranker and said, "Yippee ki-yay, mother f–"

"Fool," Donovan interrupted. He tossed me down and approached Tyson hungrily, a strange, eerie growl emanating from his chest and sending shivers down my limbs. I bonked my head on the stone, but, as if Tyson's arrival had flipped a switch, I found I could shift back into my griffin form, and I charged the vampire from behind.

He dodged easily enough, but Tyson and I worked together to attempt pinning Donovan down. We herded him up onto the sphinx's head, swatting and lunging, snapping our beaks. While I had Donovan's focus, Tyson made a risky attempt to snag his legs. But with an impatient hiss, Donovan effortlessly kicked Tyson back, and my friend somersaulted over the Sphinx's forehead, at the last second finding footing in one of the vacant eye sockets with one wing pinned and the other flapping feebly.

"Jon!" Nikki cried. She tried madly to aid us but couldn't–she was still in the middle of her own battle frenzy.

Something moaned loudly. The Sphinx. Its head rocked side to side.

"Tyson! Get out of there!" I bellowed.

Tyson half-fell out of the eye socket where the beady red pupil throbbed and winked. The head tilted sharper and sharper until it broke off and smashed sideways over its paws with a terrible cracking report. The ground quaked, and dust choked the stale air. I fanned the dirt with my wings from where I paced on the ground, calling Tyson's name.

"Here!" he coughed and emerged from where two stone tablets paved from the Sphinx's headdress had fallen on him in a tent shape. Panicked shouts and screams centered in the middle of the room attracted our attention.

A rent had split through the ground from where the Sphinx's head was cushioned. Tremors shook the pyramid; the rift grew wider as the ground became unstable, and rocks fell away from the edges, widening the gap into a fathomless black crevice. The dreamers and the rest of those gathered that actually had pulses had squashed themselves against the walls. The unsteady zombies and mummies were silently lost as they fell, oblivious to their deaths. Again.

"Noooooo!" Donovan shouted, and he fell too, along with the Sphinx.

Tyson and I took a sudden gut-wrenching plummet as the ground we stood upon vanished. We bounced into each other, but I shouldered away to give myself wing room and wrapped my talons around his forelimbs. He shrieked as my claws dug into his skin.

Muscling my way up, my wing joints popping with the strain, I saw Peter, Kayle, and Mariah dive to snatch up a couple of our warriors that had been too slow to avoid falling into the crevasse. Peter struggled to lift Marcus. It took both Kayle and Mariah to grab Flaherty. A few dreamers had also been unlucky and tumbled down into the darkness, but they vanished before descending too far, their brains rescuing them from their nightmare by waking them back up to reality.

The pyramid gave another shuddering rumble. Clouds of dust billowed up from the chasm, swallowing everything in pale obscurity. I dropped Tyson onto solid ground near the exit, but even that was beginning to crumble as the entire pyramid imploded. Together, as one great flock, we fled through the catacombs, coughing on billowing clouds of dust, stumbling on quaking ground. Tyson, Nikki, and the other dreamers had returned to their human forms, but myself, Peter, Kayle, and Mariah continued flying, keeping people together–and when the tunnels became too narrow for flight, we dropped onto talons and paws and sprinted.

"Look!" Nikki cried, pointing ahead and to the right. A great chunk of the pyramid's wall had collapsed outward with a sound like thunder, exposing dust-choked, starry night sky. We veered through it, leaping into fresh, clean air, scrambling up the steep dunes just beyond.

I didn't even look back. After making sure that those of us who remained had all escaped, I leaped into the air and glided low overhead, watching for danger as the earth shuddered faintly. I heaved a deep breath of relief and peered ahead at the broad oasis of palm and fig trees awaiting us a few miles away across a salt flat.

CHAPTER THIRTY-EIGHT:

Moving On

We gathered at the far edge of the oasis, tucked deep within the trees around the largest of three pools of water. Pinched between the collapsed pyramid and more flat desert, frigid and barren in the night, may not have been the ideal location at the moment; but Kayle, Peter, and Mariah were watching the Tencinian-facing border of our temporary sanctuary, and Flaherty and the squadron kept an eye on the desert-facing side. I was grateful that they gave my friends and me time to ourselves.

Myself, and the remaining dreamers who hadn't been frightened back to reality, had at first focused on catching our breath and quenching our thirst. Then slowly, a few of us at a time, we started to chuckle with relief. Our laughter turned into whoops of triumph, and we celebrated our success. Tyson and Lia had looped arms and danced a kind of jig. Kitty clapped her hands and hopped in place like a joyful bunny rabbit. A few kids splashed in the pool, a few others plucked some figs and popped them in their mouths with delighted smiles, and a couple of others collapsed on the sand and exchanged weary but comfortable words.

Then, as our exhaustion settled in, silence fell, and our thoughts turned. I splashed my face with water and sat back against the trunk of a tree, taking a deep breath of fruity, fresh, oasis air. A few horned lopes slipped past, staring at us curiously before deciding to imbibe from a less-crowded pool. Nikki sank down beside me, taking my hand. I looked into her eyes, and suddenly, my own stung with tears.

Vince. His name, one word, leaped to the front of my mind as if branded there.

I took a breath meant to fortify the wall between myself and my emotions, but halfway in, it hitched, and instead, I leaned forward over my knees and wept. My tears dripped into the sand, sinking into the minuscule grains. Nikki rubbed my back, and soon, her own tears joined mine. For a time, silence broken only by soft sounds of sorrow spoiled the beauty of the oasis. I sat wrapped up around my legs, my head down at the earth. For some reason, I found it hard to show my grief–I didn't want it to be seen. This was something private, from me to Vince, something personal and painful.

Memories of Vince drifted through my mind, each one bringing a fresh wave of aching sorrow through my chest; Vince convincing me to join the football team, Vince mediating disputes between our friends, Vince wordlessly taking me in after a rough few days with Dad–setting me up in his family's spare bedroom and caring for me like a big brother. I sensed Tyson dropping to my other side, then Lia, then Kitty. I reached out and clasped Ty's arm, squeezed Nikki's hand, but refused to look up; refused to see my own bereavement reflected on their faces.

Until a pair of shoes edged into my vision.

I followed the shoes up the legs and torso to Carl's face. Carl nodded and gave me a wan smile. Tears shone on his own cheeks, even though he hadn't known Vince like the rest of us had. I blinked around at the other kids, subdued, huddled away from us, but all of them joined in our mourning. We all grieved together–maybe not just for Vince, but for other loved ones that had been lost, for the loved ones we would lose before this war was over. We wept for what lay ahead, and maybe we wept for how our loss would transform us.

Someone "oohed," and we all turned to see a small group of fairies drift past overhead like colorful clumps of cotton. They shone in the night, red and blue, violet and yellow, and though it was difficult to tell past their radiant glow, their tiny faces seemed to be turned down to our own, sympathy bleak on their tiny features. Somewhere distant, so distant that I wouldn't have heard it without my griffin senses, I picked up a voice singing a haunting, woeful melody so beautiful as to bring more tears to my eyes. It was as if the Land of Dreams mourned with us.

Carl handed each of us a fig from the armload he cradled against his chest, then roamed around the clearing, passing figs out to the others present. I watched him curiously, shrugging cluelessly at Nikki. When he'd done, he lifted his fig into the air and said, "To Vince," then took a small bite.

My heart filled with warmth, and I beamed gratefully at him.

"To Vince," I echoed, raising my own fig. I touched the sweet little fruit to my lips. *I'm going to miss you, buddy. We all will.* And I popped it into my mouth and relished the sugary treat. Everyone else joined in the impromptu toast, and when the last voice quieted, a streak of scarlet flame arrowed past far overhead like a comet, as if summoned. Everyone gasped in awe. In its brief appearance in the sky, I had seen it for what it was: a phoenix, one of the most ancient dream creations, a symbol of perseverance and rebirth.

I looked at Kitty, who beamed up in the direction the bird had gone, murmuring strains of *Amazing Grace* to herself. I felt, in that moment, that Kitty understood the dreamworld better than any of us. She smiled warmly at me, and I smiled back and gave her a slight nod–of thanks and appreciation.

I thought of her faith and how her faith gave her hope and strength. Vince was gone, but maybe not forever. Maybe I'd see him again someday. The idea heartened me. And from Vince's death, something new would arise–stronger bonds of friendship between myself and the others; each of us humbled and made bolder by his sacrifice.

Little by little, the others departed, awakening to reality. My closest friends were the last to leave, fighting what I could tell was a bone-deep weariness to remain and give me company.

"So what's next for you?" Tyson asked, his voice slurred, massaging his eyes with the heel of one hand.

I traced my finger through the sand, carving whorls and loops, and looked up at each of them in turn, cherishing the sight of them, all of us together again, even if for a few moments more.

"We're stopping by the elves' realm," I replied. "They'll help us to translate what we can of the Ranker scroll. Then..." I sniffed and shrugged, anxiety coiling in my stomach just like my finger coiling in the sand. I dusted my hands and leaned back, feeling fitful. "Then... the capital city."

"The Seat of Griffins," Nikki said, and I tried to make a gentle sound of confirmation–it came out like a nauseous grunt.

"What about you?" I asked. "Have you seen any more of Ben?"

Kitty flinched, and Lia patted her back before saying, "Not recently. He patrols the streets sometimes, and he's been sending news to us through Josiah now and then, but he..." she glanced at Kitty, who finished her sentence gloomily.

"He hasn't been looking well lately."

That concerned me. There had to be something I could do to help him, something *someone* could do to help him, but nothing came to mind. I wished...well, there were a lot of things I wished.

"We're going to try to find the bodies of Kayle and Mariah," Tyson said. "If we can spread the word in other countries as we go... tell the truth about what's happening, then maybe you'll have an army of your own. The Rankers have supporters. We'll show 'em you have them too."

"Guys, that sounds incredible," I said. The concern making minced meat of my blood pressure intensified. "But how are you going to get out of the country?"

Tyson shrugged. "Josiah's taking care of it."

That assuaged some of my worries. If Josiah was supportive of this, then I knew he'd make sure my friends were safe.

Carl, laying flat on his back nearby, tossing a small stone up and down, said drowsily, "We sure showed those mummies, didn't we?"

"And Donovan," I said fiercely. "He won't be underestimating us again."

We conversed jovially about the earlier battle's finer points, exhausted by the day's trials but, for the time being, at peace. With some amusement, I considered the Oracle's final words to me and, for the first time in a very long time, truly understood and believed that I was not, and had never been, alone.

After my friends left, I fell asleep. Peter allowed me to rest for an hour or so, then roused me. We filled our water skeins and collected some of the fruit for a snack as we created some more distance between Tencina-Ahrroc and us.

By late morning of the next day, we reached the vast temperate rainforest on the far side of the desert and made camp amongst the maples and evergreens. The scent of the pine needles reminded me of home. Peter, Kayle, and Mariah remained in their griffin forms. I drifted off to sleep as they departed to scout the perimeter, and woke up early; well-rested, but with dry, bloodshot eyes sore from crying. I wondered if I had wept some more sometime in the night.

The others of the squadron, except for a pair of sentries having a low conversation, still snoozed around me. Peter was a shaggy mound of feathers and fur curled in a ball nearby, instantly ready to fight if a threat posed itself. Mariah was slung up in the boughs of an oak like a leopard, one of her hind paws twitching in sleep. Kayle lay on his back, all four legs in the air, like a cat in front of a heater. I could hear his purring from across the ashes of our campfire.

Grinning to myself, I sat up and stretched, yawning vastly, then slouched with my arms in my lap, smacking my lips. After a few moments' consideration, I emerged from my sleeping roll, crawled over to Peter's satchel, and removed the Ranker scroll.

I sat cross-legged atop my blankets, shaking some sand from my hair with a rueful snort, and unrolled the scroll, the metal links jingling. I puzzled over the images, and now that my mind was clearer after having eaten, drank, slept, and found safety, I mulled over the conversation with Donovan in the pyramid.

How much of what he'd said had been taunts, and how much had been truth? As a Ranker, his very nature was to sow doubt and manipulate the griffin-hearted, but he hadn't been lying about the clues leading the Rankers through places of power. The swamp had been a nest for nightmares, and the recipe had certainly made monsters of the local dream creations. The jungle had been tormented by the chimera, and the desert kingdom had been teetering on the edge of turmoil under the rule of the cowardly pharaoh.

However, each place had also sheltered some of my own heavy-hitters. In the swamp, we had found a talented carpenter named Joshua and several others who'd been more than willing to join the war effort. In the jungle, of course, lived the loyal tribes, and the Scarab Society had been toiling in secret in the desert kingdom since Brody's reign. If the Ranker allies had succeeded at following the clues, they would have killed a great many good people.

Our only option looked to be bracing ourselves for their next move. Peter had said that no one had ever made it to the Rankers' dark island before, but there had to be a way... The Rankers wouldn't have just sent their allies on a scavenger hunt only to find a stupid scroll with a bunch of pictures on it. There had to have been a way that they would have amassed and voyaged to the isles, where they could all plot together safely out of griffin-sight. That's what this final clue had to be; not just battle plans, but a means of showing their allies the next step—showing them where to go. But Donovan had said that actions led to the Ranker fortress, not directions...what had he meant?

I trailed my finger across the images, desperate for something to make sense. We'd lost Vince. How many hundreds or thousands of others would die just because we were powerless to reach the Ranker fortress? How many would die because we had to let the Rankers make the first punch just so we knew how to retaliate?

No. I can't let that happen. We can't lose anyone else. A small part of me knew that that was impossible–that this was war and that we would inevitably lose many more people. But the teenage kid part of me rejected that logic entirely. If I was the guardian of this realm, if I was meant to protect it, then there had to be something I could do–something I was missing.

You do not find the fortress of evil with directions; you find it with action. Donovan's voice crept into my thoughts. I ran my hand over one of the images on the scroll: that of a shadowy army standing on a field of red beside a black gate. *This is something a griffin could never understand–this is a working that your kind shall never fathom.*

I touched the army on the field of red–an oily, blackish-red as if the shadowy figures stood in a great puddle of blood. And then it came to me. I knew how to get to the fortress. I knew how to find the Rankers and destroy them before they destroyed us. But the realization didn't fill me with joy. Dread made ice of my blood. I dropped the scroll in a clink of metal. We'd never find the dark island in any traditional way. The Rankers' island could only be accessed with an action. *Our horde would have cleansed this land of your precious allies, and in so doing, the gates would have opened to them.* The very act of slaughtering so many innocents was so vile and wicked, it would have opened the gates–perhaps a portal of some kind–to the Ranker fortress.

I looked around the campsite at all the snoozing forms and thought once more of all of those dear to me who had already been affected by the war. Ben, twisted into a pseudo-Ranker, Nikki, who had almost fallen prey to Donovan... Vince... It was my job to protect them all, to make what sacrifices I could for the sake of the dream world, just as King Brody had done before me.

I clenched my fists, resolve tinged with terror coursing through me. I was going to find Garrett where he thought himself safest. I was going to kill him and finish the war before it even had to start–before anyone else got hurt.

And to do that, I would have to defy my griffin nature by performing a Ranker-worthy act; by becoming something nightmarish...

By doing something evil.

EPILOGUE

OVERLOOKING A ROCKY VALLEY ON THE RANKER ISLE IN THE LAND OF DREAMS

Garrett breathed in the smell of sweat, dirt, blood, and metal oil. The ears concealed beneath his hood were pounded with roars and shouts and steel on steel.

A castle fortress stretched miles high behind him, and he had stepped out onto a rain-slick gray balcony just below the cloud cover to get a look at his army. Donovan perched on the roof tiles beneath him like a big bat. He fed noisily on some unfortunate human from the mainland.

Garrett had not been pleased to see Donovan after the travesty in the desert, but witnessing the forces amassed below had mollified him somewhat.

Ben stood beside Garrett. His eyes were hollower than they had used to be. His skin was almost translucent, and his hair had turned white. Being a vampire double-crossing the Rankers had changed Ben profoundly and, he suspected, permanently. He had gotten better at traveling through the curtain between dream and reality physically–just as the Rankers could–without first falling asleep. Still, it was an uncomfortable process, rather like being pushed through a small, rocky tunnel filled with water and emerging temporarily senseless on the other side.

And, especially after taking the young man's life back in Firestone, Ben was forgetting his humanity more and more and found it harder to focus the more he traveled. All that he had seen in the nightmare isles had intensely impacted his health and mind. The monsters spawned from minds drenched in wicked thoughts were worse than anything he had ever seen. After witnessing the horrid things they did to each other, and to any innocent victim they caught, Ben would have to fly to the main island just to tape together his shaken sanity before returning to continue his double-life.

Even though, as a vampire, he could not sleep, the lack of it took a toll on his appearance–made him look more and more...dead. He would not sink to Donovan's level and drink the blood of innocents, so he wandered the castle at night, wild-eyed, sneaking bowls of blood drained from the animals eaten at meals.

Ben's knees shook at the collection of monsters far below gathered around their tents and campfires. Garrett's army had been arriving piece-meal since midnight a few days ago. They had sailed from far coasts in red-sailed caravels or black-sailed pirate ships. Some had flown in, and others just appeared.

What appalled him the most were the humans–the dreamers from reality that sided with the Rankers. There were thousands of them–enough so that Ben knew if he ever returned to reality, he would question every face, wonder at every passing man, woman, and child whether they had been for Garrett or for Jonathan, for evil or for good. Neither reality nor the dreamland was the trustworthy, friendly place they had seemed to be months ago.

Aside from the humans gathered below, there were Rankers, trolls, goblins, wraith Pegasi, twisted-unicorns, skeleton dragons, were-beasts, and all kinds of vermin and creatures, both imaginable and unimaginable. Even though Jonathan's "meddlesome" efforts had prevented a great many of the Ranker recruits and allies from being called to the shores of Pebble Embark, from slaughtering the griffin prince's allies along the way to the Tencinian pyramids, and from beginning an assault on the capital city while the Rankers continued working in reality, *this*...was a sobering sight indeed. The words *futile, outnumbered,* and *no chance* whispered through Ben's mind.

"Look at them, Benjamin," Garrett sighed in his horrendous, growling voice. "Isn't my army impressive?"

"Very, sir," Ben replied. "Very impressive."

Garrett watched him for a moment, his red eyes glowing even brighter than usual. Ben refused to meet that hellish gaze.

"Do you feel remorse?" the Ranker asked mildly.

"About what?" Ben asked. He wondered if he was being tested.

"For your friends. You are short one, now."

Intense, lava-hot fury, the formidable anger of a vampire, spurted through Ben's body. He had grieved for Vince, alone in the castle halls, after Garrett had braggingly relayed the story to him. But, despite Garrett's boasts, Ben knew that the Ranker was bitterly upset. If it weren't for the great many friends and allies from Firestone that had shown up in the pyramid, then Vince's death may very well have led to Jonathan being captured. Of course, Ben thought proudly, if Kitty hadn't unexpectedly interfered with Garrett's intentions to slay *more* of their friends, Jonathan wouldn't have had such powerful support when facing the sphinx in the first place.

Ben would not allow Garrett to goad himself into giving his allegiance away. This was too important. He hated himself for the words he said, but they seemed to mollify Garrett.

"Your taunts fall empty. I have friends no more. Play with them as you will."

"Will you go to them later? Will you watch them mourn?"

Now Ben looked up at him and nodded slowly. He tried not to react to the squishy slab of bloody meat that landed by his feet–Donovan tossing aside some part of his victim that he didn't like. A true vampire like Donovan could disguise himself. Subsisting on animal blood did not allow Ben the same abilities without taking a powerful toll on his already-limited energy reserves. Garrett had put Ben in charge of Firestone for the sole purpose of keeping an eye on his friends, and though Ben was honestly keeping an eye on them, even if it was for less malevolent purposes than Garrett suspected, the truth was that Ben now relayed information to his friends through Josiah, rather than speak to them directly. He didn't want his friends, especially not Kitty, to see him like this in his tortured, malnourished form.

"Hmmm." Garrett tapped his claws against the stone of the balcony. "Donovan, I think he is ready."

"Ready for what?" Ben asked as Donovan chuckled wetly beneath them.

"It is time that you had an audience with our king."

Confusion and fear washed down Ben's limbs, freezing the anger he had felt before. "I thought...*you* were the King of the Rankers?"

"I am, in a way," Garrett said. Ben could see every yellow fang in that death's-head smile. "But every king is beholden to a concept: virtue, greed, *goodness.*" His purplish tongue flickered, and he took a great hissing breath as if overcome by passion. Ben's uneasiness intensified.

"Our Nightmare King is darkness given form. He is what drives us, for it is from him that we are born. He lavishly rewards all who are loyal to him. Come, Ben, let us pay homage to our Liege Master. I know he will take *great* interest in you."

"Yes, of course!" Ben said, turning to reenter the castle, feigning eagerness. The army roared and thundered far below, and terror spun in his breast as if an unforgiving and terrible storm had swallowed him up.

Nightmare King? Darkness given form?

He had to tell Jonathan.

KAYLE, THE BLACK GRIFFIN

ABOUT THE AUTHOR

Alesa Corrin first realized she wanted to be a writer when she was in middle school. The stress, peer pressure, her mother's battle with cancer, and an impending major back surgery in the eighth grade drove her desperately to seek a distraction. Writing became an escape for her, and she soon found that she wanted to create that escape for others, creating realms of adventure through her stories.

To Corrin, writing is not merely a means of taking others through a looking-glass into a fantastic world of heroes, villains, joy, and beauty, but a mirror through which we can examine ourselves and discover our own shortcomings and strengths. She hopes that her readers are carried away on a grand adventure, driven to reflect on their own identities and, ultimately, that her book gives readers hope, empathy, and compassion for the souls around them.

If you liked this book, please consider leaving a review on Amazon!

Want to know more about the Land of Dreams? Check out acorrinbooks.com!

www.ingramcontent.com/pod-product-compliance
Lightning Source LLC
Chambersburg PA
CBHW020330030826
48979CB00021B/562

9781736560921